BABUR,
THE FIRST MOGHUL IN INDIA

In the Land of Cain

Farzana Moon

I0593014

Hamilton Books
A member of
The Rowman & Littlefield Publishing Group
Lanham · Boulder · New York · Toronto · Plymouth, UK

Copyright © 2011 by
Hamilton Books
4501 Forbes Boulevard
Suite 200
Lanham, Maryland 20706
Hamilton Books Acquisitions Department (301) 459-3366

Estover Road
Plymouth PL6 7PY
United Kingdom

British Library Cataloging in Publication Information Available

Library of Congress Control Number: 2011930712
ISBN: 978-0-7618-5629-0

For my daughter Samina,
Dearest and most beloved

Table of Contents

Preface

This book is indebted to the richness of cultures in India, brimming with the treasures of diversity and tolerance. Babur is the King of Kabul, becoming the first Moghul of India in the sequels of the six Muslim emperors in succession, to explore the treasures of art, music and architecture and to add more to the continent of Hind known in its entirety as Hindustan. He is the architect of grand highway from Agra to Kabul, ordering the planting of trees on each side of the road for the comfort of the travelers. From sixteenth to eighteenth century the Moghul era is captured in six books delineating the rise and fall of the Moghul Empire—its ascent and glory as long as the emperors remained loving and tolerant and its fall when the emperors became hateful and intolerant. Mother India in this first book in the series is much like a mystical bride, permitting its suitors to unveil its beauty, and Babur is privileged to lift the first veil to fall under the spell of its enchantment. The progeny of Babur would be tempted to unveil this bride to hold and behold its mood, wisdom and eternalness. After his death Babur's son Humayun leaves his kingdom of Badakhshan and comes to India as the second Moghul Emperor. *The Moghul Exile* traces Humayun's exile into Persia and then back to Hindustan.

1

Biblical Cain

We have learned to live with joy and to die with a better hope.
— Cicero

Babur stood gazing at the bright, stabbing star called, Suhail—Canopus. It was a moonlit night, the verdant hills of Kabul etched alive, silvery and shimmering. The moonlight itself was lending his fair, young features the aura of purity and innocence. He was standing upon one small hill in perfect immobility, a child of the night, it seemed. Immersed profoundly inside the pools of his reveries and oblivious to the starry splendor above and beyond! Donned in a robe of Chinese silk broidered with silvery stars, he appeared to be a part of this hush and pulchritude which had enveloped the glens and the valleys into a mantle of serenity. A string of pearls around his neck, and ropes of pearls around his creamy turban were accentuating one black plume, soft and glistening. His sherry-brown eyes lit by a wistful gleam were revealing volumes upon volumes of mysteries straight from his soul and psyche. Some sort of nameless desolation was within him, yet his thoughts were sailing over the waters of surface-calm, feeling not the ripples of grief, sadness or loneliness. Barely a youth of twenty-one, his expression was one of somber alertness, portraying him as some dreamy prince, who could turn himself into a poet, mystic or a scholar with the wand of his imagination, all fiery and fantastic.

The small hill upon which Babur stood was called Gulkhaneh, shrouded in its mystery of a myth that it cradled the grave of Biblical Cain. Babur was vaguely aware of his thoughts chasing this myth, as he stood gazing at Suhail, so pure and dazzling. Shades of death and shadows of grief were entering his thoughts too, almost goading him to look into his heart and tear the veil of his pain and sadness. His hands were the first ones to obey the command of his mind, snatching the black plume off his turban, as if plucking out all sorrow from his heart, still grieving and mourning. His thoughts were entering the valley of death where his mother—Khanim, his grandmother—Aisan Doulat, and his dada Khan—Khwaja lay buried under mounds of earth, sprinkled with flowers.

All had died within a brief span of one month.

Babur's thoughts were murmuring, consoling the pain of his loss and grief with an astonishing sense of relief and comfort. He sighed to himself, watching the flight of his thoughts sailing toward his queen—Zainab, who could not, and would not reward his love with love. Something within the dark recesses of his soul was awakening and foundering, searching the profoundest deeps, so very mysterious and boundless. The mystic in Babur was stumbling over some sacred road in quest of love, beauty and laughter. The eternal poet within him was awakening too, overwhelmed by the splendor of the diamond stars, so very awesome and dazzling. *He was the child of the night;* his thoughts were singing all of a sudden, *the dream-prince, the King of Kabul!* Yes, the King of Kabul possessed by this need to tear open the heart of all myths with the knife of his passion and bewilderment.

Cain—the slayer of Abel! The accursed of Allah. Wearing the mark of sin on his brow, and adopting this land as his homeland. Tilling the earth with his bare hands, and suffering the blight of the seasons. Loving life, breeding life? I might be standing right over the grave of Cain, that holy/sinful man, wretched and lonesome? Did he really trace the footsteps of Elijah over these hills, so lovely and sublime? Where could be the house of Lamech he visited?

A subtle light of mockery and laughter was alighting in Babur's eyes, his thoughts gliding back in time before he had become the king of Kabul. Another sigh escaped his poppy-red lips as he stood cherishing these rare moments of silence and solitude, away from the burdens of wars, intrigues and rebellions. He was also becoming aware of the serenity of nature all around, the majestic poplars and the mournful willows, beneath which was woven the tapestry of ravines and valleys, where streams danced and gurgled. His gaze was returning to Suhail, the meteors of time throbbing in his very eyes, arresting him on the spot when he had crossed the Upian Pass. That was when he had seen Suhail the very first time, the brightest of stars he had not ever seen before. He had stood there dazzled, so absorbed by the diamond-brilliance of this star that he had forgotten the presence of his vizier Baki standing beside him under some spell of awe and rapture.

> *How far shinest thou, Suhail, and where risesth thou*
> *An ocean of fortune to thee who beholds thee*

Baki's impromptu couplet had jolted Babur out of his reveries, and he had burst out laughing, his heart light and carefree. And now the pure sweetness of that couplet, mingled with the wine of night air was making Babur giddy, his feet carrying him down the hill with the skill and precision of a mountaineer.

I am the king of Kabul, unloved by my fair queen? How sweet is the venom of love? Babur's thoughts were mocking, and following him down the rough slope, as if hugging the soles of his shoes made out of shagreen-leather. The moonlit vistas before his sight were quiet and glorious. But the night was awakening with a seductive tremor. The wind, it seemed, had parted its lips, blowing a myriad of kisses at the ardent stars, all sparkling and twinkling. He himself could feel its kisses, welcoming the sounds of music, the rustling of the leaves and the murmur of the cataracts, singing some songs tender and unforgotten. An astonishing sense of joy and peace were entering Babur's thoughts, whisking him toward his cherished gardens, beyond which stood his palace aglitter with colorful lanterns on pillared verandahs. One of his favorite gardens, Char-bagh was still leagues away in his mind's sight as he drifted toward his palace, the mists in his head clearing a way for memories wild and unforgettable.

He was a child again, inhaling the scent of love and warmth from family and friends. He was playing with his brothers and sisters, laughing heedlessly, and getting lost in the sun-gold valleys of his homeland—his beloved Ferghana. Her grandmother was there too, her tender, loving arms crushing him to her in embraces sweet and heartwarming. The dance of love in his mother's eyes and the music of laughter on his father's lips filling his heart with the poetry of joys inexpressible. And yet, that carefree abandon of the days gone by was no more, the gentle shades and shadows of the past swallowed by time and timelessness. He was alone again, feeling the pulse of the hymnal night, his heart kneeling at the altar of nature, so awesome and benevolent. The garden of the Revered Three Friends was sprawling before his sight like a shrine most holy and awe-inspiring. This garden had acquired its name in remembrance of three holy men who had dwelt here, absorbed in prayer and contemplation. It was believed that their spiritual powers had bestowed upon this garden the gift of Arghwan—Judas trees, which had grown and multiplied, blessing the entire city of Kabul with their blooms most silken and exquisite. Another irrefutable belief was that the oak trees in this garden were due to the blessings of those three holy men, since they were not found anywhere in Kabul, but in Revered Three Friends.

Babur had grown accustomed to the mystery and reverence throbbing in each pulse of this garden, and now as he entered the grove of oaks towering on each side, his heart was freshly humbled. He was standing inert and contemplative, admiring Judas's blooms under the moonlit sky, the red teardrop petals slashed with yellow, almost saffron, luminescent and glistening. His gaze was reaching up to the gibbous moon, but his thoughts were racing back into the valleys of Ferghana. He could feel the comforting arms of his grandmother, her lips pouring a wealth of stories, while she sat hugging him and the gold in sunshine. She had nurtured in him the love for art, poetry, and nature. He could hear her voice even now, low and melodious, singing the hymns of the past, and lowering a string of warnings.

The pure blood of the Mongols runs in your veins Babur. Never forget your divine ancestors. The great, benevolent destiny awaits your courage to conquer and subjugate. You shall be the king of kings— Padishah, the Great Emperor of Hind. It is your legacy from your Great Mongol kings and emperors. Your grandfather named you, Panther of Ferghana! Do you know what it means? I will tell you, panther means, lion, in Turkish, which is your mother tongue. You are picking up the Persian dialect of the streets, I am afraid, but keep your Turkish pure and polished. Your tutors are skilled in teaching you the purity of languages in Persian and Arabic, master those with great passion and attention. Remember always, your great, glorious past, it would be your guide toward honor, justice, success. You are sixth in line from Genghis Khan on your mother's side and from Tamerlane on your father's side, both endowed with the gifts of valor and sovereignty. Genghis Khan's virgin bride, before he bedded her, was ravished by a moonbeam. She gave birth to a boy named Buzanchar, whose beautiful daughter later wedded Tamerlane. This is your patrimony, Babur, write it down, write everything you hear, see or feel, keep it preserved in writing. Greatness owes to history its own great secrets.

Revered Three Friends was left behind, Babur's thoughts whirling him further back as a five-year old prince in the vale of Ferghana. Though only five-year old, he was already betrothed to his cousin, princess Ayisha. From childhood to boyhood, exploring the hills, trails and groves in Ferghana. Going hunting with his father, Omar Shaikh, and getting lost in cherry orchards. Flying falcons and plying backgammon with guests in the palace of his parents in Andijan. Eating the juiciest of pomegranates from Khojent. Almond-stuffed, dried apricots from Marghinan. Honey-sweet apples from Samarkand. The melons and sahibs—dark grapes from Akhsi. His older sister, princess Khazanda, was with him, and he could see himself teaching her his reckless tricks in wielding the bow and arrow. Lord Kasim was there too, teaching them both the art of hard-sped arrow. He was playing polo on horseback, practicing leapfrog with Yakub, and then running wild in groves of elms, poplars and cypresses.

Babur's reveries were hurling him down the rungs of teens. Barely a lad of twelve, visiting the hill garden outside Andijan, and flying falcons with his boon companions. Suddenly, an express runner had appeared, telling him that his father had fallen off a cliff fort at Akhsi while inspecting a dovecote. His father was dead. Rudely and abruptly, Babur was wrenched out of his carefree abandon, and clamped shut into the cage of maturity, becoming the king of Ferghana. His beloved Char-bagh was coming into view, but his thoughts were still unrolling the canvas of the past. Twelve year old King Babur suffering betrayals and rebellions to preserve his birthright as the king of Ferghana. Soon after the death of his father, he had to march west toward Samarkand to confront one Uzbek foe by the name of Shaibani Khan. Lord Kasim had become Babur's mentor and advisor in warfare, and with a small contingent of army, they had succeeded in conquering Samarkand.

Alas, that victory had lasted for a brief span of one hundred days, and Babur had to march back to reclaim his Ferghana usurped by intriguing lords during his absence. But those hundred days had become his font of wisdom and knowledge, most precious and priceless. He had fallen in love with this *turquoise city* of gardens and colleges. His glorious Samarkand, he would repeat under some spell of exaltation, squeezing out the nectar of art and inspiration from its bosom rich and expansive. Much in the guise of a lone pilgrim, not as the king of Samarkand, he had visited the shrines of the saints and sages with the sense of awe and humility. Touched and humbled by the beauty of palaces grand and monuments majestic. The Hill of Kohik had become his special altar of pilgrimage, below which the river glittered like a vessel wrought out of pure silver, and he would sit there for hours, filling his heart with the waters of tranquility. Sated thus with joy and peace, he was wont to explore the gardens, but not before wandering through several gates, all ornate and imposing. His favorite ones welcoming him into their generous arms were, the Iron Gate, Lover's Gate and the Needlework's gate. He thought he had died and gone to Paradise while strolling through the gardens most lovely and serene. Bagh-i-Bulandi, Bagh-i-Dilkusha, Bagh-i-Bhisht and Naqshi-i-Jahan were calling him back to heaven this precise moment, but his thoughts were bent on resurrecting more sites worthy of the grandeur of Samarkand.

The Char-bagh lit by lanterns and moonlight, was wafting the scent of ranunculus and lily-of-the-valley, but Babur in his leisurely stroll toward his palace seemed oblivious to all, obedient only to the dictates of his thoughts. He was back in Samarkand, visiting the colleges where sages and scholars had gathered to discuss philosophy and theology. The books themselves boasting of the finest paper made exclusively in Samarkand. The tomb of Lord Tamerlane was waving its banner of invitation, throwing open the gates of Blue Palace four storey high, its halls stately and spacious. The Palace Gates were imposing, yet the mosque behind it was towering above. Upon its massive portals was carved an inscription from the Quran.

Lord, accept it from us.

Samarkand was unfolding another wonder in Babur's head, Ulugh Beg's famous observatory. It was an astronomer's dream, hosting the tables of the fixed stars—the Hyde's Syntagama and the Geographical Tables. Babur's thoughts were protesting all of a sudden, disrupted by a lone song from the throat of the hoopoe, and taking refuge in another garden in Samarkand. The Garden of Plain opposite one edifice two storeys high, called Forty Pillars. His thoughts were protesting again, weak and disjointed, gathering the soot of betrayals while he had fallen ill in Samarkand.

After gathering the blooms of beauty and splendor in Samarkand, Babur had decided to return to Ferghana. But his decision had been postponed due to a sudden illness, not even knowing that his kingdom of Ferghana was being lost to him through the deceit of a few handful of his viziers turned rebels and cutthroats. Lord Tambal and Sultan Ali were the two ingrate wretches who had devised a plan to seize and rule Ferghana. They had laid siege over the little kingdom of Andijan ruled by Babur's half brother, Jehangir, while gathering forces to take possession of Ferghana. Lord Tambal, drunk with his own ambition, had grown wild and reckless. He had hanged Babur's steadfast champion and revered judge, Khwaja Kazi, as a warning to those who might pose opposition. That was when Babur had received a letter from his grandmother, imploring him to return to Ferghana.

Babur had received this ill-fated letter on the eve of his fifteenth birthday, partially recovered from his illness and longing to drink deep of Samarkand. But the very next day he had started from Samarkand, ill and distraught. He and his companions had barely reached halfway between Ferghana and Samarkand, when the grievous news had reached them that both Andijan and Ferghana were lost to him, and that his half brother Jehangir was forced to abdicate. Crestfallen and inconsolable, Babur had continued his journey, choosing Khojent as his self-exile to deflect the arrows of betrayals and rebellions.

Khojent had become Babur's citadel of hope to win back Ferghana. Meanwhile, his grandmother and other members of the family released by the rebels, had joined Babur in Khojent. Learning from them that his uncle, Mahmud Khan, had joined Lord Tambal in his ambition to keep a strong hold on Ferghana. Wounded by betrayals and weakened by illnesses, Babur was in a state of utter hopelessness when a messenger from Ali Dost had arrived in Khojent, requesting Babur to return to Marghinan. Ali Dost with his wisdom and reasoning had succeeded in contriving a peace-treaty amongst Babur and the Lords of Deceit. Babur had become the master of Ferghana in name alone to govern its capital Andijan as far as the left bank of river Syr. His half brother Jehangir had become the puppet of the contriving foes, acceding to their demands that Andijan was not to become Babur's stronghold for warfare. Jehangir, Sultan Ali and Lord Tambal had formed a coalition to rule Akhsi, and to keep Ferghana intact from splitting into warring factions. Back in Samarkand, Shaibani Khan, learning of Babur's plight had regained his hold over the turquoise city, amassing heavy contingents to fight back if Babur ever dared return.

The marble terraces smitten ivory against the flood of moonlight were arresting Babur's gaze and thoughts, his palace looming in the distance inviting and welcoming. But he didn't want to seek the comfort of his palace as yet, cherishing the throb of solitude within and without and letting his thoughts wander and gallivant. He was in Khojent, his mother had fetched his child-bride Ayisha, and they were married. *Ayisha—the unloved bride*, a sigh of regret was escaping Babur's thoughts. Ayisha had blessed him with one flower of a daughter, but that flower-princess had died in infancy. That child-bride, unloved by him had left him, seeking the love and comfort of a home with her parents. *Taking with her the dower of her grief, misery, loneliness!*

The whiff of poetry in Babur's thoughts was permeating another scene in the past where remorse and anguish could be seen as the mists dark and swirling. While still married to Ayisha, and pressed by his need to flee and escape, he had begun to frequent one Camp Bazaar. One evening in that Camp Bazaar, his gaze had fallen on a comely youth of such exceptional handsomeness, that his heart was ravished by love and madness. He had fallen in love with that fairy-faced boy named Baburi, consumed by longings wild and forbidden. His heart in throes of agony had leaped out of his body to crush that boy into its arms. Instead, his head had spilled out a couplet to fight the fever of caprice and madness.

Desire drove me out of myself, unknowing
That this comes from loving a fairy face

Babur's very soul was singing this sad hymnal. He had come close to the front steps of his palace, and stood watching the portals in some sort of daze, his thoughts retreating into the cloister of darkness. The palace was a city itself, its myriad of windows reflecting lights, but it stood silent as the night, awakening his thoughts to bid farewell to memories. Yet memories were clinging to him like the wild creepers, his soul itself speaking in a tongue alien and feverish.

What are you seeking? Are you driven by ambition? Pressed by some mad, whirling need to know all? Wandering, always wandering?

Babur's thoughts were not heeding the cries of his soul, wrenching out the saddest of all memories which lay smoldering inside him like a brand of agony. Flashing in his mind was one vestige of a gain, and a loss precious and everlasting. Babur had returned to Samarkand, defeating Shaibani Khan, and thinking to himself that he had crushed the spirit of the Uzbek Lord. But alas, Babur was mistaken; Shaibani Khan was quick to muster more alliances with double the amount of troops than before, swooping over Samarkand like the *lord of vengeance*. Samarkand was lost to Babur this second time, along with the most precious of losses irretrievable. His sister Khazanda was taken captive, and forced to marry that lord of tyranny.

Babur himself had fled to Dizak. He was constrained to take refuge with his uncle, Mahmud Khan, who had already betrayed him once when he was away from Ferghana. Something wild and terrible inside Babur was churning forth one couplet he had written during that time of grief and hopelessness.

I have found no friend to trust except my soul
Except my heart, no confidant have I found

His heart exploding with the fury of that bitter remembrance was hurling him into his palace. He had thrown open the portals, almost colliding with his cruel beloved, but had caught her into his arms, the name *Zainab* escaping his lips like a wild caress, along with *pardon* in an attempt at gentleness.

"Pardon me, my king!" Was Zainab's startled cry from her rosy lips. Her green eyes were blazing with chagrin.

Naralla—Babur's drummer was jolted to awakening in some stupor of confusion and bewilderment by this abrupt, violent entry of the King. He had stumbled to his feet, clutching his awry turban, then falling at Babur's feet in his usual act of obeisance.

Babur kept holding Zainab to him, his eyes lit up with amusement as he noticed the Pashmina shawl over her shoulders, which she only wore when in the mood to take a walk in the garden. He held her before him, his arms still resting on her shoulders. He stood devouring her with his gaze alone, her small, white face with ruby-red lips absorbing radiance from the emeralds around her ivory throat, but her eyes remained cold and flashing.

"I wish I have to beg a thousand pardons like this every evening!" Babur laughed, ignoring the brilliant pools of hatred in her eyes. "What mad whim of yours, my beauty, is goading you to take a stroll this late in the evening? The rich, satiny comforts of your bridal chamber do not meet your approval, I guess?" He stood admiring her tiny waist, tracing the green folds of her silken dress hugging her toes. "I am at your command, my beauty, if you care to take a stroll in the garden?" He mocked, turning his attention to Naralla. "Get you to bed, my devoted fool." He commanded, offering his arm to Zainab, almost whisking her away toward the wide staircase.

The royal bed with its canopied silks and brocades was not Babur's temple of bliss, but some ruin-altar of oblivion, where he was wont to purge the rivers of hatred with his ocean of love boundless and all-consuming. And this night was no different than the rest, his kisses melting not the cold marble on her body, and the flaming torch of his desire satisfying only his lust, not his need for love sweet and sublime. His thoughts were ritualistic too, divining the cause of her hatred, for he could not and would not pardon the offenses of her family and tribe, Yusufzai.

My mountain-child! This miracle sublime with wild, green eyes. The power of my love, one blessed day, would churn her rivers of hatred into a sea of love, pure and radiant—

Babur's thoughts were murmuring, lulling the violence of his passion to rest and tenderness. He was drifting into the comforting arms of sleep and dreams.

2

Queen of Kabul

Where there is no love, there is no sense either.
— Dostoevsky

The garden of Revered Three Friends was holding Babur in abeyance, as he stood watching the astronomical clock with utmost absorption. He was wearing a blue robe broidered in pattern of crescents, which appeared to reflect gold from sunshine in silken rivulets. The afternoon sun was polishing his jeweled belt to fiery effulgence, it seemed, the bright plume in his turban encircled by carnelians glinting its aura of wealth and opulence. He was cherishing the beauty of his garden, his features suffused with the light of love, warmth, sunshine.

After the midday prayers, Babur had sought the solitary comfort of his garden, his thoughts dreamy and languid. The astronomical clock which was demanding all his attention was of Turkish origin, its miniature bronze table inscribed with the latitude of the chief cities. He was studying the gold pointer, aligned to north, and casting a shadow much in the likeness of a naked blade. A white butterfly was hovering above that shadow, as if teasing his thoughts to awaken to the loveliness of life with all its mystery and abandon.

Could one truly love? Does love change like the seasons? This one butterfly could represent our mortal hungers of the body and soul. Fluttering from bloom to bloom, deflowering many a virgin flowers, its hunger unslaked, its passion inviolate?

Babur stirred; resuming his stroll toward the orchards he himself had helped plant and nurture. In the distance, some gardeners were planting new trees, and many more pruning the bushes, or manicuring the flowerbeds efflorescent in the color of the rainbows. The sherry-brown pools in his eyes were glinting mockery and laughter in conformity with his thoughts. The laughter from the lips of the gardeners was reaching him too—this love of their labor pure and heart-warming.

Are men destined to be the victims of their lusts and moods, of passions and appetites? Is true love only the phantom of imagination inside the heads of the poets and the mystics? Some sort of dream, beautiful and phantasmagorical! Have I ever loved—truly? Do I love—yet I suffer, suffer terribly and besottedly? Zainab, Beloved, Queen of the Mountains, do I love her? Yes and no, more like a rape of the queen night after night, is that love? Where was this love when I was married to Ayisha? Not a drop to quench the bridal-thirst of her sweet passion? It was somewhere between the fires of hell and damnation, for Baburi, for Baburi?

Babur's thoughts were derisive, rather incisive. And yet, he couldn't feel the naked blade of their violence, since his heart was light and love-intoxicated. His gaze was caressing the vast stretches of his orchards most wistfully. He was remembering the gardens of Samarkand where all these fruit trees bloomed and flourished. Now the same trees were in Kabul, the exact replica of what Samarkand boasted; pear, plum, apple, peach, citron, apricot, almond, walnut, orange, and pomegranate. He was happy, the sweet-scented wine of spring offering him the libations of joy, granting him even the luxury to embrace his sadness.

Sweetness All! By the law and virtue of my nature, I cannot help but love Zainab. Love and life, spring and laughter, this sunshine, why do they remind me of death, emptiness, surcease? Oh, yes, today, the feast day in honor of my Dada Khan, mother, grandmother. Today, I cast off the garments of mourning. Special prayers and reciting verses from the Quran!

The wind-chimes of sadness were urging Babur to return to his palace, his feet already obeying the command of his thoughts. He could see the marble terraces turned pewter by sunlight, the rippling of fountains gliding over the slats of fretted stone a distant murmur. The breeze itself had begun to sing some songs of love and sadness, borrowing a symphony of music from the very sinews of Chenars and weeping willows.

The souls of the dead and the living, wandering in quest of something from eternalness to eternity! Peace in death, how wonderful and mysterious? The world of the living would follow the wheel of fate, grinding the spikes of greed and ambition. Men would always fight and command, pillaging and plundering, suffering defeats and gloating over conquests? Building and destroying, tireless and tyrannous!

A bed of Damascus roses was attracting Babur's attention, his gaze accosting the flowerbeds of gentian, the primula and the edelweiss, the crocuses peering out from against the swath of anemones. His senses were awakening to the scents from roses, and honeysuckle. The mingling of perfume from ranunculus and lily-of-the-valley was drugging his thoughts to bliss and nostalgia. His gaze was holding doves and the hoopoes in one tender embrace, and chasing golden orioles in their merry flight over his palace of red sand-stone. He was approaching close to his palace, its pavilions and balconies bathed in molten gold of sunshine accentuating the stone peacocks with carved plumage on each side of the imposing façade.

Babur's dreamy gaze was reaching up to the Himalayan tulips on rooftops, which appeared to hold in their scarlet cups the draughts of amber wine from the very flagon of the sky, so vast and sparkling. The marble steps leading up to the oaken doors were welcoming Babur into the palace. Naralla had begun to beat the kettle-drums to announce the approach of the King, and Babur had marched right into the Audience Hall amidst a sea of courtiers. The men fell to curtsying in strict decorum of the king's court, while Babur seated himself on his throne, flanked by hangings of silks and brocades. The crimson canopy above was flaunting its tassels of gold, and emulating the silk-wool splendor of Bokhara carpet under the dais, it seemed, as Naralla sounded his kettle-drums once again as a signal to commence the proceedings of the durbar.

With this signal, all decorum had vanished in a flash as was customary, lending the poets, the courtiers and scholars free rein to exchange ideas and opinions, even engage in arguments. Babur was quiet and contemplative, acknowledging the greetings of his younger half brother Jehangir Mirza, and of his youngest brother to his left, Nasir Mirza. Babur's gaze was straying over motley of groups, the Khans and the Sultans, the Emirs and the Viziers, and resting upon the Mullahs lolling against the velvety pillows, vigilant and whispering.

"Disturbing news from Bhira!" Jehangir Mirza's voice was reaching Babur in a low murmur. "Rebellion is sprouting in the south of Jehlum. The vizier Deria Khan—"

Babur was not paying much attention to the bulletin of news from his half brother, claiming his jeweled cup from Mushin, and sipping his wine thoughtfully. He was thinking about Zainab, the sparks of hatred in her lovely eyes his elixir to ambition to conquer and subjugate. Some sort of pressing need inside him was goading him toward conquests, to possess the lands, the steppes and the mountains, even the continent of Hind in its entirety. He was becoming aware of the voices, loud and skirling, rising and spluttering in arguments. Feeling lonesome and alienated as ever amidst this pool of ideation and syllogism—*a stranger in the void*, he was thinking. His poetic spirit was rebelling against this noise so harsh and discordant, and bemoaning the absence of women in his durbar at Kabul, which had set its rules of decorum in not permitting the ladies to be seated with their lords.

No wonder, goddesses are killed by men posing as gods, brandishing their wands of supremacy over the heads of women in exile in their own chambers, all perfumed and damasked. Surely, my grandmother was strong and intelligent, ruling over the affairs great or small, and taking her seat beside my grandfather in the open durbar, proud and commanding. She went riding and hunting, and even devising strategies for campaigns long and arduous. My mamma, an excellent rider and hunter! And Khazanda, my sweet sister, we played polo, and went riding down the valleys— Babur's thoughts were coming to stalemate by a fresh burst of arguments.

"My poets, scholars and philosophers!" Babur's contralto voice silenced all arguments. "Open your minds to the beauty of inspiration. Practice the art of poetry and profundity. Come, Riddler, come close to the king, and recite some of your couplets. Flattering, or unflattering, as long as they make Kabul the envy of the world!" He raised his cup, his own spilling the wine of poetry.

"My King!" Riddler stumbled to his feet, falling into one awkward curtsy before reciting.

"Drink wine in this hold of Kabul—send the cup around
For Kabul is mountain, town, river and plane in one."

A great applause broke forth from the lips and hands of all present, while
Riddler stood there flushed and overwhelmed. Babur's gaze was bestowing
compliments, laughter trilling down his lips in joyful abandon.

"Wine is forbidden in Islam!" Was Abdullah Hatifi's inebriated exclamation, as he drained his goblet of the forbidden nectar!

"The rivers of wine, milk and honey promised to us in heaven." Babur
flashed a warm smile at Hatifi, his eyes glinting amusement. "If we abstain from
wine now, in this world, we might as well be living in hell? And yet, Kabul is
heaven, even its Himalayan tulips offering goblets of wine to any who are fortunate enough to hold and behold them. You should write a mathnavi—epic poem,
Hatifi. And I am sure, it would outshine all epics, emulating even the pride of
Jam! Pray, do not stop drinking, not as yet." His attention was diverted to his
vizier, Baki Cheghanaini. He had come trundling close to the throne, neglecting
even his customary obeisance.

"Pardon my boldness, my King, but the precepts of religion are to be held in
reverence, not to be ridiculed by—" Baki's protest was silenced by one imperious wave of Babur's arm, his cup held out to Mushin for replenishing.

"You are bent on gathering a mound of offenses against your better judgment, Baki!" Babur's voice was carrying a subtle threat he didn't want to unleash. "Guard your thoughts well, one more blunder, and it might cost you your
life, worse yet, an exile from this haven of Kabul. And as to the religion worthy
of reverence, you might feel humbled if you can recite verse fifteen from Surah
forty-seven from the Quran? *A description of the garden promised to the right-
eous; therein are rivers of water which corrupt not, and rivers of milk of which
the taste changes not, and rivers of wine, a delight to those who drink, and rivers of clarified honey. And in it they will have all kinds of fruit, and forgiveness
from their Lord. Can those who enjoy such bliss be like those who abide in the
Fire and who are given boiling water to drink so that it tears their bowels?"* He
recited most reverently, the mystic-poet in him awakening to the wonder of living and enjoying. "Boiling water is not to my taste, not in this world at least, if I
can help it." He added buoyantly.

"Forgive me, my King." Baki murmured, falling to his feet like a suppliant
most lowly and wretched.

A genuine peal of laughter escaped Babur's lips, as he dismissed Baki with
an impatient wave of his arm, his eyes glinting amusement. The Audience Hall
was awakening to tides of mirth, the poets and the courtiers making Baki the
victim of their raillery and sarcasm. Babur's favorite vizier, Khwaja Kilan, was
assisting Baki to his feet, trying to be his shield against jests wild and stabbing.
Amongst the revelers most keen on teasing were Tigri Birdi, Sultan Wais, Kambar Ali, Ahmad Kasim, Sultan Barlas and Mahdi Khwaja. Baki seemed to be
crumbling against the chorus of jeers, unable to deflect the arrows of taunts,
since all voices were merging into a crescendo on the verge of exploding. As

fortune would have it, an urgent beat from Naralla's kettle-drums was enough to snuff out the symphony of mirth and raillery. Hurried footsteps outside the Audience Hall were just a prelude to the hasty approach of a messenger.

"My King." Yar Husein offered three consecutive curtsies, his face flushed and his dark eyes glittering.

"Welcome to Kabul, Yar Husein." Babur greeted gently. "What brings you to Kabul in such a whaling haste?" His gaze was searching the features of this handsome youth with a thoughtful intensity.

"Urgent matters, my King, if you grant me audience to discuss those?" Yar Husein appealed, his look baffled.

"Urgent matters better be left to the caprice of the winds, which alone has the power to hurl traitors into dungeons deep, or scatter the seeds of goodwill over the fields of unrest and rebellion?" Babur exclaimed genially. "This wounded clump of earth where all haste is governed by the laws of nature, unsullied and inviolate. And yet, the king is in a mood to untangle the knots of intrigues." He beckoned Sayyid Kasim—the Lord of the Gate, to fetch a gilt chair for Yar Husein. "Come, my son, tell us all, you won't find more attentive audience than the ones here in our durbar."

"Uzbeks are filtering in on all sides over the borders of Hind!" Yar Husein began hastily, as if afraid lest he forget the motive of his urgency. "They are already pillaging and plundering. Looting and burning all towns and villages on their way toward Jehlum. Our own little kingdom of Bhira is exposed to the assaults of their tyranny and violence. My father Deria Khan himself has entrusted me with this urgent message to plead with you, my King, to come to our assistance against the Uzbeks. We are hemmed in on all sides, unable to distinguish foes from friends, my father fearing—"

Yar Husein sat pouring out one gruesome detail after the other, but Babur was half listening, half brooding, gleaning more from the passionate urgency in his tone than from the string of his words. His thoughts were straying toward Zainab too, where she might be sitting with other begums, enjoying the idle pleasure of gossip and entertainment. *All of them, probably plotting and gloating? Un-spooling the spool of intrigues which could lend glory to the fools, if not the sense of false power to the bigots and simpletons?* Babur's thoughts were silent all of a sudden in rapport with Yar Husein's expressions, as he had exhausted his load of woes and fears. His attention was turning to his half brother Jehangir.

"What do you think, my Prince? Should we march to Jehlum and crush these maggots of violence and tyranny?" Babur asked, his eyes lit up with the stars of mockery.

"We are still in the process of strengthening our defenses, my King." Jehangir Mirza responded defensively. We ourselves are vulnerable to the assault of the Uzbeks. We need more garrisons to defend the fort of Kabul."

"Let's consult the queen." Babur opined aloud, wielding his whip of caprice. The warmth of gold in his sherry-brown eyes was falling on Pir Sultan.

"Pir Sultan, go and request all the begums to join us. I would like my queen sitting beside me while I make monumental decisions."

Pir Sultan had turned to a pillar of salt, his round eyes growing darker and rounder, it seemed. His expression was one of incredulity and bewilderment. He was getting to his feet in some sort of stupor, drifting past the stunned courtiers to obey king's command.

"The briars of zeal and stupidity!" Babur exclaimed, his voice carrying the threat of a distant thunder. "Has the lightning of my suggestion struck you all mute and terrified?" His eyes were lowering the flames of rage and mockery as he continued. "Bigotry and intolerance are our enemies, if not fear and ignorance. We wish to climb the ladder of success, longing to reach the heights unattainable, yet are pulled down by the weight of our conceit and prejudice. Do you think that Islam sanctions the imprisonment of women behind four walls? Can you recite one verse from the Quran, suggesting even remotely that a wall of separation be erected between men and women? Is it written anywhere that women's place is inside the harems, and men's outside on the fields and in battlegrounds? Prophet Muhammad's wife, Khadija, was not only a business woman, but participating wholeheartedly in the endeavors of her husband toward peace and justice. She was his spiritual guide too, dissolving his doubts with sprigs of hope, and remaining a beacon of love amidst his struggles toward peace and harmony amongst the Arabs. My grandmother sat beside my grandfather in his durbar, offering advice in matters both mundane and important. My mamma too, never abandoned the side of my baba when he had weighty matters to discuss with his viziers, in private or in the open durbar. Nothing unique or extraordinary in inviting the ladies to my durbar, only the revival of old customs to keep our hearts light and young." He smiled, noticing the approach of the ladies with great pleasure.

Men were rising to their feet, shamed and humbled. Some were offering curtsies, and the others greeting with their heads bowed. The royal servants were in a flurry of excitement, fetching gilt chairs and large pillows. The Audience Hall itself was awakening to the charm of the ladies, all perfumed and bejeweled. Amongst the bevy of Begums, Khanams and Princesses were Babur's maternal aunt, Mihr Nigar donned in a gown of pale silks, rubies and diamonds in her ears and around her throat glittering and throbbing. Shah Begum, Babur's step-mother in her pearly-green gown with pearls in her hair and around her throat was the envy of the younger princesses. Babur's half-sister, Shahr Banu in her flowing gown the color of the meadows, was looking radiant, her jewels of all gold and sapphires most exquisite and dazzling. Jehangir Mirza's wife, Ai Begum, in shimmering brocades and a gold tiara appeared to be rising above the waves of color and opulence.

And yet the cynosure of all attention was Queen Zainab, all eyes turning to her with awe and admiration. Her silken gown with its sheen of mother-of-pearls, gathered around her tiny waist with a sash studded with emeralds, was arresting her whole being in an aura of purity most awesome and ethereal. Teardrop emeralds in her ears, around her throat and in her hair were accentuating her pallor, yet lending sparkle to her eyes, most beautiful and adorable. Babur had risen to his feet, offering her the gilt chair vacated by Jehangir Mirza, into which she lowered herself most regally.

"My lovely Queen!" Babur sank into his own chair with a sigh of relief, drawing her attention to the reticent messenger. "May I present to you, Yar Husein? His presence alone has lent me the pleasure of inviting the ladies to this durbar." He dared not look into her eyes, lest the sea of hatred in there reduce his pleasure to dregs of bitterness.

"My Queen." Yar Husein murmured in a daze, offering one awkward curtsy, and then falling back into his chair under some spell of awe and confusion.

"Yar Husein is the son of Deria Khan, my Queen, as you know?" Babur's gaze alone was demanding Zainab's attention. "He is here with an urgent appeal from his father that we come to his assistance against the horde of Uzbeks intent on despoiling the peace in Bhira. What is your advice, my Queen? This matter requires quick decision, what do you suggest?"

"You are a worthy arbiter, my King, in matters great or small." Zainab intoned sweetly, almost incisively. "The King has a will of his own, a strong and mighty will, which no one dare thwart or oppose." Her eyes were sparkling like the emeralds in some ritual dance of mirth and defiance. "I am not skilled in lending advice; especially, on matters of such urgency and importance." She added, ignoring the flicker of rage in Babur's eyes, and lowering her own.

"Accept this will then, my Queen, this very moment, as a Farman of the king, and yield to its power." Babur muttered under his breath. "We await your response, your judgment, if you will? Advice, or intuition, whatever you deem appropriate?" The sherry-brown in his eyes was whipped to molten gold, his look piercing.

"My King." One tremor of a protest escaped Zainab's lips. "Uzbeks are your eternal foes, my King, none dare deny this fact. Deria Khan is in dire need of your assistance, as you tell me. I think—if it pleases you, to offer as much assistance as possible." The icy gleam in her eyes was splintering into flames of fire.

"We march to Jalalabad, tomorrow!" Babur announced abruptly, filling the Audience Hall with the sunshine of his resolve and laughter.

A volley of cheers and applause broke forth from the lips of the men, the ladies merely smiling and whispering. The Audience Hall itself with its hangings of gold and crimson appeared to be swept by waves upon waves of euphoria, since the hearts of men were rejoicing, longing for the reward of rich booty from lands alien and distant. They had been inactive for a ling time, their wild, warring spirits anticipating the challenge of danger and adventure. Yar Husein was overwhelmed, his very eyes worshiping the Queen, who had become his savior in convincing the king to come to his father's assistance.

"Who is going to rule Kabul in the absence of the King?" Tardi Beg was heard murmuring to himself.

"Time for the afternoon prayers, my lords and friends!" Babur heaved himself up thoughtfully, his arm held high commanding everyone's attention. "Look to the preparations of a swift march. And yet, in honor of this glorious day, we would have a farewell feast in the evening, praying for success and safe return back to Kabul." He turned to Zainab, holding her captive in his gaze. "The honor of your company is requested in the garden for a leisurely stroll?" He assisted Zainab to her feet, his eyes gathering the stars of desire and mockery.

Babur and Zainab were leaving the sea of jubilations, the loud beat from the Kettle-drums following at their heels out into the garden. The afternoon hush and the scintillating dance of shadows under the pines and cedars were pouring peace and serenity into the hearts of the king and the queen. They were walking in utmost silence, side-by-side, both absorbed in their silent contemplations. Babur's gaze was wooing the bridal creepers, which appeared to be hugging the spruces and the willows. His thoughts were stringing their rosary of prayers where *prayer time* in his perception meant dividing the day into astronomical hours, and listening to the music in his heart which alone was the altar and the prayer-rug of love and surrender. Right this moment, his heart was in a state of perfect gratitude, blissfully aware of the presence of his beloved beside him, even diving deep into the ocean of hatred within her without the burden of sorrow.

"Bear with me, my love, one more day and one more night!" Babur exclaimed suddenly. "I might get killed in the battle against the Uzbeks. Then you would be free from the burden of hating the king." He laughed, his features aglow with the warmth of love and passion.

"You would defy even the edict of death, my King!" Zainab sang, half earnestly, half sarcastically. "Even the fates, evil and conniving, would dare not approach the valorous lord of Kabul?" Her eyes were hosting the flames of bitterness, bright and emerald.

"The edicts of death, no one can defy, my fairest of loves!" Babur chortled merrily. "And no mortal as yet has escaped the shackles of fates, either. Paradoxically, my beauty, fates are my friends, they smile upon me, even lending me hope and comfort amidst the throes of my trials and tribulations. Though you are right, my love, in your bitter presumption. Yes, I would not die, but would conquer Hind. I am born to rule, and I will rule the world with all its wonder of galaxies and constellations! Most of all, I would rule the cold, cold stars of hatred in your beautiful eyes. These stars, so bright and stabbing—my heart, always!" One delicious ripple of laughter escaped his lips, his passionate tones on the verge of exaltation. "You are my beautiful star, my love, the star of Kabul. Why do you hate me so? Have I inspired this ocean of hatred in your beautiful soul? I would fain believe otherwise, and yet do you truly hate me?"

"No!" Zainab cried suddenly, as if her heart were breaking.

"You love me then?" Babur's feet came to an abrupt halt, stalling Zainab in her own act of taking another step.

He stood gazing into her eyes, his look ardent and devouring. Zainab lowered her gaze, trying to conceal the raging oceans of love and hate leaping into her eyes, as she stood there motionless, rather bewildered by this sudden fury of her love so wild and tainted with the soot of hatred.

"How foolish of me to ask?" Babur murmured tenderly. "Kings are as much the fools as beggars who devour even a few crumbs of food with much gluttony, knowing not that their hungers would not ever be slaked? A begging bowl in my heart, and I myself might go begging, hoping for a feast, not just the crumbs?" The tenderness in his voice was making Zainab lift her eyes.

"You know, what's in my heart, my King." Zainab murmured, the flames of love-hate in her eyes licking her misery and bewilderment.

"Yes, my love, I know too well." Babur smiled, his voice gentle as if consoling a child. "What is in your heart, my beauty, is not what grieves me, but that what is in your mind. Your thoughts refuse to efface the memory of that wretched camp. Your family and friends, my kin and kindred just the same? Those rebels ingrate! A whole horde of wretches most lawless and ruthless—" He paused, summoning the poet-mystic within him to blow away the soot of past betrayals and insurrections. "Briars of the past, I have turned my back on them. I have you, my love. My rose of the mountains, so lovely and fragrant. My only crime, or I should say *my fortune* is that I have been able to save this rose— you, my love, separating it from thorns—your family? Deny as much as you will, my beauty, but your tribe Yusufzai throbs like a canker in the heart of Kabul. My only hope and prayer is that you would understand the enormity of their assaults rigged with tyranny and savagery, once that you become the Queen of Hind. Yes, my Rose, I have a few hours to delight in your company before the gluttonous feast begins. Let's return to our palace. To our chamber of ivory and damask, to be more precise." He claimed her hand, kissing it reverently.

Zainab was mute and flushed, walking beside the king like a newly wedded bride, her heart thundering. Babur too had grown quiet, his passionate heart muttering some warnings he didn't wish to hear or explore. Yet, an inexpressible weight of sorrow was crushing his heart, murmuring this litany of a presage that he might lose his precious *rose*. His arm was slipping around the waist of Zainab involuntarily. He was cherishing her nearness, crushing her to him, almost dragging her along up the stairs toward his haven of ivory and damask.

3

Gateway to Hind

Before the phantom of False morning died
Methought a Voice within the tavern cried
When all the Temple is prepared within
Why nods the drowsy worshipper outside
— Omar Khayyam

The night air heavy with the odor of dust and humidity was assailing Babur's senses, as he stood outside his tent, trying to catch a few whiffs of cool scents from Kabul in his imagination. His tent, along with many more for his troops, was pitched on this dry, parched land of Jalalabad, the fields all around vast and barren. But the sky was glorious, lowering a canopy of stars so bright that they appeared to be slipping out of their orbs, dancing in ether before spiraling back to their city of light and splendor. Babur's heart was longing for the nearness of Zainab—his Rose, his thoughts racing ahead to arrest the beauty of his gardens in Kabul. Kabul was far away, only the city of tents before his sight dreamy and silent where his soldiers lay sleeping. Sleep was evading him this night, as it had several other nights when his spirit would be restless, and he would wander alone for hours, courting only the company of his solitary contemplations. This mood of solitary contemplation was upon him once again, and he straggled away from the silk city of his tents in the direction of a large boulder he had discovered one night, adopting it as his nightly bed to sleep or dream. His gaze was turning to the moon up yonder as if hoisted on a chariot of stars, but his thoughts were tumbling down to earth, caked with the mud of time and adventures.

Two long, grueling months had slithered past the road to conquests since Babur had marched out of Kabul with a small contingent of troops. Babur's army had not encountered any bands of Uzbeks on their way as far as the valley of Shaban, but they had materialized suddenly on the outskirts of Jagdalak. This confrontation had lasted but for a few hours, and the Uzbeks had fled as quickly as their strategy of launching a swift assault. More Uzbek rebels were encountered on their journey toward Jalalabad, but all were routed and defeated with the same energy of valor and resolve which had granted victory to the troops of Kabul on the field of Jagdalak.

The livid moon as a lamp was Babur's only guide, besides a myriad of diyas as stars, merry and twinkling. He had reached his boulder, but his gaze was returning to the moon, as if searching for secrets enshrined inside the heart of folklore. He thought he could see Cain inside the moon, holding a bundle of twigs for some sort of sacrifice, reflecting the image of a story as told by many Afghans.

Two more grueling months to journey back to Kabul?

Babur sought the sanctuary of his boulder, as if stepping into the parlor of his grand palace. Seated couchant against the polished surface of this stone, his legs sprawled over the clay-baked earth, he abandoned himself to dreaming. Zainab was with him, the ocean of hatred inside her melting, and the pools of love surfacing in her eyes, bright and beautiful. He was transported into the cool shades of his gardens in Kabul, inhaling the fragrance of Damascus roses and exploring the abundance of his fruit orchards. The oaken doors of his palace were flung open, Naralla beating the Kettle-drums, and he was scaling the palatial halls in search of Zainab. Zainab was nowhere to be found, the bevy of Begums, Khanams and Princesses were missing too, the palace all quiet and deserted, yet the Audience Hall was humming voices all loud and belligerent.

He could see his brothers, Nasir Mirza and Jehangir Mirza, inebriated and laughing. Baki Cheghanaini was lolling against one velvety pillow, towering above him in half circle were Mulla Baba, Mohib Korchi, Ahmad Kasim and Nizam Khalifa, all cheering and jeering. Babur was leaving this den of revelry, wandering and searching. He was in his chamber of rose and ivory, Zainab seated there by the window, his beautiful beloved! A play of magic and mystery was reflected in her eyes, her heart foundering amidst waves of love and hate, and her soul pure as the snow-capped mountains of the Himalayas. His heart was a cauldron of fury, ripping open its passions and bleeding. Words were tumbling down his lips in lumps grotesque and shapeless.

This searing ache inside me, my passion all wild and inconsolable! Is it different than the passions of any other men, invested with the burden of love and hate, of envy and greed, of ambition and jealousy? Our wills and moods creating the illusion of surface-calm, never penetrating the turbulent depths within, so abysmal and profound? And yet, this slumbering demon of hate, we always guard and sedate? No, I can never hate, not even an enemy! Ambition, yes, another face of love, is it? Love—Ambition, not tainted by the flame of pain or tenderness, feeling no pity or remorse, fearing neither death, nor failure, wooing only Lord of Power? Yes, I would conquer Hind! First, I would conquer the heart of my beloved, draining out the poison of hatred within her, and replacing it with the wine of love, conspiring with fates, even challenging.

Babur had fallen into the comforting arms of sleep, one clump of baked earth under him his royal bed.

The morning sun ablaze with coppery sheen was lowering its shafts over the encampment of Jalalabad. Babur was jolted to a rude awakening upon his bed of solid earth, his body drenched with sweat. The taste of dust was in his mouth, his eyes straining through the glare to reach the silk-city of his encampment. He could see quite a few of his soldiers in scattered groups, roaming or standing together. A herd of cattle, not far from the encampment, appeared to be standing motionless. Horses were there too, scrounging for fodder against the scanty verdure of bushes, a few acacia trees in the background almost bare and deformed. A whiff of roasted mutton was reaching Babur's nostrils, mixed with sweat and animal defecation.

The reek of humanity!

Babur's thoughts were awakening to the sting of reality, his gaze espying his basin-bearer, Tahir. Tahir was standing only a few paces away from him, but Babur had just noticed him, his eyes getting accustomed to the haze and glare all around. Without awaiting the king's summons, Tahir bustled forth, his eyes shining with fervor and devotion.

"My King." Tahir lowered the basin of water at Babur's feet, offering a quick obeisance. "The water for your morning ablutions, my King!"

"This water won't even wash the sins of a child, my child!" Babur leaped to his feet, waving dismissal.

Tahir stood there dejected, while Babur whistled for his horse. The devoted beast with its snowy mane, obeying the call of its master, cantered toward him most gracefully. Babur stroked its mane, noticing the warmth of affection in its liquid, brown eyes before it began muzzling his cheeks in a playful manner. Babur jumped into the saddle, and let it fly toward the canal not very far from the encampment.

Your affection, my friend, is heartwarming. No human-beast can even come close to showing such affection to another human-beast!

Babur's thoughts seemed to reach the affectionate beast, for it raced and whinnied. The canal meandering into a wide stretch was coming into view, serene and inviting. Its waters splashed molten gold were reminding Babur of his childhood in Ferghana, where he went swimming for hours, happy and carefree. Letting his horse free on one patch of an oasis with clumps of brown grass, he divested himself of all clothes, and dived into the waters with the agility of an expert swimmer. His athletic body, though stiff with fatigue and lack of exercise, was molding his muscles into the ease and rhythm of swimming effortlessly. The cool ravines of Kabul and Samarkand were luring his thoughts, relaxing his muscles and filling his heart with exhilaration. His heart was aching all of a sudden, whispering the name of his beautiful beloved and diving deep into oblivion.

"My King. This deplorable heat! The locals here advise against swimming in these waters. Many people have died here of sunstroke—" Tardi Beg's voice was reaching Babur. "This God-forsaken land, my King! May Allah preserve the health of our king." He stood holding out the blue robe, his look pleading.

Babur had emerged out of the waters laughing, wrapping his robe around him boyishly, and then struggling with his gold cummerbund impatiently. Tardi Beg was trying his best to conceal his embarrassment by recounting some recent tragedy where one man was drowned and the other dying of heat and exhaustion.

"Heat, my friend, from sun or fire, rarely kills a man! But the heat of passion, yes, a sure killer." Babur stood rubbing his hair vigorously with a towel he had claimed from Tardi Beg. "And yet, the heat in our bodies kindles many fires from within, not from without. The fires of envy and greed for one, of cruelty and wickedness a hoary blaze, of gluttony and malevolence one conflagration insatiable. Not to mention the flames of stupidity and cowardice, all licking and devouring." He caressed the flowing mane of Tardi Beg's horse before mounting his own, both riding toward the encampment.

The silk-wool tent with Bokhara carpets was housing Babur and a coterie of his generals, including Yar Husein and his father, Deria Khan. They were having a midday feast of roasted mutton on spittle and rice pilaf, their dessert the ruby-red seeds of pomegranates. Ali Kuli and Khwaja Kilan were acting as the benevolent hosts, keeping a strict watch on Mushin to keep replenishing their cups with wine from his gold flagon. Khalifa was seated opposite Babur, his gaze now and then turning toward the king, as if admiring the red plume in his gold turban, his eyes shining with devotion. Babur was eating sparsely, not accustomed to eating his one meal of the day so early, yet enjoying this repast since his heart was humming the songs of victory.

"To victory! To youth and wisdom! To King Babur!" Deria Khan raised his cup with the spontaneity of a cavalier, his dark eyes lit up with the stars of admiration.

"Youth, my friend, lacks wisdom!" Babur laughed, raising his jeweled cup. "Victory alone crowns youth with the laurels of wisdom and experience. And experience itself is the seat of wisdom. During the short span of my childhood and youth, I have experienced a flood of fortunes and adversities in such abundance that most men not ever experience during the period of a lifetime. Wars and exiles, betrayals and rebellions, and defeats and conquests, not to mention the intrigues of foes and friends alike. Somewhere in that whirlpool of experiences wild and overwhelming, I have lost my youth. By the time wisdom leaves me, I might be sitting on the throne of Hind—the Great Padishah?" He sipped his wine thoughtfully. "Guard Bhira well, Deria Khan! Look to its safety and prosperity, for me, for King Babur. We march back to Kabul tomorrow, entrusting Bhira into your hands to rule and govern. Prove yourself worthy of this trust, I shall return." His sherry-brown eyes were holding a subtle threat, revealing the gold of wisdom and experience.

"Your obedient servant forever, my King!" Deria Khan bowed his head as a token of his gratitude, smiling winsomely.

"The spoils of victory are yours, my King, to take back to Kabul." Yar Husein began under some spell of pride and euphoria. "The bales of rice and wheat, and the corn for your horses. The silks and the spices and our gifts for the royal begums. The herd of cattle I have counted myself, each one of your soldiers should get a share of three hundred goats or sheep, if not more—" He couldn't finish, flustered by the piercing gaze of the King.

"The booty fit for a king of the jungle!" Babur indulged merrily. "My soldiers' loss entirely if they couldn't carry this beastly burden with them to Kabul." He turned to his vizier, mirth still shining in his eyes. "What are you thinking, Khwaja Kilan, my mentor and advisor? Why such silence and sadness!"

"I was wondering, my King." Khwaja Kilan began reluctantly. "I have known you since you were a child, and a child-king if I can recall correctly. Valor and wisdom are your virtues, and from your noble father you have inherited the gifts of compassion and forgiveness. Not a grain of malice in you, my King, nor any intentions of greed or cruelty? Your heart is generous, and your nature kind and loving, courting neither flattery, nor ostentation. And yet, we are leaving behind a pyramid of heads, the severed heads of the enemy vanquished? Why, if I may ask, my King? Why, such a barbaric display of might and power?"

"The legacy of Tamerlane, my revered mentor!" Babur murmured, his gaze warm and ponderous. "Utterly savage and barbaric as this custom is, of making pyramids with the heads of the slain, it has a subtle message to impart. A message for both the victors and the vanquished that in this dewdrop world of illusion pride dies as well as honor, whether they are inside the head of the dead or the living. Besides, men often forget that they have heads on their shoulders, and this custom serves as a stark reminder to the ones who wish to keep theirs intact, and balanced between caution and prudence. Well, too much profundity for one day. The king is craving for solitude." He dismissed all with a wave of his arm. "This furnace of Hind we leave behind, to embrace the cool valleys of Kabul." He closed his eyes, oblivious to the slow disappearance of his guests and viziers outside his tent.

The silk standards in red and yellow were creating colorful waves, as Babur's troops rode alongside the lake Abistadeh in Ghazni, heading toward Kabul. This cavalcade appeared to be sailing in its tidal waves of gold and color, the colorful kaftans of the soldiers with setres and vembraces as a protection against surprise assaults, adding an aura of wealth and power. Babur, in his kingly attire of gold helmet and a broidered vest over his kaftan, was conscious of the valor and might of his soldiers. Recalling with a sudden clarity how the lords and jagirdars of Duki and Chotiali had trembled with fright at the approach of his troops. Thinking amongst them that Tamerlane had returned with his Mongol hordes as the lord of destruction.

How could they think otherwise? Our horses, all bedizened and caparisoned! The glint of power from kards, dhups and daggers, and the fiery blaze from jeweled scimitars.

Babur's thoughts were humbled afresh by the magic-mystery of success where the lords of the various tribes had offered their submissions, not as a result of their fears, but with their genuine spirits of love and friendship, proclaiming him their beloved sovereign. Babur's gaze as well as his thoughts were returning to the barren landscape of Ghazni, splintered by a few huts and houses in the distance, small and insignificant. He was also becoming aware of Khwaja Kilan riding beside him, quiet and contemplative.

Ghazni, where Khwaja Kilan was born and educated! Didn't I tease him once that Ghazni despite its mild and temperate climate had nothing to boast of but thorny bushes? Even branding it with the epithet of hell with not a tree to offer shade to a weary traveler! Lacking the beauty of Kabul, no verdure, no flowers, no cataracts. Babur was turning his head toward his taciturn friend, flashing him a mischievous smile.

"Your beloved city, Khwaja! Your home and haven." Babur exclaimed suddenly, his eyes gathering rills of mirth. "We are passing through it, and you haven't said a word to pay homage to your hometown?"

"Yes, my city of birth, the city of miracles!" Khwaja Kilan's features were wrinkling into a wistful smile. "Here, all wishes come true, and all dreams find fulfillment, if one is but to pray with all devotion." His gaze was reaching out to one dome of a façade with one minaret soaring above, white and gleaming. "Look to your right, my King, that insignificant dome over there is actually the tomb of some revered saint. The devotees of this village attest to the fact that the tomb itself shakes in response to the prayers. The shaking of the tomb signifies that the prayers of the pilgrims are answered. Young lovers come here, as well as the poor and the ailing, almost all finding their heart's desires fulfilled."

"What mad desires hurl men over the path to ignorance?" Another exclamation escaped Babur's lips, his gaze searching the domed tomb, painted red and gray. "And yet I am no different than the others, my curiosity if not madness, goading me to test the scale of ignorance. And yet again, I am truly in need of prayers, even willing to believe my prayers would be answered. We would camp here tonight." He announced over his shoulders, spurring his horse toward the saint's tomb. "Come, Khwaja, we would visit the revered saint. What a pity that we had to leave the rewards of our victory behind, but such is the state of life, tossed between gains and losses to keep the scale of living in balance."

An old, wooden door embedded under the dome was pushed open by Babur with a quick thrust of his hands, his thoughts impatient and reckless. He was stumbling into some dark hole of a chamber, its rotunda above admitting a few chinks of light through its crevices. Khwaja Kilan was following at Babur's heels, quiet and apprehensive, his eyes getting accustomed to semi-darkness and espying one rickety staircase. Babur too had noticed the staircase, and had begun mounting the steps boldly, the prayers inside his heart only invoking the name of Zainab, begging for her love as a suppliant most devoted. His heart was drumming presage, but he was not heeding its warnings.

Do all men carry the burden of love in their hearts all their lives? Drifting in the dream-world of their own much like the victims suffered and suffering? Do they ever think of casting away this burden, to drain out the rivers of pain from within, and to cauterize their hearts of all desires and longings?

Spiraling up the steps leading aloft one hollow blade of a minaret, Babur's thoughts as well as his steps had come to a sudden halt. Khwaja Kilan behind him stood fighting the musty odor, damp and stagnant. Babur's gaze was exploring the strange structure of a tomb within his sight, almost buried under one oaken sepulcher fanning out and down in a tooth-like canopy. The tomb itself was painted white, catching pale shadows from dusk through the oversized shutter by the landing.

"Do I have to pray aloud?" Babur folded his hands in a mock gesture, as if he was about to kneel and fall into the ritual of prayer.

"Yes, my King, that's what the devotees recommend." Khwaja Kilan murmured laconically.

"Allah, the Merciful, the Gracious, bestow upon me the gift of wisdom and understanding." Babur began earnestly, trying his best to discipline his thoughts. "My All-Loving, All-Embracing Allah, pour love into the hearts of all Muslims, dissolve the rust of zeal and bigotry in their minds, and replace them with the light of tolerance and compassion. Forgive me my faults and ignorance, my Beloved All. I stand before thee as a suppliant, seeking the light of love and justice so that I might not fall into—" Babur's prayer was truncated by a sudden convulsion in the frame of the tomb, as it began to groan and rattle.

The light of incredulity in Babur's gaze was replaced with anger and suspicion, as he noticed slight tremors on the steps behind the tomb soaring up into the heart of the minaret. In a flash, he was climbing those steps with the agility of a young boy, and landing straight in front of a door the size of a small window. With one violent kick of his heel he flung open the door, stumbling through the orifice into a dark chamber, lit only by one disk of a hole in the minaret. Straining his sight, he could see two swarthy forms in loin-cloths perched on the movable vault, which was hinged beneath and linked to the very frame of sepulcher below, very craftily and cunningly. It was like a see-saw and those men clinging on either side were suspended in their act of sending tremors down below. Babur inched closer, furious and glowering, and those men tumbled down at his feet, almost groveling.

"And I have prayed for love and understanding!" Babur cried over his shoulders, sensing the presence of Khwaja Kilan behind him. "Seize these holy rascals, my prudent lord, and whip them in front of all men, till their prayers reach the throne of Allah. Allah might forgive them their pious fraud." He swung around to face his mentor, his eyes flashing. "Or, should we leave these imbeciles here to their vocation of deceit and trickery? Ignorance and superstition, the worst of men's enemies, dangerous and indestructible. And stupidity?" He murmured, trooping down the rickety steps as if fleeing—his own thoughts, caustic and ominous.

4

Eden in Gulkhaneh

My heart, like the bud of a red, red rose
Lies folds within folds aflame
Would the breath of even a myriad Springs
Blow my heart bud to rose
— Babur

Home at last in his beloved Kabul, Babur sat enjoying the company of his family and friends inside the parlor of his palace. The words of this quatrain which he had scribbled this morning were teasing his senses, his gaze now and then piercing the sparkle of pride in Zainab's eyes, his real Beloved. His thoughts were wistful, lingering at the portals of his night-long violence of passion till the early hours of dawn, now murmuring quite besottedly that he was compensating for the past four months of his monk-like existence on the fields of Jalalabad. This morning, he was dressed in a robe of Chinese silk, the green plume in his turban matching his robe, lending his fair features the warmth of languor and tenderness.

The midday meal had just ended, a sort of feast in honor of Babur's victorious return, prawn koftas, mutton pilaf, korma garnished with almonds, pheasants stuffed with raisins, just to name a few of the gourmet delicacies. Babur had eaten sparsely as was his wont, enjoying more the taste of fruits than viands. *The choicest of melons, the juiciest of apricots, and the sweetest of plums. Golden apples and the ruby-red grapes and pomegranates!* Babur's thoughts themselves were cherishing the sweetness and freshness of such fruits, while catching the snippets of parlance, his eyes and lips pouring the wine of joy and laughter.

Babur's attention was turning to his musicians. The tunes most sonorous from the lute of Quli Muhammed, mingling with the notes from the flute of Shaikhi, accompanied by his Qubus player Hussein, were lulling Babur's heart to raptures of bliss and nostalgia. His gaze was rapt, absorbing all, even the coffer of sandalwood beside him, and the ebony table inlaid with ivory and lapis lazuli. The damask hangings over the latticed windows and the tables swathed in gold and brocade were alluring his attention, but his gaze was returning to his beloved queen, the shimmering of love-hate in her eyes carving a rivulet of loneliness within his heart, so tender and all-embracing. Involuntarily, Babur's gaze was shifting down to contemplate the poetry of songs at his feet, the Kirman carpet in its hues of blue and gold coming alive with its roses and tendrils.

One little stab of loneliness was drawing Babur's attention toward the begums, their gowns and jewels a sea of color, glittering and shimmering. Ai Begum, Mihr Nigar and Shah Begum had formed their own little circle, their coronets flaunting clusters of rubies and diamonds, or circlets of pearls and emeralds. The younger princesses, in conformity of their status as being unmarried, were wearing small silk caps broidered with gold threads or studded with jewels. Almost hidden from Babur's view was Nasir Mirza, sitting couchant against one velvety cushion, lost in his world of drinking and quiet contemplation. Jehangir Mirza's voice was grazing Babur's awareness, as if Nasir Mirza himself had begun to commune with him in thoughts alone.

"Nasir Mirza, your beloved prince, my King, in your absence had marched to Badakhshan." Jehangir Mirza was saying, abandoning his wine cup over the ebony table between him and the king. "He didn't have your permission, but was driven by his fever of caprice or drunkenness? And yet, he has a kind and passionate heart, wanting so much to conquer Badakhshan, and dreaming of a sweeping victory. He told me he wanted to surprise you with this gift of victory, my King, but nothing worked in his favor. All his hopes were shattered, and he returned to Kabul a broken man, dejected and disconsolate. His youth and inexperience, I reckon, were no match against the intrigues of the Uzbeks. Those savages like Mobarak Shah and Muhammed Korchi, so very clever and conniving. Our prince with a small contingent of troops was overwhelmed by the forces of the Uzbeks, beating a quick retreat to save his life and the lives of his soldiers. Luckily, he found refuge in Narin before returning to the safety of Kabul. Now he is nursing his shame with draughts of wine, isn't it obvious, my King?" He claimed his cup, quaffing its contents thirstily.

The wine of oblivion and the flagon of ignorance would drown my brothers into the waters of death, if not into the marshlands of betrayal and stupidity. Babur's thoughts were murmuring, his gaze fluttering over Zainab and spilling one endearment, *my emerald beauty,* before returning to his brother. *And yet, Nasir Mirza, my dear foolish brother, isn't he devoted to me?* Babur's thoughts were dwindling to the slow murmur of a cataract, his gaze alone receiving the downpour of expressions from the lips of his brother. *And Jehangir Mirza too, though gentle and brave, quite vulnerable to the temptations of deceit and trickery.*

"Beware of Baki, my King. He has the wisdom of a serpent." Jehangir Mirza was saying under some spell of urgency and inspiration. "He himself disclosed his wicked intentions to me with the hope of winning my support and friendship. I even forget now, luring me into some sort of wondrous scheme to become the master of my own fate. How to hold the citadel of Kabul under my power? How to win the hearts of all your viziers, my King, and how to conduct a durbar? Vile genius that he is, he doesn't shirk from planting seeds of discord and rebellion into the hearts of friends and foes alike. Watch him closely, my King, he may be plotting to rule Kabul himself?"

"Baki, my gentle Prince, wears the star of disloyalty over his sleeve, how could I miss noticing it?" Babur laughed suddenly. "That is his badge of cowardice, which he mistakes for defiance or audacity. And yet, he fears me greatly, daring not to test the measure of my anger or kindness. And if and when he does, he is doomed, he knows that too!"

"Baki wears daggers of enmity over the sleeves of his heart too, my King, which you have not seen! I must sound this warning." Was Jehangir Mirza's inebriated comment, than a response!

"Kings conceal warnings within the folds of their Farmans, my heedless Prince." Babur began genially. "And those Farmans have the power to reduce the kernels of all deceits and intrigues to dust and ashes. The men who carry daggers in their hearts are the most craven, dying with fright at the mere threat of danger. Hearts only groan and tremble, while minds soar and conquer. Baki's soul is naked to my perception, exposing the souls of all Afghans. They are such a querulous lot, disloyal and ungrateful. Unruly and rebellious. They would gladly sell their soul to the devil, even if it was only for winning half a patch of land." He got to his feet, his gaze arresting Nasir Mirza in its piercing intensity. "You are drinking too much, your face all flushed and bloated, more wine in your veins than blood? I like not this overindulgence. You must be wedded. Yes, I must find you a royal wife, my noble Prince! A charming princess with dreamboat eyes. It would be better if you drank from the sparkling cups in her eyes."

"I would rather drink from her lips than from her eyes, my King!" Was Nasir Mirza's giddy comment!

"Yes, you would, my bold prince, you would." Babur's eyes were shining with a mingling of reproof and tenderness. "Your boldness is making your aunts and young cousins blush with shame. But are you ashamed, no, I guess not?" He was drifting toward the bevy of begums, but his feet were stalling him midway over the group of musicians. "If I could play Qubus like that, Hussein, I could feel the kingdoms rolling under my feet." He complimented. "Borrow a tune from lovelorn to celebrate our victory this evening. You are entrusted with the task of gathering singers and dancers from glens and valleys wherever they may be, and invite all the poets and the scholars. Our viziers and courtiers too, our royal household welcomes all to make this evening grand and memorable." He drifted toward Zainab, holding dear the light of joy and gratitude from Hussein's eyes into his heart. "Come, my beauty, the glory of our gardens would lend some color to your cheeks." He held her captive in his gaze, while she glided out of her seat, her pallor replaced by a subtle flush.

A shower of molten gold from the sky, polishing the marble terraces, was left behind as Zainab and Babur kept strolling down the narrow path sprinkled with dust, pale and russet. They were walking under the shades of the poplars and Chenars, beyond which stood the groves of lemon and pomegranate. In the distance, gardeners could be seen planting the red almond saplings, but Babur's gaze was turning to the vines where the grapes in clusters shone like the rubies round and luminescent.

Summer is the loveliest of seasons in Kabul. Babur was thinking, his senses inhaling the scent of Jasmine and chambeli. The cascading jets of ripples from the fountains were bathing the beds of roses in a dewdrop serenade. The mystic in Babur was awakening to the sense of beauty in nature. His gaze was drinking the ambrosia of colors from carnations and hollyhocks. The lilacs swooping over the green arches were spilling their perfume, almost bowing in reverence to the loveliness of saffron and heliotrope. Larkspur and delphinium against the swath of love-lies-bleeding were attracting Babur's attention, his heart singing hymns of ecstasy.

"Bagh-i-Wasa would be in full bloom next year." Babur murmured wistfully, tracing the contours of marble slats edged with lychnis. "I am planning another garden, my beauty, exclusively for the two of us, for our comfort and pleasure when we grow old. Hoping, that you would learn to love me by then. I have already chosen a name for it, Bagh-i-Khilurat. Do you like this name?" He asked buoyantly.

"Sounds charming, my King." Was Zainab's generous comment, her heart moved and humbled by the abundance of scent and color in this palace garden!

"I should take you to the garden in Gulkhaneh, you have never been there, I keep forgetting." Babur's very heart, not his lips, was uttering these words. His heart, content and grateful for the mere presence of his beloved beside him. "That garden is a lover's paradise, mysterious and enchanting, as if sprouting forth from the naval of Khyber Pass, and gliding down the valleys in contours lush and undulating. Strange, that memories of old are coming back to me? My friends and I had the happiest of times in Gulkhaneh, that was before I met you. We were quite a merry group, wild and reckless, fond of playing polo or going hunting. I clearly remember the whole group when we were in Gulkhaneh one evening, Khalifa, Riddler, Tardi Beg, Khwaja Kilan, Bayziad, Ali Kuli, Pir Sultan, Mirza Kali and Khwaja Hafiz. We were playing chess and drinking wine till dawn. By that time we were so drunk that no one knew what we did or what we said, but Khwaja Hafiz kept repeating one couplet, which we couldn't drive out of our heads for days.

Ah the happy times when in ill repute
We lived a day of days in Gulkhaneh

Do you like poetry, my beauty?" He asked abruptly. His feet were coming to a slow halt by one fountain, its ripples catching cherry blossoms, and swirling them like the snow-flakes.

"Some poetry, my King, if it can challenge my heart to tears or laugher!" Zainab murmured, her cheeks flushed and her eyes glittering.

"Your heart, my cruel beauty, shuns all gems of tears or laughter, cultivating only the blooms of hatred!" Babur laughed, cutting through the blazing flames in her eyes into the fire of her heart. He stood smoothing the silk on his sleeve. "My robe is the color of your eyes, my love, it warms and comforts me, its silken touch quite close to loving and embracing. While your eyes, bright and

beautiful, wounding my heart with shafts of hatred. And then my heart feels like
a glacier of ice, much like the ice-glazed mountains in the northern parts of Kabul, where the snows never melt and the sun never warms. And yet, I hope and
wonder, if you would ever fall in love someday—with me? And wonder of all
wonders, I can't help asking again and again, why do you hate me so?" He stood
gazing into her eyes, as if awed and fascinated.

"I do not hate you, my King, I have said that before." Zainab murmured under some spell of daze and bewilderment.

"And I have asked that before, and ever so often, do you love me then?"
The sherry-brown in Babur's gaze was changing to gold amber, as if catching a
few sparks of love against the haze of bewilderment in her eyes.

"I fear you, my King." Zainab confessed, the warmth of love in her eyes
foundering against some mists of shame and misery.

"Fear—me! My sweet!" Babur exclaimed incredulously, his gaze plunging
after the foundering of love in her eyes, and his heart drumming some warnings
of presage. But he was not heeding those warnings, gathering only the blooms of
joy and hope. "Only gods inspire fear, my beauty, and I am no god. Only a simple man like any other, endowed with all the passions of lusts, desires, weak-
nesses, and yet longing, rather seeking love, your love." His gaze was ardent, his
thoughts clinging to the vine of mysticism. "If we could learn to love Allah
without the burden of fear, we would be filled with the light of love, loving all,
even our enemies. Loving foolishly and absurdly, perhaps, since love is the most
absurd of all passions, loving pain and longing for sweetness. And yet, the
power of love is great, it can conquer hearts, kingdoms, continents." He rested
his hands over her shoulders, holding her before him as if worshiping a goddess.
"Have I ever told you about the garden of Eden as perceived by the Afghans?
They think that Gulkhaneh is that garden of Eden, rather the garden of Cain. It is
the fountain of atonement, they say. It is visible to our sight and senses, refreshing our memory with the story of Fall, Redemption and Expiation. This Eden on
earth, if we can penetrate its beauty and presence, can absolve us of all our suf-
ferings, lending us the bliss of union and rapture. But my bliss is with you, my
love." He held her close in one eager embrace, kissing her hair and murmuring
endearments.

5

Love in Kabul

Sing ye people—play for me—sing the songs ye were wont to sing before your great Lord in Jerusalem

A sepulchral hush pervading the Audience Hall was splintered by a symphony of notes from lutes, flutes and cymbals. Mir Jan had begun to sing, his falsetto voice rippling forth in notes dreamy and dolorous. Babur, though absorbed in playing chess with Khwaja Kilan was catching the sad notes, and absorbing them inside his heart bereft of light and laughter. His robe of pale silks with a matching turban was accentuating his pallor, but the sherry gleam in his eyes was bright and profound. While Khwaja Kilan sat contemplating his next move on the chessboard, Babur's gaze was flying toward the groups of his courtiers and musicians. Some sort of languor was alighting in Babur's eyes, his restless gaze settling over the east wall where the display of jeweled scimitars, broad and curved daggers, and quivers bulging with arrows appeared to mock the mute surrender in his thoughts.

How sad this song? Why do I hear the sound of a distant cataract, weeping and murmuring? How exquisite is pain and silence, hovering and shuddering? Babur's thoughts, in protest against *mute surrender*, had begun to whisper and gallivant. His gaze was returning to the chessboard, the rosewood table housing this *field of combat* a sinking ocean between him and Khwaja Kilan. One wisp of a smile touched Babur's lips as he watched Khwaja Kilan's reluctant move, his thoughts drawing a line of strategy, quite daring and challenging. Swiftly, he moved his bishop carved in the likeness of a camel, replacing Khwaja Kilan's rook in its housing of carved elephant. A thin smile curved around the ridges of Khwaja Kilan's lip too as he watched the king's move, but he didn't say a word. Both were plunged deep in concentration once again, but Babur appeared to be admiring the beauty of chess pieces, exquisitely carved and embellished.

The queens molded in ivory with bouquets in their arms were peering out of their palanquins. A pair of howdahs carved out of sandalwood was hosting two kings seated on war elephants. The carvings of knights riding their horses, and the pawns kneeling in the semblance of bowmen were evoking afresh the awe and wonder in Babur's eyes for the artists who had designed each piece with the skill of jewelers.

The game of chess was progressing slowly, lending Babur a few interludes to observe his guests, viziers, and courtiers, and to grant his thoughts the liberty of making decisions which could not be postponed. The objects of his scrutiny were few, foremost amongst them Nasir Mirza, drinking religiously. Husein Mirza seated beside him was doing justice to the sweets out of silver platter. Senjer Barlas, seated not too far from them, was the victim of his overindulgence, oblivious to his insatiable passion for wine and sweets. Khalifa, Mulla Baba, Mohib Korchi and Ahmad Kasim had formed their own little circle, lolling against the large pillows while talking and drinking. Babur's gaze and thoughts had dismissed all with the exception of his uncle, Hussayan Baikara. He had come from Herat with an urgent request, seeking Babur's aid against the impending assault from Shaibani Khan.

Shaibani Khan, the inveterate lord of intrigues! Yet, my own brother, a wretched fool and a rebel!

Babur's thoughts were journeying back in time two months hence, when Jehangir Mirza had assisted him in crushing the rebellion of a few tribes in the city of Kilat. After returning to Kabul, Babur had made Jehangir Mirza the vizier of Ghazni, while granting Nasir Mirza the privilege of ruling Nur-Valley. Meanwhile, Baki Cheghanaini, equipped with the armor of hatred and jealousy, had devised a plan to hurl the Prince of Ghazni into the waters of doom and damnation. Skillful in the art of flattery and deception, Baki had begun sending letters to Jehangir Mirza, inciting him to acts of greed and tyranny. Babur's gaze alone, this precise moment, was contemplating the chess board, his thoughts racing after his lout of a brother on the road toward extinction.

Jehangir Mirza, journeying forth from Ghazni as the lord of nemesis? The besotted prince, pillaging and plundering. Shedding the blood of the innocents without the slightest of shame or remorse? Laying siege over the citadel in Bamain—

The journey in Babur's head was ending with a jolt of awareness.

Your king would be stalemated. The queen and the entire brood of your army would be slaughtered on this marble field of a chessboard. Babur's thoughts were facing a whirlwind of options. He was quick to find a solution, placing the knight in front to guard the life of the chess-king.

"A prudent move, my King!" Khwaja Kilan murmured hopelessly.

"The only move a desperate king could make against the worthy bishop!" A spontaneous gale of laughter escaped Babur's lips, his thoughts firing missiles over the head of Shaibani Khan.

That black-hearted Bedouin of a foe, brutal and heartless! For the past year and a half, that reptile has wreaked havoc over the valleys and the villages. Samarkand, the well-preserved jewel of the Mongols, he has seized, pillaging and plundering. This lord of tyranny, sweeping through Andijan, Kunduz, Khwarism, carving rivers of blood, and now approaching close to the blessed shores of Herat. Herat, the home of Art and History! We must not let it perish by the savage assaults of Shaibani Khan.

"Herat is our Jerusalem!" Babur's contralto voice boomed suddenly, startling all present out of their repose and indulgence. "It seems Nebuchadnezzar has returned? But we must not let Shaibani Khan defile this sacred city with his savage need to kill and plunder. He is killing innocent people, even the little children, and all in the name of religion? Sullying the name of Islam with his bundle of lies and distortion. Gloating over the rubbles of his tyrannies and conquests. He thinks he is guided by the very hand of divine will, whom he dares call, Allah. This prince of lies is heard of boasting that he is the direct descendant of Genghis Khan. He tells his besotted soldiers that Genghis Khan practiced the divine law of Torah. And this heathen has not even read his Quran. He must be stopped. Tomorrow, right after the morning prayers, we march from Kabul to safeguard the city of Herat against the savage threat from Shaibani Khan."

"Tomorrow! Right after the prayers?" Baki Cheghanaini stumbled to his feet, realizing too soon his breach of court manners in not adding *my king*, then kneeling double in a state of shame and confusion.

"As for you, my pious friend, you are to be exiled beyond the plains of Punjab!" Babur thundered, his eyes flashing.

"My King." Baki Cheghanaini sat there stunned. "My King, you promised you would not send me into exile as long as my offenses remained under check, never exceeding the number nine. And my offenses are only—" He couldn't continue against the blaze of rage in Babur's eyes.

"Add two more over your heap of lies, my bellicose vizier!" Babur waved impatiently. "Breach of etiquettes, for one. Were you addressing the king, or speaking with a beggar on the street? Even a beggar, despite his poverty and misfortune, holds within him the gemlike nobility of a soul, demanding respect, if not compassion. Lacking manners in my durbar is a great offense. One must conform to the laws of propriety."

"Pardon me, my King." Baki Cheghanaini implored. "I know my offenses don't amount to nine, and I try my best not to commit any more."

"Eleven, Baki, eleven!" Babur's look was piercing, the fire of rage in his eyes replaced by glints of amusement. "All your offenses could be forgiven with the exception of one, and you know which one is that? Didn't you corrupt the mind and soul of prince Jehangir, inciting him to acts of revolt, betrayal and brutality? Only an evil genius like you can turn the altar of a gentle heart into the furnace of cruelty. You have become the victim of your vile, wicked schemes. By your malefic designs alone, Khwarism fell into Shaibani's hands. You poisoned the minds of the Hazaras, instigating them to rebel and plunder. Haven't you adopted the custom of *drums playing* anytime you leave or enter your palace? Knowing fully well that this privilege is the birthright of the kings alone! By violating this rule, you become guilty of treason. You have gone as far as stealing gold and jewels from the royal treasury. Didn't you kill two young Afghans, accusing them of treachery, though you didn't have any proof? Greed and gluttony, the least of your crimes, forcing my royal servants to work in your gardens without compensation? Plotting to get me killed, once when I was away from Kabul, and the second time when prince Jehangir fled from Ghazni."

"I didn't incite prince Jehangir to—" Baki Cheghanaini's voice was sucked out by the blaze of anger in Babur's eyes.

"You weary me, Baki, be gone! The breach of etiquette once again." Babur dismissed him with one imperious wave of his arm. His attention was already turning toward his courtiers. "Kipa, Sundak, Tigri Birdi, Pir Sultan, Kambar Ali, Baba Sherzad, you all would be a part of our cavalcade on the road to Herat. And of course, my trusted friend and vizier, Khwaja Kilan. The ones staying behind to guard the citadel of Kabul would be, you, Khalifa and Khan Mirza. And Mulla Baba, Ahmed Kasim and Mohib Korchi." His gaze was shifting toward his uncle, one flicker of a smile curling upon his lips. "Do me a favor, my most distinguished uncle. Please take this burden of sovereignty over your shoulders in my absence, to rule over friends and foes, and keep an eye on rebels too, lest they disturb the peace of Kabul."

"A burden too heavy for my old shoulders, my King!" Muhammed Doghlat protested unconvincingly.

"A burden, you would make light, I am sure, with your wisdom and experience." Babur assured winsomely, becoming aware of the lyrical notes, *Allah-hu-Akbar,* from the palace mosque. "Muezzin is calling us for noon prayers. Go to the mosque, or offer prayers at home, whatever your inclination. After the prayers, look to the needs of this long journey toward Herat." He got to his feet, his gaze profound and restless. "Khan Mirza, you would make sure that Baki has left Kabul before the call for evening prayers." He drifted toward his brother, who stood drinking out of his gold cup. "And you, Prince Nasir, would return to Nur-Valley before our journey toward Heart." He snatched the gold cup from his brother's hand, and quaffed it thirstily before tossing it to the floor. "Wine, my sweet brother, is never going to quench your thirst. And what you are thirsting for, I have yet to find, and you must too? Meanwhile, abstain from drinking excessively." He got to his heels, his heart heavy and longing for the comfort-nearness of Zainab.

The evening perfumed with the promise of love and sweetness had drifted into the heart of the night, as Babur and Zainab sat on the velvety davenport, talking and laughing. Babur's fingers were combing Zainab's hair absently, his gaze admiring the pale gold sheen, which only the queen's lady-in-waiting— Maywa Jan could accomplish with her skill in brushing, *hundred strokes each night,* Babur was thinking. Some sort of bliss and harmony had settled into this bedroom of ivory and damask since Zainab had confessed that she loved him, and right this moment he was thinking he had died and entered Paradise. Her soft, white face was swimming before his sight like some houri straight from the heavens, and he pressed her close to him, closing his eyes as if he was dreaming and didn't wish to be awakened from this dream.

"Do you still hate me, my beauty?" Babur teased, opening his eyes and getting lost into the emerald pools of her eyes. *So adorable and beautiful, now that the love sits there glorious and sparkling*, his thoughts were opiate and swooning.

"I do not love you, my King." Zainab retorted, laughter in her eyes and upon her lips singing of love and surrender.

"Yes, my sweetness, yes! The king knows! Why are your eyes spilling the wine of love, and this slave is getting drunk already." Babur joined her in her mirth. "The fire of emeralds in your eyes, God's gift—most beautiful! Do you know that emerald stands for the final level of spiritual aspiration? When man has passed through the blackness of annihilation, and emerges in heaven at last able to view the world as through the eyes of God?" He kissed her hands, holding them against his cheeks. His heart was in swoon, its bliss splintering and crackling against the familiar feeling of presage. Somewhere out there was loss and grief, but his heart smitten with love dared not accost those shades and shadows. "I wish I can take you with me to Herat. But the journey is long and dangerous, though less dangerous than my entire brood of family and friends whom I am leaving behind?"

"Most of them are devoted to you, my King." Zainab consoled, her heart thundering all of a sudden. "My only fear is they would drink much too much in your absence, neglecting their duties to maintain peace in Kabul."

"My love pure and innocent!" Babur pressed her close to him, his heart longing to possess her body and soul. "Watch my stepmother closely, her heart is a jungle of intrigues. And Senjer Barlas is no less, skilled in plotting. Keep an eye on my uncle, Muhammed Doghlat too—him and my cousin Shah Mirza, when together they can't help but be swayed by their worst judgments."

"You are judging them too harshly, my King, are you not?" Zainab murmured, her heart trembling against the flood of ardor in Babur's eyes.

"Perhaps, my beauty! Why I am talking about this when my heart is filled with the sweetness of your love and my own desire." Babur held her close to him tenderly, almost reverently. Do you know, my emerald, I had always thought that no one could be happy on this wretched earth? How wrong I was? Now that I have found your love—my happiness, I feel humbled. This foolish heart, a glutton to happiness, wanting more and more—" He was crushing her into a tight embrace as if he would never let her go, kissing, kissing.

6

From Kabul to Herat

On a journey ill
And our fields all withered, dreams
Go wandering still
　　　　— Basho

The cool, easterly wind was whispering some songs dear and nostalgic in Babur's head as he rode side by side with his brother, Jehangir. Babur's green robe was gathered at his waist with a gold belt, encrusted with rubies and emeralds. These jewels were absorbing sunshine, including the red plume in his turban, and the jade hilt over his belt, but his thoughts were gathering no sunshine. His thoughts were chilled, catching only the icy glitter from past betrayals and present sadness'. Twenty days had elapsed since his journey from Kabul on the road to Herat, and much had happened like the lapping of the waves, turbulent and quicksilver. He and his brother were riding ahead of the cavalcade, the standards of red and yellow floating behind them over the shoulders of the soldiers and the courtiers. The viziers, scholars and drummers were lagging behind, letting their mounts trot or canter in rhythm with the flow of the entire cavalcade. Babur's gaze was reaching out to the gold-spangled vistas, but he was becoming aware of his brother riding beside him, his thoughts sliding back into alleys dark and mournful.

Prince Jehangir, the victim of his betrayal and foolishness, had fled west, taking refuge in the pleasant valley of Bamain, not far from the Land of the Buddhas. Babur had no intention of chasing his brother, but during his journey toward Herat, after crossing the Shibar Pass and the Tooth-break Pass, he was informed that Jehangir was hiding down the cliffs of Bamain. The fugitive prince himself, burdened with remorse, had sought the king's forgiveness, and Babur had forgiven him, exacting no punishment, only the promise of fidelity and submission.

Babur's thoughts were lost in the cliffs of Bamain, resurrecting carved Buddhas from within the very heart of the mountains, though he and his cavalcade were nearing the precincts of Khorasan—the capital of Herat. While united with his brother in Bamain, a messenger from Herat had brought grievous news that Babur's uncle—Hussayan Baikara had died suddenly. This dear loss of his uncle was a heavy blow to Babur, carving new worries that now the kingdom of Herat was exposed to invasion from Uzbeks more than ever before, since Badi-uz-Zaman and Musafer Hussayan—the sons of his deceased uncle were young and inexperienced in warfare. Shaibani Khan at the head of a large contingent was already wreaking havoc, sweeping through the cities of Balkh, Andijan, Kunduz and Khwarism with the speed of a hurricane, pillaging and plundering. This lord of tyranny was killing men, women and children, and torching the towns and valleys indiscriminately. His next move was to sack the city of Herat, but for some inexplicable reason he had decided to return to Samarkand with his booty of beasts and treasures.

Shaibani Khan! The foul reptile, hideous and heartless, Babur's thoughts were murmuring against the wonder of landscape unfolding before his sight like a dream beautiful and awesome. They were approaching close to the city of Khorasan, its five gates challenging as well as welcoming the onlookers to explore its treasures in art and architecture. Babur was leading his cavalcade toward one gateway of all sandalwood, its carved portals glinting the inlay of copper, most delicately beaten and designed. Upon approaching closer, the silver-headed bolts and the marquetry could be seen spiraling up in patterns of vines and flowers. Babur was entering the city like a lone pilgrim, becoming oblivious to the presence of his brother or of his large cavalcade behind him, his gaze drinking the glory and splendor of Khorasan. It was a city of magic and mystery, flaunting the handiwork of its artists and artisans. The slender minarets of the mosques, the marble facades of the shrines, the palaces dipped in tiles of blue and turquoise, all appeared to be sailing toward the distant ramparts turned opalescent by sunshine. Babur's sight and senses were dazzled by this mirage-like arena of form and color, so exquisite and glorious, his thoughts bursting forth in a symphony of awe and praise.

"Hussayan Baikara wrote to me once, Khorasan is the oyster shell of the world, and Herat is its pearl. He was absolutely right." Babur turned his head toward his brother, his look rapt and shining.

"If you had come to Herat by the road from Irak, my King, you would have not seen the pearls but the pebbles." Jehangir's smooth features were wrinkled into one poignant smile. "Have you forgotten, my King, that we visited Herat when we were young? I can still remember the western quarters. The squat clay hutches and the flat roofs over the houses. Once I was lost too amidst those narrow streets, all dark and labyrinthine. There were arched gates, almost crumbling, and the foul-smelling courtyards. One could see men and beasts, all huddled together, selling and bartering. So many mules and camels, laden with the cargo of rugs and bales of spices. And that noise, the pounding of chisel on ivory, quite maddening. The art of bartering, I still have to learn?" His gaze was piercing the distant grove of poplars, spruced with pines and cedars.

"All men are skilled in bartering their souls in this bazaar of greed, my sweet prince, and this art requires no learning." Babur opined aloud, his gaze sailing above the *pearl city* to the western sky, all molten and heliotrope. "We might still meet the savage Khiljis on our way to Herat? The sheep-raising Duranis could still be living in their huts, if not the warring Yusufzais, or the inveterate robbers from the tribes of Hazaras? If we are fortunate, we might see the diamond merchants from Golconda and Bundelkand, or traders from Bokhara with their bundles of Bokhara rugs, exquisite and priceless. And the hawkers selling fruits, the sweet-smelling bananas from Ispahan, the juiciest of oranges from Damascus, and the sweetest of grapes from Kabul. I must not think about Kabul, now." He sighed, feeling one pang of a longing to be near Zainab. "We can find the best Damascened swords here, our baba bought us a pair of swords when we visited Herat, if you can recall? Inset with jade and tourmaline, remember? We must buy books, the best calligraphists in the world live in Herat. And a drinking cup for you, my fool of a prince, the cup hollowed from the coral of Araby. The silks, pearls and the diamonds for begums and princesses—" His heart was murmuring the name of Zainab.

The sky had turned cobalt splashed with streaks of mauve and orange, as Babur stood admiring the palace of his cousins, looming in the distance like a miracle sublime. His gaze was returning to the garden where he stood under the pavilion of velvet, erected on golden poles, *as an emblem of greetings to welcome the King of Kabul*, Babur was thinking. He could feel the richness of Bokhara carpet under his feet, its silk-wool patterns in green and scarlet rippling forth from under the pavilion toward the steps of the palace. The soldiers and courtiers were standing behind Babur, awed and speechless, their mounts left behind in the company of the horses belonging to their hosts kind and generous.

Babur was drifting toward the palace dreamlike, his gaze fondling the jasper and turquoise flowers embedded on the marble façade. The vaulting over the front doors was hosting more jewel flowers in clusters of rubies and amethysts. He was mounting the marble steps, the cupolas embedded with jade and crystal before his sight, soaring and shimmering. A myriad of windows were lit to golden effulgence, their shades embellished with coral and carnelian. Babur's feet had come to a slow halt before the turquoise doors, their inlay of ivory and brass in koftgari designs most delicate and awe-inspiring. He turned suddenly, facing the files of his battalion, all mute and awe-stricken. His gaze was dreamy and searching. He had espied Naralla wedged between the files of soldiers.

"Beat your drums, Naralla, announce the arrival of the King." Babur's command was splintering the hush outside this palace of magic and mystery.

Naralla had begun to beat his drums, and the palace and the garden were awakened to a flurry of activity. The spell of awe was broken, unveiling more wonders of beauty and enchantment. The turquoise portals were thrown open, revealing a coterie of servants in liveries of silk and brocade. They were pouring out to greet the King of Kabul, and trooping down into the garden to offer greetings to the soldiers and courtiers. Amidst a heap of curtsies, Babur was welcomed into the bright parlor of the palace.

Badi-uz-Zaman bowed thrice before locking Babur into one eager embrace. Next came the younger prince, Musafer Hussayan, greeting Babur with the same customary bows, and a warm embrace. Babur's aunts were gathering around him too, Apaq begum, Sultan begum and Khadija begum, all bursting with joy and laughter. Prince Jehangir, followed by courtiers had entered the parlor, and all were swept into the warmth of love and camaraderie. The entire palace was stirring, it seemed, to serve the royal guests and to make them comfortable. The cooks, the cup-bearers, the basin-bearers, all were being summoned and instructed to commence their tasks with utmost diligence and swiftness. A coterie of servants had marched out to conduct the soldiers to their apartments behind the palace, while the grooms were on their way to feed the horses. The wine-bearers were filling the goblets of the royal guests with ruby-red wine from their gold flagons. Badi-uz-Zaman was in ecstatic swoon, beaming at Babur, talking and laughing.

"What is your pleasure, my King?" Badi-uz-Zaman asked suddenly, his handsome features aglow with the warmth of love and laughter.

"A bath!" Babur laughed, overwhelmed by the swift churning of fatigue in his limbs and thoughts. "I can smell the reek of our Uzbek foe—Shaibani Khan, the dust of his tyranny is settled in my very heart and soul. Before I purge myself of that reek, I need to wash the dust of this journey long and arduous from my body and garments."

"A perfumed bath for my King!" Badi-uz-Zaman clapped his hands.

One basin-bearer in a livery of red and gold had materialized before Babur, leading him into a guest chamber, vast and luxuriant. The adjoining bathroom with gleaming tiles was his refuge and sanctuary. He had immersed his aching limbs into the scented bath with a sigh of relief and gratitude. His eyes were closing against the dance-flicker of gold flames from the candelabra, the tile floor burnished blue reflecting another star-dance of memories in his head.

Behind the closed shutters of Babur's eyes, the gates of his palace in Kabul were flung open, transporting him straight into the perfumed bath with Zainab, which he had shared with her before leaving. A subtle odor of loss and grief was oozing out of his psyche in rivulets of warnings. His opiate thoughts were barring shut the windows of his psyche, humming only some tunes strange and mournful. The ghost of his dead uncle was with him, smirking and grinning. *Is the mourning period for my death past remembrance, so soon, so soon,* the poetic soul of the ghost was watching his sons with utter disinterest? Babur's thoughts were holding captive the poetic ghost of his uncle, and lowering down a rosary of words.

We are—all of us, the creatures of our habits inviolate and formidable. The slaves of our needs and greeds? Whipped by ambition? Violating the sanctity of this earth with the spades of enmity and vengeance. Doomed by the vices of cruelty and hatred. Making our hearts the battlefields of zeal and enmity. Perpetual exiles—exiled from the paradise of love and harmony, wandering, wandering—

Babur's thoughts were wading through the waters of sleep, murky and turbulent.

7

Babylonian Feast

They blossom, and then
We gaze, and then the blooms
Scatter, and then—
    — Onitsura

Babur, seated at the table with his aunts, cousins and courtiers was cherishing the taste of this Babylonian feast, while the servants were busy clearing the table of its gold and silver plates. A large platter with the remnants of carved goose which Badi-uz-Zaman himself had carved was whisked away swiftly, as well as the bowls of fruit, leaving behind only the jeweled goblets. Some sort of languor had settled in Babur's thoughts, his fingers twirling the ropes of pearls around his neck absently. His robe of green silks with a matching turban studded with an emerald in the middle was lending his boyish features the glow of warmth and profundity. His heart was aching all of a sudden, longing for the presence of Zainab beside him, his gaze slipping over the paintings in gilded frames down to the tables inlaid with mother-of-pearl.

I have prolonged my visit in Herat, and my heart is longing for the valleys of Kabul.

Babur's gaze was returning to the sparkle and glitter of jewels in the hair of the ladies and around their throats, but the tunes most sweet and tender were luring his attention toward the group of poets and musicians. Couchant against large pillows over the silk-wool carpet, Jalaluddin with his lute and Hafiz Hajji on his tambourine were creating a medley of tunes, more so for the pleasure of the dancers than to impress the hosts and the guests. The Jewish harpist, Bacha, seated in one corner, was fondling the strings of his harp for fine tuning. The voices of the poets beside the harpist were skirling aloft, loud and argumentative.

"*What are words to me?* God demanded. *Take no heed of thought or expression. I require only a burning heart.*" Binai was quoting from the dialogues of the late poet, Rumi. "Then Rumi cries in mystical madness. *I die as a plant and rise to animal life. I die as an animal to be reborn as a man, when I die as a man I shall enter life and beyond the angels I shall become what no human eyes have seen—nothingness. Nothingness in God.*" Binai's resinous eyes were challenging his poet friend, Ali Sher.

Some sort of mystic madness in Babur's thoughts was shutting the gates of all voices, the journey in his head whirling and twisting its way into the gardens of Kabul with *sweet absent* beside him, his beloved Zainab. He was lonesome amidst this ocean of gaiety and opulence, his heart longing to be near his beloved. His soul was hungering and thirsting for something greater than art and beauty, greater than song and poetry, and yet he didn't know what it was which was carving rivers of vacuity within his soul and psyche. And yet again he knew what it was, the ache and hunger for solitude, for solitary walks in his gardens, for the nearness of his beloved, his senses longing for the scent of home, love, and paradise.

Why this languor and sadness? Have I had my fill of the beauty of art and architecture? Such exquisite gardens and glorious monuments! The giddy hours of feasting and drinking. Twenty long days—centuries in this pearl city of Herat, and my heart still seeking the pearls of wisdom, harmony, knowledge? Babur's thoughts were inward bound, skirting back toward the holiest of shrines where he had kneeled and prayed with the devotion of a pilgrim lost and bewildered.

The tomb of Shah Mansur with its marble platforms was unfolding its wonders in Babur's mind. Its arches painted black swooping down like the wings of an eagle, slippery and glistening. Ansari's tomb with golden domes, and the silvery minars of Mosalla soaring up to the heavens. A cluster of golden domes inlaid with lapis lazuli over the tomb of Gohar Shadi a shuddering reflection down the crystal-clear stream, adorned with nine jet sarcophagi. Masjid Janah, a great mural of mosaics, its façade tiled more like an ocean in blue porcelain. From the distance, this mosque with its azure radiance flaunted four hundred and eight gold cupolas. Approaching closer, one had to walk half a mile to count its one hundred and thirty windows, while admiring the white columns, four hundred in all, tall and majestic. The Raven Garden and the Pleasure-House with precious blooms and the marble fountains. Babur's thoughts were halting near one white palace dipped in meadows from all sides, serene and ethereal. This was the place where Babur's aunt Sultan Begum had introduced him to his cousin, Princess Masuma.

Dear Payanda, Babur's thoughts were murmuring this endearment which he had used to tease his aunt in response to her comment, so very sweet and flattering. Sultan Begum had told Babur that his cousin Masuma had fallen in love with him, madly and hopelessly. At this recollection, Babur's eyes were lit up with an amused smile, his gaze settling on Ali Sher. Ali Sher was reciting the flowery prose of some Persian author, *probably deceased and forgotten,* Babur was thinking.

"*The whirlwind of their sighs has shattered the skies! The torrent of their tears has drowned the habitable earth.*" Ali Sher had begun to laugh, tears stinging his eyes. "This poet-star was never content with the flood of tears which the ill-starred lovers had so generously offered, so his method to madness was to drown nature into its own torrent of sorrows."

The amused smile in Babur's eyes was replaced with sadness, his thoughts communing with the much-venerated poet—Jami, whose tomb he had visited last week. But his gaze was turning to Binai, who had commenced his recital. He, in fact, was reciting a passage from the works of a court historiographer from Khandamir. The words were familiar to Babur, his thoughts expounding that this piece was written to honor the birth of Hussayan Baikara.

"At the happy birth of the glorious monarch, the light of the star of his horoscope illumined the inhabited fourth of the globe. And when the bright moon saw the glitter of his beauty, ornament of the earth, she ceased to borrow her rays from the Sun." Binai's gaze was flashing a subtle challenge at Ali Sher.

"Your dead poet, Binai, I like his metaphors better than his flatteries." Ali Sher hummed caustically. "Listen to this for the sake of critical versification. *The tree of enmity springs from the soil of discord; and, watered every day by the gardener of destiny. Its fruits ripen until they fall upon the field of unhappiness."*

"The songs and poetry dripping like wine from our gold flagons, my King, are making you sad somehow?" Badi-uz-Zaman sought Babur's attention. "Whoever said that the depiction of figures is prohibited by Islam, must be a heathen. Yes, an irreverent heathen, or a hypocrite, violating the precepts of Islam with lies and distortion." He held out the painting of Bihzad to Babur. "Our Bihzad can do wonders with his brushes, but this is God's handiwork, I say."

"Muslims recite Quran like parrots, hugging literal expressions, and exploring not the inner meaning behind words, metaphors and parables." Babur was studying the canvas with much interest. The men in colorful robes, astride their graceful steeds were coming alive before his naked sight. "One hundred and fourteen suras in the Quran, and not even one prohibiting the depiction of art, allegorical or representational. Mighty is the art of distortion, which half the Muslims in this world are adopting to conceal with the armor of their zeal and hypocrisy."

"I know the cause of king's sadness!" Sultan Begum couldn't resist the temptation of teasing. "His thoughts are with Masuma. Who could have imagined our adorable Princess smitten with love for this heartless King of Kabul?"

"My dear Payanda! Tell my fair cousin that king is in love with his wife." Babur retorted with a sprinkling of mirth. "My sweet, scheming aunt, imagine that? Love is a paradox, which only fools dare contemplate. Kings can't afford this luxury, and saints and sages can't be caught by its snares, since their hearts are filled with the love of God."

"A royal wedding, my King, won't you agree?" Musafer Hussayan raised his jeweled cup to his lips, draining its contents thirstily. "Muslims don't have to be kings to have four wives. And you being a king can certainly have as many wives as you want. A great celebration for your wedding, if you consent, and a great diversion for us in these times of wars and intrigues. Such precious boons, permitted by God's decree, we must not shun, or we would be committing grave errors in rejecting God's favors." His look was glazed, the fire of inebriation in his thoughts rushing to his cheeks in blotches of pink and crimson.

"*Permitted*, with the connotation of a choice and discretion?" Babur contemplated aloud. "As to having four wives, Prophet Muhammad elaborated on that sura that permission be granted to those Muslims who were capable of treating all their wives with equal love, with equal justice, and with equal consideration. Knowing fully well that no man, however saintly, could ever maintain the scale of love, justice and equality in perfect balance? A man—any man can't even treat his one wife with love and consideration, then how could he justify doing justice to all four of them? All men have the will and the power to mold each word, holy or profane, to suit their lusts and desires." His gaze was shifting toward the oval table to his right where a pious judge sat playing chess.

This judge was no other than Sheiul-Islam, known for his skill in playing chess with two companions at the same time, and that's what he was doing right now, challenging two players simultaneously. The gold and ivory pieces under his scrutiny were his slaves, trained to intimidate the army of one opponent, while contemplating to kill the leaders of the other, most swiftly and ingeniously. Noticing Babur's interest or distraction, Sultan Begum ventured another appeal on behalf of Princess Masuma.

"You do need another wife, my King!" Sultan Begum began coaxingly. "Zainab begum is not congenial, I have heard?"

"Zainab! My lovely star of the mountains, does she hate the king?" A spontaneous gale of mirth escaped Babur's lips, his eyes shining. "That's what you think, dear Payanda? Prince Jehangir must be feeding your lovely head with gossip straight from the court of Kabul?" He snatched one ball of majun from the silver bowl beside him, and tossed it into his mouth, swallowing it with a draught of wine. "Hatred is the most noble and virile of all passions, if you only knew? It is the seed, the kernel and the flower of all passions. By the law and virtue of its violence, it gives birth to love, tenderness and compassion. In order to appreciate the gift of love, one must commune with the demons of hate, envy, jealousy inside the dungeon of one's soul. Strange, that this verse from the Quran—Sura Four, Verse Three is coming to my mind. My baba used to recite it so often, I guess, and after his death, I couldn't get it out of my head. *And if you fear you will not be fair in dealing with the orphans, then marry women as may be agreeable to you, two, or three, or four, and if you fear you will not deal justly, then marry only one or what your right hand possesses. That's the nearest way for you to avoid injustice.*" He recited with the passion of a mystic, the sherry gleam in his eyes churning profundities. "As a king, no different than any other man, or from the slave of any man, I would most probably have a harem full of wives when my whim or caprice would dare mold the laws of religion to suit my needs of lust or desire. Surely, then, my dear Aunt, I would be disfiguring the face of truth, defying the laws of justice and donning the mantle of ignorance and all this with the blissful certainty of a hypocrite that I am a pillar of obedience under the throne of Islam. And yet, the wounds on our flesh and inside our hearts make us vulnerable. We become the victims of our noble lusts and wild desires. Yes, my beloved Aunt, I might marry? Not now, nor in the near future. I am in love, besottedly in love, with my own wife. Longing to be with her. I must journey back, tomorrow, if possible?"

"Princess Masuma would follow you to the very gates of Kabul, my King." Sultan Begum sang half merrily, half earnestly.

"You must not venture out on this long journey, my King, this time of the year. Winters come early around here." Khadija Begum flashed a smile at prince Jehangir before shifting her attention to Babur. "The roads would be covered with snow, impassable at times, and you might be stranded in the cold without shelter or provisions. Stay with us till spring, a perfect weather for traveling or excursions."

"Power of love, my sweet Aunt, it can melt even glaciers to pave the way for a lover to be united with his beloved!" Babur quipped poetically, though his heart was thundering omens dark and terrible.

"Permit the poets of Herat, my King, to indulge in their sins of divinations!" Binai exclaimed with an abrupt vehemence. "Tomorrow is not a propitious day for the King to be on the road, the stars in conjunction with your horoscope forbid traveling. Besides, if Shaibani Khan found out that you have left, he would come marching at the very gates of Herat, equipped with the armor of self-righteousness to kill and destroy?"

"King has the power to mold the stars to match his divinations, bright and favorable." Babur laughed. "And as to Shaibani's armor of self-righteousness, it would crumble too much like the armors of those fools in the annals of history, who were reduced to dust by the fires of their zeal and bigotry. Such quarrelsome race, these Uzbeks. Their excessive zeal alone would be their downfall. Shaibani, in my estimation, would hibernate during the winter months inside the comfort of his palace in Samarkand. His warring, hate-mongering spirit awakens only during the balmy months of spring and summer."

"The poets in Herat stretch their legs as far and as rudely as their thoughts!" Ali Sher groaned aloud, kicking back the heavy legs of Binai.

"Poets in Herat, even when they don't stretch their legs, impudence in their eyes leaps beyond the confines of courtesy!" Was Binai's angry retort in his act of nursing his legs!

"Shaibani Khan's vices, my King, outnumber the stars in the heavens." Saifi—the poet tossed this comment in an effort to divert king's attention from the unmannerly behavior of his poet friends.

"The slave of his zeal, he beholds his vices as virtues countless." Babur indulged laconically.

"His wicked intrigues would hurl him into the pits of damnation!" Palevan Muhammed—the wrestler was breaking his silence, his fists clenched.

"Stupidity, ignorance, and intolerance lead one to damnation, not wickedness?" Babur murmured, as if to his own self.

"Vices and follies aside, Shaibani Khan is a lover of music, my king. Difficult to believe that this formidable foe can love anyone or anything?" Badi-uz-Zaman too appeared to cover the manner-less tirade of his poets. "By the virtue of his love for music, he struck one musician over the head when he played on lute in poor taste."

"And that, my gallant Prince, is the best thing he has done so far!" Babur's eyes were gathering stars of mirth and amusement. "Maybe, the one and the only noble act of his entire life? Music is sacred, and any violation to its sanctity deserves punishment. With this merry note, I must retire. The ill-starred journey tomorrow according to the divinations of the poets might be perilous? So I must rest."

"You are not leaving tomorrow, my King?" Sultan Begum feigned ignorance, still trying to persuade the king to stay.

"We must, dear Payanda, Kabul is calling us." Babur murmured with a touch of finality.

"My King, would you please leave prince Jehangir with us?" Khadija Begum pleaded suddenly. "His constitution is weak, and he should not be exposed to the harsh conditions of this journey; especially, when winters are almost upon us." She was watching the Prince dozing in his chair with his chin wedged between his elbows on the table.

"Wine and majun, his gateway to the bliss in oblivion!" Babur murmured sadly. "His overindulgence, I fear, would never permit him the luxury of good health. Yes, my sweet aunt, he can stay, till spring, if you wish? Your love and indulgence might keep him away from the dangers of intrigues. He has forgotten how to laugh. Whoever said laughter is the best medicine, must be a physician. Though laughter doesn't taste like medicine, it has the flavor of wine, smooth and tingling, soothing the riot of discord in body and soul." He heaved himself up amidst a flurry of protests.

Sleep was continents away as Babur lay down on his bed in the guest chamber. He was missing Zainab, his heart longing to fly to Kabul. There was riot in his thoughts, louder than the rippling of music from down the parlor, interspersed with gales of mirth and raillery. His thoughts were shooting warnings he could neither catch, nor comprehend. One sliver of a warning which he could arrest was this small voice of fear, foretelling the siege of some pain intolerable and loss irretrievable.

Zainab, my love and beloved! Babur's thoughts were hugging the volcano of dreams, where all joys were sucked into the vacuum of silence.

8

Holy Grief

Morning haze
As in a painting of a dream
Men go their ways
            — Buson

Babur's cavalcade lumbering down the slopes of Zarin Pass was caught into a snow-squall, the white dunes of snow reaching up to the knees of the horses brave and tireless. The fur-lined collar of Babur's coat was stretched over to his ears, his cap of fleece almost covering his entire face with the exception of his eyes, swollen and stinging. The cold, bitter winds were chilling the very heart of nature, but the fire of love in Babur's heart was goading him to continue riding toward Kabul—to Beloved.

Allah, all the sinners and virtuous in this world would long for the warmth of hell if they were to taste the fury of this snow-storm, so chilling and blood-curdling?

Babur's thoughts were feverish despite the chills cutting through his body like the cold steel of knives sharp and ruthless. A little over than a month had slithered past since they had embarked on this journey long and arduous, and they were still fighting their way home on the snowy terrains in hope of respite and right direction. Babur could see Pir Sultan leading again, though he had lost his sense of direction, yet staying adamant that they were headed in the right direction. Kasim Beg's horse was stirring mounds of snow, while the mounts of Tigri Birdi and Kambar Ali were lagging behind, barely trotting. Babur's steed was having difficulty ploughing through this ocean of snow. His thoughts sliding back to maintain the semblance of reality in this whirlwind of hopelessness.

Herat was a distant dream lost somewhere behind the haze of Lenger-Mir Ghias and the borders of Gharjistan. Days and weeks of inclement weather were their companions, while Babur and his cavalcade had trekked through the foothills of Chekheheran, Chirghdan, Anjukan and Khaisal Koti in the direction of Zarin Pass. Pir Sultan, guiding this cavalcade had decided to take the hill-road instead of the low road passing through Farah and Kandahar. He had lost his sense of direction over the snowbound terrains, discovering too late after many hours of riding that they were back on the same slope from where they had started in the early hours of afternoon. Darkness itself had engulfed them in hopelessness, while they had kindled fires to warm themselves. In the morning, several parties were dispatched in all four directions to find the right road before continuing their journey homeward.

We would all be buried alive—or dead in these cold, white graves, never reaching home.

Babur's thoughts were scuttling out of the hardships of the past, and gazing at the dangers of the present, aghast and bewildered. The snow was rising up to the stirrups of his horse, and the pale dusk before his sight was whipping up another snow storm. He could see the narrow defile farther ahead, a whirlpool of white death, stark and glaring.

No more than one person at a time could ride through this tunnel of death. My men are already cold and dispirited, chilblains on their feet, and their noses shrinking with frostbites? Half the beasts dead or abandoned and we are still struggling to cross this valley of death?

Dark despair was clutching Babur's thoughts, his heart constricting with pain and guilt that he alone in his haste to reach Kabul, had exposed his men to the danger of death and annihilation. And yet the white purity of nature all around was lending his thoughts a semblance of peace, whispering to him some secrets divine and precious. The divine-child within him was awakening, leading him by the hand toward his bower of childhood. Showing him the wooden soldier he himself had carved. He had dressed this soldier in finest of silks, admiring his handiwork with childish pride and innocence. Within a week that soldier was forgotten, disappearing amidst the clutter of toys in favor of the new ones his father had bought or designed. Months later, he had discovered that soldier by chance, breaking it into pieces, not even remembering that for one whole week that soldier had been the object of his admiration.

The sacredness within! Is this memory trying to teach me something? Such is the fate of mankind, forgotten and neglected by God? The insignificant puppets of chance, fashioned by the Fashioner to be broken and scattered? And yet, God is gracious and merciful, loving His creatures and His Creation? Babur's steed as well his thoughts were coming to a stumbling halt at the mouth of one cave down the slope of Zarin Pass. He was becoming aware of the murmuring of voices against the howling of the winds, his gaze barely distinguishing men from beasts through the dusk-haze of roaring whiteness.

"My King, let's go inside this cave, we would find comfort in there against the fury of this storm." Khwaja Kilan's voice was grazing Babur's awareness.

"What comfort is there for the king if his men still suffer the blasts of this white fury?" Babur's voice was churning the fury of hope and hopelessness. "I am not sure how many men can squeeze inside this cave, and I would try to rest outside along with the less fortunate ones who cant' be accommodated in this sanctuary."

Shivering and shuffling, the men were taking refuge inside this cave, groping in darkness and huddling together. Khwaja Kilan had posted himself at the mouth of the cave, watching the stream of men pouring in and vanishing inside the vacuum of silence and stillness. He was still urging the king to come in, but Babur was not heeding. The king had unsheathed his sword, and was busy carving a deep bed in the snow. While the men were scrambling into the cave, Babur had managed to carve a cave of his own, seeking shelter in its depth from the fury of the storm. An overwhelming sense of fatigue was lulling him to the comfort of sleep, and he was not even aware that a rotunda of snow was erected over his head four inches high. Muffled sounds were reaching his opiate senses, but amongst them Khwaja Kilan's voice was clear and pounding.

My King, you must come out of your bed of snow, you would be buried alive. This cave is large enough to accommodate us all. We have kindled a fire, my King, come out!

Babur crawled out of his snow-cave suddenly, the white rotunda over his head crumbling over his shoulders.

"My King, we have kindled a fire. This cave is so big, we are only sixty and it can house more than a hundred." Khwaja Kilan appealed, holding out his arms to assist the king.

This cave was Babur's palace! The languor in his thoughts was murmuring lone consolation. He could see his men huddled around small fires, content with their simple meal of pottage mixed with boiled millet flour, chatting and laughing. But his thoughts were courting the presence of Zainab, she was with him already, both strolling in the palace gardens, all glorious and sprinkled with sunshine.

In fetters of passion I have sought an escape
To the path of some lone retreat

This lone couplet in Babur's head was curling in flames of desire, his arm offering a soft pillow under his wearied head, his heart longing for the touch of sweet Beloved.

Is the love of a king so precious that he deems himself blessed by some mighty powers, daring to endanger the lives of his companions? Are all men enslaved by their passions wild and untamed? Can I look into the hearts of my cave companions? Are they longing to be with their wives? Do they love as I do? What are their needs, desires, or aspirations? Oh, sweet Zainab, Beloved All! The soporific murmur in Babur's thoughts was cutting open one abyss dark and menacing.

Time itself in its endless march over layers upon layers of snow had come to a standstill for Babur, though he was riding ahead of his cavalcade. Qara Ahmed was riding beside him, the author of bringing time to a standstill—rather a messenger from Kabul, informing the king about the deceit of the king's aunts, uncles and cousins, who were holding the citadel of his palace under siege. Kabul, swathed in wintry twilight was offering Babur a cold welcome, his thoughts in anguished circles trying to escape the blaze of their rage and vengeance. He was succeeding a little, summoning the vision of a warm welcome during their journey through icy terrains, tortuous and daunting.

After leaving the sanctuary of the cave, Babur and his companions had resumed their journey, halting at the valley of Yeke-Auleng. The chief of this valley was a kind-hearted man, ruling a community of peasants. He and his men had adopted the king and his companions as their dear guests, offering them the luxury of beds and a great feast in the evening. They had slaughtered the best of their sheep, roasting them on open fires, then whipping up a grand feast with platters of rice garnished with raisins and almonds. Babur's senses were cherishing the taste of cool, scented wine supplied by those hosts of Yeke-Auleng, but his thoughts were stirring the odor of betrayals, rancid and foul-smelling. To fight that odor, he was trying to recall the generosity of his hosts, who had packed provision for their journey, including corn and grain for the horses.

One night of luxurious respite in Yeke-Auleng, and Babur and his entourage were ready to scale the mountains of ice to reach Kabul. Passing through the hill-country of Bamain where the cold was not as intense as before, they had descended down the Shibetu Pass, encountering once again the razor-sharp gusts of mountainous-winters. The Ghurbund valley down below was blanketed with snow, rigged with slopes narrow and serpentine. Emerging out of this treacherous valley unscathed, they were riding through Tutqawal toward Zammayakshi, when Qara Ahmed had materialized riding through the glittering mirage of valleys, as if pursued by demons of death and plague.

Qara Ahmed, much devoted to the king, had contrived escape from the fort of Kabul, hoping to inform Babur about the siege and the treachery. Babur's uncle Husein Mirza was the chief instigator in spreading a rumor that the king was made captive by the Mirzas from Herat, and thrown into the prison of Khorasan. Shah Begum, Babur's aunt and stepmother, was quick to add more weight to this rumor by asserting that the king would never return to Kabul, and would surely be killed in the prison of Khorasan. To validate her assertion, she had sought the help of her advisor Senjer Birlas to make her favorite grandson, Shah Mirza, the king of Kabul. Shah Mirza was installed on the throne, and *khutba* was read in his name in the mosque.

Today, the twentieth day of siege, Babur's thoughts were awakening him to the pangs of betrayal and anguish, his gaze itself cutting the snowy peaks over the Minar Hill into blades of vengeance. His heart was gathering ominous throbs, restless and fluttering. But he was becoming aware of the mute rider beside him, no other than Qara Ahmed. The scent of Kabul was in the air, and Babur's horse sensing the mood of his master, had come to a standstill down the path edged with cedars in raiments of snowy-lace.

"Qara, ride post haste to the citadel of Kabul!" Babur commanded suddenly. "The men whom we can trust are Mulla Baba, Nizam Khalifa, Mohib Korchi, Ahmad Yusuf and Ahmad Qasim. Take them into confidence, and tell them that the king is back to take the traitors by surprise. They are skilled in organizing and taking command, and would assist us in defeating the vile rebels. Here's what you need to do, you would keep watch near the east window. None of my royal rebels ever venture into that section of the citadel, and you know how to access that since you made your escape that way. When we are ready to attack, we would light a bonfire on the top of this Minar Hill, and that would be our signal to you to stay vigilant. In response, you would light a fire over the hill by the old kiosk, your signal to us that the men devoted to us are ready to assist us in any way possible to insure our victory. Now, make haste, Qara, and let the villainous fools believe that the king is imprisoned for life."

Minar Hill with its shivering pines and cedars had donned the mantle of darkness. Qara Ahmed had left hours ago, but Babur and his cavalcade were still riding uphill in search of a level ground to rest for the night. The cold blasts of winds could be heard hissing warnings, filling the hearts of men with dread and despair. Babur seemed oblivious to such warnings, the white symphony of the night reaching not his thoughts where only the citadel of Kabul could be seen melting under the spell of the traitors and the tyrants. His heart was gathering flints of warnings, and to flee their familiar assaults, he was seeking the bitter reality of nature all around, sibilant and stinging.

"One seldom experiences such intense cold during one's whole lifetime?" Babur demurred aloud, his heart reaching out to his companions with subtle warmth of love and compassion. "Never before I have witnessed such harsh weather, so violent and chilling? Who would have thought Kabul being caved in under mountains of snow?"

"The snow-storm must have hit Kabul too, my King, the paths are more treacherous than ever, and the valleys are no more." Ahmed Kasim commented low, shutting his lips tight lest the icy blade of wind slit his throat.

"This storm, probably, has saved us from perishing in the wilderness." Babur consoled, feeling a stab of empathy from deep within. "The snow drifts which filled up the hollows made our journey less dangerous. Otherwise, our horses would have stumbled down the ravines and gorges fathoms downs, and all of us would have died?" His voice was choked by the sudden drumming in his heart, longing to be with Zainab.

"My King, the snow is reaching above our saddle-girths." Ahmed Kasim moaned suddenly. "We need rest, and light a fire to warm our chilled bones. If we didn't snatch a few hours of sleep, we won't be fit to fight in the morning. Yes, we should stop right here, and light a fire."

"Must we?" Babur exclaimed, more so to drown the violence of presage inside his heart, than to confront the necessity of rest and sleep. "This glistening bed of ice is good enough as any other, we will rest here." His gaze was piercing the ice-glazed vistas, restless and searching. "Fortunately, the moon up there, and the glittering whiteness down here are lending us the clear view of our surroundings. Oh, my dear citadel of Kabul, under my very nose, I should be flying through the palace gates than waiting an eternity to punish the vile traitors. But caution is the weapon of the wise, and we must wait. Look! Can you see our old kiosk, bright and shimmering. Yes, we can wait." He was sprinting down his horse, his gaze gathering his companions in the warmth of hope and tenderness.

The fires were kindled after much patience and struggle, and now the men were huddled together, refreshing their spirits with wine, majun and mutton roast. These were the remnants of their provisions from the kind hosts of Yeke-

Auleng, and they were hoping to feast better tomorrow from the larders of the
royal palace. Babur could hear his men joking and laughing, but his gaze was
arrested to the white moon as if holding it in abeyance. His eyes were reflecting
the glitter of cold, white stars, much in conformity with his thoughts, which
were ready to scatter these gems at the feet of his Beloved. He was transported
into his palace, and inside the heart of spring, strolling with his beloved Zainab,
and inhaling the scent of home and gardens. But the odor of treason and betrayal
from the very hearts of his family was corrupting his reveries. Somewhere out
there lurking in ambush were doom and despair—the very soot of tragedies.

Is there one cruel turn of fortune's wheel unseen of me
Is there a pang of grief my wounded heart has missed

This couplet was sucked out from the very furnace of Babur's grief yet to
be, but before he could explore its pain or prophecy, he was jolted to the pangs
of awareness.

"My King. Look! That fiery blaze over the rooftop of your old kiosk?"
Khwaja Kilan exclaimed, his gaze riveted to the flames now spiraling up under
the cloud of smoke.

"Our own garrison!" Babur was startled to his feet. "They have mistaken
our night fires for our signal. Come, friends and soldiers, the fight commences
now! There is no tomorrow." He was charged with the fire of his inner resolve,
whistling for his horse.

The moon had turned livid, and a canopy of diamond stars was lowered
over the citadel of Kabul, as Babur's troops stormed through the palace gates.
King Babur is back, the soldiers cheered, their swords poised and glinting murder, if anyone dared attack or tried escape. The night guards had taken to their
heels, stunned and cowering. The traitors themselves were jolted out of their
sleep to a rude awakening, trying to hide themselves from the thunderous fury of
the king, their looks glazed and their feet reluctant to carry the weight of their
guilt and treachery. Husein Mirza, befuddled and trembling, had sought refuge
in the library, rolling himself inside Persian rugs, as if he would be left undetected as merely a bundle of carpets. Ahmed Kasim was posting guards at the
doors of Audience Hall, not even knowing that Shah Mirza accompanied by
Senjer Birlas were fleeing through the back entrance of the palace, which was
left unguarded. Babur was thundering commands, his rage falling on Tulik Kukuldash who had dared unsheathe his sword. This ingrate wretch had slumped to
the floor with a groan, as Babur dealt him a quick blow, wounding his shoulder.

"Seize all the heathens who plotted against the king, and drag them here
without delay." Babur thundered another command.

Naralla, drunk with the joy of victory had begun to beat his kettle-drum, as
if challenging all traitors to come out of their hiding, and fall at the feet of the
rightful king.

"Cease your clamoring, Naralla, and inform all the worthless rebels, viziers
and courtiers that the king desires only peace." Babur's rage was dissolving as

swiftly as it had flared. "Peace in my palace and peace in Kabul is all I desire, and from foes or friends, their loyalty and submission."

The Audience Hall itself was turned into a sanctuary of penitence as Babur stood receiving submission from his viziers and courtiers. Many amongst them were devoted to the king, only misled by the canards that the king was imprisoned by his cousins and would not return. The ones happy to see the king in good health were Mohib Korchi, Mulla Baba, Nizam Khalifa, Qara Ahmed, Ahmad Kasim and Miran Diwan, offering their customary submission with much relief and sincerity. Babur was becoming aware of the procession of begums and princesses, his heart longing for a glimpse of his beloved and his gaze searching. Shah Begum and Mehr Nigar were the first ones to offer curtsies, their features washed by pallor and hopelessness.

"Where is my Queen? Does she not know that the king is back?" The blaze of accusation in Babur's eyes was falling on Shah Begum.

"Your queen, my King. Zainab—she died." One murmur of incredulity escaped Shah Begum's lips, her eyes glinting fear and bewilderment.

"Died, how?" One anguished cry ripped through Babur's soul, his eyes gathering rivers of grief he could neither deflect, nor express.

"The Queen died of smallpox, my King." Shah Begum murmured.

Babur swayed to his feet, drifting out of the Audience Hall as if sleepwalking. He was seeking the sanctuary of his bedroom under some spell of daze and shock. The vast staircase before his gaze was endless and spinning. Literally whirled into the emptiness of his bedroom, he could feel the rivers of agony churning inside him, his heart lacerated and bleeding. He had begun to pace, buffeted by violence of grief so overwhelming that he thought he was being tortured alive inside the fires of hell and damnation.

Dead. Gone. Living in darkness? So cold, so alone, so confined? My soul, my beauty, Sweet Absent. Babur's arms were reaching out, groping for his Beloved in emptiness, hugging voids and vacuums, and tearing the weight of sorrow within his breast to wounds raw and cankerous. *My Love, my Life, why did you leave me? Come back, come back, one eternal embrace, sweet Heart, let me hold you?* Babur was abandoning himself on his bed, yielding to the violence of loss and grief. He was weeping like a child, alone and inconsolable. The torrent of grief inside him was rising and exploding, but somewhere amidst this explosion of pain and misery, one invisible shadow of mercy was lulling him to the comfort of sleep.

Self-incarcerated inside his prison of grief, Babur had lost count of days and nights. He had immured himself in his bedroom, allowing no one but Attan Mama, his old nurse and childhood confidant. Three whole days had slithered past, and she had failed to console the king, fearing for his health and sanity. Babur seemed to have become the victim of his ritual in pacing, oblivious to the state of affairs in Kabul, which demanded his immediate attention. Even this particular evening, fourth in a row, with candles burning low as his sole companions he was running ragged the Bokhara carpet with the rhythmic pounding of his feet, steady and tireless!

What pain is this? This pain abysmal and profound? Dare I name my grief, it has no name? Have I not known grief before? But this ache, this hunger, this madness? Oh, my child of the mountains! How can I forget the unforgettable? Words, words, I am wearied of words. No peace, no silence, wounds of the body and soul, violence within and without? Babur was oblivious to the pounding on his chamber door, mistaking these sounds for the rolling of thunder inside his heart. Attan Mama stood by the door, following the king in his ritual of pacing with her gaze alone, her eyes shining with the love and tenderness of a mother. She had loved Zainab too, but had let her grief fester inside her in her effort to be brave and to console the king. And now carrying another weight of tragedy, her heart was breaking. Her gaze was falling on the platters of food, cold and untouched.

And all king's favorite too, rice pilaf, mutton korma, chicken biryani and shahi tukras. Attan Mama was thinking, tears gathering into her dark eyes.

"My King." One sob of a plea escaped Attan Mama's lips, arresting Babur in his act of pacing. "You got to be brave. I have never seen you lose heart before, not like this? I have known you since you were a child, and have loved and nursed you. All those years of sorrows and hardships, you endured and overcame. Your courtiers want you, waiting patiently for you in the Audience Hall each morning. Who is to decide the fate of the traitors? And now another tragic news from Khorasan. Your brother, my King, Prince Jehangir Mirza, dead. Poisoned by your aunt Ai Begum, some say?" Her voice was choked, tears pouring down her eyes in a torrent.

"Be comforted, Attan Mama, antidote to pain is pain, and I am half consoled. Awakening to the sting of tragedies vast and inconceivable." Babur murmured, forcing back the rivers of pain in his eyes into the ocean of silence within. "Tears are a blessing, but weep no more, dear Attan Mama. Be a kind messenger to my viziers and courtiers that the king would join them in the Audience Hall tomorrow. Now I wish to be alone, and make sure no one disturbs me this evening."

Attan Mama vanished behind the doors, leaving as soundlessly as she had entered. *A bundle of hope and sorrow,* Babur was thinking, his thoughts awakening to the pain of living and suffering. He stood listening to the ocean of silence within him, strange and roaring, knowing not if he was living a dream or being sucked into the marshlands of inertia and surrender.

Pain would kill pain. Grief would swallow grief. The knotted pain inside would dry and shrivel. Calm would return after the storm of tragedies. Wounds would be sealed under the scars of memories brittle and twisted. Would tomorrow eve come? A day which never dawns—Babur was snatched into the comforting arms of sleep, the four-poster bed under him his kingdom of peace and promise.

9

Forgiveness Divine

This dewdrop world
A dewdrop world it is, and still
Although it is
              — Issa

The Audience Hall was immersed in funereal hush as Babur sat on his gilded throne, absorbing the gist of court affairs from Khwaja Kilan with utmost attention. His black robe with a matching plume in his turban was accentuating his pallor, only the sherry gleam in his eyes and the red on his lips fiery and bright. The poets, the scholars and the courtiers, all were wearing black plumes in their turbans—the color of mourning. Even the Begums and the princesses had a few streaks of black in their gowns, more so in sympathy of king's grief than to honor the period of mourning.

Zainab, My All, Beloved, would you not come back to comfort this grieving heart? Babur was thinking, while trying to catch every word which escaped the lips of Khwaja Kilan.

"Some factions in Kabul went on a wild spree in search of the fugitives, my King, after your return." Khwaja Kilan was saying. "They said they were paying homage to the rightful king by capturing all who had rebelled against the king. A strange homage, since they had begun pillaging and plundering on their way to find the fugitives, succeeding only in inciting anger and unrest. A group of young louts had emerged on the streets of Kabul, God knows from where, threatening the peace of Kabul? But our guards were quick to disperse them, showering them with a barrage of warnings that they would be arrested and imprisoned if they dared violate the peace of Kabul with the intention o looting or causing disorder! Most of the factions are devoted to you, my King, all they need is the assurance that you have returned to rule and to protect their lives and properties. And yet more—"

Khwaja Kilan's bulletin of news was truncated by the abrupt clamor of voices outside the Audience Hall, followed by shuffling of the feet and loud arguments. The Mahogany doors were flung open, the brass inlay on the polished wood shuddering, it seemed, as Ahmad Qasim stormed in, his face flushed. He was dragging Senjer Birlas with a rope around his neck, and kicking him till he fell prostrate at the foot of the king's throne.

"This wicked rebel, my King, I found cowering inside the hill-cave at Qargha Yasif." Ahmad Qasim offered a sweeping curtsy, his gaze returning to the raging, panting lump of misery and degradation. "He thinks he has done nothing wrong to earn this kind of treatment?"

"What I am accused of? What crime I have committed?" Senjer Birlas cried under some spell of delirium and stupefaction.

"What crime indeed!" Babur exclaimed, his gaze thoughtful and piercing. "Didn't I bestow upon you the Tuman of Nangenhir? A great honor any king could ever bestow upon an ungrateful wretch like you? Regardless of this great privilege, you betrayed the trust of the king by conspiring against him in his absence. What crime, you ask? The greatest of all crimes, treason, isn't it? Not only did you plot with the rebels and the traitors, but incited them to rebellion and treachery." He paused, noticing Ahmad Qasim dragging him away from the throne. "The indignity of being dragged on the floor is not a just punishment for him, Ahmad Qasim, release him. He deserves a greater punishment than this, worthy of his character. The king forgives him, granting him the punishment to live—to live in his prison of guilt, shame and corruption. Take him away, his misery alone corrupts my sight." He closed his eyes, conjuring up the faces of more suppliants who would be groveling at his feet, seeking pardons.

In fact, Babur's aunt, Shah Begum, was heaving herself up, urging her brother Husein Mirza with her gaze alone to get up and seek the king's pardon. Khwaja Kilan, perceiving their intentions, had begun whispering to Babur. *Just to let you know, my King, your worthy traitor of an uncle had concealed himself in a bundle of rugs in the store-house of your palace while you were seizing the rebels on the first night of your return.* Babur's thoughts in return were trying to quell the revolt of loss and grief within him to some semblance of peace and discipline. The ache of loneliness within him was flaring, awakening his thoughts to the sting of fresh pain and compassion. *The royal traitors, my aunt and uncle, sadness upon sadness!* Babur's eyes were opening to the scene of misery and supplication.

"My King." Shah Begum was curtsying, Husein Mirza beside her already on his knees, as if praying. "I have come as a suppliant, bringing my unfortunate brother with me, and hoping that you would grant us forgiveness."

"Hoping, that forgiveness is the seed to cultivate the fruits of love, I would scatter such seeds into the hearts of all who need to forgive." Babur murmured profoundly. "And yet I forgive you both with all my heart. And your grandson, dear aunt! Your sweet intrigues made Shah Mirza the king of Kabul for four and twenty days, and yet the rightful King returned to claim his throne. A strange evening it is, my heart gathering the soot of pity and compassion? Not the best of sentiments for an anguished heart but favorable for the ones who have played me false, breeding revolt and discord in my palace, and exposing the citizens of Kabul to riot and anarchy. And yet have no fear, my dear aunt and my dear uncle. Come, sit close to me, you indeed are forgiven." He waved at Naralla, commanding him to move the chairs close to the throne.

Naralla was quick to obey the king's command, his eyes beacons of love and devotion! Husein Mirza stumbled toward the throne, mute and bewildered. Shah Begum lowered herself on her seat regally, as if accepting the king's pardon as her birth-right, though her eyes were kindling the stars of gratitude. The Audience Hall was coming alive at the approach of another suppliant, no other than the beguiled prince himself, Shah Mirza. He drifted toward the throne under some spell of awe and dread, curtsying twice, his lips trembling. No words were escaping his lips, his look feverish and pleading.

"Come, my gallant prince, embrace the king." Babur smiled, his gaze kind and searching. "Come, embrace me." He commanded, a dry, mirthless laughter choking his pain and despair.

Shah Mirza stumbled toward the throne, shock and disbelief shining in his eyes; replaced by the warmth of devotion as he approached closer. He embraced the king with the joy of a child who had just received the most precious of gifts from a loving father.

"Sit, my foolish prince, and drown your shame in a cup of wine." Babur held out his jeweled cup to him, but noticing his reluctance, took a sip. "Never doubt the kindness of a king who has just granted you pardon, my unhappy Prince. If I had any intention of vengeance, I would have had you beheaded than poisoned."

"My King, I would gladly drink hemlock, if you offered it to me!" Shah Mirza drained the cup thirstily, prostrating himself at the king's feet.

"Ah, a trusting child is forever exposed to the evils of the world, tempted and beguiled!" Babur waved at his cupbearer. "Come, Mushin, replenish the cups of all. Especially, the king's, he needs to drown his sorrows in his cup of gold."

"My King, could you drown my fears in your cup of gold, also?" A subtle plea escaped Shah Begum's lips, her eyes shining. "Permit my brother and my grandson to leave for Kandahar. I will accompany them both, if it pleases you, my King? I am pleading for a boon, for sure."

"Strange, how the sea of pain in one's heart whips up ripples of love and compassion?" Babur murmured to himself, his gaze piercing as if searching the scheming mind of his aunt. "I would be granting myself a boon to accede to your wishes, my sweet aunt. It would be dangerous for my uncle and cousin to remain in Kabul, now that the yoke of treason hangs heavy around their necks. Even to think of such matters wearies me." He got to his feet abruptly, plodding out of the Audience Hall without acknowledging the sea of curtsies.

The sanctuary of his bedroom was Babur's pain-loving comfort and solitude. He had begun to pace, his senses numb with grief, misery and bitterness. Chilled silence was all he could feel, within and without, embracing the ocean of agony inside him, all stark and glittering. His thoughts were entering the desert of pain, beholding the wound of loss and grief, but he dared not touch it, fearing its assault and violence. He could feel the presence of Zainab in this room, all fever and madness gone from him, his anguish mute and his pacing slow and deliberate. Sadness was his dearest of companions, yet the noblest of his dreams and profoundest of his sorrows had lost their fire, leaving behind cold ashes and cinders harmless. His thoughts were sinking deeper and deeper into the chilled silence of the past where ghosts of the beloved dead were entombed in memories fond and terrible. Sweet Zainab was with his family where his childhood lay buried along with his dreams and aspirations.

A dream-illusion it was, Babur's thoughts were erecting a wall of self-defense, and cradling him into the arms of remembrance and forgetfulness so that his heart could be shielded from the splinters of grief and agony. He was with his mother, the purity of sunshine and laughter in her eyes embracing and comforting. His father was there too, taking him to the Great Hunt in the woods. The ruby-colored cistern was coming into view, his brother racing wildly, then all drinking wine, all happy and carefree. He was hurled into the valley of Ferghana, climbing on the rungs of youth and maturity, yearning to espouse Samarkand as his only bride.

Khazanda. One sob of a prayer was awakening in Babur's thoughts, resurrecting the memory of his dear sister, forcibly married to his everlasting foe, Shaibani Khan. Along with this memory the pain of his deep agony was flaring all of a sudden, but he was forcing it back, willfully and desperately.

Jehangir in Khorasan! No summons of the king would bring him back to Kabul. Death heeds not the bootless cries of the living? The wall of self-defense in Babur's thoughts was erecting more fortifications, but the *great wound of loss* within his heart was unleashing its flood of torture and violence. *But Nasir Mirza still lives—in Badakhshan, I could summon him?* His thoughts were trying to evade the assault of grief and living torment.

Zainab, Soul, Beloved. Sweet Unforgettable. One mute cry of agony was ripped through Babur's soul, his senses reeling. So savage was the agony of his spirit on the verge of physical nausea that he flung himself upon his bed, hoping for oblivion in sleep. Daze and delirium were his bliss-comfort, his lips repeating the litany of, *Sweet Zainab.*

10

Kabul The Beautiful

Love is a canvas furnished by Nature and embroidered by imagination.
— Voltaire

Kabul, with its celebrated beauty of spring was rippling with colors this particular morning as Babur and Khwaja Kilan strolled in the garden of Revered Three Friends. Marble terraces splashed with ribbons of sunshine, and clusters of hyacinths, oleanders and heliotropes were weaving a tapestry in hues vivid and exuberant. Babur's gaze was turning to the Arghwan trees decked with bell-like blooms, their pink petals slashed with reddish streaks filling his heart with awe and admiration. The scent of lilac and tuberoses was teasing his senses too, his gaze tracing the ripples of saffron and narcissi, the ache of tenderness within him wild and throbbing.

Babur had buried his grief deep within him, his wound of loss also sealed and enshrined where he could pray alone when visited by the demons of anguish and loneliness. His inherent need to seek joy and beauty had restored his spirit of buoyancy, loving life with all its caprice of pains and pleasures. Donned in purple silks with a matching turban, his pallor was intensified, though his eyes were spilling the nectar of youth and longing.

"Look, Khwaja, look at my garden! It looks much like my heart." Babur exclaimed suddenly. "Flowers blooming inside my heart—in my garden!" He kissed the lilac blooms, inhaling deeply and reverently.

"Yes, my King, I can see." Khwaja Kilan murmured as if to himself. "This heart of yours I have known since many, many seasons of joys and tribulations. It is still the heart of a happy, carefree child. Yes, a young, beautiful heart." He smiled, noticing the glint of amusement in Babur's eyes. "Your heart and soul is in this garden, my King, since you have nurtured it year after year. Four long years, has it been that long? Now the blooms are matured into perfection. The loveliest of springs in Kabul, and the loveliest of gardens I have not ever seen before! How hard you worked year after year, and this is the reward of your labors. I admire your—for the lack of a better word, fortitude."

"Fortitude!" A sudden volley of mirth from Babur's lips startled the golden orioles, other birds following their winged flight. The doves, the hoopoes and the paradise flycatchers, all were coming into view, soaring and dipping. "Fortitude, just this one word, my dear mentor, has brought back a host of memories. Your fortitude to instill in me the love for knowledge. How patiently you instructed me to admire Ibn Sina, the great physician! Had Ibn Sina not translated the works of Aristotle for us, we would have remained ignorant of the spiritual treasures, not ever opening the chests of philosophy. Out of all his works, I like Organon the best." His eyes were gathering the mists of memories, all poignant, if not nostalgic. *"The modesty and fortitude of men differ from those virtues in women. For the fortitude which becomes a woman would be cowardice in a man. And the modesty which becomes a man would be pertness in a woman.* Didn't you recite this to me, Khwaja, ten times a day one entire spring? Oh, Khwaja, take me back to Ferghana, to those happy carefree days of youth. I would make you the king, becoming your slave for life."

"The king-slave, my King, needs a wife. A wife, who could keep his thoughts in check?" Khwaja Kilan's eyes were lit up with fatherly affection, but he averted his gaze against the amused intensity in Babur's eyes.

"Need, it's a terrible word, my revered friend." Babur quipped passionately, his eyes gathering stars of mischief. "A need can make the mountains tremble when the trembling needs of the mountains need a sliver of sunshine to shake off the mantle of snow? These mountains have souls, my prudent vizier of Kabul, yes, they do. And yes, I need a wife! Had my mind not burdened with matters weighty, I would have seduced some *beauty* in my palace? And yet, the king would like to be seduced. This carnal need, falsely named love, is all dark and ugly. I have no love left in my heart, but this need, desire, hunger of the flesh— dare I name it, this abominable need is, lust. Why you are letting me rave like a fool, Khwaja, why don't you toss your sanctimonious coals of advice at me?" He sauntered past the gardeners tending the fresh saplings of Chenars. "What is the name of the bride you have chosen for me? Mahim Begum, is it?" He teased over his shoulders.

"Mahim Begum is beautiful. A rare delight to the eyes, and to the heart of any man who espouses her!" Khwaja Kilan was trying his best to hold back his excitement and to keep up with the jaunty pace of the king.

"You are wise to omit the word *soul* in your panegyric praise of the lady, Khwaja." Babur's eyes were lit up with mystic stars, his pace dwindling. "Only music delights the heart. Beauty torments both eyes and heart. Sweet torment it is if suffered for the love of a beautiful woman. Beauty in nature alone soothes my heart, dear friend. Only the beauty in nature is my love, and my kingdom. Do you hear the nature singing, Khwaja? When do you plan to wed your king to the flower of your choosing?"

"This very evening, if it pleases you, my King?" Khwaja Kilan sang, unable to contain the flood of joy within his heart.

"Surely, you jest." Babur's feet came to a sudden halt by the sun-spangled fountains, gurgling and spluttering. "You must have paved the way perfectly smooth, for it has been months since you began goading me to accept this charming proposal. A perfect day for me to put your jest to test! How about this afternoon for the wedding songs to begin? You would be going in circles to fetch my bride?" The mirthful challenge in his eyes was intense and sparkling.

"Now truly, you jest, my King." Was Khwaja Kilan's flustered response! "Maybe a few weeks, or months, perhaps? The lady has no scheming relatives." He added as a way of diversion.

"I am sure delighted to get this crumb of a consolation." Babur murmured, pain surfacing in his eyes with a quicksilver lightning. "I wish I was jesting. This dreamy spring with sweet-scented breath, and the mad wooing of the birds is wreaking havoc in my loins. You should have married, Khwaja, after your wife died. Why didn't you?"

"Even the thought of marriage I divorced years ago, making solitude my bride." Khwaja Kilan confessed reluctantly.

"An unkind, dowerless divorce, that is!" Was Babur's amused exclamation. "Solitude has been your coveted bride since years, and now that I ravish this bride of yours with constant attentions, seeking your company, you may divorce this one too? Murder, if you will, go into mourning for awhile, and then find another one! You are not old, not as yet. Fifty is half a century wasted in the cradle of childhood, another half is the nuptial bed of youth—" He paused, noticing the clouds of sadness in the eyes of his friend. "Don't be sad, Khwaja, the solitude as your bride is quite delightful. I would be jealous if you took another one, solitude alone is the dearest of links to our friendship. Though you would have the pleasure of seeing me wed, as you desire. Look to the wedding preparations, but don't make it loud and ostentatious. Despite the fact that I love music, I can't endure the din of wedding songs, and a parade of endless rituals challenging my patience!" He turned to his heels, retracing his steps toward his palace.

"The age-old customs of our ancestors can't be neglected, my King!" Khwaja Kilan followed him thoughtfully. "Rituals connect us to the memories of the past, attaining the stature of holiness in present. Our way of honoring the ones who are not with us any more."

"There is no present, dear friend, only the past and future." Babur demurred aloud. "Paradoxically, we live only in the past or the future, present itself lost in its own cauldron of timelessness. And what we have despised in the past, somehow, becomes sacred in the future, the present bemoaning only the loss of time. A time for noon prayers." He appeared to answer the muezzin's call for prayers. "Once, I tried to hold time inside the flagon of wine, but it was lost into emptiness even before the wine could be drained into cups. Allah is never going to forgive me for my thoughts dark and sinful." He was mounting the vast steps of his palace in utmost haste, as if fleeing white demons of the past and the present.

Only the demons of haze and loneliness were Babur's companions as he sat in his library, willing his thoughts to a downpour of words into his book, Babur-Nama. The warm ashes in memories were Babur's foes and friends, coughing up plumes of betrayals and sorrows, and yet he kept writing under some spell of stoic resignation. His fingers were on fire, it seemed, through which his thoughts were slipping and sliding, and yet he kept writing. For how long did he write, he had no idea, but his fingers were getting numb, and his thoughts growing wild and restless. His eyes were closing and his thoughts seeking the warmth of books and paintings in this sanctuary of a library.

The rosewood shelves hosting a variety of books were whispering their secrets to him, but his thoughts were holding dear the book of Rumi, his favorite, the Mathnavi-yi-Manavi. He could feel the gold lacquer binding of this book in his hands, its couplets with illustrated margins in gilt unfolding the spiritual wealth of mystery and mysticism. Yet, the languor in his thoughts was shifting toward the paintings on the walls, the one to his right coming alive in its large frame, all gilded and polished. The artist had captured the garden of Samarkand and the scene of wild hunt on the canvas in one scenic splendor. The Princes of the House of Timur against the background of flowers before engaging in the game of battue astride their Arabian steeds looked alive and dreamy. The bows and arrows bulging out of their quivers, all ornate and colorful. But his thoughts too were closing their eyes, murmuring and slumbering. They were seeking consolations from the books of Saadi, Bostan and Gulistan, both abandoned on the table of ivory and jade. His thoughts were plunged in darkness all of a sudden and staggering back in their jungle of dreams and aspirations.

Several brides of truth claim you as your husband, Babur, listen to them. Your most beautiful of all the brides are, Ferghana and Samarkand. You have neglected them for long! You think you can be separated from them? Another adorable of your brides, Ambition, is that not true? What about the unwedded bride of Hind you wish to seduce and abduct?

Babur's thoughts were weaving garlands of pain to deck the silent altar within him, and whispering the beloved name, *Zainab*. And yet, enveloped in darkness they were groping for the crumbs of sanity.

Poets, mystics and scholars in my court, are all men not wedded to the poetry in life? There is some vital flaw in the very fabric of this existence? Chinks of deformity plugged with the soot of illusions? What's wrong with life? The only flaw, the only deformity, it keeps on living? Isn't it even insane to think that one can gather and preserve the nuggets joy, love, purity? Life forever engaged in the battle of life and death, and everyone knows who comes out as the winner. The end, the surcease, my sweet Absent. Zainab, Zainab.

Babur, the poet and mystic was cradled into the comforting arms of sleep, contemplating the imponderables.

11

King's Wedding

Look to the laughing Rose about us—'Lo
Laughing,' she says, 'into the world I blow'
At once the silken tassel of my Purse
Tear, and its Treasure on the Garden throw
— Omar Khayyam

The Fortune Hall decked like a bride was hosting wedding guests in its sumptuous setting of Persian rugs and pillows of silk and brocade. Babur—the bridegroom, donned in finest of silks, seemed seated gulfs apart from his newly wedded bride. A large davenport splashed with velvets was cradling the bejeweled queen, surrounded by aunts and begums. The red plume in Babur's turban matching the ruby wine in his goblet was adding color to his pale cheeks, his gaze warm and wistful. This eve of the king's wedding had commenced with a grand feast, and now celebrations were at their peak with all the fanfare of singing and dancing.

Khwaja Kilan, in league with the royal ladies, had succeeded in turning this wedding day into an arena of entertainments. The dancers pirouetting on their toes were even attracting the attention of the King of Persia, Shah Ismael, who had suspended his zealous thoughts momentarily, permitting himself the luxury of drinking wine, and participating in gaiety and laughter. Maulana Kazi was the only one abstaining from wine on this auspicious occasion of king's wedding. Nasir Mirza, under the stupor of inebriation was teasing the Qubus player—Hussein, abandoning himself to mirth from some comment by the flutist—Shaiki. Khwaja Kilan was enjoying the antics of his servant Lazy, who seemed to be imitating the dancers, succeeding only in evoking jeers and hilarity. Babur's gaze was turning to his beautiful bride, admiring her dreamboat eyes and kissing her lips the color of pomegranates. His heart was aching all of a sudden, the warmth of ardor and tenderness in his eyes shifting and shuddering. His gaze as well as his thoughts was landing on Deria Khan, who sat whispering to his son Yar Husein, as if oblivious to the flood of gaiety and laughter all around. The ache in Babur's heart was flaring, chiseling its tunnel of oblivion where shadows of death hovered over the tombs of greed and ambition.

Baki Cheghanaini is no more in this world of joys and sorrows, Babur's thoughts were entering the trail of blood and betrayal. *Baki, the inveterate fool and rebel! Had he not gone pillaging the territories of Bhira ruled by Yar Husein, he would not have been killed by the orders of Yar Husein himself? Shaibani Khan still living, afflicted with the fever of killing and plundering. Boasting of conquests, and leaving behind trails of blood and devastation. Marching toward Kandahar with the fury of a storm?* Babur's thoughts were wrenching themselves free from shadows bleak and menacing. *Joy and peace in Kabul, beauty and sunshine! The wine of spring and the hearts flooded with joys, all sweet and perfumed.* Babur's thoughts were returning to the sea of gaiety, especially, by Khwaja Kilan's loud comment drowned in equally loud mirth of Nasir Mirza.

"You should abandon your gold cup, my dear Prince, and take a stroll in the garden." Khwaja Kilan was trying to dissuade the prince from drinking. "Looks like Shab-i-Barat out there, countless diyas gracing the windows and the balconies, and a full moon—the night of wonders!"

"Tonight is the night I wish my fate sealed inside the Garden of Eden!" Was Nasir Mirza's inebriated response. "You think I don't know the connotation of Shab-i-Barat? It is the night of full moon of eighth lunar month. The night when all Muslims light candles on rooftops and inside their homes. Praying and feasting as I understand. Also renewing their belief that this particular night the fates of mankind are written in heaven for the duration of the year to come; sort of balancing the scale of life and death!"

"The full moon out there is pouring lava into my blood, Khwaja!" Babur commented abruptly, more so to efface the inebriated vision of Nasir Mirza than to seek the attention of his mentor. "When are these mad festivities going to be over, my crafty friend? Since you are the author of these entertainments, along with my scheming aunts of course, you need to remind them that it's time they conducted my bride to the bridal chamber. Can't endure this din any more. A long, long wait for the bridegroom to suffer agonies of the heart and soul!"

"The night air in your garden is more conducive to your mood, my King, than to Nasir Mirza's health." Khwaja Kilan smiled triumphantly. "The hour is early, not even time for the night prayers."

"You might as well pray right now, Khwaja, that my patience doesn't run ragged." Babur intoned merrily. "Besides, if I fail in curbing my desire, I might tear the veil of decorum and abduct my own bride?"

"Patience is a virtue, my King, and you would be the first one to heed the words of wisdom than succumb to the temptation of impropriety." Khwaja Kilan began soothingly. "Just imagine if the festivities were to last for days, weeks, even a month? In obedience to your command they are reduced to one evening alone, and the evening is still young. I could recount all the virtues of patience, but wedding celebrations don't permit me such luxury."

"And I have the luxury of stalling—" Babur's voice was lost in a fresh ripple of songs, followed by dancers, floating and swirling.

Khwaja Kilan sighed relief, noticing the final round of entertainments be-fore the bride was to be conducted to her bridal chamber. The royal aunts were already assisting Mahim to her feet, her bridal gown of red satin slashed with gold stars rustling and groaning. A tiara of rubies and diamonds was gracing her hair, the matching jewels in her ears and around her throat coming alive at each step that she took, all colors on her bridal fineries dazzling and throbbing. Ba-bur's gaze was arresting her features inside the mirror of his heart, her small, white face with the glow of rose and ivory, the brilliance of amber pools in her eyes and her lips the color of pomegranates. His heart was clouded with sadness all of a sudden, the ocean of ache and loneliness within him churning a storm of need and desire. The wedding songs were an echo strange in his head, his senses swimming in some pool of daze and illusion.

The pools of daze and illusion were dissolved into the holy fires of agony and desire as soon as Babur entered the bridal chamber. He was unrobing her with the gentleness of a lover in contrast to the hunger and violence of passion within him, then smothering her with kisses wild and scalding. So savage was his need to possess her body and soul that he didn't know he was hurting her, the rapier of his desire piercing her like a blade of steel. Her pain and surrender were awakening him to the pangs of guilt and tenderness, and he crushed her to him in one loving embrace.

"My moon! My beauty and sweetness, forgive!" Babur murmured, his very heart loving and caressing.

The primal hunger-desire in Babur was appeased, and he was drifting into the bowers of sleep where the altar of his grief and loneliness could be seen slumbering and shuddering. Zainab was coming alive, laughing and mocking. She was riding on a chariot of moonbeams, and disappearing into the white mists of ether and vacuity. He was sucked into the ocean of roaring silence, his heart empty and luminous. Something inside him had died, yet longing to be born again and again into the shimmering tides of joy-pain in living.

12

Inception of Royal Harem

Sweet is the coming of the New Year
And sweet the fair face of spring
Yet sweet is the juice of fragrant grape
Most sweet the whisper of love
Ah, Babur, grasp at life's pleasures
Which, departed, can never be summoned back
— Babur

The spring morning with its ribbons of gold was flooding Babur's heart with joy as he strolled in his garden, his senses serenading the very hearth of beauty in nature. He had risen early in the morning under some spell of peace and exhilaration, gazing at the sleeping beauty beside him silently and reverently. His heart was light as if it had known no violence during the night long orgy of agony and desire, slumbering and awakening amidst tides of carnal hungers and tender longings. He had slipped out of his bed noiselessly, taking utmost care not to disturb his bride, though he had stood gazing at her before commencing the rituals of bathing and dressing.

A mantle of ethereal silence was lowered over the garden as Babur strolled past the grove of cedars, the bright plume in his turban as vivid as the Himalayan tulips left behind over the rooftops of his palace. *Like the goblets holding ruby-red wine, if not sunshine,* Babur had thought, but now his thoughts were wooing the bride of solitude. And yet the very same thoughts were inching their way back to the palace grounds where he had noticed a fresh brood of Arabian steeds not belonging to the royal stables.

Maybe some unwelcome riders from alien lands slipped into Kabul last night, one low murmur shot its missile of curiosity in Babur's head. *Or messengers of woe to unroll the tapestry of cruelties by Shaibani Khan?* Babur's feet were coming to a slow halt by weeping willow, its branches mirrored in the clear pond down yonder. *Sweet Absent,* a pair of emerald eyes were flashing mirth and mockery into the very bowl of his solitude. *Oh, yes, sweet Zainab is still the queen of my heart, and Mahim the pearl of my pain and passion,* Babur's feet as well as his thoughts were drifting into the mystic garden of poetic serenity. *To love without loving! Ah, sweet liberty! I will never fall in love again!* His gaze was tracing the citron wings of a butterfly violating the virginity of white roses while stealing their nectar and fragrance.

The cherry trees with clusters of white blooms were luring Babur's attention, his feet coming to a sudden halt involuntarily. An abrupt riot in his thoughts too was holding him prisoner in one spot, his gaze piercing the very heart of nature and sunshine. *Yes, sweet Zainab, I was fortunate to taste the soma of love once and for all! The venom of grief I have swallowed and digested. You are enshrined inside me like one altar pure and sublime. The canker of my pain and loss I have buried deep within the casket of my soul, and yet you torment me still my Beloved unforgotten and unforgettable?* So utterly absorbed was Babur inside the murky depths of his self-contemplation that he didn't notice the hasty approach of Khwaja Kilan.

"My King, I must speak with you!" Khwaja Kilan startled Babur out of his reveries by his demeanor of woe and urgency.

"Is this the way to greet a King on this glorious morning, not to mention the wedding night before that of joy and ecstasy?" Babur declared most jovially. "I must congratulate you on your choice of a bride for the king, most beautiful and most charming." His eyes were absorbing the puzzled look of his friend into their pools of warmth and merriment. "This look in your eyes, have I not seen that before? You are here to corrupt my joy by telling me that I slept with a goddess who would vanish like a dream before I returned to the palace?" He teased

Khwaja Kilan's lips were moving, but no voice was issuing forth, his look wild and pleading.

"What's wrong, Khwaja, why don't you say something?" Babur demanded with a dint of impatience and indulgence. "Let me guess, some messengers from Herat? Is Shaibani threatening our cousins once again? Am I constrained to abandon my newly wedded bride so soon, and espouse the bride of wars?" His eyes were catching shafts of sunshine and blazing.

"My King. Your aunt from Heart, Habiba Begum." Khwaja Kilan commenced rather reluctantly. "She arrived here late at night, rather early in the morning. Well, a few hours before dawn. Her daughter princess Masuma is here too. Your aunt? Well, she told me her daughter is betrothed to you, and she is here to seal the vows of marriage." His look was flustered, the ridges around his lips deepening and constricting.

"Happy Herat!" Babur exclaimed. Happier still, our Kabul. And happiest of all, the king-bridegroom. My fair cousin will be wedded to me this very day before its glory is veiled by darkness." Babur laughed, drunk by the novelty of his becoming a bridegroom once again. "And don't look so mournful, kings are privileged to have many brides. Another day of wedding celebrations and you are in charge of all the arrangements. The king wishes to sleep with a new bride tonight!"

Khwaja Kilan stood there stunned, only his thoughts racing and somersaulting. *Has the king gone mad? Is he jesting? This willful, capricious king is not a child-prince anymore? Alas, the youth of Ferghana is no more. He would be my mentor, and I his disciple?* His prudent thoughts were gathering the reeds of sanity, but no words were coming to his rescue.

"Don't look so crestfallen, Khwaja." Babur intoned gently, mirth gone from his eyes and voice. "I am not going to behead my young brides one after the other. I am no Harun-al-Rashid, though without him we would have never gained the treasures of *A Thousand and One Nights*."

"Grieved by the infidelity of his queen, King Harun-al-Rashid had no wish to marry any other, only deflowering a bevy of virgins night after night and slitting their pretty throats each morning, until Scheherazade appeared with her dower of tales incredible and irresistible." Khwaja Kilan murmured to himself, his thoughts still searching the rungs of sanity.

"Much wiser he than many a foolish kings intent only on espousing little kingdoms which they could never keep or maintain." Babur smiled, recalling those endless hours of delight when Khwaja Kilan read to him stories from *The Arabian Nights.*

"A foolish king, I should say, letting his grief become his tyrant. A sad and disillusioned king, not even knowing that he sired three sons during those dream-nights of Babylonian seduction and story-telling." Khwaja Kilan murmured again.

"No bastards in my palace!" Babur turned to his heels, retracing his steps toward the palace. "All fair and holy, holy patrimony, or to be precise, holy matrimony. A brood of princes to win victories, cultivating love for peace and unity, hopefully? Do your duty, Khwaja, make arrangements for this marriage." His gaze was following the golden orioles in their merry flight.

"You are not serious, my King, marrying your cousin—this very day?" Khwaja Kilan demurred aloud, following Babur as if hypnotized.

"Sweet fortunes have decreed this marriage this very day, Khwaja." Babur commented over his shoulders. "My decision can't be altered much like the decrees of fate which can't be averted. A word of caution, Khwaja, hide yourself from the fury of my aunt. She is likely to blame you for choosing a bride for me, while I could have been happily wedded to her daughter."

"Too late for such a caution, my King!" Khwaja Kilan murmured wretchedly. "She has already vented her rage over me. Considering your love and friendship for me, she spared me a little, but her fury, yes, has left me quite scalded. Today is not a good day to get married to your cousin, my King, you must not think about it." He almost bit his lips for uttering this thoughtless plea.

"*Must* is an odious word, my prudent advisor! Especially when it is directed against the wishes of a king." Babur began with an abrupt vehemence. "If must comes to must then I must wed princess Masuma as my priceless dowry from Mahim Begum—a dowry, her parents neglected to give to their daughter. And yet, the word *dowry* is as abhorrent to me as the word *must*, when it matches not my moods and whims. Allah knows, Mahim's beauty outweighs a hundred worthless dowries which a foolish king may ever covet?" His voice was betraying the inward riot of pain and anguish which he was trying to master and subjugate.

"How would your newly wedded bride feel, my King, if you got married one night after her own wedding?" Was Khwaja Kilan's low inquiry, his own thoughts nursing his bruised pride.

"As all the happy brides feel, my sage friend!" Babur exclaimed, as if whipping his pain to silence. "Jealous and unforgiving! Feigning indifference while trying their best to please their husbands, yet filling their vain, little heads with the poison of vengeance. And Allah help the husbands when they are constrained to swallow that poison with a draught of humility and penance?" His pace was slackening, his gaze holding dear the sun-gold purity of flowers and fountains. "My Mahim could keep me at her side if she wished, but she herself by the virtue of her wisdom and modesty would welcome my brides if I were to wed again and again. A mystery, this wedding night, something ineffable I can't explain, our souls are one, and Mahim knows I would always come back to her? I have possessed her body and soul, and yet dare I study my soul?" He stood inhaling the scent of roses hugging the pillared verandah in white clusters.

"I didn't know you were betrothed to princess Masuma, my King?" Khwaja Kilan demurred aloud, his expression a mingling of sadness and tenderness.

"Betrothed!" Babur murmured under some spell of dreamy languor. "I was betrothed only once, and wedded for life with emerald eyes, that memory alone would remain my true love, my true bride, my one and only!" He closed his eyes as if fighting the demons of grief within. "Sweet Zainab, my altar of love to kneel and pray. Well, king's marriages are arranged by friends and family for riches or alliances. Do the kings consent, mostly yes, when the brides are fair, and the passions of the kings wild and insatiable?" He paused, becoming aware of the sad, forlorn expression of his dear mentor. "Khwaja, you have changed your profession from mentoring to tormenting. You should be talking about the marriage of poetry with music. Have you noticed how dull our court has become, no one has written even one couplet since weeks? And what about sports, how long it has been since I went on a hunt? Battue, chougan, falconry would have been grand diversions for me, saving me from the grandest of follies, marriages? And now that I am cast into the mold of marriages, tell my scheming aunt that the king is longing to wed his daughter this very day!" He turned to his heels, aiming straight for the palace doors, music from within greeting his giddy thoughts.

The sweetest of notes, the happiest of songs! Are these the wedding tunes, or some subtle mockery of passions consumed and consuming? A poetic jest to greet the virgin bride of today and to neglect the happy bride of yesterday? The paradox of tomorrow itself the ignorant babe of yesterday? Today would always live, time and time again, day after day—inside the womb of tomorrow? Babur's thoughts were searching the crafty aunt from Herat, but his feet were guiding him toward the nuptial chamber to court the favor of Mahim in accepting Masuma into the king's harem.

Fortune Hall, this evening, was witness to Babur's caprice and gaiety as he sat talking with his guests with the wild abandon of an eternal bridegroom who would be delighted at the prospect of a new bride night after night. He was donned in finest of silks, his green vest revealing a jeweled cummerbund, glinting fire and sparkle. A large ruby in the middle of his turban was accentuating his pallor, lending his eyes the fire of dreamy sunsets. He had gone hunting during the day, returning with a great supply of venison which was added to the wedding feast by the skill and ingenuity of royal cooks. Now that the guests were sated with wine and viands, they were simply content to enjoy the entertainments. Babur sat watching the dancers, but his gaze now and then was fluttering from one bride to the other, as if searching for some *other* which could appease the maddening ache and void inside his soul gone wild and inexorable.

Another person in this Fortune Hall decked with flowers and feeling some sort of ache and void, was the king's advisor, Khwaja Kilan. He was seated beside the king, somewhat spent and exhausted, no more pretending to be happy, and sinking deeper and deeper into the slippery pools of imponderables. His gaze was feverish and restless, changing colors, at times shining like the dishes of chased silver, then stealing gilt and gold from the walls and attaining the sheen and mystery of koftgari designs on tables inlaid with ivory and brass. He seemed oblivious to the stream of dancers, his gaze chasing the wine-bearers, rather the gold flagons and goblets, replenished and replenishing.

A king's wedding, two brides in two days! The same thirsts, the same jubilations, only one bridegroom! Khwaja Kilan was thinking. *Such folly and shamelessness? Yet, the king is wise. Even his caprice has the power to attract awe and admiration. And yet he has mastered the art of living by the very virtue of his lighthearted gaiety and charming disposition.* Khwaja Kilan's thoughts were lost amidst a fresh burst of song and revelry.

Babur's thoughts were turning to the unwelcome guests from Herat. *My wicked aunt and the cunning princes from Kandahar, such a pitiful lot, including the courtiers from Ghazni? What need I have of such gifts*, his gaze was flashing disapproval at the piles of dowry so artlessly displayed. The silks, laces and damasks. Vessels of gold and silver, their long, fluted necks jewel-crusted. *More jewels, flaunting their riches on red velvet pillows, glinting fire and sparkle*, Babur's thoughts were fashioning these jewels into necklaces to adorn the throats of royal ladies. His gaze was turning to his lovely brides, first catching the holy communion of love in Mahim's eyes, then feasting on the beauty of his new bride—Masuma, whose eyes were lowered. *This virgin lily from Herat is going to be my bride, tonight, tonight! Pity, that I can't fall in love ever again.* Babur's attention was claimed by a merry group of princes, laughing besottedly, but before he could say anything, a low comment from Khwaja Kilan was enough to divert his attention.

"Shah Beg and his brother Muhammed Muqim are trying to win the favors of prince Nasir, it is obvious." Khwaja Kilan's gaze was searching the expressions of the brothers, whom he had dubbed earlier as wicked.

"Faithless wretches! Isn't it enough that they have corrupted the minds of many with their evil genius at scheming? They are to be watched closely lest they dare corrupt the mind of my innocent prince." Babur murmured, exchanging a meaningful look with Khwaja Kilan.

"Hope, you have not forgotten, my King, you did accede to the pleas of these wicked brothers, consenting to join them in their campaign against Shaibani Khan?" Khwaja Kilan's eyes were saying more than his lips could utter. "Are we to march to Kandahar soon?"

"Don't talk of wars, Khwaja, my heart is drunk with the nectar of love and peace." Babur got to his feet dreamily. "The king hopes for one night of pleasure with his new bride." He drifted toward his bride, oblivious to the sudden hush in this hall of festivities.

The music itself had come to one shuddering halt, all eyes following the king under some spell of stupor and fascination. Babur's gaze was lured toward his bride who sat beside her mother, both surrounded by a bevy of begums and princesses. A variety of gifts in scattered heaps were challenging his approach, rather jolting him out of his dream-passion into the pool of wealth and opulence. Suddenly, he was aware of the charged silence, awakening simultaneously to his fever of need and desire which had compelled him to break the bonds of decorum. Laughingly he turned toward his bride, ignoring the chilled stares of the royal ladies, their eyes spilling fear and bewilderment.

"My flower of Herat!" Babur assisted Masuma to her feet, turning abruptly to face his new mother-in-law. He scooped a handful of ashrafis from the tray beside her and scattered them over the carpet. "Take these worthless pebbles to Khorasan, my dear Aunt, the king needs but one precious jewel, my sweet Masuma." He paused, noticing the expression of disbelief and disapproval in the eyes of his aunt. "The king of Kabul sets his own rules of decorum, and he has no patience to wait for his bride at the whims of the begums when they deem fit to conduct her to the nuptial chamber. I myself would do this royal honor. Come, my precious jewel." He slipped his arm around Masuma's waist, whirling her away toward the staircase.

The white lily of a bride in shimmering velvets was seen floating over the steps with her king-husband. A net of diamonds in her hair was casting a gossamer halo, and the guests were awakening from their stupor of silence, clapping and cheering. The musicians were quick to claim their instruments, evoking wedding tunes, which appeared to follow the bridal couple up to their nuptial chamber.

13

Battlefield of Woe and Compassion

I have heard that illustrious Jamshed
Inscribed these words on a stone, beside a fountain
And disappeared in the twinkling of an eye
Should we conquer the whole world by our valor and manhood
Yet what part of it we carry with us to the grave
—— Saadi

At the head of his troops, Babur was riding down the terrains of Pesinga, toward the road to Kandahar. The rugged defiles on either side were cradling the red and yellow standards of the army, it seemed, as they rode onward oblivious to the discomforts of cold and fatigue. Babur on the contrary appeared immune to such discomforts, goaded only by his feverish need to avenge the rebellions of his foes and friends, amongst them Shaibani Khan who was afflicted afresh with the fever of cruelties. His thoughts were harsh and bitter, and his gaze sweeping over the barren vistas with a sense of desolation.

Fall is already here, earlier than expected, shedding its armor of blight and devastation. The odor of death and decay? Why? When the sunshine is crisp and dazzling? Babur's thoughts were leaving the steep, rugged defiles and tracing the scenic paths left behind, spruced with elms and poplars, and the streams all crystal and gurgling. His eyes were catching a few sparks of sunlight and sparkling much like the gold helmet over his head, then changing colors to vie with the scimitar at his waist, its jewels reflecting a collage of rainbows. Some sort of rage and compassion was choking Babur's thoughts, but spilling through his eyes in molten gold of memories.

Shaibani Khan with his brute force of nearly forty thousand had launched attack on the city of Herat. Taking the royal princes by surprise in their kiosk at Babu Khaki—their seasonal retreat to indulge in discussions both literary and scholarly. No measures had been taken to safeguard the city when Shaibani Khan's troops had materialized all of a sudden, pillaging and plundering. Judgment Day had arrived, it seemed, as the soldiers swept through the houses, slaughtering men and ravishing women, even killing the innocent babes and torching the houses to cinders. Prince Musafer Husayan's vizier Muhammed Berenduk was quick to devise a crafty plan to gather forces at the foot of the mountains to attack the enemy before they themselves could reach this strong-hold. In order to make this plan succeed he had to seek help from the vizier of Badi-uz-Zaman, but that vizier was in such a state of shock and paranoid that he could neither think, nor render any assistance. So the city of Herat was left at the mercy of the savage foes, and the princes had fled to Khorasan behind the walled capital, leaving behind their palaces, gardens and treasures.

And fine collection of books, Babur's thoughts were following the bloody trails of Shaibani Khan and the betrayals of his uncle and cousins, whom he had already forgiven twice over in Kabul, granting them the privilege of staying in Badakhshan. *Wretches foolish and ungrateful!* Pity and compassion in Babur's thoughts was a shuddering reality. He was thinking about his uncle Husein Mir-za whose tragic death was a living, breathing testimony of deceit and cruelty. Deceit on the part of Babur's uncle who had betrayed him once more by be-friending Shaibani Khan. And cruelty on the part of this Uzbek foe who had severed Husein Mirza's head from his proud shoulders, declaring:

Your head is as worthless as your bloody, fantastic lies.
Release to God the man who wrongs you
His vengeance is keener than your own

The poet in Babur was awakening to the rhythm of sadness and loneliness. Yet his heart was kneeling at the bloodied corpse of his uncle, and commiserat-ing with the brittle, restless souls of the dead betwixt hell, heaven or purgatory. The gates of purgatory within his heart were flung open, and he could see his Sweet Zainab embalmed in mists of death, cold and silent.

Sweet Absent

One furnace of sigh from deep within was closing shut the gates of purga-tory in Babur's heart, appealing to the child-bride of *ambition* in his mind to be his only love and guardian over the tomb of his grief so dear and intolerable. And yet Sweet Absent was the one riding with him this particular moment, sprinkling star-dust of hopes and dreams over the volcano of his pain and an-guish. She was cradling his unloved brides in Kabul in both her arms, offering him the glimpse of youth and beauty.

Youth and beauty indeed! Where is love? How does once slice hope from the solid rock of sorrow? Why do the agonies of the soul blacken the delights of the flesh, stark and merciless? Dear Masuma? Dearest Mahim, and yet the dearest of them all—

Babur's thoughts were tossed into the dust-cloud of a rider, who was gallop-ing toward him as if torn out of the very bowels of this landscape so barren and unwelcoming. This lone rider was no other than Babur's messenger, Qara, al-most falling out of his saddle, and prostrating himself on the ground where Ba-bur had brought his horse to an abrupt halt.

"My King, woeful news! Shah Beg and his brother Muhammed Muqim have left their posts unguarded, and have joined the ranks of Shaibani Khan. This Uzbek foe is plotting a massacre in Herat on grand scale. He has appointed Shah Beg and his brother the guardians of Kandahar. These brothers were heard boasting, *we would defend Kandahar till the last drop of blood in our veins remains unspilled—*"

"I myself would squeeze each drop of blood from their veins, cutting open the jugular vein of them both with my mighty sword!" Babur thundered, cutting short the delirious import of Qara with a wave of his arm. "Such imbeciles, these brothers, ensnared by the Lucifer charm of Shaibani Khan, knowing not that they have signed their warrant of death by conniving with the serpent-king of intrigues—the Uzbek foe. Yes, the Uzbek foe, he fears the might and valor of our troops, and is probably gloating over his cunning schemes that while we wreak vengeance on the besotted brothers, he would be fleeing to safety far from Kandahar? Be assured, Qara, this time the serpent-king won't escape alive." He whirled his horse around to face his troops. "My friends, a few more strips of barren land, and we would be approaching the fertile grounds of Kandahar. The travails of this long journey are about to end, lending you the opportunity to exercise your valor and to embrace victory. Victory is ours, never doubt that, for even the rapacious, mindless soldiers of Shaibani Khan are seized with white terror when they hear of our mighty approach." His voice was drowned by cheers of victory and merry applause.

The day of reckoning had arrived too soon, smitten by the dust-clouds of warfare, painting the sky in purple wounds of twilight! The right wing of Babur's troops under the command of Mirza Khan had hemmed in the Uzbek foes who were falling like moths against the shower of arrows from the unerring skills of Sherim Taogai, Yarak Tashai, Chilma Mughul, Ayub Beg, Ibrahim Beg, Alid Sayyid, Quli Charla, Khuda Bakhsh and Abu Liasan. The left wing commanded by Abdur Razaq was a whirlwind of defense, leaving man and beast wounded and stunned, the most valorous amongst them, Qasim Beg, Tigri Birdi, Qambar Ali, Ahmed Bugh, Gheeri Birlas, Sayyid Hussain, Qokan Dar and Mir Shah. The wounded and bedraggled soldiers were driven pell-mell against the onslaught of the center wing, hosting the most adept and dauntless of generals. Tireless amongst this group, and most prominent over the scene of combatants were, Sayyid Qasim, Muhib Ali, Papa Aghuli, Alah Wairan, Sher Quli, Muhammed Ali and Qasim Kukuldash. Khusrau Kukuldash, Muhammed Duldai, Shah Mahmud, Quli Bayazid, Kamal Khan, Nasir Miram, Baba Sherzas, Khan Kuli, Wali Baba and Baba Shaikh were seen racing after the fleeing horde of enemy, their cheers of *victory*, loud and exultant.

Babur himself was inside the heart of the battleground, whose swift strokes of the sword had unhorsed many a brave antagonists who had dared raise their weapons with the hope of killing the king of Kabul. But the king of Kabul astride his steed was much like a magician, appearing and disappearing in a flash to save the lives of his soldiers who were in danger of losing their limbs, if not their lives. This particular instant, Babur's flashing sword had carved a deep gash at the temple of one young soldier in his act of striking a mighty blow at the head of his brother, Nasir Mirza.

Allowing this young colt of a soldier to flee, Babur smiled at Nasir Mirza, overwhelmed by the cheers of victory and exultance. He was keenly and profoundly aware of the wounded and the fleeing, the clinking of scimitars fading into distance. His gaze was sweeping over the ocean of quivers, cross-bows, dented helmets, ripped open chain mails and blood-soaked vembraces. The injured beasts and the muffled groans of the wounded and dying were stirring the embers of his compassion while he stood catching the hissing chorus of spears, and the raucous symphony of kards and dhups, so dreadfully sibilant and mournful. His eyes were glazed with mists of anguish, as he lifted his gaze toward the sun in flight, a ball of fire, reflecting the molten gold of death and surcease. He had forgotten about Nasir Mirza beside him—who, much like his king-brother was awed by the fiery sky. Its scarlet bleeding through the lava of horizon in purplish wounds, large and throbbing.

Could this be the sun-god, hugging the wounds of the suffered and the suffering? Mournful and dying? Babur's gaze was returning to earth, suspended over the red and yellow standards before skidding over the field of woe and jubilation. *Men killing men? Innocent beasts suffering needlessly? Savage, inconceivable needs of the men-beasts? The cankers of greed and ambition? How would the victors treat the vanquished? With love and pity in their hearts? Or with the rods of tyranny and injustice?* An overwhelming weight of grief and compassion was constricting Babur's heart as he became aware of his viziers and generals, chanting the songs of victory and seeking his approval.

"Well, the songs of our pride and glory reach not the vanquished, but the wounded and the dying need our care and sympathy." One appeal of a prayer escaped Babur's thoughts, his gaze embracing all in the warmth of praise and compassion.

King Babur was heeding the low moan of one soldier, becoming oblivious to all else, but to the dream-world of his profound contemplation. Involuntarily, his hands were snatching his cape, and ripping it into lengths of wide strips. He was kneeling beside the wounded soldier and bandaging his thigh with the care and gentleness of a skilled physician.

14

Moonlit Madness

In paradise, they tell us, houris dwell
And fountains run with wine and oxymal
If these be lawful in the world to come
Surely t' is right to love them here as well
— Omar Khayyam

The scintillating dance of sunshine through the wooded terrain appeared to be chasing the entourage of the King riding toward the hunting grounds at the foothills of river Nilab. A merry group of poets, scholars, courtiers and physicians, they had nothing in common with the exception that they all loved the game of battue as passionately as the king himself. Babur astride his snow-white steed at the head of this entourage in his riding habit of velvet green with a matching cummerbund appeared more like some knight on a holy quest than the king of Kabul on his way to indulge in the sport of battue. The red plume in his turban, vivid and silken, was much like his thoughts surfacing smooth over the waters of past sorrows and hardships.

Since his return from Kandahar, Babur had cherished the beauty of Kabul with keenest of delights, grateful to be home amidst his family and perfumed gardens. A few skirmishes here and there, but seasons in hourglass of time were enchanting, sifting forth the most beautiful of summers he had not ever witnessed before. Moved by the color and vivacity of his gardens, he had planned many excursions, swimming, hunting, playing chougan, or perfecting his skills in archery. Passion and inspiration were his guides too, while making love to his brides or writing couplets under some spell of exhilaration. His carefree thoughts were soaring, embracing his dead beloved inside the cradle of a sunset, all heliotrope and sparkling. Suddenly, the shuddering reflections on the horizon were forcing his gaze back to the earthly landscape where fall had kindled the leaves to flaming ochre, some dyed with scarlet and the others streaked with mauve and orange.

Fall, the saddest of all seasons, Babur's thoughts for some reason were stirring the murky deeps of sorrows, trundling past the alleys of Ghazni, Kandahar and Samarkand.

Before returning to Kabul, Babur had bestowed his newly won kingdom of Kandahar upon Nasir Mirza. Advising him not to pursue the traitors, Shah Beg and Muqim, and to devote all his energies in building defenses for Kandahar. And yet Kandahar was not to be saved, reclaimed once again by Shaibani Khan, and buried under the mounds of his deceit, tyranny and injustice. Babur had learned about this while admiring the loveliness of his garden Bagh-i-Mahtab, where he was wont to retire for solitary contemplations. He had barely recovered from his arduous journey from Kandahar to Kabul, and this news had hit him with the force of a whirlwind. And yet, so spellbound as he was by the scent of his homecoming and gardens, that nothing could mar his joy of keeping and cherishing the beauty of peace and pulchritude! Literally sliding out of this whirlwind, his thoughts were quick to return to the Eden of equanimity, and he had penned a missive to Nasir Mirza in the spirit of hope and consolation.

Don't be grieved, my brother, I bestow upon you the kingdom of Ghazni. Enjoy the peace and prosperity of this kingdom as much as I am enjoying my Kabul. Shaibani Khan, as you say, has gone back to Samarkand, and be rest assured this vile beast would be consumed by his orgies of gluttony and debauchery. Kabul is decked with the loveliest of blooms, thanks to Abdul Razaq who guarded my citadel and gardens in my absence with perfect devotion. Also inform Abdul Razaq that I bestow upon him the little town of Ningnahar.

The grove of pines and cedars was coming into view, and Babur's thoughts were snatched out of the serene waters of optimism, trundling down the slopes of tragedies vast and incomprehensible.

Almost a month later after that brief missive, Babur was confronted with fresh waves of tragic news, vowing to himself that he would go hounding after that Uzbek viper after the auspicious birth of royal babes from both his wives, Mahim and Masuma.

Mahim is glowing with the joy and pride of motherhood, rosy and rotund, while Masuma so pale and languishing? Is she ill, she barely touched her food last night? Babur's thoughts were seeking relief from the vow of his vengeance, but the feverish link in his mind was adamant to poke the fire of recollection.

Shaibani Khan, abandoning his haven of Samarkand, had launched a ferocious attack on Herat. Pillaging and plundering, he had swept through the city like a wildfire, torching houses and murdering indiscriminately. He and his soldiers had stormed the palaces, ravishing the princesses, murdering the children, and finally killing the noblest of princes, Badi-uz-Zaman and Musafer Hussayan.

Babur's horse was coming to an abrupt halt before the field of battue, where the trainers were busy keeping the hare, the deer, the bears, the wolves, the panthers, the antelopes and many, many more beasts into a vast circle designed for the game of battue. Somewhere out there was the roar of mourning, which only Babur's anguished heart could catch and discern. His gaze was reaching down to the penciled sparkle of waters in the distant Nilab, as if he was all alone, not even aware of his merry companions who had caught up with him, bursting with glee and exhilaration. The raucous stampede of voices was penetrating his sad contemplations though, and he was becoming aware of the teasing expression of his friend and mentor.

"The kings of the jungle and the beasts of the steppes implore the mercy of King Babur." Khwaja Kilan's very eyes were jingling a subtle challenge.

"The man-beast in all of us can never claim the title of a king, remaining always a slave. A slave to one's ego fettered by the chains of lust, greed and desire." Babur demurred aloud. "A beggar in meanest of rags, or a dervish wearing his nakedness as the finest of apparels, remains still the slave to his passions noble or corrupt." He waved his arm as a signal to commence the game of battue.

At the sound of the horn, the riders had entered the arena of their favorite sport, releasing arrows from their bulging quivers with cries of elation. The wild beasts were trying to escape this mindless assault, while the royal beaters were chasing them back into the circle of death and daring. The hunter and the hunted were caught in the drama of bravado and recklessness, obeying only the law of survival. Yet beasts were marked for death, and men to boast over the pleasure in living. Babur's unerring aim had wounded one panther, but for one astonishing moment of lucidity and compassion, his heart had begun to protest and thunder. He couldn't tear his gaze away from the glazed luster of pain and surrender in panther's eyes, as it lay there supine and blood-soaked.

How wicked is life and how dignified death?

Awestruck and motionless, Babur sat astride, one agony of a prayer shuddering over his thoughts like the shroud of penance. A subtle reflection of his Beloved was meeting his gaze in the shining eyes of this panther. *Sweet Absent*, his very soul was weeping. Suddenly, he was aware of the bleating, grunting agony of the wounded beasts, mingling with the jubilations of the hunters drunk with pride at the prowess of their hunting. And yet, Babur's keen senses were catching more sounds, as if the wind itself was moaning, and the crimson bowl of a sky unleashing laments fiery and heartrending. Some sort of hopeless, helpless pain was rising within him with the fury of an impending storm, and his heart was seized by the pincers of grief and disgust.

"Cease this madness at once!" One thunder of a command escaped Babur's lips, his eyes flashing. "Yes, we all love this sport. I myself was like a child at play a few moments ago, but no more, no more. We must banish the very thought of this brutal sport from our minds, and tear out the pages of history where the name battue is mentioned. It is king's caprice, if not his compassion, which is issuing this Farman." He raced his horse out of this circle of death, aware only of the stunned silence behind him, the roaring of sorrow within him savage and turbulent.

The night air holding a canopy of stars was lending Babur the crumbs of peace and solitude as he rode along with his companions, longing for the comfort of his palace. The livid moon floating in ether appeared to be guiding the riders back toward the precincts of Kabul, their hearts saddened beyond words, and their minds baffled by the shock of ban on battue. Yet these men were not prone to sadness for long, devoted to the king, understanding his caprice much more than he—Babur himself could admit or acknowledge. The mournful hush in the air was lulling their sorrow to sleep and refreshing their hope for a night-long *mushaira*—poetry recital, which the king had promised before embarking on this excursion. The evidence of this delightful expectation could not be doubted, for the small caravan from the hunting ground was right behind, equipped with tents, carpets and provisions to erect a makeshift hall for the sole pleasure of the king and his companions. The king, this starry night, was practicing the art of introspection, his thoughts wandering down the memory lane naked and unashamed.

What whaling absurdity? Why this sudden aversion against battue? Didn't I always enjoy this sport with a sense of pride and exultation? Khwaja Kilan advised me to abandon this sport, when I was young and heedless. His admonitions reached me finally, is that it? No! I have looked into the eyes of my Beloved. The penciled eyes of dying panther, shooting green flames! Such sorrow and hopelessness! Sweet Absent is with me, don't leave me, my Beloved, my Sweetness!

Babur's thoughts were whirling themselves free of sorrow and loneliness. *Stay with me, Beloved. Help me look into the heart of the imponderables! This pressing burden of compassion! Where does it come from? Have I ever flinched from hurting a man or a beast before? Dare I say, no? But cruelty for the sake of kindness, for order, discipline, obedience! War, pride, ambition, the tyrants of time, my eternal foes and friends? Are we not the children of time, all of us, the suckling babes with monster appetites?* His thoughts were poking the cinders of another memory that of his sister Khazanda, wedded to his hateful foe, Shaibani Khan.

Must I go chasing Shaibani Khan, killing the husband of my sister, and making her a widow? Caprice and sadness, are these the brides of my solitude, or the demons of my will and desire? Why must I banish old pleasures and find new diversions? What is this need and restlessness inside me? He was jolted out of his reveries by a sudden ripple of sounds from the lips of his companions.

"The poets are longing to recite their couplets, my King." Khwaja Kilan was seeking Babur's attention. "After nursing the beasts and bidding farewell to their favorite sport, they deserve the feast of poetry, don't you agree?"

"A candle-lit mushaira, to wipe clean the soot of sadness and dejection!" Babur pulled the reign of his horse, bringing it to a slow halt. "A great site for pavilion right here, let's not postpone our pleasure for wine, majun and poesy."

A great pavilion by the banks of river Nilab was coming alive with the juggling of couplets and with cheers of applause. It was an arena of revelry and ideation where wine and majun were favored over roasted mutton and where levity and laughter were permitted regardless of rank or status. Babur seated against one crimson pillow over the Persian carpet was sipping his wine and absorbing the downpour of poetry and raillery. His warm, contemplative gaze was shifting from the dancing flames of candelabras toward the nightly splendor where moon sat livid decked with a diadem of stars, all gleeful and sparkling. More sparkling were the notes from the lute of Quli Muhammed, demanding

Babur's attention, and he was becoming aware of the two silent musicians beside the lute-player, Hussein the master of Qubus, and Shaikhi the flutist. Not far from them was seated the poet, Ali Sher, teasing the strings of his dulcimer. Another poet by the name of Sheikhem Beg had begun reciting verses strange and maudlin.

"During the sorrows of my night the whirlpool of my sight bears the firmament from its place. The dragons of the inundations of my tears bear down the four quarters of the habitable worlds—" Sheikhem Beg's recital was truncated by a loud comment from Mulla Baba.

"Is this poetry? Are you by any chance challenging the demons of the night to kill and devour us?" Mulla Baba's comments were swallowed by an abrupt plea from Ali Sher.

"My King, grant us the pleasure of listening to your couplets." Ali Sher drained his wine thirstily. "The tears and sorrows of Sheikhem Beg would drown us all, if you didn't come to our rescue. Please save us from such fate, my King!"

"Tears and sorrows express only the resilience of our hearts, my friend, and only poets perish, metaphorically, inside the flood of their grief or despair." Babur laughed suddenly. "And as to my couplets, this wanton summer has blunted my knife of inspiration, I haven't written a word."

"Take pity on your subjects, my King." Mulla Baba pleaded amidst throes of mirth. "Only your noble verses can cure this laughter, I am dying." He was clutching his stomach as if in agony. "The ghazal which you wrote, my King, something about the *world and confidant!*"

"Ah, that one!" Babur could feel the wine coursing through his veins, as he began to recite merrily.

"Let the sword of the world be brandished as it may
It cannot cut one vein without the permission of God
I have found no faithful friend in this world but my soul
Except my own heart, I have no trusty confidant."

"My King, it would be a rare feast if you could recite the one you wrote on the eve of your birthday?" Khwaja Kilan requested dreamily. "Remember Baghi-Khana and the glorious night, my King?"

"That sweet-scented night against the twinkling of stars from the hearts of fireflies!" Babur's thoughts were giddy, his head spinning a web of recollections.

"Though I am not related to dervishes
Yet I am devoted to them heart and soul
Say not that the state of a prince is remote from that of a dervish
Though a king, I am the slave of dervish."

"A rare feast indeed, my King!" Abdullah Hatifi applauded with drunken glee. "My heart is longing to hear more, some couplets sad and romantic, hearts pining in love, or lovers gone mad?"

"The hour is late. We must ride back to our palace." Babur got to his feet, laughter and inebriation glowing in his eyes like the fire of elation and ecstasy.

"Yes, the moon-bride up yonder and the stars are playing harlot with my thoughts. "To our mounts, let the pavilion stay, it might remember us in the morning with sighs and heartache." He stood whistling for his horse.

"My King, my King. A few more couplets, some farewell songs in honor of Nilab! Something about virtue, passion, painted in colors of love—" Many voices in unison were joining this chorus.

"I like but one color, the color of humility!" Babur sang ecstatically, darting out of the pavilion toward his obedient mount. "Humility is the name of the divine child within all of us. It knows our profoundest of joys and darkest of despairs. I know but one virtue, its name is compassion, and it is the most exalted of all virtues. The compassion to forgive all! And yet love is the highest of all virtues, the noblest of passions. This livid moon and stabbing stars are beguiling my thoughts." He laughed as if communing with his horse. "Sayyid Tabib, ride beside me, the stars are whispering to me that I might need your company tonight." He commanded over his shoulders.

The starry heavens looming closer over the hills were guiding the royal riders as they galloped toward Kabul under some spell of awe and silence. Babur had surrendered his senses to the beauty of the night, his thoughts mute and suspended. And yet some sort of presage was chiseling its way from deep within him, razor-sharp and challenging.

Your false sense of peace is going to be shattered when the clouds of inebriation leave and dissipate. Don't you know Masuma is ill and suffering?

"You are the chief physician, Sayyid Tabib, and entrusted with the responsibility of keeping all the members of my royal household in good health and good spirits." Babur commented abruptly as if to his own self. "Mahim Begum is carrying herself and the child in her womb most splendidly, but Masuma Begum, I am afraid? She has lost her appetite, and of late has grown pale? Have you been neglecting your duties, Sayyid?" He asked abruptly, becoming aware of the palace gates.

"No, my King!" One hushed protest grazed Sayyid Tabib's lips, his horse almost colliding with the king's while galloping through the gates toward the marble terraces. "Since Mahim Begum is a pillar of health, I have been devoting more time toward the care of Masuma Begum. She is young and prone to worry about the hour of birth, sort of bewildered by the changes in her body and moods. A normal affliction for any young mother-to-be! Once the baby is born, all her worries would melt away, and color would return to her cheeks within days."

"Such a fine physician you are!" Babur exclaimed, the simmering of rage and presage within him soothed by the splashing of fountains in the terraced garden. "What quackeries you have been practicing during the hours of your idleness? Even a simpleton with no knowledge in medicine can come up with a trite answer like *normal affliction!* I suggest you read Ibn Sina. He was born in the city of Bokhara, amongst the maidens of great beauty, who inspire songs and longings in the hearts of the young lovers. He too must have been charmed by the beauty of such girls, but he chose intellect over beauty. Wooing medicine and philosophy as his brides-to-be! Compelled by his passion to study and gain knowledge, not only did he become a great physician but a profound expounder of Arastu—Aristotle. Make sure, Sayyid, that you come up with an intelligent answer next time if I probe into the validity of your prognosis?" He abandoned his horse into the care of the stable-master, and bounded straight for the palace doors.

The king had forgotten about his night companions, pressed only by his intoxicated bliss and presage to reach the comfort of his royal chamber. *For once in my life, I am drunk, half drunk, more than drunk*—Babur's thoughts were swaying and absorbing the contours of his palace hall against the shuddering flames of candelabras. *Wine, majun and poetry, sweet seduction of the senses weak and vacillating! What did Sayyid say? Where did my night companions vanish*? His inebriated thoughts were coming to a sudden halt as he noticed his aunt Mehr Nigar, smiling and curtsying. Her hazel eyes were holding him captive, but his gaze was lured toward the beautiful girl at her elbow, also curtsying and blushing.

"The happiest of times and the happiest of welcomes!" Babur embraced his aunt, and then stood laughing. "What happier time there could be than this to have my maternal aunt in Kabul—especially, when I am about to become the father of two royal babes?" He stole a glance at the blushing beauty beside his aunt. "And where did you find such a priceless jewel, my dear Aunt?"

"I have brought you a bride from Badakhshan, my King!" Mehr Nigar cooed happily. "The fairest of all the princesses in that fair city, her name is Gulrukh."

"Thrice welcome, then!" Babur chanted merrily, his gaze espying Naralla by the arched window. "The king welcomes you, this palace too, and the very gardens of Kabul, welcome, welcome. My brides too would welcome you, dear Aunt, for the gift of this jewel-princess. These days, they can't endure my passion, such moody, delicate creatures, the fairest of the fair? They grow weary of us men too soon, while our passions grow wild and multiply?" His gaze was falling on Naralla with a flash of lightning. "Naralla, you are to be my night messenger. Go, summon Maulana Kazi. The king is to be wedded." His flashing eyes traced Naralla's flight who fled like an arrow shot from the quiver of the King's command.

"My King!" One tremor of a protest escaped Mehr Nigar's lips, horror shining in her eyes. "You are not serious? You cannot? You must not!" Fear and disbelief were choking her thoughts to silence.

"The king abhors the word *must*, my charming Aunt." Babur began half impatiently, half indulgently. "What is the reason for your sudden displeasure, may the king ask?"

"Why, a royal wedding, my King!" Was Mehr Nigar's flustered response! "What caprice? No songs, no flowers, no dancing and feasting? No time for trousseau? Where is the wedding dress—the guests, the happy rituals?" She couldn't continue against the fever of intensity in Babur's gaze.

"The kings when wedded as many times as I have need nothing to seal the bonds of a marriage, but the music of love in their hearts." Babur's eyes were lit up with the stars of mirth and delirium. "A trousseau, such worthless fineries! The sheer ritual of undressing one's bride, all tedious and frustrating—" He paused noticing the approach of Maulana Kazi, who was quick to fall at his feet in a heap of curtsy. "Get to your feet, Maulana! Don't waste this precious time in curtsies. The king is longing to get married before this night is over."

Maulana Kazi was stumbling to his feet, dazed and stunned. He couldn't move or speak, only his gaze wandering from one to the other under some spell of disbelief and bewilderment. Babur had sailed toward the Princess, slipping his arm around her waist, more so to win her trust than to soothe her visible trembling. *My Gul, my beautiful princess, the king is not going to eat you alive. He is but your slave.* Babur was murmuring endearments, his gaze tender and pleading. The Princess was falling into a trance, it seemed, her trembling had stopped, and her eyes were attaining the luster of moonbeams. Sighing to himself, Babur returned his attention to the pillar of ice as Maulana.

"Come, Kazi, pronounce us husband and wife in the eyes of man and God, and give us your blessings!" Babur commanded. "The king is in no mood to stand here all night for the angels of heavens to bless this royal wedding."

"My King!" A feeble appeal escaped Maulana Kazi's numb senses. "This time of the night? You and—" His befuddled thoughts were truncated by an imperious wave of Babur's arm, his eyes flashing.

"Spare me the levity of your advice: *you must not, my king?*" Babur's very eyes were spilling the threat of an impending storm. "Would you rather that the king deflower this vestal bloom and be damned, just because the pious mulla thinks that the marriage vows can't be sealed in the middle of the night?"

"Witnesses, my King." Maulana Kazi could barely murmur, his look glazed! "We need two witnesses."

"Beat the drums, Naralla!" Babur thundered. "Let the horns be blown, summoning irreverent pagans from the very pits of hell to witness the king's wedding this unholy night? The king's palace is bewitched, for sure, witches and warlocks lurking in the shadows? Where are the king's cup-companions, the poets, the scholars and the musicians?"

At the sound of Naralla's drum, the palace itself was jolted to a rude awakening. Suddenly, a flurry of footsteps and buzzing of sounds were piercing the silence of the night, followed by royal occupants, sleep-walking under some spell of dream-stupor. This dream-stupor was replaced with song and revelry after the king was duly married, signing his papers of nikkah ceremony most hastily and impatiently. And then whisking his bride away to his nuptial chamber against the ocean of applause and felicitations!

This strange, tumultuous night had ended too soon, its winged flight unnoticed by the royal couple, now chasing the bride of dawn. Gulrukh was cradled into the delicious arms of sleep, where desire and carnality of the wedding night dared not trespass her bliss and surrender.

Babur, in contrast, was half dozing, half sleeping. The bliss-rapture of his passion, which had later lulled him to sleep, had deserted him soon after, leaving him vulnerable to the caprice of dreams or nightmares. His newly wedded bride was a part of his dreams too, and yet he was witnessing the ebb and flow of other dreams shrouded in mists of reality, all mysterious and dissipating. Inside the mists of his dreams, he was standing in his garden, feeling the cool lips of the wind, tremulous and shuddering, and listening to the claps of thunder, wild and remote—some wordless lament from within and without. Somewhere inside the mists was muffled the cry of a newborn babe, and the scent of the earth was wafting forth the musty odor of death and decay. The mists were shifting, forcing open some mysterious doors, through which a flood of voices was surging, nondescript and formless.

Some dolorous cry from the heart of dawn! One shudder of a scream from the abyss of the night!

Babur was jolted to awakening, the pale gold of dawn cradling his new bride into a halo of bliss and innocence. He lay gazing at her as the one bewitched, but his senses were straining to absorb sounds from the very walls of his palace. The stillness of dawn was disrupted by the rills of intermittent wailing, and these wails appeared to be shooting forth from that part of the harem where Mahim and Masuma were lodged. Slipping out of his bed with utmost care so as not to awaken his bride, he covered his nakedness with a silk robe and tiptoed out of his chamber barefooted and bareheaded. Tracing the direction of the sounds, Babur landed straight into the chamber of Masuma. A bevy of begums and princesses were crowded in this room, their eyes swollen with excessive weeping, it was obvious. But Babur, in some sort of daze, was drifting toward the canopied bed where Masuma appeared to be sleeping most sweetly and peacefully, though her features were polished by the deathlike pallor of the dawn, so golden and surreal.

"Is Masuma ill?" One low query was forced out of Babur's lips, directed at Mahim who stood at the foot of the bed, mute and trancelike.

Mahim's lips moved but no sound escaped her lips, her anguished gaze stark and unseeing. Babur was edging closer to the bed as if sleepwalking and not even expecting an answer. He stood gazing at the waxen features of Masuma for a moment before touching her brow, his own features attaining the pallor of death and immobility. His hand was glued to her cold brow, icy shivers cutting through his soul like the knives sharp and relentless. Suddenly, he whirled away from the bed, facing Mahim, his sight blurred by the mists of grief profound and inconsolable.

"Why I was not informed?" One cry of agony ripped through his soul, his sightless eyes seeing nothing but the black shroud of his guilt and neglect.

Who would dare disturb the king in his nuptial bed of lust and desire? Babur's thoughts were quick to shoot a harsh reminder.

"She didn't suffer but the pangs of childbirth." Mahim Begum's eyes were gathering tears, her lips trembling. "Though prematurely born, the princess is healthy." Her attention was turning to the royal nurse. "Maywa Jan, bring the princess to the king."

Babur was awakening to the fresh assault of pain and grief, almost snatching the princess from the arms of Maywa Jan before she could settle her into the king's arms with the gentleness of a mother. The princess had begun to cry while Babur held her to him, his eyes closing and his lips moving as if offering a prayer and communing with his daughter wordlessly. A mantle of hush was lowered over all, all of a sudden, as the princess was sucked back into the comfort of her sleep, her head abandoned on the shoulders of her royal father. Babur's eyes were opening, the fever of agony there stark and smoldering. Motionless, he stood there, though his thoughts had begun swirling inside a whirlwind of imponderables.

A premature birth and untimely death, such a mockery of fate! Where is Masuma? Am I not holding her close to me? This gift of life, my princess, this miracle tender and sublime from the womb of death and darkness! Has Masuma joined the Sweet Absent? Is death larger than life, more sweet and holy by the very virtue of its being remote and unfathomable? Babur was holding out the sleeping babe to Mahim, his look glazed and burning.

"We would name her Masuma. Your own first-born, Mahim!" Babur was plodding out of this chamber of death, holding one reed of a consolation that Mahim had clasped the princess to her breast.

The king was seeking the sanctuary of his library, alone and forlorn. His heart was heavy, yet his mind was searching the crumbs of consolations. *I have left a part of myself in the death-chamber of Masuma. A part of myself which claims to love, yet not loving, and yet again greater than love and loving? What it is, I have yet to discover?* Babur had abandoned himself on the velvety depths of his chair, this library his graveyard to face the demons of grief and loss.

15

Babur The Padishah

*Love is patient and kind. Love is not jealous or boastful. It is not rude
or arrogant. Love does not insist on its own way, it is not irritable or
resentful. It does not rejoice at wrong, but rejoices in the right. Love
bears all things, endures all things. Love never ends.*
— 1 Corinthians

The Fortune Hall inside the palace of Kabul was decked with silken hangings in honor of twin celebrations this particular evening. Babur was the happiest of hosts, celebrating the birth of a son by Mahim, and the rebirth of a Turkish title which he had adopted recently, styling himself as Padishah—meaning, the single sultan of Islam. He was seated on a velvet throne with Gulrukh Begum beside him, bestowing riches and honors upon his guests while being entertained by dancers and musicians. Khwaja Kilan was seated next to him, taciturn and contemplative. Mahim Begum was absent in this hall of feasting and celebration, happily confined in her chamber with her newborn son, prince Humayun. Twice happy since she had secured a promise from Babur to invite astrologers who could divine the fortunes of the royal heir, matching his hour of birth with auspicious stars! Many scrolls with colorful Zodiac signs were unrolled on the carpet where the astrologers sat absorbed predicting the future of prince Humayun as ordained by the stars in conformity with date, hour and year of birth.

Mirth and amusement were alighting in Babur's eyes at the sight of the astrologers so deeply engrossed in their divinations, but his gaze was straying over the ocean of festivities in this hall, and arresting a variety of nuances in each word and gesture. Mehr Nigar was lolling against one satiny pillow, her attention claimed by the young dancers creating rainbows from their skirts while floating on their toes and clapping. The musicians evoking happy tunes from their lutes and flutes under the canopied stage were entertaining the begums and princesses, amongst them, Shahr Banu—Babur's half sister, the most avid and entranced. Seated next to her was Ai Begum, dreamy and contemplative. Babur's gaze was lingering over his brother Nasir Mirza who had just returned from Ghazni the night before, and now sat there drinking, the gold cup in his hand his dearest of companions.

My gentle brother has taken wine as his bride, it is obvious. The king must find a real bride for him. Babur's thoughts were feeling one whiff of sadness all of a sudden, darting off on some mad spree to search the ashes of wars and tragedies. All descendants of the Tamerlane, if not killed in wars, were murdered or poisoned by the Uzbeks? Sultan Ahmed, Mahmud Khan and Shah Rukh, all dead and forgotten! Ulugh Beg and the Khakhans, the innocent victims of murder and brutality. The Khans of Tagatai, breathing their last amidst the fogs of agony and bloodshed. Husayan Baikara, and his princely sons, Musafer Husayan and Badi-uz-Zaman slaughtered most brutally. Balkh, Hissar, Herat, Kandahar and Samarkand under the assaults of the Uzbeks now roaming the streets, pillaging and plundering! *Fortunately, my hold over Kabul, Ghazni, Badakhshan, Moghulistan and Ningnahar is strong, and I am the only one left out of the tragic brood of Tamerlane to claim the title of Padishah.* Babur's thoughts were wringing themselves free from the soot of tragedies, his gaze espying one young princess, the shock of red in her hair matching her silk gown.

This young rose of a princess, I have seen her before, where? Babur's gaze as well as his thoughts was polished by the warmth of tenderness. *When I should think, a few weeks ago, it seems likely, with Mahim in her chamber, perhaps? Another bride, a gift for Padishah!* His gaze was sweeping past the astrologers toward the heaps of gifts, all colorful and glittering. Bolts upon bolts of silks, muslins and brocades! Wooden chests with the inlay of ivory and brass! The vessels of gold and silver, the coral bowls encrusted with rubies, and the onyx figurines! A variety of jade hilts and jeweled daggers! Gold ashrafis and caskets heaped with gems precious. Pearls, rubies, emeralds, diamonds and star sapphires upon beds of lapis lazuli! Jars of spices and silver trays laden with fruits. *Ah, treasures of the world, more abundant than what we salvaged from Kandahar!* Babur's gaze was returning to the astrologers.

"Well, what do the stars of fate say concerning the future of our royal prince?" Babur flashed this query at the astrologers with a sudden burst of mirth and amusement.

"Padishah!" Muhammed Sharif was startled to his feet, bowing double in an awkward curtsy. "Venus, the most lucky and favorable of stars is in conjunction with the star of the royal prince! Yes, all the propitious signs, the riches and the kingdoms with the promise of fortunes great and enviable. He would be the king of kings. Possibly, the emperor—of Hind if I may be as bold as to predict?"

"No stars of wisdom in his horoscope, my flustered sage?" Babur laughed. "My birth sign too revealed many happy stars, and yet each star exacts a price before granting a boon. I was a happy prince once, then a wretched exile, stumbling on toward kingship, and now the king of kings and Padishah! Before my lusty prince could claim Hind as his legacy, Padishah has to become the emperor first." His eyes were gathering the stars of mysticism. "I have seen many a men stumble and fall over the rungs of fortunes, not that they lacked courage, but love and wisdom, without which we are destined to doom and misfortunes. Astrology, if free from the soot of superstition, promotes wisdom and love for learning, so keep it pure, Sharif, and exposed to the light of learning—" His thoughts were disrupted by a sudden flurry of noise and commotion.

The imposing portals on the east side of the Fortune Hall were flung open, revealing a coterie of guards dragging along some wretched prisoners, unkempt and bedraggled. Shah Mirza was coming into view amongst the pitiful lot of his companions, their coats and boots caked with snow, and their arms crossed over their breasts, as if warding off some blows invisible. Babur's gaze was riveted to his inveterate rebel of a cousin, Shah Mirza, his eyes shining with the warmth of pity and compassion. All men fell to curtsying and prostrating, numb and speechless. Shah Mirza amongst them, a heap of abject misery and hopelessness!

"Come, my worthy rebel, embrace your enemy!" Babur commanded. His gaze alone forcing his cousin to look into his eyes.

"My King!" Was Shah Mirza's stunned response, his look pleading.

"Last time when I had forgiven you, I was a king, my rebel of a cousin." Babur intoned genially. "Now, you are forgiven by Padishah. And next time with the grace of Allah, I might be an emperor? And the emperor would not brook rebellion or disobedience from any kin, foes or friends, meting out just punishments." His gaze was shifting toward his guards and servants, bright and ruminative. "Tahir, drag these stinking curs to some warm corner of the palace, their misery and plight are marring the joy of festivities. Feed them too, and some clean clothes, washed and scrubbed till they attain a semblance of human dignity. As for my cousin, fetch silk robes and warm quilts." His eyes were gathering the mists of pity and compassion. "Come, Mushin, offer my cousin a generous draught of poison from your gold flagon, which might loosen his tongue. I am anxious to poke the cinders of his lies, and to know how he escaped the claws of Shaibani Khan."

The royal guards were quick to haul away the numb wretches, while the others disappearing to fetch robes and quilts. Mushin had filled a gold cup for Shah Mirza, which he drained thirstily, holding it out to the wine-bearer for replenishing.

"Ah, your noble thirst for wine has quenched the fear of death in you, this time!" Babur exclaimed cheerfully. "Last time when you were forgiven and offered a cup of wine, you were afraid to drink lest it be poisoned? A welcome and astonishing change, I must commend. Considering, you have been drinking all your life the poison of distrust." He sighed, turning his attention to his friend abruptly. "Tell me, Khwaja, why do I forgive over and over again and always? Some inherent caprice inside me, perhaps! Or the rods of conscience holding the whips of pity and compassion?"

"Had I not known you since your childhood, I would say, *caprice*." Khwaja Kilan smiled mischievously. "But since I know you so well, Padishah, I would not divulge my thoughts concerning *forgiveness* even if you threatened me to be flayed alive?"

"In that case, my prudent mentor, Padishah must seek answers from the beautiful eyes of his wife—queen?"

Babur's flashing eyes were lured toward his cousin instead, whose very demeanor was transformed by a clean robe and a colorful quilt draped around his shoulders. He seemed more intent on drinking than doing justice to the plate of viands brought before him by the royal servants. Some sort of ache and tenderness was yawning in Babur's thoughts, but before it could awaken to the assault of painful memories, he forced his gaze toward his wife, whose sparkling eyes were absorbing the shifting of scenes with utmost absorption.

"My beauty! Do you deem Padishah foolish in forgiving his lout of a cousin?" Babur asked whimsically.

"Padishah, foolish!" Was Gulrukh Begum's startled response, color rising to her cheeks in a sudden flush. "I wouldn't utter such heresy." She murmured, all confused and flustered.

"Your beauty, my innocent flower, reveals more than what you can never voice." Babur felt awed and humbled, returning his gaze to his cousin. "My shameless guzzler, now that you have quenched your thirst, be inclined to tell us what mad audacity compelled you to come to Kabul?"

"Padishah." Shah Mirza swept his arms in one flourish of a curtsy, his eyes shining. "I would remain grateful to you eternally. It is a pity that wicked, black-hearted man like Shaibani could teach me the art of fealty, and yet true it is that he alone—the evil villain that he is, has succeeded in making me realize my follies. Here I am, Padishah, a slave to your generosity, forever and forever."

"Leave these flatteries into the jurisdiction of future, my unhappy cousin." Babur began impatiently. "Evil and black imports sit not well over the hearth of this evening marked for joy and jubilation. And yet, I must know, very briefly, the motives of your escape and return, and your plans for future. Be swift and candid in telling the truth, if you wish to escape the edict of exile?"

"Padishah!" One sob of a plea trembled upon the lips of Shah Mirza. "I would be your devoted slave forever, as I said before." His eyes were clouded by the mists of shame and contrition. "One of my companions had some jewels to bribe the guards, and we escaped in the middle of the night. Our fear to be captured again kept us moving through snow and bitter cold, such hardships! Kabul is home I have learnt, if not too late, Shaibani is no friend of the Moghuls—" His voice was choked by the sudden assault of his guilt on the verge to delirium.

"Moghul!" Babur appeared to taste this word on the tip of his tongue, his look sad and ruminative. "Words have a way to cling to their roots, no matter how many times they change and adopt new attire. Moghul is derived from the word Mongol, and Mongol is a variation of the root word Mong—meaning brave and daring. The word Mongol with its connotation of *savages and barbarians* hounded me during my days of exile, and I changed it to Moghul after I conquered Kabul, matching the wealth and grandeur of my durbar and kingdom. Words, I get wearied of words!" His thoughts were disrupted by another wave of night visitors. "My palace is becoming a den of beggars and supplicants?" His eyes were lit up with joy as he recognized his favorite cousin amidst the flurry of vigilant guards. "Welcome, Said Khan, my valorous prince! What happy chance brings you to Kabul?" He caught the prince into an eager embrace before he could manage a curtsy.

"Padishah, congratulations! I just heard, and yet I have no gifts to offer." Said Khan murmured, overwhelmed.

"The greatest gift of all, *you!*" Babur beamed. "You have brought back happy memories, the purity and innocence of youth, and giddy hours of sports and hunting." He laughed, relinquishing his hold on the prince, who was already claimed by begums and princesses, all vying to attend to his needs and comforts.

Said Khan was whisked away by the begums with the promise of a hot bath, scented with aloes and musk. Babur had returned to his throne, finding the seat of Gulrukh Begum vacant, and Khwaja Kilan grinning with pleasure. The festive evening was commencing afresh with music and songs, but Khwaja Kilan was intent upon sharing the news bulletin with Padishah concerning the warring factions. He was hoping to hold Babur's attention so that he could fairly decide as to the mode of pardon or punishment for the rebels, or to offer refuge to the fugitives who would be coming in droves to Kabul. Babur was half listening, half brooding. His thoughts were with Said Khan, longing to hear the true account of tragedies, which had reached him earlier garnished by the soot of many lies and canards. He was not consciously blocking the unfolding of rueful events expressed by Khwaja Kilan, but finding comfort and diversion from the lips of the poets and the singers. His thoughts were bent on following Said Khan though, watching him being fed and bathed, and welcoming him back into this Fortune Hall.

Khwaja Kilan had drained his bulletin of news, and now sat observing the leave-taking of guests, curtsying and bidding farewell. The singers and musicians, as if awakening afresh after the midnight hour, were evoking merry tunes, oblivious to the loss of the half the audience, and immersed deep in their arena of joy and exhilaration. Babur, after becoming aware of his ill-fated cousin, had sent him away to rest, releasing him from his stupor of guilt and misery. His gaze was straying over to the younger princesses, who were absorbed in playing backgammon. A wistful smile was curling upon his lips, his gaze wandering again, but it was lit up with the warmth of joy at the sudden appearance of Said Khan, followed by a procession of begums, laughing and teasing.

"Come, sit by me." Babur indicated the seat, dismissing the begums with a genial wave of his arm. "I had long despaired of seeing you alive?"

"And here I am, Padishah, royally fed and scrubbed clean of all grime and hardships!" Said Khan lowered himself into the seat formerly occupied by Gulrukh Begum. "The hour is late, Padishah, but before I poke the cinders of my hardships, I must warn you that more visitors might be knocking at your palace gates, in the middle of the night till early dawn?" He paused, but noticing the stars of agog and impatience in Babur's eyes, resumed exigently. "Your devoted servant Maulana Sadr has succeeded in saving the life of Haider Mirza, and they are on their way to Kabul, I have heard." He paused again, but Babur's compelling gaze was urging him to continue. "Your cousins and uncles, all those souls wise and gentle, have been murdered. Your aunts are virtual prisoners in their own palace, watched by Shaibani Khan himself and his general, Ababeker. The princely heads of Badi-uz-Zaman and Musafer Husayan are preserved as drinking cups for the sole pleasure of Shaibani Khan. Herat—the pearl city is stained with the blood of the innocent victims, and many are fleeing, some headed toward Kabul. So, sorry, Padishah, I bring sad news to Kabul."

"And yet, you are dearer to me than my life, and yet again, you and I are one." Babur murmured, gazing into his dark eyes sadly and tenderly. "I can't read from the eyes of stars, but the star of misfortune is branded on the brow of Shaibani Khan, I can see and behold it clearly. He is going to die a violent death, Allah may forgive me for saying this, but his cruelty and wickedness are tightening around his neck as the noose of nemesis. His very name is an anathema to Islam, but I do not wish to dwell on that. Tell me, my beloved cousin, how you managed to break the chains of imprisonment?"

"My recollection is a memory remote, now that I am basking under the protection of Padishah." Said Khan smiled gratefully. "Shaibani Khan sent me bound hand and foot to Andijan. From there I was delivered into the hands of Jani Beg like a foul baggage and taken to Ferghana. Jani Beg proved to be indifferent, posting guards who were not vigilant. Fortunate for me, I was able to secure a camel rope to escape through the window, but had a nasty fall. Seems like a nightmare which I wish to forget, now that I feel secure and comforted. One comment of Shaibani Khan still hounds me still: *I fight with the sword of Islam.* How that Uzbek dares blaspheme, I fail to understand?"

"Fighting is permitted in Islam only as a shield of self defense, and that too when all manner of peaceful means are exhausted." Khwaja Kilan broke his silence, his gaze commiserating with the prince.

"Fight in the name of God those who fight you, but do not commit aggression. God does not love the aggressor. Isn't that clearly stated in the Quran?" Babur appeared to recite this to himself. *"And incline thou to peace—"* He couldn't finish reciting this verse by the sudden arrival of more night visitors.

Maulana Sadr in ragged coat and cape could barely drag his feet, falling prostrate in the middle of the hall. Haider Mirza stumbling behind was caught into the loving arms of Attan Mama, who was quick to rush to the scene as if overwhelmed by sudden grief, murmuring prayers and endearments. Khwaja Kilan too was moved to action, claiming a cup of wine from Mushin and pressing it to the lips of Maulana Sadr.

"What treacherous roads they traveled to reach the haven of Kabul?" Said Khan murmured to himself, unable to move or assist.

Babur had risen to his feet involuntarily, feeling only the weight of sorrow profound and inexpressible. His heart was chilled, yet his thoughts were awakening to the fire of love and compassion. He was commanding his servants to fetch basins of warm water and trays of fruits and viands, while drifting toward the younger prince dreamlike.

"My unhappy prince, you would see many happy times yet." Babur pressed his lips against the head of the lanky youth, and turned abruptly.

He almost collided with Said Khan who had followed him at his heels, forlorn and bemused. Said Khan smiled, and Babur stood gazing into the eyes of his cousin as if contemplating his own soul, naked and turbulent.

"Let's find comfort in the oblivion of sleep, my fair cousin." Babur linked his arm into his cousin's, dragging him along toward the stairway, looming high with the promise of chambers rich and exquisite. "The stealthy dawn would break the spell of this sad-happy night, and I would be convinced in the morning of your dear presence."

16

Ninepin Doll

As leaves on trees, such is the life of man.
— Iliad—Homer

Babur drunk by the wine of scented blooms in his garden was returning to his palace under some spell of euphoria and exhilaration. This feeling of serendipity was familiar to him, suffusing his whole being with joy whenever he took a long walk in his garden, where a tapestry of colors could never fail to fill his heart with awe and admiration. He was exceptionally happy this spring afternoon since one of his cousins had brought him a gift which he valued more than the treasures of the seven worlds, not that it was priceless but crafted with love for things small and beautiful. His heart was light and his steps sprightly as he burst into the chamber of ivory and rose, cradling the gift in his hands most possessively.

Mahim lounging on her davenport against one brocaded pillow was startled as usual, still unaccustomed to his abrupt visits and moods so very unpredictable. She had just come out of her bath it was obvious, her silk robe tracing the contours of her body and her hair hanging loose, catching ribbons of sunshine from lacework windows all around. Babur stood there awed and humbled as he always did when beholding the purity and freshness of her beauty. He had not even noticed the presence of the royal nurse—Fatima Bibi seated by the bassinets rippling with lace and silk, where the royal babes rested under warm blankets. Babur stirred, drifting closer to Mahim, and holding out the tiny box, his joy and lighthearted gaiety returning.

"A gift for our little princess!" Babur pressed the jade box into her hands. "The only way I can make you jealous, my beauty, by bringing gifts for Masuma and not for Humayun?" He lowered himself beside her, watching her open this jewel of a box the size of a matchbox.

"Oh, I have never seen such a small doll before?" Mahim exclaimed, fascinated by the size as well as the beauty of this wonder. "Look, Padishah, the steely arms and needle legs! Why, it's all dressed in silks, how could one manage to handle these strips of silk and fashion a billowing gown? Oh, these bright agates as its eyes!" She sat there holding it on the palm of her hand, rapt and incredulous.

"It is called ninepin doll, Abdul Rizak told me." Babur expounded joyfully. "He bought it from some merchant in the caravan from Hind passing through the valley of Gurbund. Our princess receives gifts, but our prince holds kingdoms in the little palm of his hand. Do you know what the gluttonous astrologers—" His thoughts were truncated by the ripple of a wail from the lips of Masuma.

Babur was up on his feet with the alacrity of a young father, noticing Fatima Bibi hovering over the bassinets. In a flash, he had scooped Masuma into his arms, rocking her gently and lulling her to sleep. Barely had he pacified the princess to sleep that a loud wail from the lips of Humayun grazed his bliss-awareness. The royal nurse was caught in a paroxysm of indecision, watching Babur cradle Masuma in one arm, and snatching Humayun into the other. He stood rocking both the babes, smiling with great satisfaction after the whimpering of Humayun subsided. Triumphantly, he trooped toward Mahim, gloating over his success in making the babes quiet, and condoning the presence of Fatima Bibi who was trailing behind him like a shadow. He was about to lower the babes into the cushioned depths of the davenport, when Humayun resumed his wailing, and Masuma following suit to vie with the lusty lungs of her brother.

"What a reward for appeasing the royal lungs?" Babur laughed, relinquishing his unruly bundles into the care of the nurse and the mother.

Mahim claimed Masuma, entrusting Fatima Bibi with the task of taking Humayun into the nursery. She had joined Babur in his mirth, but was now absorbed in baring her breast to the hungry lips of Masuma. Babur was transfixed since this was the first time he was witnessing the art of suckling, recalling with a sudden clarity that Mahim had spurned the custom of sending the royal babes to wet nurses. He was spellbound as if watching some miracle divine, where beauty of life was an everlasting fountain of love and nurturing inside the very breast of a mother, churning the ocean of milk and honey. Suddenly, his heart was filled with pain, the ache and tenderness *within* conjuring up that charcoal sketch of Madonna and the Child which he had loved in the palace library of his parents' home in Ferghana. The purity and innocence of youth was entering his psyche, challenging him to kneel at each altar of beauty with the joy and rapture of a devotee. And he was just doing that, meeting the challenge of his psyche, and kissing the creamy breast without disrupting the feast of Masuma.

"Forgive me, my moon." Babur murmured reverently. "Babes have hungers and men appetites, and yet nature teaches us half the art in living."

"Can one ever forgive for *happiness*, Padishah?" Mahim's cheeks were flushed, her dark eyes spilling joy and laughter.

"Happiness!" Babur's eyes were gathering stars of mirth and mischief. "You are subtle and wicked, my beauty, wicked and profound! Don't you feel jealous that I acquire brides under your very nose? And this nose the fairest and the prettiest." He bent down to kiss the tip of her small nose. "First Masuma, then Gulrukh, now Dildar, this very evening. Do I make you unhappy? Are you not bitter or angry?"

"My mamma told me all about men and their—" Mahim could not continue against the blaze of mockery in Babur's eyes.

"And what did your dear mamma tell you, my beauty?" The sherry gleam in Babur's eyes was flashing agog and amusement.

"That kings have a harem-full of wives, and that I should leave my jealousy behind as some maidenly garment which I have outgrown." Mahim reminisced aloud, rather than responded.

"Your dear mamma, she is wise! What else did she say?" Babur coaxed. The stars of mockery in his eyes replaced by tenderness!

"I might be blessed with wisdom if I could remember all that she said?" Mahim seemed to commune with her own self, covering her breast since Masuma had fallen asleep. The little that I remember is fading too. *Kings are wedded to their moods as much as to their brides* she could never tire of repeating. *The only difference is that their moods come and go, but the brides remain.*"

"The king is Padishah now, and he would be privileged to meet this paragon of wisdom, your mother!" Babur intoned with a dint of regret as if cursing himself inwardly for neglecting to meet her family.

"She died right before—" Mahim's voice was choked against the burden of memories stark and tragic.

"Pity that such wisdom lays buried under a mound of earth." Babur murmured gently, contriving a smile, all bright and winsome. "Can't help wondering, why you don't feel jealous? Not a flattering thought for any man. Especially, not for Padishah who longs for the love of a woman with all its fire of passion and jealousy! You have schooled yourself, not ever to feel jealous, is that it?"

"I would too, Padishah, if you decided to choose your own bride?" Mahim confessed, her eyes flashing.

"I would never think of doing that! If I did, my heart would break." Babur's heart was reaching out to Sweet Absent as if he could see her reflection in the eyes of Mahim.

"Padishah!" Haider Mirza stole from behind unnoticed.

"Come, my bashful Prince!" Babur turned to him quickly as if exiled from his reveries. "Mahim Begum rarely gets to see you." He commented, noticing the jeweled sword at his waist. "Between your lessons of archery and hunting expeditions, do you get any time for studies?" He smiled, returning his attention to Mahim. "I am learning the art of fatherly duties, training Haider Mirza in war tactics and teaching him to be proficient in prose and poetry and cultivating his interest in history and languages. In a few years, Humayun would get the same lessons and training. Be grateful to Padishah, my beauty, that I don't snatch our prince from his gilded comfort and subject him to the rigors of archery?" He laughed, noticing the glints of mock terror in Mahim's eyes, his gaze returning to Haider Mirza. "Tell me, my bold prince, what compelled you to intrude upon our privacy?"

"Padishah." Haider Mirza murmured, color rising to his cheeks in red blotches. "Prince Said Khan sent me. He wants to know if you would like a stroll in the garden."

"Ah, my indolent cousin, he was still in his bed when I took a stroll. But I would be delighted to take another one since time permits me this luxury today!" He turned to his heels, beckoning Haider Mirza to follow. "Don't be surprised, Mahim, if you find jade dagger in Humayun's crib, I am planning for him to take lessons in self defense?" He commented over his shoulders.

Sailing down the polished staircase, Babur had seen the flash of a dagger piercing his heart, and disappearing. Princess Dildar with the whiff of a scented rose had flitted past the gilded foyer into some lone sanctuary. *Ah, this white flame! My red rose of a bride to be! Fortunes are mine to hold and behold! A royal heir and Padishah dreaming of becoming an emperor!* Babur was greeting Said Khan, inviting Haider Mirza to share the delights of his garden.

Mahim Begum was sinking deeper into the comfort of her davenport, watching the little princess in her lap fondly and pensively. She was falling prey to reveries, seduced by the kaleidoscope of thoughts, blazing and shifting. Babur was there, the eternal bridegroom, marrying Masuma the very next day after her own wedding. And yet, Babur was returning, needing her, enveloping her in the mantle of love ineffable and love boundless. She could look into his soul, holding dear the wound of loss and agony, and loving still the *memory* of Zainab which no living brides could ever steal or efface. Her soul could commiserate with such a memory since she too had loved once with all her heart and soul. But they had been betrothed only in thoughts, her young beau snatched into the arms of death, leaving behind the scent of vows sacred and perfumed. Her eyes were closing, and behind the closed shutters of her eyes, she could see Gulrukh heavy with child, seeking her guidance and friendship. She was dreaming a trio of wedding celebrations yet to be commenced this evening. Babur's aunt Apaq Begum was dressing princess Dildar in bridal fineries for Padishah. Shahr Banu—Babur's half sister was already seated with her bridegroom, Junaid Barlas. Shah Mirza with his bride-to-be, Sankej Banu, was being escorted into the Fortune Hall amidst chorus of cheers and songs. Zainab was there too, wearing a diadem of stars, and Mahim was awakening to the mists in reality. Fatima Bibi had lowered bright-eyed Humayun into her lap, and was taking the sleeping princess to her bassinet. *Can one possibly be jealous of the dead beloved*, was Mahim's opiate thought as she proceeded to suckle Humayun!

Char-Bagh with its glorious blooms was welcoming Babur, Said Khan and Haider Mirza, and they seemed lost in this tapestry of scents and colors. The spring air heavy with the scent from jasmine and hyacinth was carrying its fragrance as far as the groves of Chenars and Cherries where Babur and his royal companions were headed. Marble terraces flanked by bridal creepers were left behind, along with the flowerbeds of champa, carnation and heliotrope. Goblets upon goblets of tulips were coming into view overlooking a ravine spruced with wild poppies and daffodils. Babur's gaze was following the golden orioles, his concentration broken by one strident cry from the throat of a hoopoe.

"Beauty such as this has the power to tame all sounds, harsh or melodic! Nature's way of lending harmony amidst chaos and ugliness?" Babur reflected aloud, slipping his arm around Haider Mirza's waist absently. "Are you enjoying the glory of spring in Kabul, my young prince?" He asked suddenly.

"Very much, Padishah." Haider Mirza murmured dreamily. "I am very happy."

"Happy, my young prince!" Was Babur's gleeful exclamation! "Would you still be happy if you were commanded to quell some rebellion, and there is no dearth of that around Kabul?" He turned to Said Khan without waiting for a response from the young prince. "And how does my cousin find this peace-loving, sun-sprinkled paradise in Kabul?"

"Immensely blissful, Padishah!" Said Khan chortled merrily. "These are the happiest of moments in my entire life, this lovely spring. To be with you and to enjoy the glory of your gardens, a bliss supreme, indeed! These moments would stay with me wherever I go, cherishing them always."

"Don't you know, my foolish prince, you are a prisoner in Kabul?" Babur teased, drunk by the scent of Damascus roses within his reach. "You can't leave this prison, until Padishah decides to set you free. And he has no intention of doing so, for you grant him the sweetest of pleasures by being his companion and confidant."

"A prisoner, who has no wish to escape, rather dreads the hour of release!" Was Said Khan's gallant response!

"Have no fear Said Khan! Flattery has imprisoned you for life now." Babur resumed his stroll, sprinting ahead jauntily. "To lessen the burden of your life-long sentence, I would find you a bride. Kabul is the Garden of Eden, and you would find your Eve if you had the patience of Adam? The levity of my thoughts! Why do I feel giddy? I have yet to find a bride for Nasir Mirza, but he is born celibate, it is becoming obvious. An inveterate bridegroom—that's me, and that's obvious too! Princess Dildar, my new bride-to-be, isn't she beautiful?" He asked wistfully, the spurious ache within him kissing only the lips of *sweet absent.*

"More beautiful than this Garden of Eden, Padishah!" Said Khan's thoughts too were on the verge of giddiness. "An Eden where my Eve is longing to be born!"

"No celestial maiden for you, my dream-prince! We have to find you some earthly beauty to woo and wed." Babur tossed this comment to the winds, it seemed, arresting Khwaja Kilan's hasty approach in the warmth of his gaze bright and welcoming.

"Padishah." Khwaja Kilan curtsied, stealing a furtive glance at both the princes, as if seeking their support.

"Ah, my noble mentor! You have come to inform Padishah that wedding celebrations are all in readiness, and that my bride would await my pleasure after feasting and celebration?" Babur declared, the sherry gleam in his eyes spilling the wine of joy and mirth.

"Many hours before the evening celebrations, Padishah!" Khwaja Kilan began reluctantly. "I wish I can postpone this message, but it needs your urgent attention. A messenger from Shah Ismael craves your audience, Padishah. The gist of his message is that Shaibani Khan has dared challenge the king of Persia—Shah Ismael, and the king himself is seeking your alliance to fight the Uzbek foe."

"Why is it, Khwaja, that every occasion of festivity in Kabul is marred by the standards of war trooping down my palace?" Babur exclaimed histrionically. "Why do I have to abandon the peace and beauty of Kabul during the loveliest of seasons? I should be writing couplets, winning wars with words, and effacing all warring hordes from the face of this earth with the weapon of my wisdom?" He drowned his poetic thoughts in a flood of mirth, all stark and joyless.

"Padishah!" Khwaja Kilan could appeal with his eyes alone.

"How is the *lamb* going to fight with the *wolf*?" Laughter was gone from Babur's eyes and lips in a flash, his features washed by pallor.

"With dry wit, if not with sharp weapons, Padishah!" Khwaja Kilan began cautiously. "It all started a few months back when Shaibani Khan insulted the King of Persia by sending a messenger furnished with a lady's veil and a beggar's bowl—implying, that Shah Ismael had inherited the kingdom from his mother's side. This messenger had the audacity to repeat his master's command by telling Shah Ismael that he should wear the veil and leave the kingdom of Persia to its rightful heirs, meaning, Shaibani Khan. Of course, the insolent messenger was beheaded. Then Shah Ismael had dispatched the severed head along with a spindle and distaff to Shaibani Khan, which in essence was a stark reminder, mocking the contemptible trade of Shaibani's ancestors. Shah Ismael also challenged Shaibani Khan to a fair battle, and now they are to confront each other on the battlefield of Merv. That's where the matters stand now, and the King of Persia is seeking alliances from all quarters."

"The wolf would devour the lamb, I have no doubt." Babur demurred aloud, his eyes gathering the stars of poetry and profundity. "Though Shaibani is no gentle lamb, yet he has miscalculated the might of Shah Ismael. With my help, or without my help, Shaibani is doomed. The King of Persia is wise to seek my help, since I am the strongest of his allies. Pride and haste are Shaibani's worst of foes, goading him toward death and devastation." His eyes were lit up with a subtle glow of inspiration, his lips spilling an impromptu couplet.

"He who with impatient haste lays his hand on his sword
Will afterward gnaw that hand with his teeth from regret

I myself have been thinking of chastising this foe, conjuring up an evil, black day when I would avenge the deaths of many slaughtered by him most brutally and deceitfully. Such a day never dawned, and now that I have decided to end the corruption in his body and soul, this glorious spring day mocks my past inaction and neglect." The poetic gleam in his eyes was gathering more couplets, yet his lips were silent.

"Shah Ismael has requested the aid of your troops and armaments, Padishah." Khwaja Kilan breathed under some spell of fear and presage. "Would you be commanding the chosen battalion yourself, Padishah?"

"Yes." Babur contemplated aloud, his gaze reflecting the fire of his resolve. "Nasir Mirza would conduct the affairs of Kabul in my absence. Said Khan would accompany us, no doubt, and you my trustworthy mentor, can't afford to leave you behind?"

"Padishah, may I ask a favor?" Haider Mirza appealed suddenly, his eyes shining.

"Yes, my bold Prince." Babur smiled indulgently. "Padishah is in a mood to grant any boon your little heart desires."

"May I come with you, Padishah?" Was Haider Mirza's flustered request! "I don't know where we are going, but I would help."

"No, my valiant Prince, no." Babur murmured tenderly. "You are too young for campaigns, and for journeys long and arduous. Another boon, perhaps?"

"Padishah!" Haider Mirza began under some spell of fever and confusion. "You were twelve, Padishah, when you became the King of Ferghana. You fought many battles. I know how to—" He couldn't continue, fear clutching his heart all of a sudden.

"An excellent memory, my bold prince!" Babur exclaimed. "With boldness, you have earned the right to come with us. Exposed to danger you would be, but Padishah would protect you. We march tomorrow!" He announced over his shoulders, sprinting back toward the palace.

"Padishah." Haider Mirza could barely murmur, following Babur under some cloud of exultance.

"Tonight we think only of feasting and celebrating." Babur was floating ahead, aware of his companions behind, and of the beauty of his garden all around. "Tonight the songs of love, tomorrow the gongs of war!"

"You would not leave right after your wedding, Padishah?" Khwaja Kilan appeared to be poking the cinders of his fear and apprehension.

"When in heaven Roozvan asked the date of his death
I told him that heaven is the eternal abode of Babur."

Babur's only response was this fresh downpour of a couplet. He seemed drunk by the sparkling sunshine and gurgling fountains, listening only to the songs of the wind and drinking deep from the cups of spring.

17

Khazanda Dearest

And if you must be damned, at least be damned for pleasant sins.
— Voltaire

The royal tent pitched over the outskirts of Hissar was Babur's home away from Kabul, furnished with carpets, pillows and candelabras. Babur sat sipping wine from his gold goblet while conversing with his viziers, or simply brooding against the somnambulant expressions of the few who were still awake, and enjoying the repast of dry nuts and fruits. Said Khan and Khwaja Kilan beside Babur were sitting couchant against brocaded pillows, doing justice to the pellets of majun in jade bowl left at their disposal. Babur's gaze was arrested to Haider Mirza where he lay sound asleep buried under the warmth of blankets and satiny coverlets. But his thoughts were entering the tents of the Kyzylbashes in this bivouac of a silk city where he had decided to halt in hope of seeing his sister, Khazanda.

The Persian soldiers known as Kyzylbashes, also nicknamed Red Hats had recently joined Babur's army, boasting of reclaiming for Padishah the lost kingdoms of Ferghana and Samarkand. Their leader Najm Sani had brought the news of Shaibani's death a day before yesterday, and had returned post-haste to Herat to deliver the news of victory to Shah Ismael. Babur was spared the need of fighting his foe, for Shaibani Khan had died a wretched death on the battlefield of Merv, lending Kyzylbashes the impetus to engage in more battles with the sense of pride and exultance. Shaibani Khan's troops were routed and dispersed, and he himself had tried to escape by jumping down from the parapet of his citadel, but was crushed to death by the weight of his wounded soldiers who had landed over him in one heap, most bloody and grotesque.

My own valiant princes, they have yet not seen the ugliness of wars, merely coasting over the waters of tragedies as surfed by the Kyzylbashes. Babur's gaze and thoughts were inward bound, his heart teasing the strings of compassion. *Shaibani, though my foe, was a valiant soldier. Had he been the victim of my vengeance, I would have given him a decent burial with all due rites and prayers.* Mushin, ever vigilant of Padishah's need was replenishing his gold cup, one lone couplet within him awakening and shuddering.

Do thou resign to fate him who injures thee

For fate is a servant that will not leave thee unavenged

Babur's poetic contemplation was disrupted by an abrupt volley of mirth from the lips of Shah Mirza. His face was flushed, words flushing down his lips in a torrent.

Shah Ismael has turned Shaibani's head into a drinking bowl, I have heard. Shaibani's body torn from limb to limb by the order of the King of Persia! Each limb of this fallen foe dispatched to different parts of Persia. One half of his arm sent to—

Babur had ceased to heed, his own thoughts clamoring for attention.

How can any man of understanding pursue such a conduct as, after the death of his foe, must stain his fair—black fame? The wise have well called fame, notoriety, a second existence? Babur's soul was awakening to the pain of memories, recalling with a sudden clarity that Shah Ismael was sending Khazanda to him, his dear sister—the widow of Shaibani Khan. *Khazanda, Khazanda, how long we have been separated? Would she recognize me, or would I—* his heart was a cauldron of pain, hugging Khazanda. And yet, a pair of emerald eyes was blinding his sight, awakening from the very sinews of his pain and wielding bolts of lightning. Sweet Absent had come back, arrayed in white mists of death, and digging the wounds of his grief with her sweet hands.

"Padishah needs to stretch his limbs, a long walk, if not a rigorous exercise?" Babur got to his feet, his look wild and feverish. With an impatient gesture of his arm, he stalled both Said Khan and Khwaja Kilan in their act of rising. "Alone. I want to be alone." He trooped out of his tent straight into the arms of dusk, golden and scarlet.

Haloed by the ethereal beauty of the evening, Babur stood still, only his gaze wandering and arresting colors from silken tents, which appeared to rise like domes, bulbous and glowing. From the very fabric of dusk, a face was emerging—not that of Khazanda. Sweet Zainab was with him, he could feel the nearness of his Beloved in each throb of silence over the tapestry of this silken bivouac. No one was stirring in the encampment, the evening itself enveloped in silence, most blissful and wondrous.

Everyone is sleeping, the birds and the beasts, and even my soldiers? Probably drunk, or knocked out by sheer fatigue? Babur was stirring, strolling toward the silvery ghat, flanked by pines and poplars. The evening sky had turned crimson, slashed with streaks ochre and violet. An island of white clouds had appeared from somewhere, fringed with gold from the dusk, floating and expanding. Babur's gaze and thoughts were racing past this dying sunset, cutting open the heart of a dawn adorned with stars dreamy and sparkling. *A dawn of hope with the promise of joy and fortunes!* He thought he heard the murmur of a distant thunder, holding in abeyance the fury of an impending storm. But his eyes were witnessing another storm amidst the whirlwind of dust-clouds from under the horses' hoofs, revealing stiff riders with conical turbans of twelve points, their long banderoles fluttering in the wind like flames, scarlet and restless.

These bold riders were no other than the Kyzylbashes, their Arabian steeds swift and dauntless, matching the Persian pride and implacability of their masters. Babur's thoughts were trooping forth to meet these riders, but his gaze was searching the dear, long-cherished visage of his sister. Khazanda had materialized amongst the cortege of the Kyzylbashes like an apparition in black silks, her hair woven in ropes of pearls. Najm Sani was quick to dismount, lending royal guards the privilege of assisting and escorting Khazanda Begum with all due propriety. Babur was standing there motionless, vaguely aware of Najm Sani's litany of pride, his gaze reaching out to his sister, prayerful and dream-like.

*Padishah, the King of Persia wouldn't trust the safety of your sister with anyone, but me, under my strict guidance. Entrusting me with this message that the King of Persia sends Khazanda Begum—the widow of Shaibani Khan with all due courtesy and protection! My duty and my honor—*Babur had ceased to heed, absorbed completely in watching the apparition approaching closely, so lovely and graceful.

"Padishah." Khazanda bowed her head, her blue eyes kindling the flames of joy over the pools of sadness.

"Khazanda!" Babur could barely murmur, crushing her into one eager embrace. He was kissing her hair, brow, cheeks, and murmuring endearments. Then he stood holding her before him, as if bemused, his eyes gathering the mists of joy and disbelief. "Let me look at you. So much sadness in your eyes, my dear, even the kindling of joy can't consume it?" He stood gazing into her eyes, oblivious to all.

Said Khan, Shah Mirza and Khwaja Kilan had followed Babur at a safe distance undetected, and were now making their presence known by approaching closer, silently and unobtrusively. None could utter a word, their eyes searching the stern faces of the Kyzylbashes standing by their mounts, ramrod and vigilant. But what had rendered them speechless was the tender scene of reunion between the royal sister and brother, lost to the world inside the fogs of their thoughts and memories. Babur was awakening to the world around him, his gaze holding Shah Mirza captive in its profound intensity.

"Shah Mirza, you are to be my messenger, delivering my heartfelt thanks to the King of Persia for sending my sister to me with all due honor and courtesy." Babur began thoughtfully. "Yes, Herat awaits us, but you would be the one reaching there earlier, entrusted with the gifts of rugs, silks, spices and jewels. Along with these tokens of gratitude, you are to inform the King that Padishah and his troops would join him soon in quelling the rebellion of Uzbeks. Najm Sani and his soldiers would be your guide and companions."

"Padishah." Shah Mirza could barely murmur, despair written all over his face, and his head bent low.

"Lift your head, my gallant prince, let me pluck out the reeds of misery from your eyes." Babur commanded with a mingling of rebuke and indulgence.

"Your obedient servant, Padishah!" Shah Mirza raised his head slowly, color rising to his cheeks from some bellows of shame and wretchedness.

"Did you assume that we would be marching back to Kabul? No, my craven prince, no!" Babur's very gaze was cutting through his soul, it seemed. "Consider yourself fortunate for this opportunity to prove your valor and loyalty worthy of my trust." He shifted his attention back to his sister, slipping his arm around her waist. "You need rest, Khazanda, how inconsiderate of me. We would talk tomorrow to our hearts' content. Come, I have a special tent prepared just for you." He made her walk beside him toward the city of silken comforts.

Those silken comforts, as if by a magic wand, were effaced by the city of Herat, as soon as Babur and his cavalcade had reached the palace gates where Shah Ismael had greeted him with great pomp and ceremony. Time had crawled into the tunnels of weeks and months, and it had been a year since Babur had left Kabul and he was still here in this war-torn purgatory of tyranny and vengeance by no other than the King of Persia himself, Shah Ismael? This particular evening, Babur seated with Shah Ismael in the familiar hall of this palace, was overwhelmed with sadness, remembering his cousins who were murdered most brutally by Shaibani Khan, their treasures looted and their women violated. His gaze as well his thoughts were restless, peering beyond the gilded walls and communing with the ghosts of the past, so very alive and surreal. And yet his poignant thoughts were forcing him to acknowledge the presence of the King of Persia in Shia regalia of a conical turban, all scarlet! And a white robe billowing at the sleeves! Babur was becoming aware of his own green turban, adorned with ropes of pearls and a black plume, his gaze stumbling over the waves of conical turbans over the heads of the Persian poets, musicians and courtiers. Babur's gaze was arresting one marble chess table under a canopy, all gold and brocade. Poet Bainai and his rival Ali Sher were lolling against velvety pillows, watching another poet Saifi engaged in chess game with the famous chess player, Shaikhul Aslam. Beside them sat the poet-wrestler Palevan Muhammed, seemingly avid and interested, but Babur's gaze was tearing open the confines of this palace, and reaching out to the *pearl city* of Herat, where it lay in utter ruins, silent and mournful.

The poetry and laughter of the mystics and the scholars is gone from this city ravished by wars and cruelties. Once, inspiration alone was the breath of life for Herat, and now inertia and languor reign over here like the mighty tyrants. Babur's thoughts were hovering over the marble facades of this palace, cold and unwelcoming. *Didn't he sit in the same room with his gentle cousins, Badi-uz-Zaman and Musafer Hussayan, eons ago, centuries in succession? The blue marble halls and the artwork of lapis lazuli, all grown dull and frozen! Even the lofty minarets out there stand chilled, if not shivering?* Babur's thoughts, suddenly and surreptitiously, were encountering the fire of zeal inside the heart of Shah Ismael, recoiling against those flames of bigotry and intolerance, as they had done so many times before, and choking inside the prison of their inaction and paradox.

Shah Ismael had held the city of Herat in pincers of grief and devastation even before Babur and his cavalcade had arrived, forcing its citizen to adopt Shia customs and doctrines, including the dress code of wearing conical turbans.

And the Sunnis who disobeyed were killed most brutally, their homes burnt and their corpses mutilated. Babur was shielded from this horror for several months, finding the King friendly and hospitable—eager only to fight the Uzbeks till the roots of their rebellion were plucked out and destroyed. Convincing Babur to win back Ferghana and Samarkand was no great fete on the part of Shah Ismael, since he knew these were two *lost loves* of Padishah. True, that Babur had dreamed of reclaiming his lost kingdoms, and Shah Ismael's offer of winning those back with the help of Kyzylbashes had moved him to tears, resulting in a solemn pledge of friendship and alliance. But tears of blood were congealed within his heart when the truth about Shah Ismael's savage treatment toward the Sunnis could no more be concealed. That was when the Persian King had offered Babur the irresistible gift of two Circassian slaves, more so to keep the pledge of alliance intact than to flaunt his will and power in winning alliances and kingdoms.

Ah, the goddesses sculpted in gold, Gulnar Aghacha and Nurgul Aghacha, my blue-eyed jewels with flaxen hair! Babur's thoughts were kindling a bonfire with hungry, licking flames. *How many concubines would I acquire if I stayed in this den of deceit and hypocrisy? The hypocrite! This King of Persia has succeeded in keeping me chained to his dull wit of false piety and self-righteousness, while I have failed to remove the rust of my desire and ambition. Deluded as I am I know what Islam means—peace and reconciliation. It is the religion of love and unity. I am born a Sunni, and the Persian King a Shia, where's the scathing difference? We are the two mighty arms of one absolute Whole, embracing the One, obedient to the Law of the One, seeking Oneness! Sunni, Shia, what do the sects signify? Nothing but names under the hearth of Islam! Oh, my Perfect All, why this hatred and contention?* The ache of loneliness was in Babur's heart, his thoughts reaching out to Khazanda for solace and answers. He had not seen his sister for two whole days and his heart was suddenly implacable and rebellious.

"My King!" Babur's tone and gaze were a subtle challenge to the throne of sanctity which the Persian King had created around himself as a shield of power and invulnerability. "Can't explain this sudden longing to see my sister right away? Could you please send a page to her room, requesting her to join me in this hall of poetry and ideation?"

"Padishah!" Shah Ismael exclaimed, his expression one of shock and disbelief. "I thought you were grown accustomed to the customs in our court? Muslim women are not to appear before men unless they wear a veil. Khazanda Begum refuses to obey this injunction, so I can't allow her to join us here. You would not grudge me this virtue of a discipline, Padishah, I hope?"

"Islam, bled white of all truth and virtues, my King, that much is obvious!" Babur's thoughts were lit by the fire of impatience, unable to swallow the flames of lies and distortion reflected in the eyes of the Persian King. "Subjecting Muslim women to practice the customs of the heathens, is that Islamic? History stands witness to the fact that Arab, pagan women wore veils as marks of wealth and distinction. Prophet Muhammad, to cultivate the virtue of equality forbade

Muslim women to wear veils. That's why, even to this age, women are not al-
lowed to cover their faces while performing hajj in Mecca. Is there any injunction for Arab men to wear a head-dress, and yet they do so to protect themselves
against the heat and violence of the desert climate? So dressing has nothing to
do with religion but to feel comfortable in a certain place, and to be a part of the
culture where one chooses to live, isn't that the holy truth, my King?"

"Your heresy could cost you kingdoms, Padishah." Shah Ismael murmured
piously, unable to defend his pious views with the rod of his zeal.

"Even the kingdom of Allah, my King?" Babur's eyes were spilling the
gold of mirth and profundity. "A note of interest to you—concerning veiling
from the Christian point of view, my King! My baba read to me the epistle of
Paul translated into Turkish, and I still have a copy of it in my palace library. *I
want you to understand that head of every man is Christ, the head of every
woman is her husband, and the head of Christ is God. Any man who prays or
prophesies with his head covered dishonors his head, but any woman who prays
or prophesies with her head unveiled dishonors her head—it is the same as if
her head were shaven. For if a woman will not veil herself, then she should cut
off her hair, but if it is disgraceful for a woman to be shorn or shaven, let her
wear a veil. For a man ought not to cover his head since he is the image and
glory of God, but woman is the glory of man! For woman was not made from
woman, but woman from man. That's why a woman ought to have a veil on her
head, because of the angels.* My baba used to read this epistle to his friends during open discussions about religions."

"Your baba was a pious Muslim, Padishah, may God rest his soul in heaven." Shah Ismael began pontifically, searching desperately for expressions to
defend his zeal. "His only error—if not his sin was, that he chose Khwaja Kilan
as your mentor. You seem to know more about the pagans and the Christians
than about Muslims." He was losing the thread of his thoughts, forgetting about
the issue of *veil,* and reciting involuntarily. *Allah created men from a clot of
blood—created He both man and woman from a single clot of blood—*" He bit
his tongue, feeling the noose of his holy blunders around his neck. "Women are
to be veiled by the law and virtue of sheer modesty! They are proud, jealous and
sharp of tongue. Veiling offers them protection against men who—" His
thoughts were choked by the sudden kindling of mirth in Babur's eyes, his own
spilling anger and reproof.

"I myself would be wearing a veil, my King, if I stayed in your company for
long?" Babur teased, encouraged by one flicker of a smile on the lips of the Persian potentate. "But the women from Ferghana and Samarkand would never be
constrained to wear veils, they are endowed with free spirit and love outdoor
sports, including horse riding. As for my baba, he was the kindest of men ever
lived, and he didn't commit any error while cultivating in me the love for reading and writing. Khwaja Kilan himself learned from him the interpretations of
Torah, Bible and Quran. One snippet from Talmud is grazing my memory. May
I share that with you, my King?" He smiled, beholding the mingling of consent
and suspicion in the eyes of the King. "Nothing to do with veils, I assure you.

The Lord considered from what part of the man He should form woman, not from the head, lest she be proud. Not from the eyes, lest she should wish to see everything. Not from the mouth, lest she might be talkative, nor from ear, lest she should wish to hear everything. Not from the heart, lest she should be jealous, nor from the hand, lest she should wish to find everything. Not from the feet, lest she be a wanderer. Only from the most hidden place, that is covered even when a man is naked; namely, the rib."

"How admirably you quote, Padishah?" Shah Ismael's gaze was lowering the daggers of mockery and challenge. "Are you as fluent in quoting from the Quran as from the other Scriptures? Have your noble thoughts ever touched the hem of Shia doctrines?"

"One of my favorite books in that category was Amm-al-Kitab." Babur murmured in response. "I am getting wearied of quoting, but I must satisfy the curiosity of the King of Persia. The Shia texts of Gnostic affinities in Persian, and I literally swallowed their contents with much greed. Here's one excerpt: *When God concluded with men a covenant at the time of His creation of the material world, they prayed to Him to show them Paradise. He showed them, thereupon, a being ornamented with a million, varicolored shimmering lights, who sat upon a throne, head crowned, rings in the ears, and a drawn sword at the girdle. The radiating rays illuminated the whole garden; and when the men asked who this was, they were told, it was the form of Fatima as she appears in Paradise. The crown was Muhammad, the earrings, Hasan and Husain, the sword was Ali, and her throne, the seat of Dominion, was the resting place of God, the Most High."*

"Splendid!" Shah Ismael chanted with a sudden burst of fervor. Missing, or rather condoning the fact that women in this particular text had the exalted status of being close to God. "Hope, your valor shines as bright as your wisdom, Padishah? Tomorrow we march back to Hissar. By the Grace of Allah, we would win your lost kingdoms of Ferghana and Samarkand, marching forth to conquer Tashkend and Seiram, if the—"

The muezzin's call to prayer from the adjacent mosque had sealed the lips of the King. All heads were bowed in reverence, the music truncated, creating a vacuum only to be filled by the voice of the muezzin. Babur was overwhelmed by a sudden wave of sadness, recalling the sweet notes of a prayer call in Kabul in contrast to this one, filling the bowl of silence with the weight of command and urgency. Shah Ismael's voice was loud and commanding as soon as the call to prayer was finished.

"Fetch the prayer rugs. We would pray right here, facing the east, united in brotherhood." Shah Ismael waved his arm, his eyes kindling lamps of fervor.

"The prayer rug in my sinful heart is commanding me to pray in the seclusion of my chamber." Babur murmured, turning to leave. "After my prayers, I am accustomed to reciting this sura quietly to my self, which reminds me of my duty, or the lack thereof, toward man and God. *Piety lieth not in turning one's face to East or West, but true piety is his that believeth in Allah and in the last day, and in His angels and in what he hath, for the love of Allah to his relations and to orphans and to the poor and to travelers and to beggars and for the ransom of prisoners, his it is that prayeth and payeth the tithe, who keepeth the promise he hath made, who is patient in pain and suffering and in time of famine, those are the sincere, these fear Allah.*" He was leaving behind the pulse of his recitation, stark and throbbing.

The marble hall, flecked with sun-gold from the windows was chilling Babur's heart as he floated toward his chamber. The ghosts of the past were following him at his heels, his aunts, uncles and cousins. He could hear their voices, soft and gentle. Their poetic spirits communing with him, carefree and loving! His thoughts were reaching out to Khazanda, yet his feet were carrying him toward the chambers of Gulnar and Nurgul. Deep and abysmal was the pain within his soul, cutting open one long-forgotten rent, unfolding the saddest and profoundest of memories. Sweet Absent was with him, hugging his loneliness. A canopy of white mists was lowered over his head, his soul arrested in an act of fleeing, stunned and dazzled!

18

Samarkand Lost Again

Tell whoso hath sorrow
Grief shall never last
E'en as joy hath no morrow
So woe shall go past
— Arabian Nights

The hills and plateaus of Samarkand were coming into view under the moonlit sky, as Babur rode ahead of his cavalcade. The Moghuls in their blue coats and the Kyzylbashes in red were riding together, the park of elms and poplars on both sides their respite against the November chill and a great camouflage in their stealthy march toward the city of Samarkand. Babur was wearing a woolen coat, the heavy armor underneath his shield great protection against surprise assaults, but he was expecting none, welcoming only the stealthy assault of his thoughts. Haider Mirza riding beside him was awed by the beauty of the silent night with glittering stars, his heart catching the rhythm of the horses' hoofs as some melodic symphony from the very heart of nature. His heart was reaching out to Babur, longing to know the secrets of this night, but Padishah seemed oblivious to all, as if he was riding all alone, serene and contemplative. Bewitched by the glorious vistas unfolding before his sight, Babur indeed was alone and lonesome, letting his thoughts surface and dissolve inside the waters of wars and conquests.

Victories had fallen Babur's way with a domino-affect since his departure from Herat. Shah Ismael had accompanied him as far as Kunduz, returning to his own kingdoms in Persia, and leaving him—Babur the sole master of his fates and strategies. Within a span of few months, the kingdoms of Hissar, Bokhara, Tashkend and Seiram had become Babur's conquered dominions. But he was sorely concerned about the presence of Red Hats in his army, who were prone to acts of cruelties if not checked. In order to check their need for violence, he had issued a Farman that the vanquished were to be treated with respect and kindness and that any act of cruelty on the part of the victors would not go unpunished under his strict command. All the hard-won battles of the past were coming alive in Babur's contemplations with a surge of renewal, as if seeking validation.

The Uzbek rebel, Mehdi Sultan of Hissar had died of a lance wound in the heart by one of the Kyzylbashes. Sultan Mahmud of Bokhara had fled in sheer panic even before the Moghul army could penetrate his weak defenses, so Bokhara was added to Babur's conquests without the taint of war or bloodshed. Ferghana too was added to Babur's conquests without the spilling of blood on either side, since Jani Beg—the leader of Ferghana had sued for peace, sending his envoys beforehand to sign a peace-treaty. Another Uzbek rebel, Sujek, had not fared well in Tashkend since he had confronted the Moghul army, boasting of victory. But after many of his soldiers were wounded and the rest fleeing pell-mell, he was quick to offer submission. The army of Khazej Sultan in Seiram was routed and scattered, granting the Moghuls another laurel of victory. The dominions of Bokhara, Seiram and Tashkend were left under the command of the Persian generals to protect and safeguard against any attacks or insurrections. Hissar was to be ruled by Shah Mirza, and Said Khan was made the governor of Ferghana.

You have won supporters for life, my valiant prince! Babur had complimented Haider Mirza, his thoughts now evoking fresh visions, though he was still not aware of the valorous knight beside him who had become the subject of his contemplations. Haider Mirza had become the center of attraction in Bokhara, when the supporters of his late father had gathered around him, cheering and applauding. *Ferghana, Ferghana!* Babur's thoughts were now repeating this beloved name, transporting him back into the warmth and sunshine of his victory and exhilaration.

Reclaiming Ferghana as his own was like returning home after a long, long separation from his beloved, and he had hurled himself into its arms with the passion of a lover seeking bliss and consummation. He had feasted on the beauty of spring and had wooed his love for swimming in the waters of river Syr under the canopy of summer, all gold and sparkling. Visiting the marble palace of his parents at Andijan was like going on a pilgrimage, kissing the ribbons of sunshine under the gazebo, and circling around his ancestral kiosk with the awe and fervor of a lost pilgrim. He had even trekked the dusty roads on horseback, stopping at inns in remote villages, and talking with the farmers, artisans and merchants. The scents and smells of those places were coming back to him, painted vivid in his imagination the colors of tunics on men and women. His gaze was touching the fabric of dusk on the horizon, all colors blending onto the tapestry of past and present. A new dawn with the brushstrokes of an artist's dream slashed with colors all rosy and violet was awakening Babur from the comfort of his reveries. His thoughts were reaching over his shoulders, and sliding down the rhythmic trot of his cavalcade to reconnoiter the mood and morale of his soldiers.

Red Hats outnumbering the Moghuls. The Kyzylbashes, these men of barbaric stock, though pliant and subservient, are compelled by their need to pillage and plunder. A bonfire of wild passions within the heart of humanity to kill, maim and torture? The fires of vengeance, rape, murder and devastation! Men-beasts, are we all not guilty of ambition, hatred, hypocrisy? Babur's gaze was appealing the snow-capped mountains in the distance for wisdom and understanding. Yet the vast, looming landscape before him was lending him no guidance, stark and glittering.

True to its glorious name as the *turquoise city*, Samarkand was coming into view against the white haze of the morning. Babur's cavalcade, furling its standards of red and yellow, could be seen floating into the city under the frolic-dance of snowflakes. The blue domes and minarets slender and silvery were playing hide-and-seek before Babur's gaze as he led his cavalcade toward the Iron Gates, beyond which lay concealed the turquoise palace, flanked by winding foothills. White heavens were Babur's guide, it seemed, filling his heart with the scent of homecoming. Suddenly, one blinding squall of snowflakes went whirling down the foothills, arresting his attention, his gaze following the caprice of nature. Down below, barely visible were the Uzbek soldiers threading their way in a laborious retreat into the heart of the mountains, cavernous and inhospitable.

An ocean of roaring silence had cast a spell over the entire cavalcade, it seemed, as Babur reined his horse to a standstill. This awful hush was crackling all of a sudden, sibilant and rippling. Babur's keen senses could not miss these familiar sounds, his thoughts alone coaxing his horse around half a circle as he sat astride watching the disciplined flanks of his soldiers. The Kyzylbashes had unsheathed their weapons, their swords, daggers and scimitars glinting murder and vengeance. Some of these Red Hats were slicing air with the naked steel of their kards and dhups, and a few amongst them opening their quivers to unleash a shower of arrows over the wretched horde of an enemy in flight. Cross-bows poised for shooting and the naked steel of spears and lances from the middle flank were absorbing Babur's attention, his eyes flashing. He had seen the fire of hatred and vengeance in the eyes of the Kyzylbashes, his heart thundering and his gaze searching the flanks of the Moghul soldiers. The violence of thunder within his heart was fading to a distant murmur by the sheer light of devotion in the eyes of his faithful soldiers, his heart grateful for their solid pact of obedience in keeping their weapons sheathed until commanded.

"My friends and soldiers, we are not to attack the fleeing enemy!" One thunder of a command escaped Babur's lips, his eyes piercing the very souls of the Kyzylbashes. "The Uzbeks are in retreat, as is obvious, and there is no need for confrontation unless facing a direct assault. I have ruled Samarkand twice, and hold its people in great esteem for their kind and loving hearts. They are friendly and generous, living in perfect harmony with riches and beauty of this land—a land where our ancestors lived and prospered. Prudence demands that we conquer this city peacefully and without bloodshed. No killing or looting is permitted, and certainly not aggression. We have come to rule Samarkand, not plunder. Anyone violating these rules would be punished severely, and this is my Farman and warning."

"Padishah!" Najm Sani goaded his horse out of the middle flank, facing Babur defiantly. "Muslim conquerors, they slaughter their enemy wherever they find them, lest, in times of peace they return and kill the victors in sleep?" His eyes were ablaze with the fever of zeal and hatred.

"Men who rule without the *grace of guidance* become tyrants, Najm Sani, whether Muslims or non-Muslims! No religion permits killing, save alone, injury, by word or gesture." Babur's eyes were shooting bolts of lightning, keeping in abeyance the storm of warnings. "Khwaja Kilan, my mentor, whom I revere, would be suited best to guide all men and nations, especially, the Kyzylbashes, toward peace and restraint!" He stole a glance at Khwaja Kilan in the right flank before returning his attention to the bold warrior. "Prophet Muhammad was the only conqueror worthy to rule in the name of Islam, shunning wars even when fighting was permitted in self defense, and constrained to engage in war when all means of peace-making were exhausted. *Do not commit aggression, fight in the cause of Allah who fight you, but do not commit any aggression. Allah does not love the aggressor.* Isn't that what is written in the Quran? Prophet's own life speaks this truth by the example of his actions how he lived, loved and forgave. None of you, my brave soldiers, are in danger of being persecuted for your Faith, so march on and offer thanks to Allah for the gifts of life and virtuous living." He whirled his horse around, flying toward the gates of the city, his troops riding behind, silent and fearless.

The exultant citizens of Samarkand who had hurled insults at the fleeing Uzbeks just half an hour ago, were now transformed into a horde of revelers at the approach of the Moghul troops. They had poured out onto the streets, snatching any weapon they could find in their homes, even spades and shovels. A few were equipped with spears and javelins, some carrying sickles and the other hatchets. But none of these weapons were put to use against the fleeing Uzbeks, and now espying the standards of red and yellow in the distance, they were moved to a flurry of action to offer a hearty welcome to their former king and benefactor. Poised for cheering and applauding, the large groups on both sides of the streets could see the ocean of helmets, all gold and polished. Suddenly, the beating of kettle-drums, followed by the rhythmic galloping of the steeds were revealing the brave riders, at the head of which Babur could be seen waving his jeweled sword as a signal of peace and camaraderie.

Padishah, Padishah! The King of Kabul! Babur the Lion! Our King is back, our Great Lord has come home! A volley of cheers went skirling high, ricocheting down the valleys, and then swirling into a crescendo.

Babur was overwhelmed, sucked into a flood of brilliant colors. The woolen jerkins worn by the cheering crowds were reminding him of his own youth and carefree abandon. Waves upon waves of color in robes and turbans appeared to be fluttering before his gaze, citron and crimson and red and green, all vivid and shimmering. More men women and children were pouring out into the streets, carrying rugs, silks and any colorful materials they could find in their homes, to make the homecoming of the king a festive bazaar of jubilations. The sky itself was lowering white streamers of snowflakes, while the jubilant crowds were rushing forth to deck the palace windows with silks and to roll out the varicolored rugs over the carpet of snow for a royal welcome. And a royal welcome it was, drumming the pulse of joy and euphoria. Babur and Haider Mirza were snatched from their mounts over the heads of the wild crowd, and carried over the waves of shoulders toward the palace steps, now covered with rugs of varied hues and designs, displaying a tapestry of flowers and medallions. Babur appeared to be riding on the chariot of dreams, though down below he could see men dancing and singing. The front of the palace was turned into an arena of entertainments, some men were juggling their spears, others making a canopy of javelins over their shoulders, even the ones equipped with maces and spades were enacting some ritual dance of spring and harvesting. Amidst a fresh chorus of cheers, Babur and Haider Mirza were welcomed into the gilded hall of the palace, giddy and exhilarated.

The day of great victory and jubilation was dissolved into an early evening as Babur and his companions sat inside the palace amidst heaps of gifts from the lords of Samarkand. They had rested, bathed and feasted before returning to this opulent hall lit by candelabras, and furnished with exquisite array of carpets, pillows and davenports. Babur's gaze wandering over the gilded portraits and tapestries on the walls was returning to the marble hearth, arresting the dance and crackle of flames underneath as if divining secrets from the tongue of each flame, all hypnotic and fascinating. A low hum of voices was grazing his awareness, his gaze restless and shifting once again before lingering over the gifts which were piled against the windows in shimmering assortment.

Bolts upon bolts of silk, linen, damask and brocade! An array of rosewood tables with the inlay of ivory and mother-of-pearl. The vessels of silver and gold embedded with jewels priceless. Turquoise bowls and onyx ink-stands! Swords embellished with jade handles and trays laden with jewels and ashrafis. Oyster shells revealing pearls, large and glowing. Silk-wool rugs and bales of spices, musk and perfumes! Baskets of nuts and fruits which lay within reach of his friends and courtiers, who sat lolling against the pillows, doing justice to the variety of snacks while talking and laughing. Something inside Babur was stirring, the ache of nostalgia and loneliness, his thoughts seeking refuge in the library where he had spent a couple of hours before coming to this Audience Hall. He could still smell the musty odor of books, his mind reaching out for crumbs of knowledge, but his thoughts were disrupted by the stormy approach of Khwaja Kilan.

Khwaja Kilan's eyes were shooting sparks of anger and disgust. He was shoving and pushing Ayub Khan before him, whacking him in the rear all of a sudden, and the befuddled victim fell sprawling over the Bokhara carpet. The silk pouch which Ayub Khan was clutching flew out of his hands, spilling gems all fiery and priceless. A treasure chest was snapped open, it seemed, scattering pearls, rubies, sapphires and carnelians at the very feet of Babur.

"This ungrateful wretch has been busy looting, Padishah, taking advantage of the inebriated hosts fast asleep in their homes!" Khwaja Kilan declared with the vehemence of an angry lord.

"I thought only Red Hats needed the whip of discipline and restraint?" Babur rose to his feet, his eyes flashing. "Gather these pebbles of shame, you lizard, and return each gem to the rightful owner." He thundered a command, the blaze of anger in his eyes falling on his courtiers. "Drag this sniveling worm of a thief back to the house from where he stole this treasure. And after these gems are restored to the rightful owner, strip him naked, and make sure he walks up and down the street this cold night till dawn. A chilling reminder for all who dare disobey Padishah!" He turned to his heels, seeking the sanctuary of his chamber, willing the hands of sleep to lull him to the comfort of oblivion.

The white purity of winter was dissolved into the beauty of spring, and the scent of renewal was absorbed by the warmth of summer, and Babur was still in Samarkand. This particular afternoon, he was seated on a makeshift throne in his palace garden, and imprinting each scene on the canvas of his mind. His heart was aching, rather swollen with protests that how could he even think of bidding farewell to this turquoise city, since it was the trinity of his passion, his home, his hearth and his beloved? *More than one beloved,* he was thinking, watching his Circassian beauties—Gulnar Aghacha and Nurgul Aghacha, seated not too far from him, besides a host of friends, cousins and courtiers.

And yet I have to leave?

Babur could see one missive from Kabul on a silver tray beside him, its rubric script on a gold-sprinkled paper teasing his thoughts about the happy news from Mahim Begum. But his thoughts were courting sadness, strolling down the lanes of past few months to gather precious memories, which were already fading like the mists in dreams, floating and shuddering. The rustling of wind through pines and cedars was awakening him to the sweet-scented glory of this garden with its abundance of champa, chambeli and tuberoses. Before his gaze was a tapestry of colors, saffron, oleander and larkspur, all vivid and flaming. In the distance, he could see the fountains, gold-sprinkled from sunshine, and reflecting the purity of Makrana marble in prismatic dance of splish-splash.

How our minds conjure delusions? Each color in this garden a breath of peace, beauty, mystery! Could this be the Garden of Eden? Another dream, illumined by the lamp of imagination! Dearest of my loves—this Samarkand, loveliest of gardens, this delusion grand and dazzling? Could I pour all into the flagon of time, and take it with me to Kabul? Babur's thoughts were cutting the mists in past and drifting aimlessly.

The grand reception offered to Babur and his companions on the day of their entry in Samarkand had lasted but for a few months. Soon, the citizens of Samarkand were becoming aware of the intrusive presence of the Red Hats, sensing the fire of zeal and pride in their eyes and demeanor, and getting annoyed by their outward display of prayers and supplications. The lords of Samarkand had sent a delegation to Babur, complaining about the stiff and arrogant behavior of the Kyzylbashes and requesting him to send them back to Persia. This request had come to Babur at the time when he was informed that several Uzbek factions had formed alliances, and were gathering at the borders of Samarkand to launch a massive assault. Babur was disheartened by such news, and possibly could not comply with their request, since his troops hemmed in on all sides could not defend this city without the help of Kyzylbashes. With or without the Kyzylbashes, Babur had no choice but to leave, since the lords of Samarkand had become impatient and restless, filled with anger and resentment at the mere sight of Red Hats with their turbans of twelve points, *conical and scarlet much like the daggers of hatred in their hearts.*

Babur's thoughts were deflecting such hateful comments paraded by the denizens of Samarkand, seeking peace and wisdom from the men of genius in this city, who had died with the promise of living eternally. One amongst many was Ulugh Beg, whose red sandstone observatory he had visited when he was young, and once again could not help revisiting with a renewed sense of awe and reverence. Feeling much like a lone pilgrim, he had returned to the shrines of those dearest to his heart, evoking sweet remembrances of his father who had been his guide and friend many times over whenever they visited Samarkand. Ibn Sina—the writer, physician, and expounder of Aristotle in its tomb of blue marble was arresting his thoughts, but the journey in his head was flashing a monument of white marble, housing the remains of Al Farabi, a famed ascetic and a philosopher.

Somewhere deep within, an ache of loneliness was piercing Babur's heart, abysmal and profound. The beauty of this garden with all its color and perfume was mocking him, it seemed, his gaze searching Sweet Absent inside the very void of ether between earth and heaven. But it was alighting on the gold-sprinkled missive before him, its contents trickling down his head with the murmur of a distant cataract. Mahim had congratulated Babur for becoming the father of a prince and a princess, expressing great joy, as if she herself was the mother of these royal babes. Gulrukh Begum had given birth to a healthy prince, and Dildar Begum was the proud mother of an adorable princess. After conveying this happy news, she had requested Babur that he choose propitious names for the newly born, and respond to her at the earliest possible.

What is this dream-illusion? My new-born babes must be over the rungs of one year old by now, if I can recall correctly. The pulse of new life in each leaf, each bloom and in countless beams of sunshine, and yet surcease is not far behind? This sparkling mirage of peace, color, beauty! His gaze was alighting on Ismael Khan—Khazanda's son who had come from Kunduz to join his mother. Ismael Khan and Haider Mirza were seated side-by-side, being schooled, rather being entertained by Khwaja Kilan under some spell of awe and wonder.

"What should we name our royal prince, my worthy mentor?" Babur broke Khwaja Kilan's concentration with this abrupt inquiry.

"Padishah!" Khwaja Kilan's eyes were kindling the lamps of devotion and inspiration. "I have always favored the name of Kamran, if it pleases you, Padishah?"

"Prince Kamran, it is, then." Babur announced happily. "Mahim Begum would bless you for choosing such a princely name." His gaze was sailing past Gulnar Aghacha and Nurgul Aghacha toward Khazanda. "What should we name our little princess, my sweet sister?"

"I might think of some name, if all the royal mothers promise to send their blessings my way?" Khazanda Begum teased. "I am beginning to enjoy the court gossip straight from Kabul, the enchanting palace and the lovely gardens. Mahim Begum wielding the wand of power and discipline, and trusting no one with the care of prince Humayun and princess Masuma! Shouldn't she ask Gulrukh Begum to choose the name of her son? And Dildar Begum should be the one choosing the name of her daughter?"

"You favor the mothers, not the begums, it is obvious." Babur demurred aloud, his look wistful and endearing. "Not all the court gossip has reached you, dear Khazanda. You don't know Mahim. Her love is deep and boundless. Princess Masuma claims her love more than prince Humayun, and she deems herself the mother of all royal babes, born or unborn. Strange and mysterious that Dildar and Gulrukh stay bewitched by her charm and authority, obedient to her wishes or commands. All the begums and princesses stand in awe of her, happy to do her bidding. I myself feel compelled to satisfy the least of her whims, strange indeed!" His gaze was shifting to Nurgul Aghacha and Gulnar Aghacha. "You are commanded to choose a name for our royal princess, my beauties, since my rebel of a sister deigns not to favor Padishah?"

"Any name beginning with Gul, Padishah, I have been thinking." Gulnar Aghacha sang joyfully, her agate eyes sparkling. "Nurgul and I have Gul in our names, and we think it is beautiful. Since Gul means rose, Gulrose, I think would be a lovely name for the little princess?"

"Gul is lovely as it is, without the real rose piercing its heart!" Nurgul Aghacha protested, her cheeks flushed by the fire of her poetic expression. "Roses have thorns, and thorns bruise. No royal princess should have a name which reminds one of pain or wounds—" She couldn't continue against the gleam of ardor and amusement in Babur's eyes.

"We could add color to the beauty of Gul?" Khazanda Begum ruminated aloud. "Gulrang! Soft and silken as the rose petals, and no thorns to prick and stab." The blue pools in her eyes were gathering stars of mirth and mischief.

Gulrang! Both Nurgul and Gulrang chanted in unison.

"Both Dildar and Gulrang would bless you for concocting such an exquisite garland of a name!" Babur exclaimed, his joy draining at the stiff approach of Najm Sani.

"Padishah." Najm Sani curtsied, allowing a little pause before delivering his message. "A messenger from King of Persia just arrived entrusting me with this message to be delivered to you personally. Shah Ismael requests Padishah not to abandon Samarkand. The King also confirms our reports that Uzbeks indeed are gathering their forces at the borders of Hissar, Kunduz and Ferghana. He has expressed his concern, awaiting your assurance that Persian and Moghul troops under your command would strive with all their might to defeat the Uzbeks, strengthening first and foremost the borders of Samarkand."

"My command!" Babur left one threat of a pause as he heaved himself up slowly and deliberately. "My command to my devoted soldiers is to march back to Kabul. Samarkand is not to be the battleground for Moghuls against Moghuls. The lords of Samarkand are well equipped to defend their beloved homeland as they have stated, expressing most candidly that we leave, lest the general populace turn to violence and rebellion. We came here peacefully and we would depart peacefully. We might be able to save Ferghana from the war-mongering hordes on our way back to Kabul? A long, long journey rigged with dangers and hardships, we would start early at dawn tomorrow." He waved dismissal. "Right now Padishah's only wish is to indulge in the luxury of a quiet stroll." He turned, but not before noticing the daggers of hatred directed at Najm Sani straight from the eyes of Ismael Khan and Haider Mirza.

So, that's what the Red Hats do, inspire hatred inside the hearts of even the young princes? Was Babur's one rag of contemplation before he lost himself into the profusion of flowers, serenading the sparkling waters where the fountains gurgled and spluttered.

Samarkand was vicissitudes away as Babur's cavalcade lumbered through Ghaj ravine, threading its way toward Hissar. He was riding ahead of the Moghul troops, the Red Hats in front of him an ocean of helmets and shields, polished by the flood of autumnal sunset, all saffron and luminescent. Babur's horse padded with a quilted cuirass and cloth of mail was lending him a sense of warmth and protection, but his thoughts were exposed to rage and rancor against the Red Hats, who, despite his warnings, could not be restrained from their pressing need to slaughter and pillage.

An undisciplined lot, defying my commands, and moved only by their fiendish instincts to kill and plunder! I have lost control over them? Had it not been for my need to save Ferghana from the claws of Uzbeks, I would have hurled these hounds—Kyzylbashes to perdition? And beloved Ferghana lost too!

Babur's thoughts were cutting open the wounds in seasons since he had left Samarkand. This turquoise city was now occupied by the contentious clans of Uzbeks under the nominal rule of one leader by the name of Ubaid Khan. Bokhara and Ferghana were also fallen into the hands of the Uzbeks, who were concentrating more on quelling the riots than choosing a leader amongst their warring factions. At this recollection, Babur's heart was ripping open one familiar wound of loss and grief, his gaze reaching down to the valley of Ghazhdewan cradled by the foothills of Hissar. Somewhere deep within him, a rent of ache and loneliness was startled to awakening, longing for the scent and beauty of Kabul. He could breathe the perfume of his gardens, his very thoughts gathering Mahim, Gulrukh and Dildar into their arms and hugging and kissing Humayun, Masuma, Kamran and Gulrang.

Babur was jolted out of his reveries by an abrupt chant of war cries from the lips of the Red Hats. Kyzylbashes had espied an army of Uzbeks down the slopes of Ghazhdewan, and was rushing toward the enemy with the vengeance of warlords. The Moghul soldiers, following the lead of Padishah, had brought their steeds to a sudden halt, sensing his rage against the Red Hats who had commenced fighting without his express command to launch such an assault, pressed only by their zeal and beastly instincts. A great pandemonium was unfolding before Babur's sight as he sat astride, his own soldiers behind him suspended under some spell of inertia and wonder. Against the shower of arrows and clattering of swords, the Uzbeks were the ones suffering losses, the groans of the wounded and the dying shrill and heartrending. The Uzbek leader was urging his soldiers to flee, while one of his men with a gash running down from his cheek to chin was being trampled in the melee. The scene was shifting in a flash, the Uzbeks now overpowering the Kyzylbashes, hacking them down under some spell of blind fury and hopelessness.

The infidels are dying under the scepter of Islam! Haider Mirza's gleeful comment hurled at the Kyzylbashes was condoned by Babur as he spurred his horse toward the field of combat. He could see Najm Sani who had broken his lance, his hand reaching down to the hilt at his waist to retrieve his scimitar. He was unscathed, the malicious gleam in his eyes following the Uzbeks in their desperate flight toward safety.

Follow the heathens! Najm Sani cried exultantly, his face suffused with the fire of fanaticism.

"Cease your bleating cry, Najm Sani, lest you become the object of pity for your horse weeping over your death?" Babur thundered a command. "Moghuls or Kyzylbashes, none of our soldiers are to follow the fleeing wretches. Attend to the wounded. *Fight only those who fight with you*, does any one amongst you remember this injunction?"

"Padishah!" Najm Sani's unvoiced appeal was silenced by one imperious wave of Babur's arm.

"Blood of zeal and hatred is in your eyes and in your heart, Najm Sani!" Babur's very eyes were flashing accusations. "From here we part, not as foes but as strangers. Gather your horde of zealots and depart at once. You are free to go anywhere you like, but make sure our paths are never crossed." He whirled his horse around, racing back toward his troops, leaving the Red Hats to their own schemes or conjectures.

Homeward bound, Babur's cavalcade was entering the frontiers of Balkh. Without the presence of the Kyzylbashes, the Moghul troops were seized with a sense of euphoria, marching through Kunduz singing and joking, and even now were riding jauntily. *Longing for Kabul*, Babur was thinking, his thoughts following the Kyzylbashes. *They are probably in Khorasan by now, where the King of Persia is lodged?* He was becoming aware of Haider Mirza riding beside him, a subtle smile curling on his lips at the recollection when the prince had labeled Kyzylbashes the *infidels* and the Uzbeks as the *scepter of Islam.* The smile was fading from his lips, his thoughts suddenly a whirlwind of sad contemplations.

Whoever comes to the gate of death knows the value of life, each breath a pearl of victory inside the oyster of wars, perils, conflicts. What is this insufferable need to rule and conquer? Why must men fight? And yet their warring spirits are getting sustenance from the beginning of creation. Fighting for land, faith, and legacy! Religion, any religion, the curse of time, cultivating hatred and violence, tearing nations apart, pilfering love and joy from the hearts of mankind? Why are lands sacred and gods jealous? Are we not condemned for sins we did not commit? What mercy in salvation which holds the whip of tyranny and oppression? What virtue in love which cripples? What wisdom in prayer which offers not the crumbs of compassion? Babur's thoughts on the verge of heresy were crushed by the weight of sunset unfolding before his eyes like a tapestry most exquisite and awesome. Humbled and bewildered, he appeared to be galloping toward the sky where the prayer-rug of multifaceted colors gleamed and shuddered. An ocean of gold, slashed with streaks violet and crimson was cradling in its bosom the continent of Hind, *a pearl of hope* to be polished and redeemed.

19

Perfumed Garden

Nirvana is where the manifestation of Noble Wisdom expresses itself in Perfect Love for all. It is where the manifestation of Perfect Love expresses itself in the Noble Wisdom of enlightenment for all—there, indeed is Nirvana.
— Buddhism

Babur at the head of his cavalcade was riding toward his palace, the tapestry of Kabul unfolding before his sight with the scent of homecoming. They had rested in the valley of Gurbund by the river Nilab the night before, and were now carrying the glory of the hills and the flowers in their eyes, longing to be with their friends and family. The cavalcade itself was diminished considerably, each soldier availing of the opportunity of Babur's consent to leave for their homes along the way whenever convenient. Babur himself seemed unaware of the group of his close companions riding behind, his expression dreamy and wistful, only the blue plume in his turban dancing merrily in the wind. Peace and emptiness were his companions, the lush groves of his garden receding, and exposing the palace in the distance, large and looming. White terraces edged with spring flowers were coming into view, and he thought he could hear the gurgling of the fountains.

Suddenly, his beloved garden had come alive with the sound of the kettle-drums, a group of courtiers materializing on the sun-spangled terraces, cheering and welcoming. Soon, a sea of color could be seen surging forth, the men with bright plumes in their turbans, and women in panels of silks and brocades, all vivid and shimmering. Babur leapt down from his horse, surrendering himself to the waves of joy and laughter. He could see Nasir Mirza racing toward him, and he caught the prince in one eager embrace in his very act of offering a curtsy.

"Padishah!" Nasir Mirza gasped for breath, shaking himself free from Babur's embrace. "Welcome home. Kabul welcomes you, your palace, your gardens, your household, all welcome you. And I the most humble of your slaves welcome you most heartily."

Babur stood there overwhelmed, his face suffused with the light of joy and sunshine. Prince Humayun, barely six years old, was racing ahead of his brother prince Kamran, a year younger than him, both dressed in Moghul fineries of silks and jewels. Both were swept into the loving arms of Babur before he could turn his attention to princess Masuma, trying her best to hide herself in the billowing gowns of the begums. He was sweeping all in warm embraces, hugging and kissing, Mahim Begum, Dildar Begum, Gulrukh Begum, and a bevy of princesses. The ropes of pearls around Humayun's neck down to his waist were attracting Babur's attention, his gaze shifting to his wives with a kindling of mirth and ardor.

"Save these jewels for the princesses, dear Mahim!" Babur declared cheerfully. "Valor would be the only jewel for Humayun when he could prove himself worthy?"

"Your baba wore jewels, Padishah, and he was the most valorous of all kings." Mahim Begum quipped, her smile radiant and challenging.

"Ah, the wit of women! How they dig out jewels from tombs dark and silent?" Babur laughed, marching past the ocean of jubilations toward his palace of marble and sandstone.

The molten gold of the afternoon was swallowed by an early dusk as Babur sat with his friends and family inside the Pleasure Hall, all gilt and damask. Donned in purple robe of silk with a matching plume in his turban, he was feeling royally entertained in the familiar surroundings of warmth and opulence. His gaze was absorbing all colors, from Bokhara carpets to the tapestries on the walls, from rosewood furniture in koftgari design to brilliantly lit candelabras. The chests with marquetry in ivory and mother-of-pearl seemed to throb and sparkle with the life of their own, as if moved by the sweet notes of flute by the flutist Shaiki in accompaniment with the lute played by Hussain. A bevy of dancers were entering the hall, creating waves upon waves of rainbows with their skirts gossamer and gleaming. Babur's gaze was shifting toward the splash of jewels and colors on the ladies lolling against pillows round and velvety.

Mahim Begum with a tiara of sapphires and diamonds was envy of the begums, her blue silk gown stitched with pearls and carnelians. Dildar Begum was radiating the fire of rubies in her ears and around her throat. The fiery glow of agates and emeralds was making the face of Gulrukh Begum bronzed and flushed. Gulnar Begum in her gown of turquoise with matching jewels looked ethereal as if ready to float up to the very heavens. The gleam of admiration in Babur's eyes was replaced by sadness as his gaze alighted on his sister Khazanda Begum. She was wearing pale silks and a string of pearls around her throat as her only ornament. Enveloped in her aura of serenity, she was busy embroidering the bodice of a silk gown, oblivious to her half sister Shahr Banu, who was watching the needlework with rapt wonder. A royal scuffle was commencing not far from them where Nasir Mirza sat drinking in his world of silent contemplation.

Prince Humayun and prince Kamran were tugging at one toy drum, both struggling to snatch it from each other, but not succeeding. Princess Masuma had joined them, prancing and cheering. The little princess Gulrang was not to be left behind, sliding right under the drum and beating it with her fists. The brothers were thrown into utter confusion, their eyes locked in silent combat, and their knuckles turning white by the sheer force of holding on to the rope strung around for tuning.

"A royal entertainment indeed! Don't you agree, my celibate brother?" Babur laughed, claiming Nasir Mirza's attention. "Watch my royal brood making this Pleasure Hall a field of combat!"

"Padishah!" Was Nasir Mirza's startled response! His look was dazed, and he couldn't speak, averting his gaze to watch the little combatants.

Prince Kamran had succeeded in claiming the drum from prince Humayun, and was now racing toward his mother Gulrukh Begum. Humayun was not following his brother, standing there impaled in one spot like the lord of nemesis, his eyes flashing. Prince Kamran had found refuge behind his mother, peering from behind her, his own eyes glittering. Babur's gaze was returning to his brother who was holding out his jeweled cup to Mushin for replenishing.

"Any reports of rebellion in my absence you might like to share with me, my taciturn Prince?" Babur asked, his eyes kindling reproof at his brother's overindulgence in drinking.

"A few, Padishah." Was Nasir Mirza's inebriated response! "Aimaks, Hazaras, Afghans, always making raids, always plotting and scheming. A few spurts of riots here and there, but I quelled them all, restoring peace and discipline." He quaffed his drink thirstily, his eyes following Mushin.

"Come, Mushin, fill Padishah's cup, and don't serve the Prince anymore this evening." Babur commanded, returning his gaze to his brother and noticing in there the silent plea for wine and oblivion. "I admit that in my absence you have managed the affairs of Kabul with utmost prudence, my charming prince, but it doesn't mean you have earned the privilege of overindulgence in my presence." Babur began thoughtfully. "Your reward for valor and loyalty is the kingdom of Ghazni, which I bestow upon you to rule and keep intact. Practice moderation in everything you do, especially in drinking? That look in your eyes, Nasir Mirza, of a wounded bird—well, just this evening?" He turned to Mushin. "You may fill the cup of prince one more time, and if he needs another, don't be in a haste to refill."

The Pleasure Hall brimming with song and gaiety had claimed Babur as its prodigal son, bestowing upon him the gifts of love and laughter. The giddy hours replete with raillery and feasting had slipped past unheeded, and still the air was charged with the rills of music and festivity. Babur's keen senses were awakening to the sound of music outside his palace, the mystic in him longing for the poetry of his gardens. Though engaged in parlance with his wives and cousins, he could hear the serenade of the fountains, and could see the night sky studded with stars, almost inhaling the fragrance of flowers while hugging the scented air in his imagination with aching tenderness. His gaze was dreamy and wistful, his thoughts suspended somewhere in ether, hovering over his wives, and unwilling to decide as to which one would serve his pleasure this first night of his homecoming. And yet his gaze was settling on his concubines.

Ah, the houris straight from Paradise, Gulnar and Nurgul, the goddesses with gold hair and eyes the color of night skies! They have been my bliss-

comfort during my journeys long and endless? Who would be my houri tonight, Mahim, Dildar, Gulrukh? Babur's gaze in its sweeping intensity was settling on his sister Khazanda, and a familiar ache of sadness was rising within him with the windswept fury of a rainstorm. A sudden revelation was dawning upon him that Mahim was discomfited by the presence of Khazanda, as if his sister would pose a constant threat to her rule of authority and judgment in this royal household? This revelation alone was splintering Babur's need for solitude, his heart reaching out to Mahim with tenderness akin to grief and agony. Grief—for this insufferable longing for Sweet Absent, and agony for the absence of love which had once been wild and passionate, now buried under the tomb of *great loss*, permitting him not the gift of another beloved.

"Would you fancy a stroll in the garden, dear Mahim?" Babur abandoned his gilt chair with an abrupt alacrity, drifting toward her dreamlike.

"Padishah!" Mahim heaved herself up slowly, joy washing over her features in a rosy flush.

"It would be a bit chilly out there, my beauty." Babur smiled, flashing a command at her lady-in-waiting. "Maywa Jan, fetch a shawl for Mahim Begum, the finest and the warmest."

Maywa Jan, who was coaxing princess Gulrang to sleep, let the little elf slip out of her arms, and plodded away, grumbling relief and prayers. Princess Gulrang raced toward Mahim, hiding her face in the soft ripples of her gown. Princess Masuma could not be left behind, darting out of Dildar's lap to claim attention from Mahim. Mahim stood there laughing, hugging and kissing the princesses effusively. Babur's attention was diverted toward prince Kamran and prince Humayun who were now seated together, the object of their contention abandoned near a heap of pillows. Rapt and spellbound, they couldn't take their eyes off the treasures displayed by Haider Mirza and Ismael Khan. Swords and daggers inset with jewels most exquisite and priceless. The hilts of jade and ivory, revealing scimitars, all polished and craftily designed. Maywa Jan had returned, holding out a Pashmina shawl woven in a bouquet of colors with a fine border in pink and turquoise. Babur was quick to claim the shawl, wrapping it around her shoulders with utmost absorption before leading her out of the hall, his step quickening. Sayyid Qasim was ahead of the royal couple, throwing open the imposing portals into the heart of the night.

A blissful hush all around with brilliant stars overhead and the moonlit mists over the elms had cast a spell over the royal couple as they strolled in silence. The machalchis had lit a myriad of diyas over the terraces and along the manicured paths leading toward the grove of Chenars, spruced with flowers both wild and exotic. Babur's senses were suspended in some sort of ecstatic swoon, dancing in a wild abandon over the slats of fretted stone which were left behind, and where the fountains danced and gurgled. The blue-white blooms of plumbago were claiming his attention, his thoughts escaping most cunningly into the fragrant valleys of Ferghana and Samarkand. And yet the sudden profusion of scent from Rat-ki-Rani was whirling him back to the night beauty of his garden. He could see the bridal creeper peering out from behind a spruce, its deep-green foliage polished by moonbeams. Awed and humbled, he was drifting along, his heart aching once again, longing for something more precious than this beauty and silence. *Sweet Absent*, his thoughts had snuffed out this candle of a longing, awakening him to the warmth and beauty of sweet present beside him, quietly and blissfully adorable. Without stopping and without looking at her, he began to speak, as if communing with the vast silence within and without.

"Strange, that these recollections are coming back to me, vivid and lifelike, as if straight from the pages of the Holy Scriptures Khwaja Klan used to read to me after I became the king of Ferghana. *Life is a shadow, the shadow of a tower or a tree. The shadow which prevails for a time? No, even as the shadow of a bird in its flight! It passeth from our sight, and neither bird, nor shadow remains.*" Babur paused as if a shadow of presage hovered low over his ruminations. "Strange indeed, that now Nasir Mirza is invading my thoughts in this garden filled with beauty and enchantment. He must leave for Ghazni, though I would rather keep him here with me. By the virtue of being my half brother, he must learn to rule and defend small kingdoms, if not aspire toward becoming a king? Shah Mirza is another concern of mine! Once a scheming prince, now he professes loyalty to me, so I have left him in Badakhshan to rule wisely and peacefully. Time flies ahead of our thoughts. Soon Kamran and Humayun would be old enough to be dispatched to lands alien and distant—" He stopped abruptly, facing Mahim. "Why this silence, my beauty, you haven't said a word since we came out? You should have buckets of court gossip to share with me? What kind of welcome is this, donning a veil of silence and mystery?"

"Padishah!" Mahim Begum murmured, her eyes glittering with the violence of some inward passion she could not voice. "I missed you so—we all missed you. Hold me close to you, Padishah! Lie to me, if you must, but tell me you care for me." She felt paralyzed, her cheeks flaming, one agony of a prayer inside her silenced.

"My beauty, my moon!" Babur snatched her into his arms in one crushing embrace, kissing her face, eyes, and lips! "I would be lying if I told you I didn't care for you." He held her before him, gazing into her eyes.

"And love?" Mahim Begum's feverish eyes were ardent and implacable.

"That would be a mighty lie, my beauty." Babur smiled, reading volumes from her eyes, his own revealing the pain and loss of some old grief he could not suppress.

"I never thought I could be jealous of—" Mahim Begum could not utter the name of *Zainab*, as if it would scald her lips.

"And I never thought I would fall in love again?" Babur stood gazing into her eyes under some spell of stark wonder and fascination. "I have never seen such brilliant stars—in your eyes, my love. Diamonds with their fiery blaze and stars with their stabbing brilliance, I have seen, but not this dance of light, not ever before!" He folded her into his arms, murmuring endearments. "You are trembling, my love?"

"With joy, I assure you, Padishah." Mahim Begum could barely murmur.

"Now I am trembling—with desire." Babur held her close as if he would never let her go. But his gaze was fixed to the moon, catching in its livid face the reflection his true Beloved. He released Mahim gently, slipping his arm around her waist, and retracing his steps toward the palace. Sweet Absent was with him, his heart embracing only one memory ineffable. *Beloved, Beloved*, his very soul was singing this hymn unforgotten and unforgettable.

20

Dervish of the Steppes

Our state cannot be sever'd, we are one
One flesh, to lose thee were to lose myself
— John Milton

Kabul with its glorious summer this particular afternoon was filling the palace with scented breeze, as Babur sat at the rosewood desk in his library, filling his journal with entries for his memoirs, Babur-Nama. This oval library furbished with rose and ivory damask was his gilded cage he did not wish escape, loving its treasures of books and paintings. One of his favorite paintings was a silk masterpiece on the back wall, wedged in between two columns of bookshelves. Some Safavid artist had caught the princes of the house of Timur on silk with brilliant robes and turbans, graceful and lifelike, as if challenging other artists to dare duplicate such beauty and passion. The tapestry on the wall overlooking his desk was Babur's next favorite, the scene of hunt woven in silk-wool knots most exquisitely, but right now he was oblivious to all with the exception of thoughts and the flowering of the Turkish script which his fingers molded on the gold-sprinkled paper with the objectiveness of a court historian.

Many wondrous summers like this had slipped past on winged flight since Babur had returned to Kabul after losing both Ferghana and Samarkand. The frolic of time had swallowed some lives and had given birth to some new ones, but Babur had not changed much with the exception of acquiring a thin goatee and a thick mustache. Donned in silk robe of ochre with an orange plume in his turban, he looked as young as half a decade ago. Only the poetry of mysticism in his eyes had attained the purity of sunshine, reflecting his inner quest for wisdom and knowledge. Right now his thoughts were rebelling against the monotony of stating facts, his jeweled quill poised in an act of scribbling, yet spilling a couplet instead which had been simmering in his head with the promise of a ghazal.

What faith can one but in the things of the world, my heart
What good can you hope for, from souls that ignore the truth

Babur dipped his quill in the inkpot impatiently, snuffing out this inspiration with his practiced will to get back on the track of journal entries, but his thoughts were escaping into his gardens and orchards. The fig and the orange trees, the peach and the almond, and the largest grove of lemon trees, all were seeking his joy and praise. His gaze was leaping down from the window in front of his desk into the garden below, admiring the tapestry of colors and inhaling the scent of flowers. The great riot and profusion in nature were attracting the golden orioles, and each particle of earth-scent was exploding into songs, Babur was thinking. His practiced will was coming to his rescue, and the quill between his fingers was resuming its dull task of stabbing and recording.

> *Kabul is becoming the city of gardens, the most beautiful amongst many; Shahr-Ara; Shahi-Jahan; Char-Bagh; Baghi-Jalua; Aurta-Bagh; Surta-Bagh; Baghi-Mehtab—meaning moonlight. Baghi-Ahu is favored by the princes, since they can see the deer roaming freely and fearlessly. Kabul has its share of unrest too, seditions by various clans, the ever-rebellious Aimaks, Afghans and Hazaras. And tragedies, Nasir Mirza died. His death resulting in rebellions inside Ghazni. The chief rebels, Shram Taghai; Masid Wakeh, Kul Nazer and Baba Beshagheri routed and dispersed by Kambar Ali. The death of Shah Mirza in Badakhshan came suddenly, his son Suleiman Mirza is at our palace in Kabul, finding much comfort in the company of prince Humayun, since he is of the same age as our prince.*
>
> *Mahim Begum has had several miscarriages. She is brave and resilient, and possessive of all the children in my harem. Gulrukh Begum is the mother of our youngest son, almost three year old, prince Askeri. Princess Gulchihra—almost two is our youngest daughter by Dildar Begum. Mahim Begum adores our little princess, barely a year old, and dotes upon the mother Dildar Begum since she is heavy with child again. Khazanda Begum is married to Mehdi Khwaja. Princess Masuma, on the rungs of twelve summers, is married to Zaman Mirza. Princess Gulrang is betrothed to Aisan Timur.*

Babur's quill slipped from his fingers, a flood of tenderness welling inside him for all his children; especially, for princess Gulchihra, whom he called *lily of Kabul*, wishing to arrest her childhood eternally, so that he could keep her with him always. The warmth and languor of the summer afternoon was reaching him in little whiffs of breeze, teasing his senses to woo the beauty of his gardens. But the tingling of fatigue down his legs and behind his back was making him feverish and restless. He had been sitting in his chair since hours, completely engrossed in filling his journal with entries, and now his limbs were protesting all of a sudden, almost hurling him out of his seat as he lumbered on his feet to gain balance. Some sort of ache and tenderness was yawning within him as he commenced the ritual of pacing, his thoughts etching the mournful expression of Mahim at the prospect of Humayun leaving for Badakhshan.

Suleiman Mirza is accompanying Humayun on his journey to Badakhshan and our prince is not alone to rule this little kingdom. Babur had consoled Mahim, condoning her pleas that Humayun should stay in Kabul. Both the princes were leaving this very evening, and the grief-stricken face of Mahim was invading his thoughts, but he was diverting his attention toward the mahogany shelves hosting a variety of books, all lacquered and neatly stacked. He knew the title of each book by heart, and their location. His mind was taking inventory of the books he loved the most, the titles moving in his head with the rhythm of his pacing.

The works of court poets: Reseter-Sefa by Mir Khan; Habib-es-Syar and Kholsasd-Akhbar by Khand Amir. Gulistan and Bostan by Saadi. Shah-Nama by Firdausi. Rubaiyat by Omar Khayyam. Zafar-Nama—Timur's book of victory. The collection of poems by Rumi, Hafiz, Jami and Ibn Sara. Babur's feet were coming to a sudden halt in front of the gold-illumined volumes, the names Kisai and Al-Thurthusi grazing his awareness, yet his hand was reaching out to the odes of Faizi. He stood flitting pages, reading aloud randomly.

My dear son, consider how short the time is that the star of good fortune revolves according to thy wish. Fate shows no friendship—Babur flitted more pages. *Although life far from thee is an approach to death, yet to stand at a distance is a mark of courtesy.* He replaced the book reverently on the shelf, the sound of voices and laughter from down the hall disrupting his perusal and solitary contemplations. His heart was awakening to the poetry of living, rocked by oars of memories; his feet carrying him down the gleaming staircase.

Floating through the parlor, Babur was sucked into the fragrance of the Pleasure Hall. A flurry of curtsies followed by protests and requests from the lips of the begums, and the princes and the princesses were pouring joy and warmth into Babur's heart. Princess Gulchihra had bounced forth from behind the rustling gowns, and Babur had snatched her into his arms, hugging and kissing. She had abandoned her head on his shoulders, as if drifting into the comfort of sleep, while his gaze was shifting from one face to the other, his lips as well as his eyes spilling words and laughter. His heart was fluttering all of a sudden, escaping into the joy-warmth of his gardens, but before his feet could obey his heart his gaze was arrested to Humayun.

Humayun was standing under one canopy suspended over the windows, and sweeping down at the sides in pleated brocade. The pet cockerel—Humayun's favorite, was perched upon his shoulders, nibbling on the pearls around his neck down to his waist. He was standing still, his gaze dreamy, only the red plume in his turban, his gold vest matching his breeches and shoes of yellow shagreen all vivid and shimmering. Mahim Begum, following the gaze of Babur, was discomfited by the stark immobility of her son, her lips spilling one wail of a request.

"Padishah, somehow it doesn't feel right that prince Humayun should go to Badakhshan. May I go with him, I am afraid—" Mahim Begum couldn't continue against the flash of mirth and amusement in Babur's eyes.

"A mother's heart, my beauty, possessive and clinging!" Babur smiled. "You flatter the prince too much, Mahim, and with your indulgence he is turning into a superstitious dolt. Look, how he fawns at his pet cockerel! A propitious day for his journey, he is thinking, since the gracious pet has favored his right shoulder? Don't you agree? I was twelve, the same age as our prince is now, when I became the king of Ferghana. No mother to watch over me, only a grandmother, both kind and ruthless, keeping me steadfast in every move which I made, in every gain which I anticipated, in every loss which I encountered. Pity that our parents are no more, and our children would never know the love and blessings of grandparents!"

"Padishah—" Mahim Begum attempted another plea, but couldn't voice her fears against the flash of ardor in the eyes of her husband.

"You would splinter the beauty of peace-loving summer with you sighs and laments, Mahim, if you didn't go with Humayun?" Babur abandoned the sleeping princess over the shoulders of Mahim, her arms cradling her lovingly. "You better hurry, and get your things ready if you want to go with the prince?" He laughed, his very feet guiding him toward his cherished gardens.

The terraces splashed with sunshine were gleaming as Babur skipped down the steps edged with wild creepers, beyond which the gardeners labored, planting new saplings of peach and almond. The riot and the scented blooms in the garden were teasing Babur's senses, his heart fluttering into realms abysmal and mysterious. His thoughts were humming the familiar songs of ache and longing. Something dear and lost was coming back to him, making him giddy, and filling his whole being with the joy-pain of nostalgia on the verge of exhilaration. He was inhaling deeply, drinking in sounds and colors from the crystal cups of nature. His heart was trembling all of a sudden, as if moved by the harp of love from within and without. Somewhere in the abysmal deeps of his soul was the mating of joy with grief, and yet his inner self was kindling the lamp of bliss and surrender. His thoughts were soaring aloft, but his gaze was falling down the winding slope, and arrested there with a sudden jolt of awareness.

He had espied prince Askeri squatted there on the grass, exploring the nozzle of a musket! *A dangerous weapon in the hands of a child*, anger and disbelief was alighting in Babur's eyes with a quicksilver awakening. He couldn't mistake it for any other but the one designed by his master-gunner, Ali Kuli, an Afghan musket named jezzail. Prince Askeri was still absorbed in exploring this strange object, when Babur snatched it away, his eyes shooting flames at prince Kamran and Maywa Jan whom he had seen approaching in a flurry of haste and consternation. Prince Askeri was quick to find refuge into the arms of Maywa Jan, while prince Kamran curtsied, flustered and trembling.

"My undisciplined colt of a prince!" Babur vented his rage on his son, sparing Maywa Jan. "How would you in times of war, keep watch on the enemy under cover, when you couldn't watch your own child brother in danger of hurting himself with this musket?"

"Padishah!" Guilt and chagrin were choking Kamran's voice. "There is no powder in jezzail. Well, I was practicing—when I heard a cannon shot. Ali Kuli, he showed me the Victory Gun he has designed. Forgive me, Padishah." He murmured against the flaring of anger and impatience in Babur's eyes.

"Get you gone, Kamran, and study the art of mindfulness, not neglect!" Babur waved dismissal, his anger subsiding. "Learn wisdom from the tongues of the poets and the sages, and gather as many pearls of knowledge as you can before I send you to Kandahar. That little kingdom awaits one worthy sovereign." He turned to his heels, resuming his stroll.

Babur's gaze was stealing molten gold out of sunshine, but his thoughts were molding guns, jezzails and cannons. He could smell the reek of looming assaults across from the borders of Kabul. Besides the ever-querulous, ever-scheming Afghans, the clans of Yusufzais were plotting raids, Babur was recently informed of their secret oaths to pillage and plunder the villages whose leaders were weakened by the deluge of their rifts and conflicts amongst various factions. *To conquer Hind, is this some imperative need within me, or the curse of ambition or temptation? And yet the kingdom of Kabul must be sustained, its holy mountains to be protected against marauders and its people to be provided with opportunities to enrich themselves, lest they die of sloth, if not afflicted with despair and poverty?* Babur's thoughts were absorbing their blaze of sunshine, pain-filled and dazzling. *To be sure, I am trying to quell the warring restlessness of my subjects, or finding means to appease their wild, scalding instincts of adventure? Where does this all lead to? Where does one go? Does anyone get anywhere except closer to death?* His gaze as well as his thoughts was wandering, much in rhythm with his steps, slow and ponderous.

The fountains bordered with violet and jasmine was wafting a potpourri of scents, mingled with the heavy perfume from tuberoses and ranunculus. Some sort of warmth and seduction was in the air, colors leaping out from the very bowls of edelweiss', daisies, primula' and marigolds. A majestic array of spruces, Chenars and poplars were greeting Babur, but his gaze was reaching to the distant groves of loquat, tamarind and pomegranate. He could see kingfishers amongst the company of doves and hoopoes, and the smooth sailing of the golden orioles and the paradise flycatchers. Suddenly, his heart was bursting open with an astonishing surge of joy, as if something awesome and incredible was in store for him down the very rungs of time before this day could melt into another night of silence and darkness. This intensity of feeling within him was akin to the one he had felt but once in his lifetime. And yet that feeling was of grief and despair, forewarning him of some tragedy, and that same day his father had died in an accident. This feeling, in contrast, was of joy and celebration, cradling the promise of miracles and mysteries, and holding in abeyance all sorrows of the past, alive and cankerous.

A host of tragedies, one could always remember, hugging the pain and clinging to sorrows, Babur's steps as well as his thoughts were tracing back the paths familiar and unforgotten. *And yet joys are numbered few, easily abandoned and forgotten. What would make me happy, really happy?* If Zainab could come back and he could not think beyond the absurdity of such hope—dream.

The glory of the day was swallowed by a moonlit night, as Babur paced in his library, still intoxicated by that *feeling* which had teased him all day, its intensity now a throbbing presence and a challenge inscrutable. Mahim Begum had left along with prince Humayun, leaving behind a vacuum quite large and boundless. Babur had filled that vacuum by having a lengthy discussion with Khwaja Kilan about the looming threat from the clan of Yusufzais who were plotting rebellion. After Khwaja Kilan had left, Babur's thoughts were marooned on an island of inspiration, devising a quick plan to test the validity of the reports as to the stealthy designs of the Yusufzais. This plan was now uncoiling its form within his head like a tide wild and ubiquitous. His childhood wish of roaming in the guise of a mendicant was coming alive, goading him to knead his wishes into the mold of reality. He was heeding the voice of caprice and curiosity, his thoughts hurling him straight into the chariot of action and adventure.

The library of rose and ivory could have been a fantastic dream of the past, Babur was thinking, as he found himself standing outside the humble quarters of his basin-bearer, Tahir. His thoughts themselves had whisked him into the small room, startling Tahir to his feet. The incongruity of this scene against the lone, flickering candle had turned Tahir into a statue of fright and bewilderment, his lips uttering one low moan of an appeal, *Padishah.*

"Padishah is not going to eat you alive, my son!" Babur consoled against the fever of his elation and impatience. "Find me one robe suitable for a dervish or a beggar and a beggar's bowl. Don't just stand there like an unblinking idiot, fetch me the robe and the bowl." He commanded, his eyes shooting bolts of lightning.

Tahir was whipped to action by the flash of anger in Babur's gaze alone, searching through the pile of clothes in the corner. His fingers were deft, spilling a shower of clothing right and left, and retrieving one ragged robe rolled into a ball the size of a watermelon. He was quick to unroll this ball of a robe, revealing a wooden bowl, all cracked and shapeless.

"Padishah." Tahir held out the robe and the bowl, his look still glazed and uncomprehending. "This robe was worn by a Kalendar, my baba told me. This bowl belongs to the same holy man too, who—" He could not continue as Babur snatched the proffered articles and turned to his heels, only his laughter trailing behind over his shoulders.

Galloping toward the valley of Darium like a hooded thief, Babur was exhilarated by the novelty of his caprice and freedom. Each muscle on his face was tingling with pleasure by the whiffs of night air, cool and fresh, but he was pulling the hood over his face to conceal his identity. He was inhaling deeply the scents of the earth and the pines, his thoughts trying to explore the *feeling* of pain-bliss and pain-sweetness. The moon was caught in a coronet of stars, diamond-bright and sparkling. His gaze was skidding ahead over the purplish hills, at the foot of which the tents of the Yusufzais were pitched, as his spies had informed him earlier. His thoughts were clear, and his imagination vivid as he approached closer, coaxing his steed diligently and cautiously. The hazy glow from bonfires down below was becoming visible, and he dismounted briskly, stroking the white mane of his horse fondly before tethering it to one poplar.

Gathering his coarse robe around his waist, and tucking his beggar's bowl in the crook of his arm, Babur proceeded down the slope, looking exactly like a beggar, bent double against the pangs of hunger and deprivation. And yet, within him was surging a fountain of joy so wild that he could barely breathe, as if his heart would explode on the brink of rapture and surcease. Surfing on the waters of agony and elation, he seemed to be sailing toward the stars, but his feet were grounded before one large tent hosting a bonfire, upon which sizzled mutton legs strewn on crude spits, almost roasted for a great feast. He was hungry all of a sudden, but this hunger had nothing to do with food, this was the hunger of the soul. The parched, savage hunger of the soul awakening to the pangs of spiritual longings, to die for a glimpse of *beauty and beloved*!

They are prolonging the feast of the Ramadan, I presume? Babur was searching for a suitable spot to watch the inveterate rebels, and to snatch a few nuggets of information from their conversations. His gaze was catching the frolic-dance of feasting inside the white tent, furnished with yak wool rugs and candelabras polished and gleaming. The men with caps and vests embedded with tiny mirrors, and the women in colorful silks were absorbing his attention. He was about to turn when a familiar voice grazing his awareness was making him search the owner of that voice. His gaze was gathering more than he had hoped for, or imagined.

The leader of the Yusufzais clan, Shah Mansur, tall and handsome, could not be mistaken for any other. He was talking with his brother, Malik Ahmed, whom Babur had recently forgiven for his misdeeds, his generosity extending as far as bestowing upon him a perghana, and trusting him for his oaths of loyalty and obedience. Many more faithless rebels were falling under his gaze, the most prominent amongst them, Dost Beg, Muhammed Ali, Baba Cochi and Dingdong. He was averting his gaze, and assuming the humility of a lowly beggar as he noticed one young Pathan swaying toward him under some weight of hilarity. The tiny mirrors on his cap and vest were reflecting their mirth as he approached closer, tossing a chunk of roasted mutton wrapped in flat bread into the begging bowl of Babur, and laughing.

"You are lucky, fakir!" Was the young man's inebriated exclamation! "Bibi Mubaraka herself sent you these victuals. A houri, she is, fair and beautiful!"

"Houris dwell in heaven, my friend!" Babur chewed on one large morsel, smacking his lips, and watching the drunken lout with covert amusement.

"Fakirs are such simpletons, satisfied with crumbs, and blind to the beauty of the world!" The fair youth roared besottedly. "Bibi Mubaraka is the houri of this earth, adored by all. Especially by her father Shah Mansur, since she is the youngest of his daughters!"

Babur stood biting on his share of food with affected greed and hunger, his senses alert and vigilant to catch each word or gesture from the lips of this young man, so deliciously drunk and callow.

"Bibi Mubaraka is not only beautiful, but has a kind and generous heart too!" The young man continued; his look glazed and happy. "She took pity on you, wrapped this meat in bread with her lovely hands, bidding me to feed the starving fakir?"

"Could I see her from here?" Babur murmured, hoping to keep the youth talking, and divulging if possible. "Could you point her to me, I would like to thank her for her generosity."

The young man tried to focus his attention on Babur, and then turned his head, his gaze searching for the houri of the earth amidst the glitter of silks, jewels and brocades gracing the lovely forms of the ladies.

"There she is!" The young man exclaimed suddenly, his whole form transfixed. "The one in the blue dress, diamonds sparkling in her ears and around her throat! Can't you see, she is talking to her father?" He was drifting back toward the tent, oblivious to the silent torment of the beggar, who stood there stunned, dazzled.

It couldn't be true, if only my heart could cease its thundering? Babur could not tear his gaze away from the apparition named, Bibi Mubaraka. *Zainab incarnate, born again? Living, breathing, laughing!* The mad, shattering pain of loss and grief buried deep within him was wrenched free in his soul, spewing bolts of lightning and swirling with the violence of a thunderstorm. *A miracle sublime, sweet absent has come back? Beloved, my sweetness all!* He could feel his soul sobbing, something inside him was splintering, lacerating. *My love eternal, my bride everlasting has returned, I would not ever lose her again.* Stricken with madness he wanted to snatch her into his arms, but the serpent of propriety in his head was wagging its lethal tongue, warning him of his folly and indiscretion. The sting of agony in his soul was goading him to possess the jewel of his desire, but the wound of sanity in his head was bleeding, seeping down to the very soles of his feet, and urging him to flee, to think, to seek reason.

Delirious with pain and longing, Babur had returned to his lone steed, oblivious to the moon shadows lapping after him, sad and receding. He had forgotten why he had come to the valley of Darium, but he had not forgotten the gift of hope in his begging bowl. Before mounting his horse, he pressed the last morsel to his lips as if tasting the bread of life, and consecrating the food of love. He was drunk with the soma of love and agony, worshiping the very morsel in his hand which *her* sweet hands had touched and blessed. Pulling the hood over his head and saving the *bread of life* in the pouch of his robe, Babur was riding back like a pilgrim lost who had forgotten his self and surroundings in this wilderness of time and timelessness.

Time itself, in fact, had slipped out of proportion as he left the purplish hills behind, finding himself seated on a boulder not far from his palace, his horse grazing indifferently. He was trying to splinter the joy-shock of his experience with thoughts feverish and bewitched, and succeeding only in beholding Zainab being transformed into Bibi Mubaraka. The diamond stars and the dark woods were whispering to him the secrets of the heavens, and yet the pit of grief and anguish within him were pleading for rest and sanity. His gaze was reaching up to the livid moon, snatching one reflection of a word, *Yusufzais*, which was etched there like a brand of destiny, illumined and scalding. By punishing Yusufzais, he had earned the hatred of his one and only beloved, Zainab, and now Bibi Mubaraka? One cry of agony ripped from his soul, cutting the stillness of the night to blades of derision. The cold stars were blazing all of a sudden, he thought, raining coals over his flesh with the fury of a vengeance savage and nameless.

No, I must not repeat my follies. I must make peace with Yusufzais. Sweet Zainab has come back! Bibi Mubaraka, Beloved! One life, one soul, one memory great, ineffable and everlasting! I must remold, cherish, possess. Madness had left Babur, he was enveloped by an astonishing sense of bliss and misery, feeling wretchedly alive and hugging the blows of his mute suffering with joy and gloating. Anguish was no more, and yet the mists of pain and tragedy from the tombs of the past were cradling him with such tender solicitude that he didn't even notice the approach of Khwaja Kilan until he fell to his knees at his feet, murmuring, *Padishah.*

"What mad whim of yours compels you to address a lowly beggar with the title of, Padishah?" Was Babur's comment out of the clouds of his mystic reveries!

"Padishah." Khwaja Kilan murmured again, his look wild and pleading. "Alas, gone are the days when I could keep you under the mantle of my guidance and protection! You were a young prince then, but now Padishah. Your vagaries, Padishah, if I may be as bold as to say, would not only endanger your life, but the safety of your kingdom?" He sat nursing his knee, his gaze still pleading.

"You worry needlessly, Khwaja." Babur smiled. "Padishah went spying over Yusufzais. I didn't go courting danger or entertainment, if that's what your fear?" He heaved himself to his feet, his gaze dreamy and wistful.

"You are planning a siege then down the valley of Darium, where all the leaders of Yusufzais are gathered?" Khwaja Kilan murmured to himself, getting to his feet laboriously.

"No." Babur averted his gaze, whistling for his horse. "I would sign a peace treaty with the Yusufzais. I want to marry the daughter of Shah Mansur, tomorrow at the latest." He stood stroking the white mane of his horse, who had obeyed his summons promptly.

"Padishah!" Was Khwaja Kilan's stunned response, his hands in an act of nursing his knee falling limp to his sides!

"You have the honor of being my messenger, suing for the hand of Shah Mansur's daughter in marriage to Padishah." Babur mounted his horse, not meeting the gaze of his mentor. "Consider this my holy Farman. You might as well start right now, and return to me posthaste—with bride-to-be." He was flying toward his palace, his heart a cauldron of joy-misery, he could neither dispel, nor contain.

21

Afghan Lady

Now I know what love is.
— Virgil

The mid-afternoon sun under its canopy of gold appeared to be taking a siesta, as Babur emerged out of his garden out onto the vast field where Ali Kuli was working on the Victory Gun. His robe was the color of violet hills in the distance, and his thoughts as light as the matching plume in his turban, welcoming the sun-spangled vistas with the sense of joy and freedom. To his right were the groves of spruces and poplars. The emerald valley curving down the slope was luring his attention toward Mustafa Khan who was immersed deep in testing a set of mobile culverins, but Babur's, feet were obeying the commands of his mind. Stepping ahead of his thoughts in the direction of his master-gunner! Intoxicated by the scented blooms in his garden, he was carrying the scent of hope and anticipation, holding and beholding the beauty of his newly born beloved in each pulse of color and sunlight. Some sort of sun-spangled dance in his head was cradling Bibi Mubaraka in its aura of ache and tenderness.

Early in the morning, Khwaja Kilan was sent posthaste with all necessary gifts and instructions to win the hand of Shah Mansur's daughter to be wedded to Padishah. In fact, he was commanded to fetch the intended bride to Kabul without delay, so that the Padishah could be married before sundown.

What do I see in this shuddering disk of a sun, joy and fulfillment, then pain and banishment? The sky was spilling gold, and reflected in there were Babur's contemplations. But his thoughts were swirling over the Mahara Hill, then swooping down the valley where the palace of Shah Mansur stood gleaming by the very virtue of its fair occupant—Bibi Mubaraka. With this lone thought hovering over the hills, Babur's heart was suspended over some ocean of sadness so abysmal that his whole being was sucked into the ether of ache and longing, vast and nameless. He would have remained in this state of dull vacuity, had the loud shot from the cannon not jolted him out of his inertia on the brink of oblivion. He could see the cannon ball hitting the intended target before exploding into a cloud of smoke and cinders. The odor of gun-powder hung heavy in the air as Babur stole behind the master-gunner, who, it was obvious, was overwhelmed by his success, and had turned into a statue of immobility.

"This brilliant shot, so precise and affective, is worth a silk robe and one hundred ashrafis, and you have earned these by the virtue of your ingenuity." Babur's generous praise startled Ali Kuli, as he whirled around, curtsying.

"Padishah! One shot from the cannon, and no one from the clan of Yusufzais would ever dare rebel!" Ali Kuli beamed with joy and pride.

"No guns have the power to dissolve the forces of evil and malice inside the hearts of men, least of all the fires of rebellion?" Babur laughed, dispelling his sadness with rills of hopes and dreams. "Your cannon have much noble service to render yet amidst threats of wars and insurrections. Kabul longs for peace, its land much sacred to be violated with guns and cannons. Kabul is the Jerusalem of all sects and faiths! More like a shrine of love, striving toward nurturing the kernels of beauty and harmony. The warring dust in Hind needs to be settled and your cannon might accomplish the task of creating order out of chaos?" He turned to his heels abruptly, retracing his steps, leaving Ali Kuli standing there mute and bewildered.

Babur was vaguely aware of the gardeners working in the orchards of pear, peach loquat and apricot as he piloted his way through the narrow paths, inhaling deeply the scent of the earth and ranunculus. His thoughts were feverish and restless, visiting the tomb of his dead *beloved. Desecrating the shrine of love, embracing the sweet absent, and kissing the lips of great memory*—he was thinking. The pomegranates sparkling like jewels on the trees were luring his attention, but his feet had a mission of their own, aiming toward the fretted slats and marble thrones over which the fountains rippled and gurgled. To his right were pavilions open and lofty, splashed with colors from coxcomb, larkspur, campanula and amaranthus, all inviting him to pause and rest, but his gaze had chosen the marble terrace in front as his abode of solitude. Overlooking the terrace were roses as big as the sun-disks, their scented beauty claiming Babur's attention, rather filling his heart with awe and surrender. So utterly beguiled was Babur by his sense of wonder and tranquility that he didn't notice the stealthy approach of Khwaja Kilan until his voice penetrated his pool of serendipity. Turning abruptly, he almost collided with his mentor, his gaze searching the wearied expression of Khwaja Kilan.

"Come out with it, Khwaja, what does my future father-in-law demand?" Babur's look was piercing, his thoughts raging and somersaulting. "A traitor and a hypocrite!"

"Padishah." Khwaja Kilan murmured, curtsying. "Shah Mansur objects to this alliance on the grounds that the daughters of Yusufzais married to Ulugh Beg and Thin Lord—your uncles, were unhappy marriages. Besides, he says, Bibi Mubaraka is already betrothed to one wealthy Khan, and regrets that—"

"Regrets!" Babur's eyes were kindling sparks of rage and impatience, his thoughts snatching one fragment of his ghazal and pouring disdain.

"Ulugh Beg, the ocean of science and learning
Who was the protector of this lower world
Drank from Abbas the honey of martyrdom

Shah Mansur! The malefic liar, how he forgets that the daughters of Yusufzais were treated with utmost respect? They lived like the queens—of fortune! He dares tarnish the memory of fame, glory and wisdom? Ride back, Khwaja, and tell that lizard of a rebel that Padishah would efface the very name Yusufzais from the pages of history, if he honors not my command to marry his daughter. And a command, it is!"

"Padishah!" Khwaja Kilan could barely murmur, dwindling against the blaze of rage in Babur's eyes.

"Better yet, kill that lout of a wealthy Khan, and fetch me my bride!" Fever and madness in Babur's thoughts were flashing through his eyes, his gaze unseeing. "Yes, you are commanded to bring Bibi Mubaraka this very evening, otherwise, the whole horde of Yusufzais would never see the dawn of another day. This is your message from Padishah to the maggot of the mountains." He turned to his heels, leaving behind the stunned messenger who had no choice but to carry the burden of this threat back to the door of Shah Mansur.

An early dusk with its haze of gloom was flooding the library where Babur had paced for hours, dousing the fire in his soul with thoughts liquid and quicksilver. But now he was seated at his desk, looking out of the window, the book of Faizi's odes before him neglected and forgotten. The chased gold flagon of wine was within his reach, but that too lay there neglected, unable to penetrate the dark sea of his contemplations. His thoughts were cutting darkness inside his soul and psyche with the blade of agony mute and naked. Sweet Absent was with him, a throbbing wound of loss and grief, and yet fate had molded that wound into a flower of joy and hope—Sweet Absent had returned in the form of Bibi Mubaraka. The wait was intolerable, his hand reaching for a ball of majun in the silver bowl, and his thoughts waving pennants of fear that he would surely die if he couldn't reclaim his gift of love in the form of Bibi Mubaraka. *Better yet, kill that lout of a wealthy Khan*—his mind was polishing the blades of derision with such abrupt zeal that the sea of darkness within him was splintered into knives of pain and contrition.

Oh, my Creator! I have tyrannized over my soul, and if Thou art not bountiful to me, of a truth I shall be numbered amongst the accursed. The violence of his inner guilt and agony was so stark and savage that his very soul could be heard pleading with age-old wound of his loss and grief which felt so alive and lacerating. He thought he could hear the gong of destiny, sounding its alarm, mocking the face of fate, drumming the drum of paradox.

How I have lived? What I lost and what I conquered? What would I find, how, when, where? What is this Great Love, grieving and exulting, mourning and rejoicing? Is it Zainab, lending breath of life to the hope in living? What is this hunger inside me, this violence inconsolable? Could love penetrate the depths of truth? Could truth separate the waters of joy and grief? Truth, love, beloved, the pulse of time and illusion!

The mystic in Babur was awakening to the need of guidance, snatching the book of odes from his desk, and flitting through its pages reverently.

Oh, Thou who existest from eternity and abidest forever
Sight cannot bear Thy light, praise cannot express Thy perfection
The light melts the understanding, and Thy glory baffles wisdom
To think of Thee destroys reason, Thy essence confounds thought
Science is like blinding desert and sand on the road to Thy perfection
The town of literature is a mere hamlet compared with the word of Thy
knowledge
Human knowledge and thought combined can only spell
The first letter of the alphabet of Thy love

The ache and longing in Babur's heart was goading him to read more odes and explore the mind of Faizi.

Thy fame contains the image of the heavenly and lower regions
Be either heavenly or earthly, Thou art at liberty to choose
Do not act against thy reason, for it is a trustworthy counselor
Put not thy heart on illusions, for heart is a lying fool
Be ashamed of thy appearance, for thou pridest thyself
On the title of, sum-total, and art yet a marginal note
If thou wishest to understand secret meaning of the phrase
To prefer the welfare of others to thy own
Treat thyself with poison and others with sugar

He sighed to himself! Flitting the pages randomly, and arresting wherever his gaze rested and lingered.

The companion of my loneliness is my comprehensive genius
The scratching of my pen is harmony for my ear
If I were to bring forth what is in my mind
I wonder whether the spirit of age could bear it

A mantle of sadness was lowered over Babur's shoulders as he sought more words, gleaning no consolations.

It were better if I melted my heart, and laid the foundation for a new one
I have too often patiently patched my torn heart
I cannot show ungratefulness to Love
Has he not overwhelmed me—sadness and sadness
I cannot understand the juggler-trick which love performed
It introduced Thy form through so small an aperture as the pupil of my eye
Into the large space of my heart, and yet my heart cannot contain it

Babur's very heart was donning the mantle of sadness, but the ocean of agony in there was hushed, as if aghast, dazzled? Dazzled by the magic of music from within, some melodies sweet and familiar, striking the tunes of wedding songs, the lover greeting the beloved and the bride united with the bridegroom. An astonishing sense of bliss was seething in the very fabric of his soul and psyche, his face transfigured with joy, and yet his heart was shuddering against the tempo of rapture deep and inexpressible. His gaze had caught the glimpse of destiny, and the music which he thought was from within his soul was actually throbbing over his lawn below his window, where the wedding procession of the Yusufzais rippled with songs and lights.

Leaping to his feet against the magic of the evening, Babur sank back into his seat, his gaze holding dear the feast of sounds and colors. The musicians with their lutes and flutes were pouring down the notes of a lovelorn, while trumpets in the background were asserting their rhythm on the brink of explosion. A group of machalchis with their torches raised high were ahead of the procession, while the Afghans behind them twirled their bhutans and swirled. Men in colorful turbans were balancing a palanquin over their shoulders, all brocaded and garlanded. The women in long skirts stitched with tiny mirrors had begun to clap, while the palanquin was being lowered, concealing the bride of Padishah. Padishah, this precise moment, was turned into a heap of awe and wonder, as if witnessing the purity of love in the breast of Adam when he had gazed upon the nakedness of Eve before his expulsion from the Garden. That's how he was feeling, a great surge of awe and exaltation before the ultimate Fall, ordained and inevitable, his thoughts were whistling a litany of aphorisms. So abysmally absorbed he was inside the honeycomb of his emotions and so magnificently alienated from the marshland of reality that his senses were utterly at rest, neither witnessing the unfolding of scenes down below, nor admitting any sounds until Khwaja Kilan's voice jolted him out of his restful state of bliss-oblivion.

"Padishah, your bride awaits your pleasure." Khwaja Kilan announced, trying to slough off his burden of duty and fatigue.

"Welcome, my friend!" Babur leaped to his feet, his gaze dreamy and ardent. "My sage, my patron saint! You have made me so happy, I am grateful." He locked him into one fervent embrace, and then stood back, laughing. "Ask of any boon, my friend, and it would not be denied."

"Too wearied to think of any right now, Padishah!" Khwaja Kilan smiled. "But I may need it as a ransom for something in the future."

"If I were as wise as you, Khwaja, I would not leave the boon waiting to the whims of future." Babur smiled in return, his heart thundering. "Thank you again, my friend and mentor. I would like to hear the success story in the morning. Right now my longing is greater than my curiosity." He waved dismissal.

The phantasmagoric evening with its promise of joy and consummation had finally struck the gong of reality as Babur stepped into his royal chamber. His gaze was reaching the canopied bed where he expected his bride to be seated against the satiny pillows as was customary. But she had chosen to stand by the bed, much like a white apparition against the glow of the candles burning low in the silver candelabras. Her eyes were closed, and her face appeared to be molded alive in ivory as she stood in perfect immobility. *Some celestial crea-*

ture, not of this world, Babur was thinking, unable to move or speak. She was wearing a gold dress broidered with vines and flowers. It fell at her feet in shimmering folds, lending her the semblance of a statue of gold and ivory, since she seemed not to breathe, enveloped in some mist of peace and purity.

Babur's heart, lurching and somersaulting, was holding him prisoner in one spot, only his thoughts flying and hovering over the odyssey of the Greek gods and goddesses. *The noble Penelope, or beautiful Helen, but she is Zainab, Sweet Absent has come back,* Babur's thoughts were goading him to claim his Beloved.

"Love, Beloved, my child of the mountains." Babur swayed toward her as if drunk, the violence of desire in him sharp and lacerating. "You have cast a spell over me, my beauty! Open your eyes, and break this enchantment."

"Padishah." Bibi Mubaraka's eyes were fluttered open, though she lowered her gaze, shielded by eyelashes, amber and silken. "This mountain child desires a boon, which would break this enchantment. The Yusufzais seek your pardon, Padishah. The flowers on my dress represent their love and oaths of fidelity."

The voice is that of Zainab! Yes, sweet Zainab has returned. Babur drifted toward her like one moth to a flame, the fever of longings inside him reaching to his eyes and blinding his sight. He was aware only of the blaze of hunger and passion inside him, parched and maddening.

"My love, I would pardon the whole world, if I could beg a few crumbs of love from you in return?" Babur slipped his arms around her waist, and was suspended there as if stung to the very cores of his sanity and madness.

A pair of blue eyes, most beautiful and dazzling, had impaled him alive in his act of embracing his *beloved*, while his own were searching the emerald depths in the eyes of *sweet absent*. His eyes were closing, as if lowering the shutters of prayers over the tomb of loss and grief. *The mockery of fate!* Something inside him was wading through the ocean of agony, while he was being sucked into the voids of death and living torment.

"Are you ill, Padishah? Have I offended you by requesting pardon—" A cry of despair ripped through Bibi Mubaraka's heart, choking her thoughts, and jolting Babur to awareness.

"No, my love! A thousand times, no!" Babur folded her in one crushing embrace, his heart carving fresh wounds of love and agony.

The animal passion of a man gone stark mad had possessed Babur while consummating this marriage, but afterwards he had held her close to him most reverently, murmuring endearments. His thoughts too, humbled by the flood of pain and rapture, had lulled him to sleep, choosing one dark spot for silent contemplation. *What is love? It is pain? Or agony! Could be despair—and hatred? Hopelessness all! Certainly not true and absolutely unfathomable?* He had possessed Zainab, not Bibi Mubaraka, yet love had possessed him—entirely.

22

Naming of a Prince

Love is a canvas furnished by nature and embroidered by imagination.
— Voltaire

The city of Bajuar, hemmed in by the borders of Hind and Kabul, was the abode of Bibi Mubaraka this sultry afternoon. Babur had conquered this city, bestowing it upon Khwaja Kilan before taking him along for further conquests. Dreamy and listless, Bibi Mubaraka was trying to woo the comforts of a siesta, but the odor of dust and heat was keeping her awake. The canopy of lace over her four-poster bed and linen sheets under her were offering her a little comfort, her thoughts finding refuge in the shaded glens of Kabul and drinking perfume from the goblets of wild flowers.

A tapestry of joys was unfolding in Bibi Mubaraka's head, colors blending into days of enchantment with Babur, and enchantment turning into sparkling gems of bliss supreme, a rosary of sweet moments lapping after months—seasons. And yet, that fabric of joy and bliss was concealing the knots of pain and bewilderment. She was startled by her dreamy thoughts, holding them in comparison with the cotton-silk trees down the window of her bedroom. Envisioning the beauty of the deep scarlet blooms, against which the ugliness of sun-scorched land could be blissfully forgotten. She could feel one flicker of a smile upon her lips at this sudden revelation, her thoughts reaching out to Babur in an effort to explore the mysterious blooms of love and longings. Time could be seen flapping its wings under the closed shutters of her eyes, flashing the brief span of her wedded life in a collage almost ethereal and gossamer.

Her thoughts were transparent and swirling, baffled by the wild passion of her poet-husband—his passion, so wild and intoxicating. Those thoughts themselves bewildered by the power of his great love, which appeared to devour her body and soul, still hungering for more, for something profounder than life and beauty. She had fallen in love with the poet, the mystic—not Padishah, cherishing the *mystery and the mysterious* in love and surrender. At times, she was saddened by his moods, whims and appetites, which would come hovering over him like the dark clouds, shrouding him in mists of needs nameless, larger than ambition, conquest or subjugation. Endowed with the spirit of light-hearted gaiety, she had been successful so far in dispelling those dark clouds, but lacking the perception to explore his need for gains and possessions. Now as she lay supine on her bed in her pale muslin gown, her bare arms moist and her thoughts liquid, one hot spark of a revelation was throwing open the gates of her perception.

My poet-mystic of a husband, is he suffering? Some sort of inner conflict where my love can't reach or appease? The violence of his passion, the mingling of love-hate, as if he hates me! No! His love for me is pure and boundless! Strange and possessive, worrying about my health, safety, comfort! Becoming impatient and restless when I am gone even just for a few hours. Courting fear and despair when he has to go on campaigns without me, afraid that somehow he would lose me? And yet, he is driven by the very hands of fate, by the rod of his need-ambition to conquer the world? Exposing his life to danger, challenging fate, wooing death? No, that is not true! He loves life as much as I do, loving laughter and sunshine. Mahim, Gulrukh, Dildar, Nurgul, Gulnar, all jealous of our great love, and yet they are all kind, even loving. Poor, Mahim, always missing Humayun and longing to be with him! The daughters of Padishah, Masuma, Gulrang, Gulchihra, so very adorable! Padishah's sons, Askeri and Kamran, gallant and handsome. My baba and uncle have made a covenant of peace with Padishah. Great conquests of Padishah, Kandahar, Bajuar, Bhira, Parhalech! Where is Padishah now, what is he doing? Bibi Mubaraka was drifting into the bowers of sleep, her fingers teasing the large diamond on her ring finger as if looking into the face of a crystal ball to dissolve the gulf of separation between her and Babur.

Babur's lonesome abode this evening was the city of Chandawal which he had conquered this very afternoon. His royal tent was pitched at the slope of the hills, while the tents of his army were scattered below, guarding artillery and ammunition. The early shadows of the evening aglow with violet dusk had lured Babur toward his tent, whipped by his need to court solitude, while the others were still drinking and feasting to celebrate the victory over Chandawal.

Sitting couchant against one crimson pillow, Babur had been writing since hours, and of course drinking, the gold flagon perched right beside him on the Persian carpet his boon companion. The gold-sprinkled papers were scattered all around him, upon which he had written the details of the conquest, interspersed with couplets and comments. He could feel a whiff of cold breeze before the flickering of candles attracted his attention, his heart longing for the nearness of Bibi Mubaraka. His gaze was tracing the names of Khwaja Kilan, Shah Mansur and Malik Ahmed which he had just scribbled as a prelude to further entries, but his thoughts were skirling high, matching an abrupt stab of agony-violence within him for the offense of separation from his beloved.

The Afghan Lady, as Babur called Bibi Mubaraka, had become the altar of his pain-love, painfully sublime, and exquisitely painful. He was carrying this altar within him as some canker of love-hate, hugging the mockery of fate in the realm of love irretrievable and love unconquerable. He had fallen in love again, with Zainab—the Afghan Lady. Sweet Absent was snatched out of her cold tomb, transformed into the mountain-bride, carving rills of hatred within him which he had not ever known before, and becoming his everlasting torment. One imperceptible shudder shook Babur's frame at the inception of such thoughts, and he dipped his reed pen in the inkpot. This jade inkpot itself appeared to be mocking his thoughts, rather infusing the fever of memories long buried and banished.

What did I tell Zainab once which made her blush with shame and chagrin? Wonder, if she truly hated me all those years? Did I say I could not hate anyone, not even an enemy? And now this blister of hate! This canker of love, my searing, scalding passion! Madness and sadness! Love and pain, this paradox, something inside me corrupted and corrupting? Bride and beloved, sweet absent and sweet present, are they not one and the same, kneaded from the dough of affliction, adorably near, dearly inseparable? A familiar sense of ache and longing was cutting through Babur's thoughts with a razor-sharp swiftness, and he abandoned his pen, his gaze falling on the couplet he had written this afternoon. He snatched this paper out of the clutter, his other hand reaching for his wine goblet, but he was distracted by the breezy approach of Khwaja Kilan. Khwaja Kilan was quick to install himself opposite him unceremoniously, since court etiquettes were not practiced during the times of wars and campaigns.

"Ah, read this couplet aloud to me, my friend!" Babur held out the paper to his mentor. "Your rich voice would lend it life and passion."

"Do I have to, Padishah?" Khwaja Kilan claimed it reverently, his gaze already absorbing its essence before he began to recite.

"Say sweetly O breeze to that beautiful fawn
Thou hast given my head to the hills and the wilds."

"Splendid, Khwaja!" Babur applauded. "Now fold it carefully. Keep it safe in the pouch of your robe, and then fly to Bajuar on the fleetest of mounts you could choose. Read this couplet to Bibi Mubaraka Begum with the same passion as you did just now. You are to be her escort, bringing her back with you, this very evening!"

"Padishah!" Khwaja Kilan exclaimed. Disbelief shining in his eyes! His hands fumbling for a sealed envelope which he had just received from a messenger from Kabul! "A letter from Mahim Begum—I meant to deliver it as soon as I came in?"

"Your wisdom is your enemy, Khwaja." Babur's look was thoughtful and piercing. "If I were you I would not wish to ignore the commands of Padishah?" He claimed the letter held out to him, tossing it aside. "You might as well start right now, and you would be back before I finish reading this letter? *A foolish command*, I know what you are thinking. Ah, but if you ever loved as I do! Love is madness of course, yet it is a noble madness, making one bold and reckless. Sanity, on the other hand, is surrounded by fears, making one dumb and cowardly. And yet again, my thoughts are driving me insane, if not the cries of longing and loneliness?"

"This hour of the night, Padishah!" Khwaja Kilan began cautiously. "How would I be able to protect Bibi Mubaraka Begum against the bands of bandits, who spare neither man, nor beast? Besides, these hills and plains are infested with rebels and robbers alike, waiting for any opportunity to kill and plunder."

"So, Padishah is doomed to imprisonment in his royal tent?" Babur exclaimed, infusing a spark of cheerfulness in his voice and manner. "I neither can court solitude, nor have the pleasure of my beloved beside me. What I must not do, I would, drink myself to oblivion." He procured another gold cup from behind his pillow, his hand reaching for the gold flagon.

"You could read the letter of Mahim Begum, Padishah, it might unleash a string of diversions?" Khwaja Kilan heaved a sigh of relief, claiming eagerly the gold cup brimming with wine.

"Night is too young to be despoiled by wives' tales." Babur quaffed his wine thirstily. "Let's talk about the conquests and the treasures which we amassed. And yet, if wars were fought within the hearts rather than on the battlefields, there would be no bloodshed. Wounded hearts of course, which could be consoled and bandaged without the loss of limbs or lives? How many of our men succumbed to death and how many to disease?"

"We lost a few hundred of our soldiers, but the losses on enemy's side outnumber ours." Khwaja Kilan's voice was low and distant. "Dost Beg, along with a dozen of his companions died of burning fever." He couldn't continue against the sudden flaring of sadness and compassion in Babur's eyes.

"Who are the friends and who the enemies?" Babur demurred aloud. "Foes and friends, all enemies to themselves and to many countless others. The imponderables beyond thought and imagination! And yet we value the booties and the treasures. All the gold, rubies, ashrafis and diamonds! The treasury of Kabul would be replenished for one whole year before we return to conquer Hind. The streets of Hind are paved with gold, I hear, its silks and spices most rare and exotic, and a wealth of gods and goddesses. What do you say, Khwaja, if we scatter our rich booty to the winds, and let the people of Chandawal gather what they may? We would return to Kabul as beggars!" The tinkling of mirth in his eyes landed on his lips in a gale of laughter.

"Beggars are not welcome in Kabul, Padishah!" Khwaja Kilan resorted to mirth and raillery. "Disguised as a beggar, you earned nothing but dry mutton wrapped in stale bread, not to mention a scornful rejection from Shah Mansur."

"Don't gloat over your dry wit, Khwaja, or you would be hoisted on a windhorse to Bajaur this very night?" Babur retorted, his thoughts dissolving the gulf of separation from his beloved with the rod of ambition. "Ali Kuli's cannons and Mustafa Khan's culverins are our riches not to be despised by any lords proud or rebellious. The power of such riches has gained us the kingdoms of Bhira, Bajuar, Kandahar, Pharhalech and Chandawal. Now we return to Kabul with all the treasures, but first I would reclaim the most precious of my treasures at Bajuar, early at dawn!" His eyes were lit up with stars of tenderness at the mere thought of Afghan Lady.

"Your victorious return to Kabul, Padishah, would be rewarded with more joys if you could tell Mahim Begum that you read her letter?" Khwaja Kilan ventured, more so to divert Babur's attention from dreaming than to satisfy his curiosity.

"Such persistence, Khwaja! I know you favor Mahim over all the rest of my wives, but still? But I would read, and yet?" Babur's hand reached for the neglected envelope, claiming absently one of his folded papers upon which he had scribbled a verse. "Mahim is superstitious, and I fear her influence is already turning Humayun into a superstitious dolt? Hoping, this is only my fear, or perception. He is valorous, nurtures his intellect with knowledge, and is loving and compassionate." His fingers appeared to be unsealing the note which he had mistakenly claimed as Mahim's letter. "I am guilty of favoring Mahim in her superstitions at times just to make her happy. Though I detest superstition as much as bigotry! And yet, Mahim's superstitions are more like whims, innocent and harmless, and I am accustomed to satisfying each little whim of hers with curiosity and indulgence." He laughed, noticing his own scribbled note in his hand than Mahim's letter.

"Oh, Allah, kingship is thine alone
Thine to give when thou pleasest
Thine to take away at thy pleasure."

Babur recited aloud, retrieving Mahim's letter laughingly. He unsealed it impatiently, and was quickly absorbed in reading, his features suffused with the glow of joy and amusement. A beatific smile was curling upon his lips as he sat absorbed in the contents of the letter he had postponed reading. With a boyish toss of his head, he lifted his eyes, dreamy and wistful.

"Bless you, Khwaja, though you didn't succeed in goading me to read this letter sooner!" Babur teased. "Dildar Begum's time of delivery is approaching sooner that expected. Mahim Begum predicts that the baby is going to be a boy. Why not a girl, if one may ask, but listen to this—her whim or superstition, she wants me to choose a name for the prince before he is born? No wars to fight this night, and no music to appease my longings, so we would spend this night choosing a name for the unborn prince. Not any ordinary name, mind you, but a propitious one as Mahim requests. Do you still remember that game of choosing names our ancestors practiced so diligently?"

"How could I forget, Padishah, since I was the one reviving it for your indulgence or amusement." Khwaja Kilan responded cheerfully. "I would whip up as many names as you desire."

"As many as you could whip up till the break of dawn!" Babur challenged. "A handful would be enough if they could be worthy of consideration?"

"Akbar, Anwar, Javed, Hindal, Jamshed." Khwaja Kilan spewed forth a few, concentrating to gather a battalion worthy of praise and admiration.

"Your fingers won't be as swift as your thoughts, once you begin the task of writing?" Babur held out a sheaf of gold-sprinkled paper to him. "To begin with, you need to tear each paper into little squares, one for each name, filling a bowl with water shouldn't be difficult, but kneading little balls out of wet clay might require skill? You are entrusted with this whole task of choosing a noble name. I would rest meanwhile, and if we are lucky a name would surface before dawn?" He slipped a pillow under his head, longing for rest and for the nearness of his beloved.

Khwaja Kilan, grateful of the task at hand since he was spared of the night journey to Bajuar, was quick to perform his duty to the best of his abilities. With utmost caution so as not to disturb Padishah, he had worked diligently, cutting the paper, writing the names, and folding each paper into four-fold creases. A glass-bowl which he was looking for, he had espied in the corner of the royal tent! It was already filled with water for Babur's personal use, and he had slipped out toward the rear pond to fetch the wet clay. Most of his time was spent in wrapping each square of paper into wet clay and kneading it into a ball. Finally, he had managed to drop the clay balls into the bowl of water noise-lessly, and had placed it at a spot from where Babur could see it as soon as he opened his eyes.

Outside the royal tent, the night itself appeared to be sleeping under the canopy of stars. Khwaja Kilan's eyelids were getting heavy, but he sat vigilant, fascinated by the tenacity of clear water, slowly turning murky while holding the clay balls at the bottom. Suddenly, the clay balls were surrendering to the pressure of disintegration. One muddied square had found release and was wading its way to the surface. So absorbed was Khwaja Kilan in watching this lone square that he didn't know Babur too was watching until his hand reached the murky waters, snatching the first tiny square before others could follow.

"A miracle, Khwaja, and it is not even dawn yet!" Babur exclaimed, unfolding the square reverently.

"I didn't knead the clay properly, it shouldn't dissolve so quickly." Khwaja Kilan sat lamenting to himself.

"Stop fretting, Khwaja. This paper itself has the scent of rain and fecundity. Wafting forth the perfume, promise of birth and renewal." Babur unfolded the paper, reading aloud the name. "Hindal, yes, Hindal it is. One fortune of a name, Khwaja, and you would be rewarded generously by Mahim Begum."

"Hindal, meaning, the giver of Hind!" Khwaja Kilan sang happily. "A propitious sign for Padishah, for his future conquests!" His heart was sinking all of a sudden, his thoughts gathering gloom and weariness.

"I would save this paper as a souvenir for Mahim, a gift she would love more than any jewels rare or precious." Babur folded the paper into its original creases, completely immersed in his act of folding and thinking. Suddenly, he looked up, his gaze profound and piercing. "What gloom sits on your brow, Khwaja?"

"Age itself sits heavy as gloom on a person's face, Padishah, no matter how happy one feels." Khwaja Kilan smiled. "I am growing old—I am old. Too old to travel, I guess."

"*Ripe age is the garden of wisdom, and wisdom remains young forever*, didn't you tell me that when I was a young prince?" Babur ruminated aloud, his look opiate and profound. "A decade or so separates us in years, Khwaja." He was seeking the comfort of his pillow once again. "If you were to grow old, I would not be far behind. And yet I would never grow old, then how could you? Let's sleep and dream young. We would wake up with the vigor of youth, and with the promise of joys and hopes, which never grow old or wrinkled."

23

Love Consecrated

Now in my heart
I see clearly
A beautiful face
Shining
Etched by love
           — Sappho

The entire Kabul palace was alive with the sound of music and laughter this evening as Babur stood by the hearth in his bedroom, listening to the crackle and splutter of Holm-oak firewood. His back was toward Bibi Mubaraka seated on the davenport, but he could feel the caress of sparkling blue from her eyes with his senses alone in rapport with his love and vivid imagination. He stirred the logs with iron poker, its knob of serpent-head stinging him with a fresh awareness that he was to march back to Hind early in the morning. Almost four years had elapsed since his victorious return to Kabul, and he was returning to Hind to claim his legacy, if not the jewels of his ambition.

What is this fear commanding me not to take my beloved with me lest I expose her to danger? My heart too roasting in the fires of fear that I might lose her if she was left behind? This ache and desire, am I disciplining myself in the art of denial so that I could endure the pangs of separation for days, months? An ocean of pain was raging inside Babur as he knotted his hands behind him, his back still toward Bibi Mubaraka. His thoughts were gazing at the ruined altar of love within his soul where Sweet Absent had settled permanently, erecting another altar of love-hate there for the living beloved. His sight always searching for emerald depths inside the blue pools of eyes most beautiful and adorable! *Profanity of love,* he could hear his thoughts murmuring, but before his thoughts could turn into fresh splinters of pain, he diverted their flow toward the peace and glory of Kabul.

Kabul, since the past four years had become a haven of peace, each season bringing new sprigs of joys in abundance of flowers and prosperity. The night air scented with Rat-ki-Rani from below the window was entering his bedroom, teasing the green plume in his turban, his knotted hands reaching up to his jeweled cummerbund as if to make sure that he was not dreaming this subtle whiff of peace and perfume, that reality was as resplendent as recollections gossamer and shifting. *Mahim has grown plump, resigned to the fact of Humayun being away, rather happy that he is ruling the kingdom of Badakhshan. Besides, she has adopted Hindal as her son, three and a half now! Doting on Dildar once again since she is heavy with child. Askeri, the youngest of my princes, pampered by his mother Gulrukh, now that his brother Kamran has gone to Kandahar.* Babur's hands knotted behind his back were relaxing as he kept his pain in abeyance by letting his thoughts frolic and wander.

Bibi Mubaraka, unlike Babur, was utterly at peace with herself and with her surroundings. A canopy of lace dripping over the rose-wood bed was her altar of love and prayer. She could see the happy, tender moments of her wedded life woven in the silk-wool flowers of the Persian carpet. Her gaze was turning to the oval mirror above the dresser embellished with koftgari pattern of vines and creepers. Reflected in the mirror was a set of tables with marquetry of gold and ivory. The pale flames of candles from candelabra were also arrested in the mirror, ethereal and flickering. White tuberoses in a silver bowl were attracting her attention, but her senses were absorbing the notes from lutes and flutes down the hall, the tunes almost dreamy and nostalgic. Suddenly, her heart was drumming its beat of sorrow abysmal and nameless.

Babur, oblivious to the riot within the heart of his beloved, was transported body and soul over the mountains overlooking the valleys, drinking pure gold from sunshine and catching whisper of love from the breath of breeze, sweet-scented and frolicsome. The poet-mystic in Babur was awakening, though he himself had turned into a statue of immobility. His thoughts was flitting the pages of his diwan which he had written during the past three years, the collection of his couplets, ghazals and quatrains in this book coming alive in his recollections. Amidst these recollections was blooming forth a familiar longing to carry his beloved into his arms to the loftiest of mountains, reciting his poems to her alone under the moonlit heavens. Loving her under the canopy of stars, and worshiping her everlastingly!

How can I read poetry to her, when she herself is the loveliest of poems? Babur's thoughts were reaching out to Bibi Mubaraka, though he was standing still, surrendering himself to the feeling of love and inspiration.

Bibi Mubaraka's gaze now was fixed to the white knot of Babur's hands behind his back, her repose suddenly diving deep into the inner sanctuary of her heart where she dared not enter lest she be lost inside the fogs of despair and darkness. And yet, rare as it was, she was sucked into the fury of mists dark and swirling.

What is Babur thinking? Why did he abandon the feasting? What does his silence portend? Why is his passion so wild and insatiable? Can love fester and corrupt its essence of purity and desire? The mingling of hatred, violence, tenderness, could this be called love? What madness is this, he worships the very air I breathe?

"Padishah!" One agony of a prayer escaped Bibi Mubaraka's lips, her eyes reflecting the flames of her inner anguish and bewilderment.

"Yes, my sweet." Babur murmured over his shoulders, turning abruptly.

He was startled to see the rivers of pain in the eyes of his beloved. His heart lurched as he stood there stunned, dazzled. The sparkling blue in her eyes was cutting his reveries to chunks of torment, all wild and inconsolable. His heart was aching to fold her into his arms, but he could not stir, only worshiping her small, white face flushed by rubies in her ears and around her throat. Like a devotee, he stood entranced, his gaze alone hugging her tiny waist draped in pale silks, rippling down to her feet, *so precious and adorable,* he was thinking.

"Do I make you unhappy, my sweet, my dear Afghan Lady?" Babur murmured, as if to his own self.

"No, Padishah, no!" One sob of a protest trembled upon the lips of Bibi Mubaraka. "I was just wondering why you abandoned the feasting so abruptly." The periwinkle blue in her eyes was kindling the sparks of happiness.

"Ah!" A tender smile grazed Babur's lips. "Only to suffer the sting of pain—with you—without you, when the break of dawn hurls me toward continents far and seasons inclement." He began to pace, as if trying to arrest the chaos in his thoughts.

"I am the cause of this pain then, Padishah. I am the one making you unhappy." Bibi Mubaraka's heart was fluttering again, returning to that mysterious darkness where her pain lay ensconced. "Yes, I do make you unhappy. I am barren. I can't give you sons—" Her voice was choked against the sudden trilling of mirth upon Babur's lips, his eyes spilling libations of love as he flashed a glance most tender and enveloping.

"I have enough sons to conquer Hind, my beauty!" Babur was saying, his pace not slackening. "Humayun, the kind-hearted! Kamran, the contentious! Askeri, the gentle schemer, I am taking him with me to Hind. Hindal, just a child prince, not yet ready to match the valor of his royal brothers. Lovely daughters too, I have, the darling buds of joys! And yet, they bloom quickly into flowers of youth and are gone, eager to warm the hearths of their husbands. Masuma, already a married woman! Gulrang betrothed, and dreaming of a home away from home. Gulchihra, quite young to be married as yet? I wish I could arrest her childhood and keep her with me always? Daughters are a blessing, and if I want any more children, it has to be a daughter, just like you, to cherish and adore."

"A daughter I cannot give you!" Bibi Mubaraka murmured wretchedly. "Our love, Padishah, it seems, lacks the bloom of fulfillment. Now I understand why you hate me so!" She sat hugging the mysterious darkness within, the blue flames in her eyes licking pain and shuddering.

"Hate!" Babur swung on his feet to face her, his look glazed and incredulous. He appeared to be stung to the very cores of his soul suffered and suffering. "You are twice loved, twice worshiped, many countless times over and above!" He drifted toward her as if crushed by the weight of his sorrow and disbelief. "I love you more than life. You are my life! My soul and my mountain-bride! Without you I am nothing. Without you, I see only death and darkness. If only I could tear open my heart, suffering torments savage and formidable?" He held her to him gently and tenderly.

Their lips were locked in one eager embrace, tasting the holiness of union and oneness. He was kissing her, not with the fury of violence and anguish, but with the tenderness of a devotee, shuddering with fear lest he desecrate the altar of his love. Gently and slowly, he released her, humbled by the sweetness of her youth, all pure and radiant.

"I have wronged you, my unhappy love." Babur murmured, gazing into the brilliant pools of her eyes reverently.

"I am not unhappy, Padishah." Bibi Mubaraka sang charmingly, the dance of joy in her heart deepening the blue in her eyes to nightly heavens.

"Has anyone kissed a houri before?" A breath of ineffable prayer was upon Babur's lips as he kissed her eyes. "I have, and the dancing stars too." Babur got to his feet, and resumed his pacing.

"In what way you have wronged me, Padishah?" Bibi Mubaraka tossed this request as if not interested in knowing.

"By falling in love with you twice, or thrice I should say?" Babur seemed to be ruminating aloud, not meeting her gaze. "Witchcraft of your beauty is compelling me to confess. Some sort of absolution, a healing balm to dull the pain of separation? Do you remember, my love, a beggar begging alms?"

"A mendicant I pitied with all my heart, how could I forget?" A tinkling of laughter escaped Bibi Mubaraka's lips, her gaze following Babur.

"This mendicant still deserves pity, if not love!" Babur joined her in her mirth. "If you only knew the hungers and appetites of this beggar?" He kicked off his gold-pointed shoes and drifted toward her as if approaching a shrine. "I just want to hold you lovingly and blissfully, without the violence of passion wild and corrupt." He held her close to him, tenderly and wistfully. "I need to find my own self, and to know your *presence* alone, feeling only the bliss of your nearness. To consecrate our love as one soul, one essence, complete and inseparable! Ah, the agony of temptation to be near you, and not touching or kissing you, could this discipline teach me to endure the knives of separation?" He released her, pillowing his head under his arms, and abandoning himself to the luxury of round pillow which cradled both him and his beloved.

"Do you love your other wives as much as you love me, Padishah?" Bibi Mubaraka teased, watching him close his eyes, his pallor stark and luminescent.

"I loved but once! One unforgettable? I still love her, in you, my beloved." Babur murmured as if communing with his soul, aghast and bruised. "Zainab is the name of my love. She was my second wife. Strange, that I fell in love—with my own wife. When she died, I was grief-stricken, inconsolable. That fateful night, when I saw you I thought Zainab had come back to absolve me of my grief and living torment. Yes, I was blinded by love, crushed and dazzled. Alas, when I looked into your eyes, searching for the emerald depths, your sparkling blue came alive, mocking, laughing. Stunned, I thought again that Zainab had returned only to rekindle the fires of my pain, madness, loneliness. In that one moment of shock and betrayal, my thoughts had begun swirling. Hating, rejecting the very essence of love and beauty. I had loved Zainab even when she hated me, and when she learned to love me she betrayed me into the hands of the world, empty and hateful. And here I was, that blessed night, hating—you? My soul sobbing out this litany of love, which I had offered as an offering of peace to Zainab once, I could not ever hate, not even an enemy?"

"How did she die?" Bibi Mubaraka could barely murmur, tears welling into her eyes, not due to Babur's painful confession, but as a conduit of release from her pain in loving this man more than she could contain or endure.

"Smallpox." Babur murmured back, his eyes still closed. "In some mad moment of despair I had prayed that if Zainab could come back to me as a lump of deformity, her body disfigured with scars, I would still love her." His arms were groping for the living beloved beside him, drawing her close to him, his lips grazing her hair, her eyes. "You are weeping, my love?" His eyes were shot open, the taste of salt in her tears scalding his lips, his heart a cauldron of desire.

"Tears of joy, Padishah." Bibi Mubaraka buried her face over his shoulders, his arms encircling her in a tight embrace.

"The most precious of pearls which I would preserve in my heart as the gifts of love to comfort me during my hours of loneliness!" Babur kissed her eyes again, surrendering to the violence of his need and desire. "I would taste the forbidden fruit, my Eve! For tomorrow, I would be hurled out of this heaven, while you would abide here bright and beautiful. Am I the tempter, and you the tempted? Me, the sinner, forever in exile! But I would return to claim you back." His senses were welcoming the fever of agony and desire, his kisses hot and searing.

I would never let her go, not ever! Babur's senses were reeling against his need to enter the lotus of her reckoning, yet consummation was bliss supreme he had not experienced in years. *Yes, we would never part. No tears, no parting sorrows, no sweet farewells.*

"No dawn to separate us from loving everlastingly, my love. No such dawn would ever dawn. We would be together, forever and forever." Babur was murmuring, drugged by the perfume of her body and by the sweetness of her love. Somewhere, beyond this moment of intoxication was the sacred road to rest, peace, and oblivion!

24

Jewel-Hind

A thousand kisses on your eyes, your lips, your tongue, your heart
Most charming of thy sex, what is thy power over me
— Napoleon Bonaparte

A silken city was erected right inside the heart of Lahore, which Babur had conquered with all its wealth of gardens and colleges. He was lying this particular afternoon in his damasked tent, fighting the sickness of yellow fever, which he had contracted a few days ago, succumbing to its assault of nausea and delirium. Tahir stood fanning Padishah with a fan made out of peacock feathers. Babur was drifting between the fogs of sleep and wakefulness, his physician Sayyid Tabib seated couchant against one round pillow, alert and vigilant. Khwaja Kilan was there too, talking in low tones with Mir Jamal, the brother of Bibi Mubaraka. Khazanda Begum's husband, Mehdi Khwaja, sat not too far from Babur, forlorn and contemplative.

A low moan escaped Babur's lips, all eyes turning to him, but he seemed to be resting peacefully, as if his fever was abating. His fever, indeed, was abating, for he could feel the trickle of sweat slithering down his spine, his senses awakening to the familiar riot in his thoughts, healthy and vigorous. And feverish, of course, exploding forth with a sudden violence to celebrate the freedom of speech which had been denied to him during the days of his convalescence!

My soul, not my body is on fire. This hunger and longing, sweet absent divorced and sweet presence espoused. The inseparable one buried deep within, the long-separated continents away in Kabul? Babur's thoughts were shutting the gates of his pain and loneliness, commencing their perilous journey on the road to ambition and victories.

The thundering of invasions was entering Babur's feverish thoughts against the smoke-clouds from guns, jezzails, muskets and culverins. The cities of Lahore, Multan and Serhind were conquered, and yet the vanquished had conquered the hearts of the Moghuls, welcoming them with joyful cheers, and offering them rich tributes along with their oaths of fidelity.

All peoples, regardless of their caste, creed or colors are to be treated with utmost respect and kindness. No injustice or plundering. No violence or treachery. Babur's Farman which he had issued after his conquests was imprinting

each word into tablets of law inside his head, as he lay wading out of the marshland of his fever and feverish thoughts. *This continent of Hind is a world within
worlds, brutal and awe-inspiring. A strange, mysterious world with all its beauty
and ugliness, hugging its rags and riches with equanimity, honoring even the
meanest beast with reverence, yet repulsing their own kind, who, without any
fault of their own were destined to be born as a race within race of low caste?
And yet again, most of them, old or young, rich or poor, healthy or misshapen,
radiate the aura of serenity, untouched by the violence of man or nature?* His
thoughts were floating aimlessly, languid and awestricken.

*Lovely, dark-skinned girls in silken saris with colorful tilaks on their brows
and gold studs in their noses! The taste of dust in one's mouth and the oppressive heat go unnoticed here against the glitter of gold and jewels, even the wrists
of the poor women adorned with gold bangles. No wonder, Hind has suffered so
many invasions, the lords of greed within and without still contemplating plunder and devastation. I would build gardens here, and pavilions of gilt and marble. And colleges and libraries!* Another low moan escaped Babur, his lips dry
and parched. His eyes were fluttering open, red-rimmed and searching.

Tahir was quick to heap pillows behind Babur's back as he tried to sit up,
his gaze wandering from one to the other with a glint of impatience. Sayyid
Tabib also leapt to his feet, snatching a gold cup from the carved table, and filling it with his concoction of lemon and rosewater. He had told Babur earlier that
this was a proven remedy for yellow fever, and now he held out the cup to him
as if offering some rare nectar from the very rivers of Paradise.

"My fever is gone, my good physician." Babur waved away the cup impatiently. "Nothing would quench my thirst but wine. Ah, Mushin knows the needs
of my soul." He claimed the goblet of wine from him, draining it thirstily. "I do
not wish to bathe in my sweat. Prepare a bath for me, well, no such luxuries
here. I would go swimming in the cool waters of Ravi." He was distracted by the
arrival of Abdullah Hatifi who was shooting straight toward him, smiling while
curtsying.

"Happy tidings, Padishah!" Abdullah Hatifi squatted himself at Babur's
feet, holding out a missive. "A letter from Mahim Begum, but the messenger
already told me, announcing the birth of a beautiful princess."

"May Allah shower blessings upon our little princess!" Babur waved away
the missive as he had waved away the gold cup before. *I must tutor my Afghan
Lady in the art of correspondence*, he was thinking. "Read the letter to me, Hatifi, or better yet tell me briefly its import, I feel drained." He leaned his head
against the pillow, his gaunt features accentuated by the grey streaks in his beard
and mustache.

"Padishah?" Abdullah Hatifi unsealed the missive as if committing an act of
heresy. "Dildar Begum has given birth to a beautiful daughter. Mahim Begum
says she has adopted the princess and has named her, Gulbadan."

"Gulbadan, meaning literally, rose-body!" Babur appeared to inhale the fragrance of this name upon his lips, his eyes closing. "How exquisitely tender is
this name, wafting the scent of peace and purity. A new birth, the flowering of

love within one's heart, the perfume of surrender, and a new beginning!" He was drifting back into the arms of sleep.

The city of Lahore this evening was rosy with the promise of a new dawn when Babur and his troops would be journeying back to Kabul. Babur's spacious tent was lit to effulgence by candelabras, hosting a privileged few to watch the play written and produced by the sole ingenuity of Abdullah Hatifi. He had erected a make-shift stage where a narrator was poised to herald the changing of the scenes. The men acting male roles seemed comfortable, but the men disguised as females were dying of stage fright, it was obvious.

Babur, couchant against one velvety pillow was watching with half interest, half amusement. His silk turban with a yellow plume was accentuating his pallor, his gaze shifting from Shaikhi the flutist to Hussein, who sat practicing his lute as if oblivious to the drama on stage. Naralla disguised as female protagonist Laila could be seen crouching in one corner, trying to melt the red silks draped around him with his fiery gaze alone. His face was painted black with charcoal in semblance of Laila known as Black Beauty.

"A triple celebration this evening, Padishah!" Abdullah Hatifi was saying, honored to be seated close to Babur. "First, the honor of celebrating your victories! And then khutba being read in your name in the mosques at Lahore, Multan and Sirhind. The second, to celebrate your recovery from yellow fever, and the third, the birth of a royal princess! This masnavi Laila and Majnoon is my share of gifts to rejoice and celebrate. I hope, the actors do justice to my script, which I think I have written with the blood from my heart, though nothing as precious as the blood of the martyrs who died valorously."

"*The ink of the scholars is more precious than the blood of the martyrs*, Prophet Muhammad told his disciples." Babur smiled, his gaze still fixed to the stage. "You are the author and architect of these celebrations, Hatifi, and your genius is beyond compare, bringing to life this tale of woe and spirituality." He complimented, listening to the narrator on the stage with a profound interest.

Laila, dark as the starless night, was the daughter of Banu Amir during the reign of Caliph Hashaam, whose power in Arabia was at its peak in the Year 724 A.D. A young poet by the name of Kais fell in love with this daughter of the night, as if she was the fairest of houris straight from heaven. He began to serenade her black beauty with songs full of longings and lamentations. Laila, in return, fell hopelessly in love with this angel of a poet, her heart restless and fluttering. Banu Amir, upon discovering that his daughter had fallen in love with a lowly poet, was quick to force her daughter into marriage with a young man by the name of Assad from the tribe of Ibn Salem.

The news of his beloved married to another man had fallen upon Kais like a bolt of lightning, his very heart ripping the heavens asunder with its cries most painful and heartrending. The stark mad lover had lost his sanity, running wild on the streets, singing love songs, and finally abandoning his pain into the heart of a forest. Wilderness alone

had become his refuge and purgatory, and beasts of the jungle his fam-
ily and friends. He had become a living, throbbing vessel of grief and
inspiration, writing tragic verses and pinning them on the trees for his
beloved to claim and preserve.

Occasionally, he would return to town, singing verses and roaming
aimlessly, followed by a horde of children throwing stones at him and
laughing. He had espoused Laila as his madness supreme, his very soul
pouring couplets, his voice raspy and cracked.

The narrator was caught in his flood of recital, while the actors enacted their
roles in harmony with the description of the scenes. The lovers had parted; the
weeping bride was being carried in a doli over the shoulders of men on their
way to the home of the bridegroom. Kais had stumbled back into his forest, reciting a quatrain under some spell of divine inspiration.

In heaven we are joined, on earth we are apart
Nor death, nor fear or decay can separate our hearts
Our souls wander freely and choose for all eternity to combine
Mine is yours, yours is mine

The narrator paused, and then continued with an abrupt urgency.

Kais, the mad lover is now branded with the appellation of, Ma-
jnoon—the demented one! See how he reads his verses to the lions,
wolves, panthers and gazelles? In truth, Majnoon is the divine lover,
seeking his beloved. He has attained release from the fetters of sanity,
and has entered the bliss of madness. Laila is his darkness supreme, his
black purity, his one and only love and beloved. He has possessed her
noble beauty inside the wound of his soul, welcoming his night bride
with a sigh of rapture. Look, how he embraces death, consumed by the
consummation of love with madness! The unloved bride of the de-
mented one, upon learning of his death, utters a piercing cry, her soul
departing after him for the bliss of union in afterlife.

The narrator drugged as he was by his voice missed one whole page, causing confusion on the stage. Kais was still alive, visited by his cousin Salen from
Baghdad. The men carrying the doli in an attempt to flee the stage had lost their
balance, and the bride—Naralla dressed as Laila came tumbling down, evoking
a volley of cheers and laughter. While Naralla sat nursing his buttocks against
the sting of pain and embarrassment, the garlanded doli was being hoisted upon
the shoulder of the men, all seething and flustered. Majnoon, in his jungle-scene,
was oblivious to Salen who was saying: *O Demented One, I am the pilgrim, and*
you are the Mecca. But Majnoon was busy pinning verses on the trees, his eyes
glazed and unseeing.

The narrator had found his voice, commencing, as if nothing was amiss and the actors performing in conformity with his narration.

The Demented One is the soul of all souls, a great soul, longing for love and beloved. Seeking the Unknown and the Unknowable! He is Light, embracing Darkness, losing himself in the colorless pool of oneness, attaining bliss and union. Behold, how the mortal lover is wooing death for the sake of love—for beloved!

The men-deer were chanting the name of Laila in unison in accompaniment to the doleful notes from lutes and flutes. Majnoon, with one last cry of agony, had fallen prostrate on the stage, his lips still repeating Laila's name in a litany of supplications. Laila too, with much-too genuine cries of pain, had abandoned herself into the arms of her dying lover. A great applause broke forth as the dead lovers scrambled to their feet to flee the stage. Babur sat laughing, and showering compliments on his beloved poet.

"Your masnavi, Hatifi, would outlast any torrents of grief ever suffered in the past, or likely to be suffered in the future!" Babur scooped a handful of ashrafis from the silver tray beside him and scattered them at the feet of the poet. "A thousand ashrafis for your talent and a thousand more for your sweet labors, but you yourself have to count and claim when we reach Kabul. And yet, your genius is priceless for choosing black beauty as your protagonist for such a fair lover as Majnoon! The tale of course is much older than we could ever surmise, but you have brought it back to life with all its paradox of fair truth blackened by ignorance. This reminds me of another tale my baba could never tire of telling—that of the king of Thebes. Oedipus was the name of that king, who plucked out his eyes in sheer grief, exclaiming: *O darkness, my light!* Subtle and profound! Darkness revealing light and darkness itself concealing the essence of pure light!" He heaved himself up, his eyes shining with the warmth of longing and profundity. "Early at dawn, we ride back to Kabul! But now I wish to say farewell to Hind. We would come back, for sure, for more riches and conquests." He turned to his heels, his gaze alone commanding all not to follow. "Solitude, I cherish. Beauty, I worship. Ah, but love, I hold in reverence." He murmured over his shoulders.

Clusters upon clusters of stars were Babur's night companions as he strolled away from the silk city of his encampment, his heart aching and luminous. All about him were peace and stillness, the mystic poet within him awakening to the sense of duality inside the very heart of nature and mankind. Each star which his gaze had plucked out of the heavens, he had sealed with kisses, blowing it away toward Kabul to steal the nectar of love from the lips of his Afghan Lady—his Beloved.

The sweet seduction of reality and illusion! Day—night, evil—good, love— hate, light—darkness. Such dewdrop pairs of imponderables. A lover following the path of destiny, beloved knowing she is destiny? Why do we go warring, lusting after lives and possessions? How tragic is death, and how sad the lust for living? Yet, the saddest of all, the faces of the living-dead. How many people walk on the face of this earth, pregnant everlastingly with sorrows mute and nameless? Feeling neither joy, nor pain. Acknowledging neither comfort, not aware of the discomfort. Neither touched by the light of beauty, nor repulsed by the sight of ugliness. Why it is that I too am carrying the gloom of the soulless and the sightless?

The bright, sparkling eyes of the stars were holding Babur prisoner, mocking his thoughts and entering the portals of his dark contemplations. His quick strides were tracing back the forlorn path toward his city of tents, where his soldiers slept and dreamed of home—Kabul. The livid moon up there was dreaming its dreams, lowering ribbons of revelations, and almost carrying Babur over its chariot of moonbeams, laughing and shuddering.

Yes, I am destined to come back, to claim the legacy of my ancestors! Hind itself is waiting for the first Moghul emperor to rule with love and kindness? But I cannot rule, or conquer without the love of my Afghan Lady. His thoughts were kneeling at the grave of his grandmother, heeding her prophecy that one day he would be the emperor of Hind. Padishah—not the emperor, was entering his tent, bewitched and exhilarated.

25

Gypsy Dance

My bounty is boundless as the sea
My love as deep, the more I give to thee
The more I have, for both are infinite
— William Shakespeare

The glens and valleys of Kabul donned in the mantle of snow were quiet and chilled, but the library of rose and ivory in Babur's palace where he sat writing a letter to Humayun, was aglow with warmth from the blaze of fire under the hearth and from the abundance of candles from the candelabras. More than two and a half years had elapsed since his return to Kabul, and still he was not sated with the beauty of the seasons, longing for spring with all its renewal of scents and colors. As soon as he had arrived in Kabul he had learned about Humayun's marriage with Bega Begum in Badakhshan. The prince had sent a brief note to Mahim that he loved the girl and that they were married without any pomp or ceremony.

Pomp and ceremony were very much a part of the triple celebrations this evening in Babur's palace, foremost amongst them prince Kamran's wedding. A chorus of wedding songs surfing over the notes of music from down the hall were foiling Babur's attempt to write a letter to his son, his thoughts stealthy and straying. Without fail, Afghan Lady was the first one to invade his solitude, making his heart molten with desire, and yet he was forcing his thoughts toward his other wives, aiming to understand his royal brood through them than to unscramble the puzzle of their moods and whims.

Mahim is possessive and superstitious. My Gulrukh, wild and mischievous! Happy like a song-bird is Dildar! Gulnar and Nurgul, my golden butterflies. Beloved is only one—Afghan Lady, my mountain bride. Why do I see the dance of ice and fire in her eyes these days? Ah, but half her love is diverted to princess Gulbadan, my precious, precious Rose-body! And yet, I must write to my heedless prince? Babur dipped his pen in the jade inkstand, his thoughts a mingling of pride and reproof.

Dearest prince, Humayun, best beloved, my son,

A thousand congratulations for the auspicious birth of your first son—Alaman! I am the happiest of grandfathers. You do possess good taste in choosing names, and have chosen a name worthy of praise. Perchance, your wife chose it; offer my love and compliments to Bega Begum. Alaman, meaning, the ever-faithful, may he live and prosper. I am sitting in the comfort of my library, handsomely dressed in a silk robe and satin vest studded with carnelians in honor of wedding celebrations. Wish you were here? My heart is longing for your presence. I would have arranged great wedding celebrations for you too, if you were not hasty and heedless, many, many gulfs apart—in Badakhshan? Princess Gulbadan is two and a half year old now, strange to say that she is already the aunt of sweet Alaman. Kamran is getting married to Bega Begum. Three weddings we are celebrating in one evening. Khalifa's daughter Gulbarg Begum is getting married to Hasan Khan. His son too, Muhib Ali is marrying Nahid Begum. Mahim is driving the cooks insane with her demands. Only five hundred dishes to serve the wedding guests, she keeps complaining and fretting. I have chosen the wedding presents for each bride, equal portions of silks, jewels, damasks and one thousand ashrafis. To you, I am sending the most precious of gifts—books. These books are priceless since I claimed them as the gifts of my conquest. After I conquered the kingdom of Milwat, their leader fled, leaving behind his wives, mother, brothers and sisters, along with his books and treasures. When the ignominious wretch was captured, I pardoned him, restoring his family and treasures, but kept the books.

You must cultivate your taste in reading good books, and practice the skill of writing. Don't try to impress me with words, just let your thoughts flow as well as the strokes of your pen, and you would achieve simplicity, elegance. Now something of interest to you! In Kandahar, down the slopes of Biserhuch hill cradling the imaret of Pustak, I have chosen this rock for building a lofty dome. Seventy stone cutters are already working on it, fashioning tablets, upon which my name and the names of all my sons would be engraved.

Seek wisdom, my son, and court friendship. Practice the art of generosity, and be merciful to both foes and friends. Fill your heart with love and compassion, for these are the highest of virtues in remembrance of Allah, Who Himself is loving and compassionate. Have respect for each man, woman and child—especially, for children for they learn from the example of our own living. Nurture and multiply your love for your wives, sisters and—

Babur's thoughts were truncated as Khwaja Kilan stumbled into the library, curtsying and smiling.

"You are becoming intrusive by the hour, Khwaja, making it your habit to come unannounced?" Babur replaced his jeweled pen in the inkstand, his eyes flashing.

"Don't you know, Padishah, at weddings all kind of levities are permitted and everyone feels privileged to deviate from formality or etiquette?" Khwaja Kilan beamed. "Besides, I only take the liberty of intruding when I know you are happy."

"If you only knew, I was communing with my son and with Allah!" Babur laughed. "And yet, you are welcome. Does this flatter you?"

"Much more than that, Padishah! I feel honored and flattered!" Khwaja Kilan intoned merrily. "The guests would be flattered indeed if you joined them in their merry-making. The begums are requesting the pleasure of your company in the Fortune Hall."

"Pleasure is entirely mine, Khwaja, yet I am greedy of time. I have been meaning to send felicitations to Humayun for days, but do I get a few moments of respite from my royal duties, no!" Babur's look was thoughtful and piercing all of a sudden. "Has Humayun grown more superstitious than ever before, I can't help but thinking?"

"Superstition, *is*, neither less nor more! That's how I feel, Padishah." Was Khwaja Kilan's laconic response!

"You are profound, Khwaja, wickedly profound!" Babur exclaimed. "Superstition is more when it bodes evil, and it is less if it prophesies good. Let me put it this way, do you think Humayun is compassionate?"

"Padishah! Prince Humayun loves his cockerels with as much passion as he would his children, I had often thought while watching him. Yes, he is compassionate." Khwaja Kilan murmured against the blaze of amusement in Babur's eyes before he turned his gaze to the fire under the hearth. "He is loving and kind-hearted. Trusting and forgiving to the point of a fault, for he would be condoning the conceit and ingratitude of his subjects, and becoming vulnerable to unrest or seditions."

"Why do my thoughts drag me back to the valleys of Ferghana, Khwaja?" Babur returned his gaze to his friend. It was warm and wistful, as if carrying the cinders of memories. "The days of my youth, I was barely twelve, we had gone hunting. Do you remember that, Khwaja? I killed a deer with first shot from my cross-bow. I was proud and gloating, while you looked sad and crushed. I can still remember the look in your eyes, and I can never forget that story from Hadith you began telling gently and dreamily. *A man walking down the road got very thirsty, and finding a well on the way managed to reach the level of the water by shifting his weight from one jagged stone to the other until he could balance his feet on one rock as big as a boulder. After having his fill, he climbed out of the well, feeling light and refreshed. He had gone only a few paces when he saw a dog panting under the burden of heat, his tongue hanging out and his body sagging. I have quenched my thirst, and this dog is dying for the lack of water, the man thought and retraced his steps toward the well. Filling his shoe with water, he returned to the dog and satisfied his thirst. Allah was pleased by this man's single act of compassion, and He bestowed upon him the bounties of this world and the world hereafter.* This is how you planted in my young heart the seeds of compassion, Khwaja, plucking more gems out of Hadith and polishing them with the warmth of your expression. *There is a reward for every living creature. A man's true wealth hereafter is the good he does in this world to his fellowmen. Work for this world as if you live in it forever, and work for the other world as if you are to die tomorrow.* Sweet memories and sweet treasures, Khwaja, which can never be sold or bought in this world of gains and losses, but cherished always!" He was turning his attention to the letter abandoned on the desk unfinished.

"If we didn't enjoy the present moment, Padishah, there won't be any trace of pleasant memories to sustain us in our future hopes and aspirations." Khwaja Kilan murmured as if to his own self. "A time to think, and a time to rejoice! And now is the time to rejoice with your family in the Fortune Hall, Padishah."

"If you would, Khwaja, spare me a few moments to commune with my son and with Allah. I can't let this letter of felicitations to be postponed for another day, and then it might linger for weeks, months, a year, most probably?" Babur was already dipping his pen in the inkstand. "The luxury of the present moment evades me somehow in this conduit of wars, intrigues and rebellions, and of course the feastings. The festivities would last till dawn, I am sure, much to the despair of the bridegrooms. Throw a few more logs to feed the flames, Khwaja, before you leave." He began to write, becoming oblivious to all, but to his Turkish script flowing neatly on the paper.

Superstition is the worst of all evils, my son, for it corrupts not only the senses but the soul itself, shun it completely. I hear you have started believing in portents? Shunning society, and daring not to step out of your palace until some auspicious sign waves its consent to lift your royal feet in search of fortunes great and fleeting! Have you plucked out knowledge out of the heart of posterity? Is it true that you believe in omens? What is this oracle which I hear through the lips of the messengers? You inquire the names of the first three men whom your princely eyes behold, and then you begin the process of shuffling their names to fashion words to suit your whims. So far, your faulty intellect has whipped up three words out of the collection of many names. Desire, Well-being, Triumph, are these the jewel words you have acquired through superstition? Desire, my son, begins with the innocent appetite of a suckling babe, multiplying later into a marshland of desires corrupt and insatiable. Well-being takes root in the sapling of youth, growing into a tree of illusions, all twisted and gnarled. Triumph is nothing but a grain of serendipity, growing cankerous within the shell of ego and pride. Desire, any kind of desire, study all its stages from birth, to infancy, to maturity, then experience its need with the purity of your heart. Crave not well-being until you have mastered the art of living without fear and prejudice. Seek not triumph unless you are ready

to nurture it with compassion. Write to me, and tell me that all I hear
are rumors, and I would believe. Mahim misses you. Kabul longs for
your presence, and I do too, I must—

Babur's thoughts were silenced once again by the breezy approach of another intruder. This time it was Mir Jamal, the brother of his dear beloved, Bibi Mubaraka.

"I have a feeling that I would never be permitted the luxury of solitude even if I chose some Himalayan retreat for prayer and meditation?" Babur exclaimed genially.

"Padishah, begums are requesting—rather demanding your presence in the Fortune Hall!" Mir Jamal bowed double, his features lit by a boyish smile.

"I obey only the commands of your sister, my gallant messenger." Babur smiled in return. "A thousand begums, not to mention the countless houris in heaven, can't make me obedient to their commands, but my Afghan Lady. I am waiting for summons from her alone. But don't be hasty in conveying my wish to her lest she comes too soon? Better yet, stay guard at the door, and let no one enter the library, so that I could finish this letter to my happy prince." He returned his attention to the letter once again, dismissing Mir Jamal with a wave of his arm.

You have a burden of kingdom upon your shoulders, my son, carry it with
pride and honor. You would be ruling many more kingdoms when we conquer
Hind. Stay well, and don't forget to nurture your valor and intellect. Warm hugs
and kisses to Alaman, and love to Bega Begum. Loving always, Babur.

Babur sealed the letter slowly and deliberately. His thoughts rocketing all of a sudden into realms sacred and profane! He could feel the stab of grief and agony within where Sweet Absent was buried alive, awakening to the life of love and longing. He leaped to his feet as if stung, whirling on his feet and espousing another stab of illusion. Sweet Absent had materialized before his gaze, the fire of love-hate in her emerald eyes ablaze, glowing. For one flash of a moment he stood there bewitched, dazzled. But it was no illusion! Bibi Mubaraka was standing not far from him, bright and radiant. The blue pools of her eyes were sparkling much like the blaze of diamonds in her ears and around her throat. Donned in pale silks, matching her complexion, she almost looked ethereal, luminescent. Babur drifted toward her dreamlike, becoming aware of the flickering of pain in her gaze so pure and dazzling.

"My mountain beauty, where does this pain come from, dimming the sparkle in your eyes, so very beautiful and adorable?" Babur held her captive in his gaze as he stood facing her, awed and spellbound. "Am I the cause of this pain, Beloved?"

"No, Padishah." Bibi Mubaraka smiled sweetly, the purity of joy and love in her eyes warm and embracing. "A silly doubt in my head, at times, murmuring lies that you do not love me?"

"Lies most blatant and unpardonable!" Babur slipped his arm around her waist, gazing into her eyes. "How could I prove my love to you, my love? I could jump into a pit of fire if that were your wish and command? And yet, I don't need to prove it, since my love for you is my religion, holy and personal. It's the only truth I hold sacred inside the altar of my soul." He kissed her softly and reverently. "Your beauty would drive me mad with desire if I held you close to me a moment longer?" He released her slowly and reluctantly. "Propriety demands that we join the guests and the begums." He murmured, linking his arm into hers with the swiftness of a cavalier.

Fortune Hall decked with festive colors was turned into an arena of gaiety and laughter. Babur and Bibi Mubaraka, against the flood of music, were whisked away into different circles by the whims of family or guests. Bibi Mubaraka was claimed by the aunts, assigned the task of supervising the platters of food being brought in by the servants in liveries of gold and crimson. Babur was snatched by the begums, all seeking his approval and attention. Mahim, donned in emerald silks with matching jewels was bubbling with joy and pride as if her own son was getting married. Dildar, Gulrukh, Gulnar and Nurgul, all arrayed in opulent of gowns were flaunting their jewels while mingling with the guests and spilling laughter.

The guests sated with wine and music were now content only on nibbling sweets, or watching the dancers. Babur had eaten sparsely, feeling alone and restless amidst this sea of color and sparkle, his heart aching for peace and solitude. He had succeeded in snatching Bibi Mubaraka away from the everlasting rituals of wedding ceremonies, making her sit beside him to appease his fever of loneliness and restlessness. Now as he sat with his beloved, sipping his wine, his gaze was reaching out to his sister Khazanda, who was offering brides the gifts of pearls and rubies. She herself was decked with pearls, her blue velvet gown accentuating the sparkle in her eyes and lending her pallor a subtle glow of radiance and youthfulness. Babur sighed with pleasure, recalling with a sudden wistfulness that she had abandoned her mode of dressing severely in silk-wool gowns, at least for just this evening? His gaze was turning to Kamran with a warmth of admiration as to his being dressed as the perfect of bridegrooms, but before he could fully admire his son's satin vest broidered with gold, princess Gulbadan sneaked herself into his lap, poised for a usual hug and a kiss.

My Rose Princess, Babur's very heart was singing with joy, as he kissed her, squeezing her into his arms most blissfully. *Her agate eyes, exactly the color of her mother's, so precious and adorable! Yes, the purity and innocence of Dildar's heart shines through the eyes of my Rose Princess.*

Babur appeared to be drugged with joy, squeezing his daughter into a warm embrace and aware most profoundly of his beloved beside him, radiant and beautiful. He was transported into a world of his own, where only the princess and the beloved existed for him, all the rest were some dewdrop illusion, ethereal and phantasmagoric. Though apparently responsive to the tides of music and laughter, his thoughts were soaring beyond the confines of gaiety and celebration. He could envision the silence of snow-capped mountains under the canopy of stars, all stark and shimmering. So real and peaceful was the silence of the night in his imagination that he could see the moon hovering above with the pulse of beauty so serene and awesome that he could almost feel his whole being kneeling under the spell of reverence and surrender. And yet, this spell was broken, his thoughts were communing with Humayun, gazing into the eyes of the starry vastness where Hind lay buried like a jewel unpolished inside the casket of timelessness. This spell too was shattered by the sudden frenzy of the music skirling high with the rhythm of a Gypsy Dance.

Babur was whirled into the ocean of dancing, changing partners as swiftly as the beat of the drums. It indeed was an ocean of color and jubilations! Waves upon waves of silks and brocades slashed with the sparkle of jewels could be seen throbbing and shimmering. The men with colorful plumes in their turbans and their hands tied behind their backs in knots were vying with the ladies whirling on their feet with the agility of trained dancers. Babur and Bibi Mubaraka were arrested in a circle of pairs, men clapping and the women floating on their toes with a wild abandon. But they were weaving their way out of this madness, and before the music could reach to a delirious culmination, they had succeeded in swirling out of the thunder of clapping and pirouetting.

The large bedroom with its damasks and paintings was a cherished haven for both Babur and Bibi Mubaraka where they had escaped, the music still following at their heels. Babur stood holding her in one crushing embrace, murmuring endearments, and listening only to the violence of desire and hunger in his body and soul.

"Yes, Beloved, you do drive me insane with desire. My love for you is an ocean profound and boundless, yet raging and hungering for the sweetness of your love and beauty." Babur's very soul was murmuring as he carried her to the bed, its canopy of gold trembling against the ardor of his need and passion.

26

Gulbadan—The Rose Princess

*Through snow and frost a flower gleams. As my love does through ice
and evil weather of life. I believe that I love your more than yesterday.
But that belief grows with every single day.*
— Wolfgang Von Goethe

Babur, seated on the balcony of his Kabul palace this spring morning,
though absorbed in writing an urgent missive to Humayun, was aware of the
Rose Princess beside him, equally absorbed in memorizing the Turkish alpha-
bets. He could inhale the scent of rose and lilac from his garden down below, his
senses reflecting the colors of flowers in his Char-bagh, which he had admired
earlier before making his own self comfortable to write letters and his memoirs.
Dog roses and forget-met-not cradled against the jasmine bushes were dreamy
and bashful in his mind's vision. The riot of hyacinth, anemone and narcissus
was arrested with all its glory and perfume. And ebony trees with scarlet little
buds could be seen flowering in the backstage of his imagination while words
poured out of his thoughts in a downpour. Two hasty years had merged into the
rivers of time since the marriage of his son Kamran, and since his fortunate dis-
covery in choosing this balcony as his sole retreat for writing and contemplation.

Actually, this retreat was his gift from Gulbadan from the treasures of her
innocence and imagination. She had, one balmy summer night, expressed her
wish to Maywa Jan that she would like to sleep on the balcony. Maywa Jan, in
return, had appealed to Babur for his consent, and Babur had not only granted
his consent, but had turned this balcony into a royal pavilion for both him and
his dear princess. Furnished with Turkish rugs and pillows, it was further embellished with a canopy of gold and crimson. For Babur's personal use, a gilded
chair and a desk were added, inviting more amenities such as carved stools and
tables with the inlay of brass and ivory. This particular morning, Himalayan
tulips in their brass pots could be seen basking under the sun on this balcony,
vibrant and blazing. He had compared their color with the shock of red in Gulbadan's hair, and now with this sudden recollection a smile was unfolding upon
his lips, impressing upon him the dullness of his own attire, a white robe gathered around his waist with a green cummerbund. He could feel a whiff of breeze

over his bare head, its gentle touch neither ruffling his hair, nor disturbing the sheaf of papers over his desk.

At least the jewels on my cummerbund shine graciously over my dull attire, Babur's thoughts were taking flight aimlessly and surreptitiously. A few weeks ago Dilawar Khan had journeyed from Lahore to Kabul by the sole virtue of his youth and perseverance. He had been a virtual prisoner in his father's home before contriving escape. His only mission was to warn Babur about the imminent threats of rebellion in the kingdoms Padishah had conquered and left under the care of his father, including other leaders capable of ruling and defending. Upon hearing such grievous news, Babur had decided to invade Hind, but now while writing to his son, his thoughts were vacillating. Some sort of fear and sadness within him were shooting warnings that he shouldn't leave Kabul lest he become a prisoner in Hind—to his ambition and conquests. That he might not ever return, longing for the beauty of Kabul, and dying there in grief away from his home—his haven? This tyrannous thought riding over his shoulders was compelling him to resume writing his letter to Humayun.

> *Sultan Ibrahim in Delhi, who deems himself to be the overlord of Hind, is conspiring against me with the intention of ruling over my conquered domains of Lahore, Multan and Sirhind. Alam Khan—whom I left as the governor of Multan and Sirhind, fearing Sultan Ibrahim's stealthy designs, sent his son Lion Khan to my viziers Doulat Khan and Ghazi Khan, requesting their aid against the covert designs of Sultan Ibrahim. But these craven and shameless wretches in return sent a message to Alam Khan that he should make himself the lord of Multan and Sirhind. Doulat Khan went as far as imprisoning his son Dilawar Khan who opposed his father in becoming an accomplice to unrest and rebellion. Matters have come to such a pass now that both Alam Khan and Doulat Khan have turned traitors, each claiming to be the rightful lord to rule over the fractious clans and kingdoms. Encouraged by the rivalry between these two simpletons, Sultan Ibrahim is sending large contingents at the borders of Lahore, Milwat, Sirhind, Sialkot, Sultanpur, Shahabad, boasting to conquer the whole of Hind since he is already the lord of Agra and Delhi. Stupidity, ignorance and ingratitude are the vilest of sins I have learned not to pardon or condone.*

Babur's pen poised for expressions was suspended between his fingers, his thoughts straying. Something deep and abysmal inside him was stirring, goading him to scorch the pages with coals of reprimands for Humayun, to jolt him out his state of ease and luxury.

Not that I am angry with him, but that I love him the best. Babur abandoned his pen in the jade inkpot, and sat brooding. *I expect more from him than from any of my sons and daughters. By chiding him, I exact from him his obedience as well as his antagonism? Am I getting old, bilious and intemperate?* His gaze was climbing up the citadel and sweeping down into his garden where the gardeners were planting the saplings of chenar trees. Down yonder in the open field were flanks of Moghul soldiers, practicing their morning drills, happily and diligently. He forced his attention back to his unfinished letter, but couldn't think of a word, his thoughts flashing the loveliness of his Afghan Lady, along with his ache and longing for peace and nearness. *What is this apathy, vacuum, emptiness? Pain is gone from me, joy has lost its warmth, and love is divorced from my heart and soul? When one ceases to love, one ceases to live. Have I become like one of those living dead? No, a thousand times no, my undying love for my beloved, or is it still Sweet Absent? How can one express the river of silence in one's soul?* His chain of introspection was broken by the voice of a muezzin calling the faithful to noon prayers.

Ah, this music divine from the lips of mere mortals! The recitation of Quran too can move devout Muslims to tears, and yet what charm lies in those words which never fail to fill my heart with awe and reverence? Some sort of revelation was lowering its command over the puddle of his ruminations.

Am I commanded to seek omens, to search the rags of superstition? One mockery of a challenge in Babur's thoughts was holding him prisoner to its sense of the absurd and mysterious. *Yes, superstition could be molded into one priceless gem if it seeks only the jewel of wisdom, shunning always the chaff of ignorance.* His mind was already concocting a wish, and stuffing it with the sand of hope and anticipation. *Today of all days, if Dilawar Khan came to me here, offering me pan and murraba while requesting again that I invade Hind, my decision to do so would bear the seal of finality, no more delay or indecision? Has decision not already been made, and yet I keep postponing the hour of departure? What do I fear? Oh, yes, my fear to be separated from my beloved? What a fool I am, I have decided to take her with me—*

"Look, Padishah! Drums, horses, soldiers? Are you going to ride with them, go away again?" Gulbadan sprang to her feet abruptly, her white dress in silken ripples lending her the appearance of a doll molded out of porcelain.

"Yes, my flower! Soon." Babur held out his arms, and she slipped into his lap with the familiar ease of a much beloved princess.

"Could I ride with you, Padishah?" Gulbadan sang her wish, her dark eyes sparkling.

"No, my lovely Rose. You would wilt." Babur laughed, teasing her red curls absently. "Only soldiers go with me. Young princesses, absolutely no! Bibi Mubaraka Begum, perhaps?"

"You would take *her*, Padishah?" Gulbadan's voice had the echo of hope and jealousy.

"If she is as eager as you, my sweet, then I might?" Babur could see the kindling of accusation in her eyes, and he laughed again. "But I can't take you with me, my love."

"You do not love me, Padishah!" Gulbadan half cried, half pleaded. "I will not love you, Padishah."

"My fairest of loves, I love you the most!" Babur exclaimed, kissing her hair and cheeks. "And yet, I love Bibi Mubaraka the best. You are too young, only four and a half, we would talk about love when you are a little older." His thoughts were peering down the abysmal agony and sweetness of love, but he shook his head, fondling the red curls over her shoulders. "You need pearls and rubies in your hair, my Rose, to soften this flaming riot, I should tell Mahim? Mahim loves you, and your mamma Dildar, and your aunt Khazanda, and all the begums, your brothers and sisters and everyone!'

"Mahim Begum is in Bad-a-kh-shan—" Gulbadan was flushed, failing in her attempt to pronounce this word correctly. "She only loves prince Humayun, Padishah. Mamma loves prince Hindal, he told me so. She doesn't love me." She was trying her best not to cry, knowing with the preciosity of an intelligent child that her father loved not tears, but laughter. Her heart was clinging to Khazanda begum whom she called, Dear Lady, feeling intuitively as any precocious child could, that her aunt loved her more than anyone else. "My Dear Lady, I don't know, she makes me sad. I know she loves me! You make me laugh, Padishah, and I love you, love you this much!" She extended her arms, making a circle over her head, and laughing with glee as Babur hugged her.

"I can hear the ripple of wisdom in your laughter, my love, and see the stars of poetry in your eyes." Babur could see over her shoulders the ceremonial approach of Dilawar Khan.

The sunlight itself had attained a dreamy glow, it seemed, as Dilawar Khan drifted closer followed by Ahmed, both enveloped in some halo of haze and mystery. Babur sat there transfixed, his eyes kindling disbelief and astonishment. Ahmad, carrying a silver tray, was quick to lower it at Babur's feet, curtsying and leaving. Gulbadan had slipped away, but Babur didn't notice, his attention claimed by the contents on the silver tray with utter absorption. Dilawar Khan had curtsied too, and now sat attending to his task of preparing a pan out of the jeweled pandan. A subtle hush was all Babur could feel, golden and surreal, much like the half-ripe mangoes preserved in honey in a glass dish on the tray, which appeared to be a rare treasure possessed by Dilawar Khan. No word had been spoken, though smiles were exchanged and eyes telling volumes which could not be expressed in words.

Dilawar Khan had begun the ritual of pan-making, lifting the lid of the jeweled pandan with much care and reverence. A layer of chuna—lime was spread over the betel leaf, and a coat of katha—red vegetable extract was added to the first layer, then a sprinkling of supari and fennel seeds, colored and sweetened. With great precision, he rolled the betel leaf into a triangle, and offered it to Babur along with a spoonful of murraba. Babur chewed on this delicacy, smiling approval.

"This pan tastes better than the one I had in Lahore." Babur's eyes were lit up with genuine pleasure. "You have brought the most delectable of appetizers—to whet my appetite for wars."

"Padishah!" Was Dilawar Khan's cheerful exclamation! "That means you would march on Hind, soon?" He commenced the ritual of making another pan.

"That means I would conquer Hind, extinguishing the fires of rebellion in the wake of my conquests. Hind must not bleed to death by its briars of contentions." Babur's eyes were kindling the stars of divinations he could witness inside the mirror of his psyche.

"Allah-uh-Akbar!" Dilawar Khan chanted with the fervor of a young recruit.

"Allah loves not war but peace, not tyranny but compassion, my valorous son." Babur murmured with a touch of gentleness. "You are too young to explore the tragedies of death and devastation. Men often use the name of Allah to justify their passions for greed, cruelty and ambition. Most of us who lack the wisdom to understand the will of God become mighty tyrants in their quest for power and possession, but a few fortunate ones with a rare gift of understanding conquer for the sake of peace and harmony, becoming the vessels of God's love and justice." His look was profound, his thoughts indulging in the luxury of mentoring a youth as he would his own sons. "Allah is all love, but mankind in its ocean of vanity and ignorance utters the Holy name in vain, clinging to vice while preaching virtue, and nurturing evil against the mask of goodness. Well, I digress? You have brought a paradox from Hind, my son! A paradox which weighs heavy on my conscience! Night after night I have lain awake to peek through the heart of this paradox, but you alone hold the key to unlock its portals." His look was profound and piercing. "The first and foremost duty of a virtuous son is to remain loyal and obedient to the wishes of his father? I can't stop wondering why you chose to favor Padishah against your father, seeking my love and approval than his consent and affection? Does not your conscience revolt against this act of betrayal?"

"Fathers make mistakes too, Padishah, much like their own fathers." Dilawar Khan murmured with implicit regret, his young features washed by sadness. "I think, my father's only mistake lies in the fact that he taught me to choose the right path in the first place. This might be the cause of my disobedience, though I don't feel a sense of betrayal. I am young, but I know the difference between right and wrong. Why my father chose to rebel, I don't know, but I fear he would lose all in his ambition for power by the hands of the same warring lords who have incited him to sedition. You are the rightful heir to rule Hind and to dissolve all rifts, and bring peace where discord reigns. Your kind and generous heart, I trust, would forgive my father when you return to reclaim your kingdoms." He stopped abruptly, overwhelmed by the warmth of tenderness in Babur's gaze.

"Your sweet flattery could cost you life-imprisonment, my son, though it has become a haven for exiles and dervishes!" Babur intoned cheerfully. "Your purity of heart is a mighty ransom to gain liberty from any misfortune, I must admit. Now it's time for my siesta, and I would dream of conquests." Babur got to his feet, waving dismissal. "Ten more days and we march to Hind. Prince Humayun is joining us in this campaign." He murmured over his shoulders, disappearing behind the balcony doors under some spell of haste and euphoria.

The afternoon spell was dissolved into a pool of siesta, yielding to the flurry of evening schedule with all its court affairs, followed by dinner and parlance amongst the royal household. It was dusk now as Babur and Bibi Mubaraka strolled in their palace garden, spellbound by the hush and beauty of nature spilling forth color and perfume. The pine-scented paths and the sweetness of wine in the air were drugging both with the bliss in silence. A coppery veil of clouds was lowered over the sun, its rays spun with gold, dancing and shuddering. Babur's thoughts were shuddering with a sense of loss, bidding farewell to Kabul, to his gardens. A dull stab of grief and sadness was piercing his psyche, cutting open the wound of a grave where Sweet Absent lay resting. He couldn't abandon her in eternal neglect—in Kabul, his psyche was raising a shrill cry, constricting his heart and soul with a warning that he would never return to Kabul.

What madness compels me to entertain such thoughts? I have always returned to Kabul, no continent on earth, not even Hind can hold me prisoner forever? This jewel of a Hind, I would polish and preserve, and then—Babur's thoughts were coming to a sudden halt by the sweet voice of his beloved.

"How long would you stay in Hind, Padishah? When would you come home?" Bibi Mubaraka broke the spell of silence, hugging her green silks as if holding dear the poetry of this scented garden.

"You would know, my mountain beauty, you would know!" Babur teased, slipping his arm around her waist. "I can't leave you behind in this Eden all by yourself, my love. No wars could ever separate us anymore. Your sweet presence would be my talisman to conquer, and to live—with joy, forever and forever!" He kept strolling, his arm tightening around her waist, their feet falling in rhythm with the great love in their hearts.

"Padishah!" Joy and disbelief trembled upon Bibi Mubaraka's lips, her heart dancing and rejoicing.

"Do I detect a scent of betrayal in your voice, my love?" Babur teased again. "You would rather roam free in the pine-scented valleys of Kabul than come with me to Hind?"

"Padishah!" Was Bibi Mubaraka's trilling protest! "You would provoke the jealousy of all your wives. Already, they are jealous of your love for me?"

"Jealousy is sweet elixir to love, my love! They seem drunk by its sweetness, and would stay in happy swoon till we return!" Babur held her in one tight embrace, both clinging to each other like a pair of young lovers. "To undress you with my eyes alone suits not my passion mad and formidable. And yet I would fain hold you dear to my heart and soul, shunning the violence of my passion wild and insatiable." He crushed her into his arms, his kisses wild and searing.

27

Rani's Koh-i-Noor

The gorgeous east with richest hand
Pours on her sons Barbarie pearl and gold
— Milton

The Moghul standards of red and yellow were a rude blaze against the morning sun as Babur rode through the ranks of his troops, vigilant and inspecting. The chain mail over his breast and helmet on his head were glinting their commands while he commanded courage and obedience from his soldiers. The sun-baked earth was the field of combat where the Moghul troops were gathered against the army of the Sultan of Delhi, Sultan Ibrahim. Outnumbering the Moghul troops, the Sultan's army stood their ground on the plains of Sirsawa facing the Moghuls, along with their army of war elephants. Further down below river Jamna gleamed under the hot sun, its turgid waters churning ripples, as if goading the inactive armies to commence their fighting and to replenish the veins of mother earth with blood, so that the wheel of life and death could continue grinding to maintain the balance of renewal and eternalness.

Thou art my shield, my strength, my protector, O Allah! Lend me hope, courage, victory. One anguished throb of a prayer escaped Babur's heart as he reconnoitered the great river of army opposite, against which his own looked like a pond, harmless and insignificant. *Hope for mankind, to appease pain and suffering, to extinguish the flames of cruelty, treachery and malfeasance, to entertain reverence for life, to efface the passion for killing?* His thoughts were hovering over the long trails of his journey from Kabul, splintered with wars and conquests on the way to Delhi.

The Moghul contingents, journeying from Kabul through Khyber Pass, had halted at Ali Masjid, where Babur and his troops had offered noon prayers. Days were merged into weeks when they had reached the black waters near Bigram. Several boats and rafters were employed to cross the river till they had reached the foothills along the river Indus leading toward Sialkot. They had to cross two more rivers, Jhelum and Chenab, before they could reach Sialkot. In Sialkot, the Gujars—peasants of this city, on the breach of stealing bullocks and buffaloes from the Moghul encampment, were punished severely by the leaders of the troops without the approval of Babur. At the junction of this thought, Babur's heart was filled with sadness, but he was quick to whip his thoughts back on the trail of conquests. The cities of Bihat, Lahore and Milwat were conquered. The leader of Milwat, Doulat Khan, unable to defend his claims, was brought before Babur as a humble suppliant. Two swords suspended from his neck affirming his absolute submission—the swords, which he had boasted he would employ in killing the Moghuls. Babur had forgiven him of course, his thoughts now following the inveterate rebel, Alaed-din who had taken refuge in the castle of Kinkutch after the sweeping conquests of the Moghuls in Serhind and Punjab. The cannons and the movable breastworks were claiming Babur's attention, his gaze assessing the stacks of artillery, but his concentration was broken by the sudden appearance of prince Humayun, who came galloping toward him, looking more like a shining knight than a Moghul soldier.

"Do you think, my Prince, that six moveable breastworks between the gun-carriages would leave enough room for matchlock-men to fire their guns with great—" Babur's concern for safety and efficiency was swallowed by the fury of a war-cry from the ranks of the Sultan Ibrahim's soldiers. "The glory in this battle belongs to you, my valorous Prince, and you would wear the laurels of victory!" He spurred his horse toward the battleground, thundering commands and instructions.

The battle had raged only for a few hours, but now the fiery sun was showering its arrows upon the fleeing enemy as prince Humayun headed the pursuit across from the field of Panipat. Twelve thousand Moghuls against one hundred thousand of the enemy's soldiers had gained victory, not by their valor alone, but by the use of the mighty cannons. The impact of the cannons had thrown the war elephants of Sultan Ibrahim into absolute frenzy, and they had become his own nemesis, causing much panic and confusion amongst his ranks, unhorsing many soldiers, and trampling over the fallen with much rage and ferocity. The offenders were hemmed in from rear and front, from right and left from the disciplined ranks of the Moghuls, suffering most piteously the assault from arrows and artillery. The battlefield of Panipat had turned into a pandemonium amidst the flashing of kards and dhups, and the vanquished were fleeing pell-mell, trying their best to escape the blows from daggers and scimitars, while javelins whisked after them mercilessly. The odor of pain and sweat was heavy under the pall of smoke from the cannons while the wounded and the dying moaned and groaned. Burning vividly against the haze of the sun were the standards of red and yellow, fluttering carelessly over the corpses of men and beasts, all caked with dust and blood.

Pity and sadness! The mute agony in Babur's spirit was awakening to grief and compassion. Still astride, he seemed to be contemplating this field of affliction, his senses sifting the sound of laments from that of rejoicings. Suspended between the ether of his inertia and silence within he was transported for one flash of a moment in the world of his beloved, seeking guidance from her sweet presence. *Many wives, mothers, daughters, sweet beloveds are waiting for their men to return home? Sad and tragic indeed! These men would suffer no torments on Judgment Day, for they have suffered enough.* The songs of victory and jubilations were grazing his awareness, and he was riding toward the tides of revelry, thinking only of rewarding his soldiers with boons and compliments. *The vanquished hope only for mercy,* his thoughts were marching back into the bowers of peace and presence where Afghan Lady alone reigned and commanded.

The palace garden at Delhi was swathed in golden haze of the evening as Babur sat there on his throne under the makeshift pavilion of velvet and damask in the company of his viziers and courtiers as the first Moghul emperor of Hindustan. Bibi Mubaraka was seated by Babur on a gilded chair, both feeling a little respite from heat by the diligence of Tahir who was fanning with a fan made out of peacock feathers. At the foot of the throne was a Persian carpet, hosting close friends, most prominent amongst them Khwaja Kilan, Dilawar Khan, Mehdi Khwaja and Abdullah Hatifi. Prince Humayun was absent since he was dispatched to Agra right after the battle to guard the treasures of the Raja of Gwalior—Bikermajit, who had died on the field of Panipat while fighting valiantly.

Babur donned in white silks with a red plume in his turban and the fire of rubies on his belt, was indeed the first Moghul emperor of Hindustan, khutba being read in his name at Jami Masjid in Delhi by Maulana Mahmud. Bibi Mubaraka beside him in pale silks and diamonds in her hair and around her throat was radiating her aura of power, which only the pure in heart could retain and possess. Another person blessed with the purity of heart in this assemblage was Tahir, though he was proud of his gold turban this evening, but simply happy to serve Padishah turned Emperor. The courtiers were rapt watching the olive-complexioned maidens with dark eyes, their colorful saris lending them the semblance of houris, serving wine and fruit from the very bowls of paradise. And paradise it was—a jewel garden, not in blooms, but in treasures. Bales upon bales of gold, silver and jewels were torn open to be assessed and recorded. The scribes who had recorded earlier the number of lives lost, were now busy writing the worth of treasures gained. Besides gold and jewels, the silver coins in currency of tankas, ashrafis and shahrukhis were heaped in separate mounds to be distributed amongst the soldiers and courtiers. Several piles of equal value were set aside to be given to the poor and the needy in Hindustan. Babur, though apparently present in this ocean of jewels and jubilations, was seeking the sanctuary of his solitude. His thoughts were following Humayun inside the palace of Agra, but the silent journey in his head was disrupted by the loud comment of Dilawar Khan.

"The valor of the Moghuls has struck deep terror into the hearts of the Hindustanis!" Dilawar Khan, peering over the shoulders of the scribes appeared to be boasting. "A stunning victory, number of slain on the enemy's side, what, sixty thousand?" He turned his head abruptly, seeking the attention of Babur. "Your valor alone has gained this victory, my Emperor." His expression was cut short by the intensity of amusement in Babur's eyes.

"Prince Humayun's first victory, my young flatterer, his very first and great victory!" Babur indulged kindly. "No valor of ours could have won this battle without the boon of some divine assistance." His heart was constricting with sadness, yet his thoughts were expanding inside the realm of inner knowledge. "I have been thinking, in consideration of my reliance on Divine aid, the Most High Allah did not suffer the distress and hardships that I have undergone to be thrown away, but defeated my formidable enemy, and made me the conqueror of this noble land of Hindustan. This success I do not ascribe to my strength, nor did this good fortune flow from my efforts, but from the fountain of the favor and mercy of Allah." His hand and heart were reaching out to Bibi Mubaraka. And he claimed her hand before returning his attention to the young flatterer. "Your father has my forgiveness, but I must send him to Bhira in Kabul till the injuries he has received through his rebellious heart are somewhat healed." He appeared to think aloud, the profound look in his eyes falling on his poet and scholar. "You should write Fateh-nama, Hatifi, now that you have witnessed with your own eyes our victory at Panipat. Your masnavi, Laila and Majnoon has earned you the title of a great writer. Since you could write so well through vicarious experience, this one should make you perfect your genius?"

"It was easy to write about the agony of the lovers, my Emperor." Abdullah Hatifi glowed with joy and pride. "To crown this miraculous victory, I have to write with the blood of my inspiration."

"Yes, if I ever did believe in miracles, this would be the one, a victory most—" Babur's thoughts were left unexpressed by the sudden approach of a messenger.

"I bring you sad news, Padishah." The messenger fell into a hasty curtsy before unfolding his bulletin of news. "Shah Ismael of Persia is dead. His younger son, Shah Tahmasp, is the successor to his throne. The news of king's death has reached the Uzbeks on both sides of Sirr, and they are plotting to invade Khorasan."

May the bigotry of Islam die with him! One thought bubbled in Babur's head, but aloud he said. "May his anguished soul rest in peace! My heart is with prince Humayun at Agra, but my mind is sailing over the hills toward Khorasan. A clashing of cymbals within my soul?" He dismissed the messenger, his look both sad and profound. "The emperor of Hindustan is needed at Agra this evening, and yet he wishes to fly to Khorasan to secure that kingdom for prince Tahmasp." His gaze was alighting on his mentor and advisor. "You would prove me wrong, Khwaja, I know, since I thought Uzbeks would never rise in sedition after the death of their mighty despot, Shaibani Khan?"

"Foes never die, my Emperor. They live through the pages of history, casting a spell of vengeance in the minds of their disciples, ever belligerent!" Khwaja Kilan smiled ruefully.

A group of men approaching in one solemn procession was attracting the attention of all present. Amongst them was one soldier carrying a silver platter, displaying a severed head, all bloody and grotesque. He stopped a few paces away from the throne, holding this gruesome prize under Babur's icy gaze, his own eyes glowing with pride and fervor.

"The living proof of Sultan Ibrahim's death, my Emperor!" The soldier's face was flushed with exultation. "We found his body under a heap of corpses, almost several thousand, it seemed?" His expression was deflated all of a sudden by the look of murder in the emperor's eyes, kindling rage and disgust.

Babur was more afraid than disgusted. He had noticed the sudden pallor of Bibi Mubaraka, who had closed her eyes, clutching his hand feverishly. A mantle of ominous silence had fallen over all, all eyes riveted to the object of pity and revulsion.

"Remove this vile trophy away from the sight of all!" Babur thundered, shattering this glass of silence. "He was a valorous man, give him a decent burial with all due respect and honor. *Better to forgive than to avenge an injury*, my baba used to say." He watched the men retreat in haste before he closed eyes, his heart thundering its commands to efface all with the exception of his beloved.

"Dead have attained the glory of peace, my Emperor." Khwaja Kilan began soothingly. "The rites and honors, especially in times of wars, better be left unpracticed."

"A decent burial is for the solace of the living, not for the benefit of the dead." Babur's eyes were shot open, his look smoldering. "My thoughts are with the aged mother of Sultan Ibrahim, Khwaja. The bereaving mother of the unfortunate son! You are entrusted with the task of bestowing upon Buwa Begum the perghana of seven lakhs from our treasury."

"I feel honored, my Emperor." Khwaja Kilan began rather tumultuously. "What puzzles me if I may dare to question your wisdom? In honor of victory at Bajuar, severed heads of the slain were piled together to erect great pillars, honoring neither the dead, nor the living? Why such change of heart now?"

"My wisdom if I claim to be wise, my wise Khwaja, is the result of your gracious teaching in the art of living and warring." Babur's eyes were kindling the lamps of amusement. "The method to my madness is to cater to the needs of time, not to the reason in sanity. It knows when to spare the vanquished, and why subdue the proud. Why, when, where, who, all such imponderables fit in the scheme of this world-puzzle somehow and somewhere—a paradox in wisdom indeed! More paradoxes, if you will! Wisdom without compassion is ignorance and forgiveness without love, arrogance?" He got to his feet, assisting Bibi Mubaraka to her own, as if oblivious to his surroundings!

"Make arrangements for our journey to Agra. Prince Humayun needs our wise council, if not our compassion?" He commanded over his shoulders, entirely absorbed in leading his beloved toward the palace.

The secluded garden in the back of the Delhi palace was the sanctuary for both Babur and Bibi Mubaraka as they strolled hand in hand, much like the lovers reunited after centuries. This garden with only a few rose bushes and swaths of bougainvillea on trellises was certainly no match for the gardens in Kabul, but the colorful zinnia and marigold in unkempt beds were vibrant and delightful under the haze of the evening sun, all gold and metallic. A hum of voices and laughter from across the palace where soldiers had gathered to tend to the mounts for the night journey to Agra, was reaching the privacy of this garden, as the royal couple kept strolling under some spell of bliss and silence. The air was stifling all of a sudden, and Babur could feel the tingling of sweat down his spine, his heart aching for the beauty and comfort of his homeland.

"How my heart longs for the cool wine in the air!" A prayerful exclamation escaped Babur's thoughts. "Gleaming terraces and the fountains perfumed with the scents from the flowers! This heat sure drains one's energy, inducing languor and dullness." He released her moist hand, slipping his arm around her waist. "You are the child of the mountains, beloved. You do not belong here. Even this Delhi palace is dismal and airless. A monument of ugliness, I should say. But inside my heart I have erected a palace for you of all marble, lofty and grand. Just for you, perfumed with love, to pay homage to your beauty! Would you be happy in such a palace, my love?" His feet came to an abrupt halt before one olive tree, gnarled and twisted, but his gaze was finding rest in the dazzling blue eyes of his beloved.

"My happiness is wherever you are, my Emperor. The most charming of palaces wherever you take me?" Bibi Mubaraka sang joyfully, her face flushed and radiant.

"I am your slave, my miracle of loveliness!" Babur stood there gazing, awed and humbled, dreamily aware of the reflection of Sweet Absent in the very radiance of her demeanor. "Why I have this fear, my love, always this fear that I would lose you? And with this fear comes the sense of desolation that without you there would be nothing but grief and darkness. Agra is not far, only one day journey at the most, but it seems like continents apart without you by my side. I would fain take you with me, but the heat and the dust and the danger of raids. The roads are infested with rebels and bandits." He cupped her face into his hands, kissing her and holding her to him fiercely, and wondering why the hunger of his love was never slaked.

Time and distance were left in abeyance back in Delhi, and now Agra palace was the abode of repose for Babur, as he sat in its great hall, sipping his wine tranquilly. All night journey, followed by a few hours of rest, had restored Babur's spirit to joyful anticipation. Before going to bed he had commanded his servants to furnish this hall with luxurious carpets and cushions, and the result this morning had astonished him to his heart's content. Not only was floor furnished with Persian carpets, but the bare walls of green tiles adorned with tapestries and gilt paintings. His gaze this particular moment was hovering over the rosewood chest, hosting flagons and goblets of wine, all gold and encrusted with jewels. Several caskets of jewels were within his view too, the most precious of gifts presented to Humayun by the Rani of Gwalior. Lolling against pillows, not far from the jewel caskets were seated Khwaja Kilan and Mehdi Khwaja. But Babur's gaze was turning to Humayun where he sat guarding a rare treasure as he claimed it to be, reserved as a surprise gift for him—Babur, he had commented mysteriously.

This surprise gift was concealed in a red pouch of creamy velvet, seemingly alive and truly mysterious. But Babur's gaze as well as his thoughts was studying his son with a keen perception. Humayun was impeccably dressed as always, the sparkling jewels in his turban with a green plume aslant. His silk robe of pale hue was absorbing the shade of emeralds. A tender smile hovered over Babur's lips, his thoughts turning inward to flaunt the reflection of his red plume and his cummerbund encrusted with rubies and diamonds. *He is in love*, one rude thought spiraled in Babur's head, piercing the shade of poetic melancholy blending so well with Humayun's features, pallid and glistening. Prince Humayun feeling the warmth of Babur's gaze was lifting his eyes up to him brimming with love and devotion.

"You have proved yourself worthy of valor and wisdom, my dear Prince." Babur flashed him a wistful smile. "I must commend you on your judgment in lending protection to the family of late Raja Bikermajit. It makes me proud that you didn't force them to relinquish any of their treasures, and accepted only what they gave of their own free wills. Your kindness would lead you to success, always, if you could keep your heart free from greed, malice and cruelty."

"You taught me to be kind, my Emperor, and all which I possess comes from you, the wisdom and the compassion and much more." Was Humayun's gallant response, as he held out his goblet to Mushin to be replenished!

"Your flattery is superfluous, dear Humayun." Babur smiled, his eyes kindling stars of reproof. "You have been drinking too much, I have noticed. Excess in anything is harmful to health, both physical and spiritual. Practice moderation in everything you do, that's the universal law to healthy and harmonious living." His thoughts were striving toward making his son the model of virtue and strength. "A lesson in generosity, you must learn, this very day! All these treasures which you have received are yours to keep or give away. But sharing these with others would keep your heart free from the evils of greed and avarice. Divide this wealth into four portions. One as a reward for your valor and hardships, one for your troops and friends who have helped you achieve this victory. The third one for the poor and needy in Hindustan, and the fourth one to enhance the beauty of this land we have come to rule with all justice and fairness. The ill-paved road from Delhi to Agra is to be repaired, rather to be built into a great highway. We would plant gardens in Agra, channel the water through canals, and build dams and palaces. Agra is to be my capital." He paused, becoming aware of the deflated expression of Humayun. "What strange light of misery I see in your eyes, my son? Does the lesson in generosity not suit your princely needs? You deem my suggestion unwise and extravagant, is that it?" He demanded half incisively, half indulgently.

"No, my Emperor, no!" Humayun protested, the look of misery in his eyes deepening. "The only wealth I desire is to stay in Badakhshan, or in Kabul." He lowered his gaze against the fire of intensity in Babur's eyes. His eyes were riveted to the velvet pouch before him, his senses accosting fear and sadness.

"You do not plan to stay in Hindustan, my Emperor, do you?" Was Khwaja Kilan's incredulous exclamation, adding flint to Babur's simmering rage.

"We have no affinity with the barbarians who came here for the sake of plunder, carrying away the riches of this land, and leaving behind death and devastation." Babur thundered. "Have we conquered this land only to abandon it to the warring factions of rajas, sultans and ruffians? No, Hindustan would be our home! We would make it a beautiful, welcoming home, taming its hot climate with shaded trees and fountains. The beauty of Kabul, Samarkand, Ferghana, we would bring here, planting orchards and kneading the dust of this land into nuggets of gold for riches in trade and revenue." His rage was drained by the dear remembrance of Ferghana, his beloved homeland.

A subtle lull was settled over all in the great hall, none daring to speak lest they invoke Babur's anger. Yet Babur's eyes were lit by tenderness all of a sudden as he sat sipping his wine, his gaze settling on Humayun. The Prince was lost in his world of silence, rather absorbed in retrieving the jewel from the velvet pouch, his features washed by pallor. He was thinking about the Rani of Gwalior who had stolen his heart, his thoughts screaming that he had lost a treasure much more valuable than the one bestowed upon him by the Rani. This rose-tinted diamond, weighing almost three hundred and twenty ratis—as the Rani had told him now throbbed in his hand as he carried it to Babur, offering it to him with all humility and reverence.

"My gift of love and devotion to you, my Emperor, this diamond rare and precious!" Humayun seemed to be in a trance, unaware of the fact that the dazzling beauty of this gift enveloped all in a mantle of awe and shock. "This is Rani's favorite diamond, her great gift which she insisted that I must accept. She has named this diamond, Koh-i-Noor, meaning, the mountain of light."

Babur claimed this diamond with equal reverence as it was presented. He sat there rapt, watching this diamond sparkle on the palm of his own hand. Its radiance almost dazzling, and spell-binding! *Reflecting many stars, sunsets, rainbows*, Babur was thinking, overwhelmed by the beauty of this jewel and by the rare nobility of his son's sentiments.

"You are worthy to rule the world, my beloved Prince." Babur held out the diamond to his son. "Rani of Gwalior gave it to you, and I give it back to you. Your love and devotion are the most precious of jewels you have given me to gladden my heart for ages to come." He smiled as Humayun claimed it back reluctantly. "Precious as this diamond is, it's worth nothing if coveted as a vainglorious prize by men of greed. And I am sure many would covet it, not for the sake of its beauty alone, but to cut its heart into many sparkling gems to gain fortunes." He paused, his look profound and piercing. "That wretched look in your eyes again, my son? Rani of Gwalior, indeed! Did you win this jewel as some amorous gift, or did you steal it from some holy temple—in someone's heart?" He teased.

"My Emperor, for sure, Rani of Gwalior bestowed upon me all these gifts, including this diamond." Humayun laughed, trying his best to keep the agony of his love within his breast. "She was probably expecting someone savage and ruthless, but finding me affable and courteous, she began showering upon me all sorts of gifts and compliments. Actually, I had done nothing to deserve this! All I did was to offer her and her family protection from plunderers and cut-throats, granting her the privilege of taking all her treasures with her to the home of her parents. Also, promising to safeguard her possessions to be transported later at my own expense." He averted his gaze, resorting to humor to safeguard his pain of love which might escape his eyes. "She was charmed by my gentle manners I would like to think, if not moved by my handsomeness?"

"Yes, an amulet of love, this diamond, my son, you would never forget." Was Babur's low comment, his keen perception discovering the secret of his son's misery and sadness. "Strange and yet not so strange that my son and my dear mentor wish to return to Kabul." His gaze was sweeping all in one profound embrace. "Let no such proposal, *to return to Kabul*, come from any friend of mine. But if amongst you there be found anyone who does not wish to remain with me, let him depart. He has my full consent, unconditionally." He closed his eyes, summoning the vision of Afghan Lady inside the great palace at Agra his mind had already fashioned.

28

Emperor of Hindustan

And thence
To Agra and Lahore of Great Moghuls.
Oh, Allah! Kingship is thine alone
Thine to give when Thou pleasest
Thine to take away at thy pleasure
    — Milton

Babur scribbled this verse on the new page of his treatise on poetry—a treatise, which he had begun writing a few months after his victory at Panipat. He was seated this bright morning in the library of his newly built palace in Agra. From its lofty chambers, the waters of Jamna could be seen flowing tranquilly, though the river itself meandered and disappeared against the contours of the hills, verdant and voluptuous. He was dressed in white silks, the color of his breeches matching the yellow plume in his turban, and his shoes of Moroccan leather with tips pointed inward, studded with pearls and agates. Seated at his desk by the window of marble latticework, he could see the palace grounds down below where the gardeners worked diligently and laboriously.

Abandoning his jeweled pen, he sat twirling the ropes of pearls around his neck, his gaze sailing down to arrest the work in progress and to imagine more to fit his canvas of imagination. The saplings of pipal and chenar trees were already lifting their heads to sunshine. Far from this grove could be seen a group of gardeners, planting orange, loquat and tamarind trees, their faces swarthy and glistening. A few leagues away from the fruit orchard was a gazebo made out of red bricks where three young men labored over the trenches for the sole purpose of planting plumbago, bridal creeper and Rat-ki-Rani. Close to the palace gates, some men were preparing flower-beds, while the others digging deep the sun-baked earth for latticed water jets and fountains to be designed by the Moghul architects.

Flower-beds for fall flowers, which would be early winter over here, one cloudlet of a thought was surfacing in Babur's head, behind which lay a storm of his fear and restlessness. His prime fear was for Bibi Mubaraka, who had contracted yellow fever, but was recovering now, but he still worried about her health, driving his physician Sayyid Tabib insane with his demands and com-

mands for the comfort of his beloved. He himself had just recovered from an
evil assault of enteritis, but its ill affects of anxiety and depression were still
with him, quick to surface and linger, if he didn't dispel them with the rod of his
volition and discipline.

I am getting close to death, Babur leaned his head against his gilded chair,
his eyes closing. Behind the closed shutters of his eyes were opening the portals
of his new palace, tall and imposing! Bibi Mubaraka had crept into his thoughts,
standing beside him, facing the façade of this new palace, her gaze riveted to the
decorative pillars and the arches embellished with the art of calligraphy. She
was awed by the carvings of stone in the shape of lion, snake, griffon, nil gao
and elephant. Her cries of delight and admiration had brought tears into her
eyes, while she had stood caressing the banisters etched with the motif of lotus
and palmetto, all bright and glistening.

I am in bliss and much-too-much in love with my Afghan Lady. The sprinkling of joy and sadness in Babur's head was making his senses opiate, sucking
his thoughts into a river of imponderables. *My beloved is with me, yet why my
spirit is restless, longing and searching for something unattainable, thirsting for
the hemlock of sweet unforgettable? Yes, my spirit is inching closer to the dark
abode of the Sweet Absent, welcoming death, anticipating an accolade? No, I
am living for love, loving Sweet Present, knowing Sweet Absent.* His thoughts
were leaving this dark abode, stirring the dust of the past months into torches lit
by the flames of rebellions. The wildfire of rift and violence had run havoc in all
parts of Hindustan, outliving the summer, hot and searing, and lingering after
the monsoon, wet and stifling, but all hurdles were torched to oblivion against
the flint of Babur's wisdom.

Babur had become the lord of Northern Hindustan, his empire stretching
from the Himalayas to Gwalior, from Oxus to Bengal, including the kingdoms
of Kanauj and Luchnow. Eastward, his empire extended from Badakhshan and
Kabul through Punjab and Lahore, to the borders of Bengal. The leader of Gwalior, Tartar Khan had submitted to the authority of the emperor Babur. Prince
Humayun had succeeded in quelling the seditions of the Afghan leaders, Ali
Fermuli and Bayezid Fermuli, in the kingdoms of Oudh and Jaunpur. Amidst
those little skirmishes, one son of Ali Fermuli was captured as a prisoner of war,
but Babur had ordered his release unconditionally.

*And yet Rana Sanga is asserting his claim over my conquered domains of
Chanderi and Ranthambor, challenging us to a war?* Babur's thoughts wearied
of wars were turning their back over the battlefields of rifts and dissentions.
*Everyone is leaving me? Why did I bestow upon Khwaja the kingdom of Ghazni,
and why did I give him the permission to leave Hindustan?* His heart was aching
all of a sudden, cognizant of the fact that his friend—mentor was leaving this
very evening. *My soldiers are wearied of heat and dust, of wars and discomforts,
longing for home, for Kabul. Strange, my soul too hungers for Kabul, for its
beauty and fragrance, for the scent of home! And yet, Hindustan is fascinating
with all its relics of sacred and profane, hosting a pantheon of gods and goddesses, garlanded and bejeweled. Even the poorest of brides in this land can*

boast of gold studs and gold bangles. He was opening his eyes, his gaze fluttering over the Makrana shelves laden with books he had acquired during his conquests. These books were his priceless treasures, the only treasures he had kept
to himself, the rest distributed amongst his friends, soldiers and the poor and
needy of Hindustan. This benevolence of his had earned him the title of king-
Kalendar, lending him the privilege of ruling with justice and kindness.

Kindness! Babur's thoughts were flashing one reflection of a scene where
one young bride was hurled into the blaze of fire over the pyre of her husband
for the sake of honor. *The honor which was denied to her in life, would it not be
denied to her in death also?* His very heart was peering into this rite of suttee,
aghast and shuddering. *And yet, these rites are sacred. Even if I were to snatch
the brides away from the pyres of their husbands, they would kindle their own to
immolate their lives? Death made beautiful by the rites of wedlock in life and
death?* He heaved himself up, and began to pace, forcing his thoughts to discipline, rather guiding them on the road to newly built gardens and highways.

The highway from Agra to Delhi was made wide, all ditches filled, and all
bumps smoothed. Another highway, four hundred mile long from Agra to Lahore was under construction, where pipal trees were to be planted on both sides
for the benefit of shade for travelers. The plans for four gardens in Agra were
being drawn, and another one for the city in Dholpur.

*A great palace at Sikri would be a splendid addition to the glorious gardens
in that city!* Babur's thoughts were seeking the beauty of Baghi-Zar-Afshan—
the gold scattering garden, where he had glimpsed the loveliness of nature for
just one day during his visit in spring. *The crow imperial with its orange flowers
as if clusters of sunshine sat glistening on the lush branches!* His thoughts were
rapt with admiration as if he was sitting in that garden. *Ah, but the gul mohur,
another rare tree, its yellow and scarlet blooms shimmering, much like the jewels exotic and precious. How blissful to sit under its shade in spring while taking
a shower of gold from its scented blooms? I must take Bibi Mubaraka there
when gul mohur and crow imperial are in bloom.* His thoughts were whirling
back in time, peering into the loneliness of his heart where his tragic love still
sat mourning the loss of Sweet Absent. But he was awakening to the need of
paying homage to the greatest of all his loves, his Afghan Lady, his beloved
present and living. His feet were obeying his thoughts, leaving the comfort of
his library, and seeking his bliss in the rose and ivory bedroom.

The marble foyer with gilt paintings was left behind as Babur hastened toward the bedroom. His steps were light as he approached closer so as not to disturb his beloved since she might be sleeping. Outside the door, he paused to
admire a set of tapestries in gilded frames, and then stepped inside with utmost
caution. He paused again, noticing his royal physician busy offering some sort
of concoction in a silver cup to his beloved, which she drank obediently. They
didn't notice him until he drifted toward the bed, his eyes flashing laughter and
amusement.

"My Emperor." Sayyid Tabib bowed double.

"Are you forcing my wife to drink that deplorable extraction from rose mixed with borage tea?" Babur arched his eyebrows. "Some sort of spicy concoction recommended for fevers? A panacea for all ailments, is that it?"

"No, my Emperor." Sayyid Tabib protested. He was relieved to see the emperor smiling, for since the Begum's illness he had received nothing from him but commands and reprimands.

"I hope not." Babur smiled, stealing a look at his beloved. "For, if Bibi Mubaraka Begum's health doesn't improve at the end of this week, you would be tossed alive on a pyre of some luckless fellow who had the misfortune of dying celibate!" He laughed, noticing glints of fear in the eyes of his physician. "Did you, or did you not feed Tahir the balls of dough kneaded with rose seeds? Another one of your exotic remedy for dysentery!"

"Yes, my Emperor. He was cured!" Was Sayyid Tabib's flustered response against the tinkling of mirth from the lips of Bibi Mubaraka.

"And belladonna mixed with charras which you made poor Kabir drink?" Babur began under some spell of inquisition. "Yes, that poet from Banaras whom I befriended! After one draught of that drink and the poor wretch couldn't even recite a couplet worth one tanka. Now begone, no more experiments with the aphrodisiacs. I want to hear music and poetry in my court in the evening, make sure that Kabir is sober." He dismissed him with an impatient wave of his arm.

Sayyid Tabib after offering consecutive curtsies to begum and the emperor disappeared behind the door, while Babur caught in another spell of awe stood gazing at the pale rose of a beloved couchant against one pillow on her bed, its canopy swept aside in silvery knots and sashes.

So soft, so tender, so adorable, so irresistible! Babur's very thoughts of denial and suffering were murmuring these endearments.

"My mountain Lily!" Babur claimed her hands, pressing them to his lips reverently. "You need a sprinkling of snow over your pallor, if not the blush of a rose!" He released her hands reluctantly.

"Your cheeks need more snow than mine, my Emperor." Bibi Mubaraka sang sweetly, the blue oceans in her eyes sparkling.

"Your slave, my love, not your emperor." Babur intoned caressively.

"My love, then!" Bibi Mubaraka murmured back against the flood of ardor in Babur's eyes.

"My sweetness All!" Babur leaned over, kissing her lips, and holding her close to him for one brief moment. "How do you feel, my love?" He appeared to drink deep from the blue oceans of her eyes, thirstily and wistfully.

"Wonderful, just now!" Bibi Mubaraka quipped joyfully.

"Your wit is better than your health!" Babur laughed, feeling her pulse, and kissing her again. "You do need rest, and good nourishment." Babur turned away, crushing his desire within him, and praying silently for her health and strength. "You better get your strength back quickly to see the progress of a garden in Dholpur for your pleasure alone. One hundred men, including gardeners and architects are employed to design one jewel of a garden. Since you love lotus flowers, this garden is to be named, Lotus Bagh."

"Thank you." Bibi Mubaraka murmured, joy and love in her eyes washing her features with a subtle glow.

"When you regain your strength, love, I would take you to Sikri." Babur knotted his hands behind his back, more so to restrain his passion than to discipline his thoughts. "You would love the gold scattering garden in Sikri. We would sit under the gul mohur tree, and I would read you my couplets. You would literally see a shower of gold at even the slight rustle of breeze. The most exquisite of flowers you have not ever seen before, not even in Kabul. Those yellow, jewel-like flowers attain the glitter of gold under the sun." He couldn't contain his passion, crushing her in one warm embrace, kissing her eyes, lips, face. "Rest, my sweet, rest!" He could barely murmur, releasing her and fleeing.

The spiral staircase under Babur's feet appeared to be whirling as he glided down, encountering midway Sayyid Tabib.

"You are to stay with Bibi Mubaraka Begum, and dare not leave until her fever is completely vanished. Maywa Jan would attend to your own needs." Babur commanded, dismounting past him in blind haste.

Naralla had begun to beat the kettle-drums as soon as Babur entered the feast-hall called the Mystic House. It was throbbing with the presence of poets, scholars, dancers and musicians. Rajas and nabobs were the most prominent of guests amongst many other from distant provinces of Hindustan. A flurry of curtsies and greetings followed at Babur's heels as he approached his throne flanked by damask hangings. The wall behind his throne was hosting a collage of broad daggers and curved daggers, the quivers bulging with arrows and jeweled scimitars. To the right of the throne was a gilded davenport for the comfort of the begums, unoccupied at present, its velvets and brocades inviting and shimmering. Gilded chairs were placed in front of the davenport, occupied by prince Humayun, Khwaja Kilan, Mehdi Khwaja, joining the trio was the poet Kabir. Jade vases filled with tuberoses were set over the tables inset with mother-of-pearl. The chests with koftgari designs were hosting gold flagons, from which the goblets were replenished with wine for the pleasure of the guests and the dignitaries.

A bevy of dancers with gold studs in their ears and tilaks on their forehead were evoking gasps of admiration from the guests, but Babur seemed oblivious to all, the wine in his jeweled cup still un-sipped. His hand was reaching out for majun in the silver dish beside him, and his gaze resting on Khwaja Kilan.

"Why is it, Khwaja, that wine tastes like dust and ashes in my mouth, while you and others seem to enjoy, thirsting for more?" Babur commented, rather than asked.

"You have just recovered from a prolonged illness, my Emperor, and your taste buds are still fighting the reek of nausea and retching." Khwaja Kilan sipped his wine contently. "In deference to my age, the ailments of this land have stayed away from me, sparing my old body the torments of boils, fevers, sciatica or dysentery. Wine is my weakness, but if it started to taste like dust, I would renounce this habit of drinking."

"To replace vice with virtue is the only way to renounce any habit, no matter how bitter it grows. Even if the wine has lost its sweetness, I cannot renounce drinking unless some mighty cause presents itself as an antidote?" Babur smiled, knowing full well his friend's distaste for everything in Hind, but he continued heedlessly. "Nothing tastes good in Hindustan. In this land of plenty, grapes are smaller than marbles, oranges without juice, and meat without flavor?"

"That's why I am leaving Hindustan, my Emperor!" Khwaja Kilan exclaimed, his heart already flying toward his beloved Ghazni.

"Yes, I seem to forget that you are deserting the emperor! Your last feast in Hind!" Babur quipped. "Since you are leaving me, I am entrusting you with a Farman for the citizens of Kabul. *Whoever there may be of the blood of the Lord Timur and of Genghis Khan, let them come to our court at Agra and seek prosperity together.*"

"No wonder you have attained the title of King-Kalendar, my Emperor!" Khwaja Kilan beamed with a dint of paternal affection. "Not one tanka or an ashrafi is left in your treasury. The wealth of the five cities gone by your Farman, and all those treasures to be distributed amongst the poor and the sages! Now would anyone be willing to share the poverty of the emperor?"

"The treasures which I bestow upon others are returned to me multiplied ten times over in wealth of joy and gratitude—a wealth, much more precious than any jewels or ashrafis." Babur smiled. "See, Khwaja, how your disciple has perfected the lesson of generosity from you, and yet I have kept some gifts to be sent to Kabul. The dancing girls, who are delighted to journey to Kabul, make sure Mahim Begum gets the first choice of dancing girls for her sole pleasure. Supervise all the preparations for my royal household to come here before you retire to Ghazni. Tell the begums that for the comfort of their travels in the future, the work on a nine hundred mile highway from Agra to Kabul is already commenced. Every nine mile a minar would be erected as a measure of distance and a post-house would be built every eighteen miles apart for the comfort and convenience of horses and couriers. Also, guard well the gifts of jewels and ashrafis, though Mahim Begum would be pleased more with the news of Humayun's victories. That jeweled scimitar is for Kamran; send it to him with a note that he must strengthen the defenses of Kandahar. Gulrukh Begum is worried about Askeri. Tell her that her gallant prince is enjoying the luxury of kingship in Bengal. For my blind servant Asas, I am sending the largest ahsrafi with a hole in the middle to hold a string of pearls. But tease him first that the emperor has sent him nothing. He would curse his fate, for sure, but when he is finished lamenting, tie that string of pearls around his neck, and he would feel the gifts with his hands, crying with delight."

"How do you expect an old man to remember all this, my Emperor?" Khwaja Kilan protested.

"You would remember to send me grapes and melons from Akshi, I know." Babur murmured, sensing the sadness of his friend, his heart saddened beyond expression.

"The very best, my Emperor!" Khwaja Kilan could barely murmur back, averting his gaze.

"Yes." Babur's gaze was falling on Kabir. "You are exceptionally quiet this afternoon, Kabir, and gloomy, why?"

"My Emperor." Kabir was startled out of his dark contemplations. "Since morning I have heard nothing but an ocean of silence!" He declared poetically, stealing a look at the musicians. "The Qubus player over there, I can't catch his rhythm, even the notes from Shaikhi's flute and Hussein's lute are muffled. Silence is everywhere, in this court, on the streets of Agra, over the waters of Jamna?"

"You are hallucinating, of course." Babur breathed indulgently. "Jamna could never rest in silence, its raging waters deep down roaring and clamoring."

"Today is a holy day, my Emperor. Devotees seeking the gift of inner silence!" Kabir's eyes were shining with some inner glow of poetic inspiration. "Most of the people have gone to river Ganges to bathe and pray."

"Cleanliness is next to holiness." Babur recited, his eyes flashing amusement. "To wash out the soot of impurities from their bodies, if not from their hearts!"

"Perhaps, my Emperor?" Kabir's very eyes were spilling the wine of poetry. "Purity of heart is of more importance than a bath in the Ganges."

"This epigram of yours is worth ten ashrafis, my worthy poet!" Babur scooped a handful of ashrafis from the coffer beside him, inviting the poet to receive his reward. "You wouldn't forget that evening, Kabir, when you couldn't win a tanka's worth of praise for your couplet, would you?" He teased as the poet claimed his gift, curtsying back to his seat joyfully.

"My Emperor, since you are in a generous mood, may I ask a boon?" Humayun pleaded abruptly before Kabir could return to his former seat.

"I know what your heart desires, my beloved prince." Babur flashed him a warm smile. "You are eager to fly back to Badakhshan, much like Khwaja, longing for his Ghazni." His gaze was profound and piercing. "You have my permission, but you have to earn this privilege by performing your duty in Hind first. Rana Sanga is our foe most formidable. He is bold and valorous, and I would rather he was our friend. He doesn't accept my offer of peace, so we have no choice left but to fight."

"For his insolence alone, he would suffer defeat, my Emperor!" Humayun began with a sudden vehemence. "In conformity with his wishes, I desire not peace, but war and victory. Command me, this very day, my Emperor, and I would present myself as a victor before you tomorrow."

"Is that your valor speaking, my son, or your zeal, or your longing for Badakhshan?" Babur tossed a ball of majun into his mouth, his expression sad and contemplative. "If you are to rule wisely, my young prince, then you must know that wars neither spare the victor, nor the vanquished, both suffering the tragedy of death and devastation. Victory itself becomes a burden if one learns not to rule for the sake of peace alone." He paused, becoming aware of the deflated expression of his son, his heart aching and his thoughts churning the foam of humor and cheerfulness. "The Moghuls are born victors, and you would be victorious, I am sure. But one look at your foe and you would scream with fright as if you have seen the devil himself. Rana Sanga is blind in one eye, which he lost during a brawl with his brother. His left arm is missing which was amputated after an injury while fighting with the king of Delhi, Lodi Sultan. A cannon ball wound has left him crippled in one leg. Besides eighty sword wounds on his body, there is not much left to count the scars of his comeliness. Age and experience would guide you toward wisdom, my valorous prince, and you would learn from the misfortunes of others as well as from the gifts of your fortunes." His gaze was shifting to Khwaja Kilan who was watching him with the tenderness of a fatherly affection. "Won't you postpone your journey to Kabul, Khwaja, to witness Humayun's victory?"

"My years are numbered, my Emperor." Khwaja Kilan intoned sadly. "If I stayed in Hind another week, my old bones would crumble along with my dream of returning to Ghazni, Kabul too receding further from my dreams?"

"Your wisdom compliments my own age, my friend, and you are yet to live another century!" A ripple of dry mirth escaped Babur's lips. "I would never understand why you hate Hind despite the fact that the climate here is certainly not conducive to a comfortable living. I would be confirming your feelings by saying things which are better left unsaid. But since you are leaving, I am constrained to confess that the three things which oppress me the most in Hind are heat, dust and violent winds. And yet we would put the gardens of Babylon to shame by turning this continent into an Eden of perfume and flowers. The saddest of truths is that wars become the luxury of age and time, but we would channel our energies in molding candles than cannon balls. These diyas and deutis here waft the odor of oil, besides ruining the finest of rugs with their smoke. As a start, Khwaja, send me a life-supply of candles from Kabul, your ransom for freedom?" His attempt at cheerfulness ended in a sigh he could not suppress.

"No dearth of candle-makers in Kabul, my Emperor." Khwaja Kilan succeeded in infusing the warmth of joy in his voice. "Not only would I send boxes and boxes, but would instruct the men to light candles every mile of the highway from Kabul to Agra yet to be constructed."

"Deny as you will, Khwaja, you admire the grandeur of art and architecture in Hindustan?" Babur laughed. "Have you paid homage to your beloved shrine in Delhi, the Kutb Minar? Your last farewell to the shrine in marble and red sandstone!"

"As much as I admire the grandeur of those giant Buddhas northwest of Kabul in the valley of Bamain!" Khwaja Kilan murmured. "I have already visited that shrine, my Emperor." His eyes were lit up with a mysterious smile. "Also, I took the liberty of inscribing one couplet on its wall, which I dare not recite. Your intellect would hold that expression of mine in eternal contempt, I am sure."

"Ah, those statues of ineffable beauty carved by Cyclopean hands! I might adorn them with gold and jewels as they were centuries ago." Babur murmured back. "Do you accuse your royal pupil of *dullness* as that of *intellect*, Khwaja?" He teased, smiling in return.

"I would not dare accuse you of anything, my Emperor." Khwaja Kilan beamed. "What do you mean by *dullness*, if I may be as bold as to admit my ignorance?"

"Intellect, my wise mentor, corrupts one's sense of wit and cheerfulness! And I dread even the thought of becoming witless and cheerless." A volley of laughter escaped Babur's lips, his gaze bright and challenging.

"Intellect is the child of wisdom, my Emperor, and I—" Khwaja Kilan's protest was left unfinished against the surge of Babur's mirth, and his gesture of a command.

"Tell me, Khwaja, what wisdom made you inscribe a couplet on your beloved shrine? No, no need to answer, just recite that couplet."

"You would gather only the levity of my expression, my Emperor. I don't want to expose myself to ridicule." Khwaja Kilan murmured as if communing with his thoughts.

"I would match your levity with my caprice." Babur goaded, his eyes flashing commands. "My poetic mood doesn't permit me the luxury of anger, but if you don't recite your couplet now, you would be forced to sign an edict that you would stay in Hind as the hostage of your disobedience."

"I might as well choose the gallows." Khwaja Kilan poised himself to recite, his lips curling into a pale smile.

"If safe and sound I pass the Sind
Damned if I wish again for Hind."

"Ah, my unhappy sage, you should know that Ghazni is likened to hell for its bitter, bone-chilling temperatures." Babur's eyes were spilling the gold of poetry, his thoughts letting loose the pearls of his inspiration.

"Babur, give thanks that the mercy of Allah
Hath given thee Sind and Hind in royalty
Khwaja, if thy strength fails under heat
Turn thyself aside to Ghazni's cold.

I would have this verse inscribed right under your couplet, Khwaja." He got to his feet abruptly, commanding Humayun to follow him.

The ocean of cheers and applause was left behind as Babur sought the gleaming terrace overlooking his garden. Humayun trailed behind, aloof and taciturn.

"Have you abandoned your love for the Rani of Gwalior, my prince? Or, is it the hopelessness in love which goads you to flee Hindustan?" Babur commented over his shoulders.

"Your son is vain, my Emperor." Was Humayun's inebriated response! "If I was not afraid of being repulsed, I would hurl my body and soul into the lovely arms of Rani."

"You would never taste the hemlock of true love, my happy prince!" Babur laughed, wending his way toward the palace instead of the terrace. "Consider yourself fortunate, for the snares of love are vicious." His mirth was enveloping him in its own mantle of pain-sweetness he dared not explore.

29

Defeat of Rana Sanga

*Life a passing shadow, say the scriptures. The shadow of a tower or
a tree, the shadow which prevails for a time! No, even as the shadow
of a bird in its flight, it passeth from our sight, and neither bird nor
shadow remains.*
— Talmud

A large boulder of stone was Babur's throne upon which he sat immersed
deep in his lone contemplations. Oblivious to the beauty of dawn with its streaks
of ruby and opal, he looked like a carved statue, his elbows dug solid over his
knees, and his head cradled into his hands, only his chain mail and jeweled belt
glinting life and color. Last evening, seated on the same boulder he had vowed
to himself to abstain from wine. The same evening he had issued a Farman that
after the decisive battle at Kanahwa all his gold vessels were to be distributed
amongst the poor who could benefit by selling such items with the hope of making a living.

Now the field of Kanahwa lay sprawled wide and far under his feet, awaiting the longed-for challenge of a combat with Rana Sanga! Rana Sanga had entrenched himself and his garrisons in his fort of Chanderi right across from Babur's city of tents pitched on level ground under the fiery gaze of sun. Two
whole weeks had crawled past since the Moghul troops had arrived at the field
of Kanahwa to meet the challenge of Rana Sanga, but so far he had made no
move to attack despite his grand army of one hundred and twenty thousand men
and five hundred elephants. In contrast, Moghul army consisted of only of seven
thousand men, their morale low and their spirits deflated, mainly due the inactiv-
ity and mostly due the disparity in numbers. This thought alone stung Babur like
a poisoned arrow. Freeing his head from his hands, his gaze was falling on his
possession of elephants, numbered few, though well maintained and gold caparisoned. They were being fed on water and sugar, he could tell, watching the mahouts looming over the tubs, content and vigilant.

Medina Rao—the vile Rajput, joining Rana Sanga! Babur's thoughts were
swelling into blisters of rage and desolation. *He is not the only one though, nine
Raos, seven Rajas and one hundred and four chieftains have formed alliance
with the Rana—the blind rat! Why he is still hiding in his hole when his soldiers*

outnumber ours and his supporters flaunt their riches in swift steeds and war elephants? Stupidity and cowardice! Babur's thoughts were rising in accusations against his troops, his gaze arresting the sky now polished by orange and purplish streaks. He had risen early, seeking this favorite rock of his as his lone sanctuary where none disturbed him with a few exceptions here and there, or if he himself summoned others depending upon his need or whim. Right now he needed only the mantle of his solitude, condoning the flurry of activity in the silken city of tents below him, his thoughts simmering and smoldering to raise the morale of his soldiers and to consecrate his decision of offensive with the whip of will and action.

No, Moghuls are neither stupid, nor craven, only afflicted by the gluttony for pain and pleasure, and revolted by the very thought of inertia and inaction. Even the men of Hindustan are brave swordsmen, yet extremely ignorant of the art of war, thus lacking the skill of commanding a battalion. His thoughts were sailing back to Agra, hovering over the palace walls where his beloved lay protected, awaiting his return. He wanted to be near his Afghan Lady, borrowing hope and courage from her love, begging the crumbs of inspiration, so that he could infuse fire and passion into the hearts of his soldiers for valor and victory. And yet his thoughts were plotting revolt within themselves, straying if not slumbering.

Mahim's fears and superstitions, even far from Agra, are right here, alive and palpitating? Babur's thoughts were reminding him that she is on her way to Hind. He could hear the loud chuckle in his head, envisioning the dull-witted astrologer Mahim had sent to choose an auspicious day for the battle. *She has the instinct of a tigress, wild and vigilant to protect her cubs—in this case, her adored son, Humayun?* His thoughts were materializing before his sight as if ripped out of the glinting sunshine. The astrologer from Kabul was grating his way toward him, wearing the shroud of piety and paranoid. Babur heaved himself up from his boulder, tossing a quick query at the astrologer as he approached closer.

"Is this a propitious day for battle against the indolent enemy, my friend?" Babur's gaze was profound and piercing.

"No, my Emperor." Was Muhammed Sharif's startled response!

"No, you say?" Babur smiled indulgently, though his eyes were gathering clouds of rage and impatience.

"Yes, my Emperor." Muhammed Sharif bowed his head, his look flustered.

"Would you contradict your own superstitions, my fool of a sage?" Babur indulged impatiently. "Tell me your reason for saying, *no*." He commanded.

"My Emperor." Muhammed Sharif ventured forth under some spell of fear and misery. "Sakkiz Yidoz—a cluster of eight stars is a sign of ill-omen for the Moghuls. Mars too in the west with stars orbiting in the opposite direction bodes misfortune. If the Moghuls were to engage in battle today, defeat is—" His expressions were cut short by the thunder of rage in Babur's exclamation.

"You foul reptile!" Babur's very gaze was shooting flames. "You lie like the cicadas. Stupidity is another name for superstition, and you are being crushed by its weight. Begone! You would serve me better by delivering my Farman to the troops. Let everyone know that we wage war today, and make sure you carry not the weight of superstition with you." He turned away in disgust, donning the mantle of his decision as his weapon of valor and victory.

The noon sun with its trumpet of gold had arrived too soon as Babur astride his horse gauged the morale of his troops. Beyond the sea of men, beasts and war-elephants, he could see the mighty cannons poised for shooting. The disciplined flanks of soldiers equipped with kards, dhups and scimitars were waiting silently for the emperor's command to commence the fighting. Against the standards of red and yellow, Babur could sense the mingling of fear and anticipation in the eyes of his soldiers, waiting anxiously for some words of encouragement. He raised his jeweled scimitar as a signal to speak, his eyes gathering all in one warm embrace.

"We would annihilate our foe. This is not a boast, but one sacred oath to win or to die. Let this inspiration from the lips of your revered poet, Firdausi, guide you toward valor and victory.

Let me die honorably and I die content
To the earth my body, but to the heavens my honor."

Babur recited with the flare of a poet-star, his very eyes gathering the stars of inspiration. "Soldiers and Noblemen! Every man who comes into this world is subject to dissolution. When we are passed away and gone, Allah only survives, Who is unchangeable. Whoever comes to the feast of life, must before it is over drink from the cup of death! He who arrives at the inn of mortality, one day inevitably take his departure from that house of sorrow—this world. How much better it is to die with honor than to live with infamy? Let the drums beat and charge." He commanded.

In a flash, the strident notes from kettle-drums had ripped the sky, the sunshine itself lowering golden beams to strike the combatants. The sun-baked earth was pounded by the hoofs of the horses as the Moghul cavalcade advanced toward the fortress barricaded by Rana Sanga's battalions. Rana Sanga was nowhere to be seen, probably entrenched inside his fortress along with the cream of his soldiers and generals. A fierce battle had begun in all earnest with cannon balls roaring and striking to breach the defenses. Against the billowing of dust and smoke clouds, Babur could see the foes flying pell-mell, his scimitar glinting murder at any who dared meet his challenge. The enemy was thrown into utter panic, and the battlefield was turned into a pandemonium, the wounded and the unhorsed in throes of agony and dying.

Time had turned quicksilver under the fiery gaze of the sun, measuring the victory at hand in moments as if the battle had just begun, though fighting had lasted for three whole hours, and the fortress was hemmed in by the Moghuls intent on gaining complete victory. One dauntless soldier by the name of Nur Beg was seen pounding the gates of the fortress with his mattock, and succeeding in throwing it open with a cry of exaltation. Joining him were other Moghul soldiers, holding sacred the code of war ethics while challenging the foes to come out and engage in fair fighting, for they would not attack the vanquished if they were unarmed or unprepared.

What transpired after this challenge, the Moghuls were unprepared. A great tide of Raos, Rajas and Hindus, naked and unarmed, was emerging out of the gates, swollen with pride and malevolence. A quicksilver awakening it was for the victorious and the appalled. What followed next was the nightmarish reality as the tide of men enveloped the Moghuls under some spell of suicidal frenzy, engaging in a fist-to-fist fight, knowing fully well that they would be killed. Pressed by the weight of honor, the Moghuls were abandoning their weapons and meeting the challenge of the death-intoxicated foes with their bare hands. Soon, the battlefield was strewn with naked lumps of humanity, oblivious to the clattering of the drums and braying of the horses. While the Moghul standards were being raised in splashes of red and yellow, the stealthy escape of Rana Sanga and his few followers was unnoticed, their swift steeds carrying them toward the lone refuge in Rajputana.

Oh, the demented fools, making life the harlot of death! Babur closed his eyes, recalling the age-old rites of sanctifying pride and honor. *These lily-livered heathens have murdered their babes and women, and have come out to flaunt the rags of their anguish and lunacy.* Babur's eyes were shot open by the groans of a wounded soldier.

Babur was upon his feet in a flash, noticing Humayun who was ministering the wounds of this young soldier. *It's all an illusion, this death and tragedy, even my own son?* Babur's senses were reeling against some hurricane of sorrow, but he was blocking away the sounds of agony and the cheers of jubilations, summoning one reed of a reality that Humayun longed for the cool climes of Badakhshan.

"You have earned your freedom to fly to Badakhshan, my son." Babur murmured against the haze of illusion, trying his best to envision the sprigs of peace and sanity. "Remember, my Prince, tragedy of life is that men prefer to remain in their prison of pride and ignorance, incapable of learning from their mistakes since they believe they have made none. No wonder then, men would always fight, justifying death and devastation as the reward of valor and right judgment?" He straggled away, his mind witnessing only the white sea of desolation within him, his heart cutting open the wound of memories stark and gruesome. *Yes, men would always embrace the tyranny of their desires. They would kill, plunder and subjugate, wooing wars and serving the masters of their greed for power, ambition, and possession!*

30

Agra of the Moghuls

Come, fill the cup, and in the fire of Spring
Your winter garment of repentance fling
The bird of time has but a little way
To flutter—and the bird is on the Wing
— Omar Khayyam

Babur seated at the rosewood desk in his library was taking a reprieve from his royal duties, and poised for writing a letter to his friend, Khwaja Kilan. Spring sunshine from latticework window was accentuating the color of his robe matching his pallor. The bright plume in his turban and the red cummerbund around his waist were infusing some color into his cheeks, his demeanor one of profound contemplation. Some sort of ache and hunger was rising inside him, rather a deep-rooted thirst for wine, his hand reaching for a pallet of majun in the silver dish. Absently, he tossed it into his mouth, dipping his pen in the jade ink-pot.

> *Dear Khwaja, my friend and mentor,*
> *I am sitting at the desk in my palace of red sandstone at Agra, filled with this need to commune with you like some heedless child of the mountains, and sloughing off the mantle of sovereignty as the emperor of Hindustan. This continent of diverse cultures and religions is as peaceful as one can ever hope it to be, despite the flaring up of rifts and conflicts leading to skirmishes. My heart longs for Kabul. You are fortunate to stay in your beloved Ghazni and Humayun doubly fortunate to rule Badakhshan which is his home and haven. I would fain visit you both, but time doesn't allow me such luxury, keeping me in fetters of duties countless and challenging. The beauty of Kabul, I should say, is taking root in this soil, since I am keen on designing the gardens. Agra already boasts of three gardens, Ram-bagh, Dehra-bagh and Zahar-bagh, hosting the loveliest of blooms, chamba, chambeli, tuberoses, just to name a few, and delphiniums and heliotropes. Jasmine is blooming right under the window of my library, and saffron is ready to burst into color. I have abundance of lotuses where the fountains dance and gur-*

gle. Terraces of Makrana marble gleam under the sun, hosting pots of carnation and oleander. Chenar trees are budding early, and kingfishers have made a permanent home in my garden. I am longing to take a stroll in my garden with Bibi Mubaraka Begum, but she is fluttering downstairs somewhere in the palace, issuing orders and getting the rooms ready for my harem from Kabul expected to arrive here this very evening. A grand welcome is awaiting my household in Delhi. I have sent ten elephants furnished with howdahs of silk and brocade hangings, and soft cushions for the comfort of the princes, begums and princesses.

An overpowering sense of fatigue was crushing Babur's thoughts, along with his need for wine, sudden and formidable. Since his vow at the battlefield of Kanahwa, he had not touched wine, but had been unable to quell the need to drink, his very soul parched and thirsting.

How many times I have been on the brink of breaking my vow, but have persevered! After our victory over Rana Sanga, my soldiers bestowed upon me the title of Ghazi. I do not deserve this title. This title belongs to them, for they too had joined me in this solemn vow to abstain from drinking. Many of those men wish to break their vow, and some do, but then repent and do penance, while my abstinence itself is punishment enough for me since I cannot pray to appease my suffering.

Renouncement of wine has bereft me
And will to work has left me
Others, repent, and vow to abstain
I abstain and impenitent remain

The mystic in Babur was awakening to the downpour of couplets in his head, but he was in haste to share all with his friend lest he forget.

Paradoxically, Khwaja, I do drink—the old wine of history and architecture. I hope you can read my Turkish script which is losing its shape and color. To share this wine with you is a pleasure rare and exotic which stays dormant under the burden of royal duties and engagements. Mandars at Gwalior are awesome except for their idols they resemble the religious schools of Islam. Even the idols with the exception of their naked privities, are a great source of wonder and inspiration. The dark, spacious halls of these mandars are filled with treasures exquisite and beautiful. Man Mandar alone is a tourist's dream, hosting rows of stone-carved peacocks with snakes spiraling out of their beaks at its very entrance. I have been to many Hindu temples, intricately designed and gloriously heartwarming despite many attempts from hordes of zealots to despoil and demolish, amongst them our ancestors, Mahmud and Sultan Sikander. Under my rule, no one is per-

mitted to desecrate the beauty of these temples, holy and precious. Man Singh's palace at Gwalior is my favorite, boasting of a silver roof and lofty pavilions. Inside, its walls are etched floral designs embedded with lapis lazuli and with other gems, all fiery and colorful.

I would send you bows made out of buffalo skin and arrows molded from reeds, if you wish to hone your skill in archery? Your letters to me waft the odor of medicinal herbs and potions, my friend, stop worrying about my health. I am immune to all ailments, fearing only the assault of age and ambition. Yet, old age is more the malady of a soul, than of the body and mind? Last week, I was afflicted with a mild cough, and Sayyid Tabib concocted a potion of violets dipped in lemon and mixed with clarified sugar—a concoction so evil-tasting that its taste still lingers in my mouth.

Babur was overwhelmed with sadness, realizing with a sudden flash of pain that he missed his friend and mentor. Recalling also the discomforts of his previous illnesses, sciatica, frequent boils on arms and legs, just to name a few, making him impatient and intemperate, if not plunging him straight into a pit of melancholia.

My title, King-Kalendar is pulsating with a life of its own, though one man in a hundred becomes a Kalendar in Hindustan, which—in fact, is the monastic order of the Turks, and Terdi Beg has become a Kalendar. Prince Humayun is happy in his beloved Badakhshan. Prince Askeri is a little despotic, I think, in ruling his little kingdom of Bengal. Prince Kamran is enjoying his rule over Kandahar. The son of our Thin Lord in Samarkand, Suleiman Mirza, and prince Hindal are ruling Kabul. Poetry and Art are flourishing in my court at Agra along with poetry contests every month where the poet-stars flaunt their talents in ghazals, couplets and quatrains. Sheikh Zain is writing Fateh-nama to honor our victory at Kanahwa, since Abdullah Hatifi is drunk with inspiration to spill couplets alone, abandoning his duty as a court scribe. More than a hundred safinas are at my disposal for pleasure excursions, which could be used as military boats if needed; especially, for quelling the tides of rebellion in the villages scattered not too far from the banks of river Punjab. One mile long patch of melons across from the banks of river Jamna is yielding much fruit, but the melons don't taste as good as the ones you sent me last year. I literally had tears in my eyes when I tasted the gift of first melon from Ghazni, eating all of it and reaching for another one—

Now Babur's thoughts were tasting the salt of tears, overwhelmed by the deluge of memories sweet and unforgotten. He was signing the unfinished letter, his thoughts goading him to write to Humayun lest he postpone it for several more months amidst the ocean of his royal duties and engagements.

My beloved Prince
Your neglect to write to me is inexcusable, since couriers are posted
with fresh postilions every eighteen miles from Agra to Kabul to deliver
the letters most swiftly and punctiliously. Your writing style has become
cumbersome as if you are trying to impress me—your father and em-
peror. Try writing simply and honestly, and the effect would be delight-
ful. Friends supply me with all the news concerning my family, and
what I hear about you is rather disturbing. You are becoming a recluse
day by day, is that correct? Taking solitary walks, if not shutting your
own self behind the harem walls? You would be the next Moghul em-
peror of Hind, and emperors can't indulge in the luxury of seclusion.
You would be required to appear at the window of your palace, morn-
ing, noon and evening as an affirmation that you are well and capable
of insuring the well-being of your subjects.

Reproof and impatience were guiding Babur's thoughts, though he was trying his best to tame his expressions into a mold of loving kindness.

Your beautiful wife and your tender bloom of a son are reminding me
of my gardens in Kabul, hopefully, beautiful and blooming? The gar-
dens in Kabul, all ten of them are more precious to me than all the gold
and jewels in Hindustan. Char-bagh, Surat-bagh and Mehtab-bagh
yield the most exotic of blooms, though Shahara-bagh, Shahijahan-
bagh and Aurta-bagh are the most colorful all spring and summer.
Baghi-ahu is your mamma's favorite garden, and she wishes she could
carry it here to Hindustan? Alas, reports reach me daily that you have
left the gardens under the sole supervision of the gardeners who have
no skill in nurturing the new varieties, or in enhancing the beauty of the
gardens. You have espoused vanity and ostentation, I hear, decking
yourself with jewels and indulging in night-long bouts of feasting and
drinking. Write to me, tell me that all these reports are base lies to tar-
nish your character, and I would believe you.

Babur's fingers were loosening their grip over the pen, his thoughts opiate
and restless. An overwhelming sense of fatigue was his pillow and retreat as he
abandoned his head at the back of his chair, letting his thoughts drift into ether
of memories. Enveloped in mists emerald and gossamer, he could feel the presence of Sweet Absent, yet the scent of Afghan Lady was pervading the mists
and the dream-languor. Love was a shining mirror balanced between his heart
and soul, reflecting harmony and wholeness despite his sadness in feeling the
gulf of separation between Hind and Kabul, between him and Humayun. Khwaja Kilan was drifting further from his dreams, yet hope was creating waves upon
waves of joys, welcoming his royal household, inhaling the scent of Kabul, embracing the beauty of hills and valleys.

Babur was lost into the world of dreams, not knowing that Bibi Mubaraka had come up, watching him tenderly before gliding out of the library. His dog Pummock had curled up at his feet, snoozing contentedly. The pale lengthening shadows of the late afternoon were long past effaced as Babur opened his eyes, watching the smoldering sunset through his latticework window under some spell of awe and fascination. He was becoming aware of Pummock at his feet, stroking the double coat of white over his neck absently. The Pomeranian barked happily, his fox-like eyes demanding attention.

"Settle you down, Pummock!" Babur commanded. "The Moghuls would flay you alive on the breach of disturbing the emperor." His eyes were closing, his heart expanding to welcome his royal household.

They would be here soon, loving Hind as I have loved, replacing squalor with neatness, servitude with pride and despair with aspiration. Almshouses are only for the weak and the ailing. The able and the indolent must work, taking pride in earning their living, and learning to enjoy the beauty of this land and its abundance. Babur's thoughts were entering the subtle realm of perception rigged with joys and premonitions. *Can happiness be ever complete without the threat of sorrow, dark and looming? What is this white cloud of grief, hovering above and beyond?* He must have dozed off, following the currents of his subconscious, for he was startled to awakening by the loud yelps of Pummock posted at the latticework window, his ears erect and his tail wagging.

In a flash, Babur was at the window, looking down at the parade of elephants with gilded howdahs entering the palace gates with their trappings of damask and brocade. His heart flooded with joy, Babur swung around, aiming for the grand staircase.

"Your royal household has arrived, my Emperor. They are—" Mir Jamal's words were swallowed into a vacuum as Babur sprinted down the steps into the foyer and into the open, gliding toward the palace gates under some spell of dream-haze and euphoria.

The palace itself was coming alive with the sounds of drums and cymbals, accompanied by sweet notes from lutes and flutes, and the sitar humming welcome in the background. Babur was oblivious to all, only aware of the garlanded ladders lowered down the howdahs, revealing the beloved faces of his wives and children.

"How sweet is the scent of Kabul? The perfume of my beloveds!" Babur was sweeping all into eager embraces, hugging and kissing.

Gulrang and Gulchihra were the first ones to bounce into his arms, then Gulrukh and Dildar. Gulnar and Nurgul were sailing over the tides of joys, Apaq Begum inching closer, overtaken by princes and princesses. Next came Mahim, her eyes sparkling, and her corpulent figure concealed under layers of silk. Her smile was radiant, but her eyes were squinting disbelief at the stark grey mustache of her husband who had barely turned forty-five, though his features had still retained the glow of youthfulness.

"You have robbed me of the pleasure of welcoming you royally, my moon!" Babur held her close in his loving embrace. "I was to ride to the very gates of Agra on my caparisoned horse to lead you all to the palace with much pomp and gallantry."

"We surely would have fainted inside our howdahs, my Emperor, if you were to greet us in such a manner?" Mahim declared. "We are already overwhelmed by the abundance of riches with which you have furnished our howdahs. Such wealth and opulence!"

"The emperor is not wealthy, my beauty." Babur laughed. "All this wealth belongs to Hind, and I its mendicant borrowing its riches to make this land the envy of kingdoms vast and distant."

"I don't know what to believe, my Emperor?" Was Mahim's flustered response! "All the way from Delhi to here, crowds cheering and chanting: *Babur, the Lion. Babur, the Tiger, King-Kalendar. The First Moghul Emperor, we welcome his royal household.* I was not sure which stranger would be greeting us at Agra?"

"Just your husband, my beauty." Babur espied his sister amongst the bevy of Begums. "My dear, dear Khazanda." He swept her into his arms. "How I have missed you!" He caught sight of princess Gulbadan behind his sister, the red shock of her hair escaping her velvet cap and gleaming. "My dearest, my sweet Rose!" He was quick to snatch her to himself, kissing her hair, her cheeks. "My Rose of Kabul, you would be happy in Hind."

Amidst the fanfare of music and cheers, the royal cortege was invading the palace halls where Bibi Mubaraka stood greeting much like an apparition from the starry heavens, arrayed in white silks and diamonds. Babur stumbled toward her as if drunk, slipping his arm around her waist, his heart lurching and somersaulting.

"This angel, my loves, has relieved me from the weight of entertaining, even arranging for a great show this evening, called tamasha." Babur confessed endearingly, his gaze alone sweeping all in one tender embrace. "Rest a while, and then get ready for feasting and a glorious evening."

Naralla had begun to beat his drums with a great zeal, while the royal servants were escorting the ladies to their gilded chamber for baths and refreshments, whatever their moods dictated.

31

Emperor Poisoned

Dying Praim at the shrine
Staining the hearth he made divine
— Virgil

The blue bowl of a sky studded with diamond stars appeared to be enveloping the coliseum at Agra in magical mists where the sporting event called tamasha was unfolding with all the fanfare of music and splendor. Babur seated with his royal household under the awning of damasked pavilion was transported into a world of awe and wonder where beauty could be seen serenading nature from heavenly sky to earthly paradise. The pavilion itself with its railings secured with gold knobs was furnished with divans and carpets, divided into several tiers, reserved separately for poets and musicians, for courtiers and scholars, and for the guests from all parts of Agra. Mahim was seated to Babur's right and Gulbadan to his left, this Rose of Kabul separating his Beloved—the Afghan Lady, one tender thought was claiming Babur's attention. The merry wives of Babur behind him were talking and laughing all of a sudden, the voices of Gulnar and Nurgul clear and sparkling, while the voices of Dildar and Gulrukh were muffled in laughter. A show of lights was appearing on the field of the coliseum with machalchis balancing diyas on their palms upturned, creating circles of lights, and converging in the middle in the formation of moon and stars, suspended and twinkling.

"Where is tamasha?" Gulbadan murmured, seeking Babur's attention.

"Tamasha is the Hindi name for this show with all its pageantry, my lovely Rose." Babur laughed, slipping his arm around her waist and pressing her closer. "You have to learn new words in Hind, new customs and new etiquettes." His gaze was riveted to Wali—his cheetah-keeper, leading a flock of cheetahs into the arena proudly and jauntily.

The scenes were shifting in phantasmagoric flashes of light and color, the show of lights cascading into tendrils and flowers. A thunder of applause, followed by joyful anticipation was stirring the night wind to whiffs of ecstasy. The scent of tuberoses was in the air, and the audience was spellbound. A group of men were entering the arena, gold turbaned and flaunting their jeweled cummerbunds. Half of these men were leading camels, their humps covered with splashes of velvet and brocade, the other half were the mahouts in charge of the elephants, all garlanded and caparisoned. The camels fed with opium were goaded to fight the elephants. It was a swift, raucous fight, in which the elephants drunk with rage were the victors, forcing the inebriated camels to retreat and surrender. Another fight was commencing with equal swiftness, that of heavyweight wrestlers, wearing nothing but loincloths, their skins oily and glistening. The winners in this competition had nothing to boast about, but bruised faces and bloodied noses!

A stream of dancers and musicians were flooding the arena, joined by acrobats and musicians. A pageant of men in silk dhotis were not only spinning on their toes with staggering speed, but balancing colorful hoops around their necks, in their hands and over their waists, creating ringlets of color, all allusive and fantastic. The show of lights was splintering to make room for the gymnasts. Sprawled flat on their backs, these athletes were balancing thin poles over their stomachs, upon which the young acrobats were climbing with the dexterity of monkeys. The tides of gymnastics were receding, replaced by a surge of gallant riders, taking their separate posts to show their prowess in polo, archery and javelin throwing.

The evening itself was suffused with the glitter of gold and jewels, it seemed, as Lambardi dancers spilled into the arena, exposing their anklets from under the saris of silk and chiffon. The studs in their noses and tilaks on their foreheads were creating their own sparkle-dance as the dancers whirled on their toes, while they balanced tiers of clay-pots in their arms, all bejeweled and garlanded. A crescendo of music from tablas and thillances was commencing its beat to welcome the Garba dancers from Gujrat. Layers upon layers of silk panels around the waists of the young dancers down to their ankles were flaring like the peacock feathers, as they floated in a circle within a circle, going round and round while clicking their bhutans with their partners, floating and whirling. Suddenly, the bhutans were abandoned at the beat of the drums, and the men in plumed turbans were joining the ladies for a bhangra dance, their hands knotted at the back and their feet tapping in rhythm with their partners!

The festive galore of the evening was turned into a night of feasting as Babur reached his palace along with his family and a few chosen guests who had the privilege of dining with the royal household. This evening, Pleasure House was the feasting hall, preferred by Babur as opposed to the Mystic House which somehow made him feel cold and lonely by the sheer size of its vast, lofty columns, so aloof and intimidating. There was no lack of warmth and friendliness in Pleasure House, lit to effulgence by silver candelabras. Besides, Bibi Mubaraka seated to his right at the table was suffusing his whole being with the warmth of her love and purity. Mahim was to his left, rather quiet and contemplative.

The tables were being laden with choicest of viands and gourmet dishes by a parade of royal cooks, while Babur waited for his dishes after they were approved by the tasters, fit to be served to the emperor. He stroked the ears of Pummock, making him sit obediently at his feet, shifting his attention to the dancing girls on the stage, enacting some ritual of a prayer dance. Their henna-dyed hands were held over their heads in shape of lotuses, and they were bending down as if offering flowers at the shrines of the gods and the goddesses. The aroma of food was teasing Babur's senses, and he could see the dishes of mutton curry garnished with almonds, and chicken korma with chunks of cashews. A platter of chicken Biryani was being lowered in front of Gulbadan seated across from him, but his gaze was turning to the next dish beside it, his favorite, roasted mutton over hare stew, topped with shami kabobs, fish cutlets and fried carrots. He was feeling hungry all of a sudden, his gaze straying toward the table piled with desserts where sweetmeats of several varieties were cut into shapes of stars, daisies and diamonds. In the center of each dessert table was a fruit arrangement, piled high, exquisite and tempting. Sighing to himself, Babur was about to comment upon Mahim's silence when his gaze fell on Gulbadan, who sat there devouring the dishes before her with her eyes alone, her face flushed and glowing.

"You have my permission to eat, my Rose! I would not allow anyone to reprimand you for the breach of etiquettes." Babur smiled, holding the startled expression in her eyes inside his own with the warmth of tenderness. "It seems, Kabul has deprived you of feasting in my absence. I am famished too, but I am at the mercy of the royal tasters."

"Thank you, my Emperor." Gulbadan chanted happily. She was about to fill her plate, but Khazanda Begum's little cough of a warning caught her attention. "Yes, Dear Lady, I would wait." She murmured in response to the stern reproof in the eyes of Khazanda Begum.

"Are your cooks honest and faithful, my Emperor?" Mahim was quick to catch Babur's attention, her heart a cauldron of anxiety and foreboding. "Who supervises the kitchen? Can you trust the cooks and the tasters?"

"Still the queen of superstition, my moon?" Babur laughed. "Yet I am happy, your sweet concern means that you love the emperor? You fear for my life, that much is obvious! I can't forget how in Kabul you supervised the food and the cooks, and by the time food was brought to me, I felt like a mendicant. My fortunes have not improved in Hind, I still feel the same way—a fakir in Hind, getting crumbs from the plates of the royal tasters." He turned to Bibi Mubaraka, his eyes spilling mirth. "Isn't that true, my Afghan Lady?"

"Not in the least!" Bibi Mubaraka teased. "The royal tasters fill your plates with choicest of meats, my Emperor. Even your devoted Pummock gets its own royal share!"

"Ah, the unhappy emperor!" Babur sighed in mock despair, his gaze sweeping all in the mirth-dance of his eyes and heart.

The trilling of laughter from the lips of the ladies was meeting Babur's gaze, splintering his mirth and air of mockery. Dildar's laughter was like the tinkling of bells, and Gulrukh's the clapping of castanets. Gulnar and Nurgul were joining this sea of mirth, and venerable aunts were imitating the merry wives of the emperor. Shad Begum and Apaq Begum's comments were lost in tides of mirth, while Fakhri Begum and Khadija Begum seemed foundering inside the currents of lighthearted gaiety, only Sultana Begum's appeal for sobriety was having affect, drawing attention to the parade of royal cooks.

Ahmed was at the head of the other cooks, assigned the privilege of carrying the silver platter for the emperor. He lowered the silver platter before Babur, and stood removing several layers of silk napkins, each napkin bearing a seal of individual cooks who had tasted the food, confirming it safe and healthy to be brought before the emperor. The royal feast began in conformity with Moghul etiquettes, the emperor initiating the commencement of dinner by taking a morsel out of his plate. The great feast had begun in all earnest, everyone enjoying and praising the cooks for their culinary excellence in cooking and presentation. Babur had tasted almost all the varieties of dishes from his platter, reserving his favorite one for final taste and savoring. That favorite dish of his—hare stew, garnished with carrots was tempting him even before he could finish eating the first serving. Scooping a generous portion of hare stew beside other delicacies on his plate, he gave in to the pleasure of eating only what attracted his palate.

One bite of his favorite stew, and Babur's taste buds were on fire, as if he had swallowed some sort of powdered glass soaked in vinegar. The acrid taste in his mouth was almost burning his tongue, and his whole body was seized by a spasm of pain and retching. In a sudden fit of convulsion, vomit spewed out of his mouth, his hands clutching the table, and toppling the dishes before him over the carpet of blue and gold. All were suspended in shock, unable to move or speak, with the exception of Pummock who had begun licking the royal feast most blissfully until he attacked the hare stew. Suddenly, he was going in circles, then crashing in one shuddering heap, a stream of viscid fluid dribbling down his tongue, and settling down in a pool of dollops, slimy and greenish.

This spell of shock against the fogs of nightmarish silence was ripped open by a shrill cry from Mahim's lips, agonized and piercing.

The emperor is poisoned!

In a flash, a hurricane of laments had exploded. Mehdi Khwaja was the first one leaping to his feet, and cradling the emperor's body before he collapsed into his arms.

The doors of the Pleasure House were thrown open, voices commanding help, and princes storming down the halls in search of the royal physicians. The begums were swooning, the princesses shutting out the horror by closing their eyes, yet Mahim Begum was molded alive into a stature of fire and ice, her expression chilled and her eyes blazing. While Babur was being carried to his chamber, Bibi Mubaraka was falling limp into the arms of her brother much like a mountain-lily, white and smooth, the fire of diamonds around her ears and throat melting not her bliss-oblivion.

The royal physician, Sayyid Tabib, was ministering Babur with utmost diligence and concentration, sweetening his purgatives with prayers and keeping at bay the frantic suggestions of Mir Jamal and Mehdi Khwaja. Adjacent to this chamber lay Bibi Mubaraka, tended by another royal physician, surrendering her soul to the violence of grief and despair. The mere sound of the word, *poison*, had poisoned her will to live, her very soul dying of grief so profound that her mind dared not imagine a life without Babur in a world bereft of love and laughter.

Mahim in contrast, though racked by the agony of her spirit, was endowed with that rare virtue of inner strength which could not ever be thwarted, even by a mountain of tragedies. She was beside Babur heart and soul, watching each ministration of the physician anxiously and suspiciously. Paradoxically, the feeling of foreboding within her was gone, replaced by the furnace of rage and vengeance against the culprits who had dared poison the emperor. Her heart was pumping hope against the bellows of her resolve to punish all traitors. Amidst all this violence within, her heart was light, knowing intuitively that Babur was going to live and regain his health and strength. No physician on earth could convince her of this fact, not even Sayyid Tabib, but her innate core of wisdom and perception.

Once assured of Babur's safety under the care of Sayyid Tabib, Mahim had drifted back into the House of Pleasure, oblivious to the coterie of servants, cleaning and scrubbing. Pale and distraught, she stood there in the middle of the room, only the fire of rubies in her hair and around her throat alive and sparkling. She was becoming aware of her thoughts in a seesaw of contemplations, comparing her great love for Babur with the tragic love of Bibi Mubaraka for him, which had hurled her into the abyss of despair and hopelessness.

Who poisoned the father of my beloved Humayun?

Mahim's profound love for her son was rising within her, erecting a wall of defense over her thoughts, confirming her love for her son as grand as Bibi Mubaraka's for the emperor. A quick shudder coursed through her spine by the sudden violence of her thoughts, raging once again, adding flint to her resolve to find the culprits and to hurl them into the dungeon of torture and damnation. She was trembling now, trembling with rage, her thoughts holding the whip of vengeance. Her pallor was replaced by blotches of color as she sprang to her feet, knowing not where she was going, or what she was thinking. Only her heart was thundering commands, guiding her through the maze of gilded halls into the very stillness of the kitchen, bright and intimidating. Her entrance was so sudden and her eyes blazing so menacingly that the royal cooks were startled to their feet, their faces etched with misery as a result of the grinding inquisition, though they had confessed nothing. They were curtsying, numb with shock and guilt, seized afresh by stark terror and hopelessness.

"You all would be flayed alive if you didn't confess! Who poisoned the emperor's food?" Mahim demanded, her eyes flashing flames and her gaze settling on Ahmed. "You are the head cook, Ahmed, failing in your duty toward the emperor. You would be hanged for such vile neglect. Make peace with Allah! For now, only truth could save you from the fires of hell." The fire of rage in her eyes was holding him prisoner. "Speak, you ingrate wretch, who tampered with the food of the emperor?"

"My La—dy." Ahmed stammered, the wild, tormented look in his eyes speaking volumes. *He didn't think the emperor would die, he didn't want the death of the emperor.* "Sultan Ibrahim's mamma—Buwa Begum! The mother of that Lodi lord who was killed at the battle of Panipat." He began incoherently, rather deliriously. "She approached the junior royal taster, Bekawal." He indicated the miserable wretch on the polished floor, hugging his knees most piteously. "Buwa Begum also took into confidence Yasmin and Rukhsana. She herself pounded belladonna into a powder, but they didn't know, and he—" His voice was choked by the thunder of one bitter exclamation.

"Allah be my witness!" Mahim's exclamation was more of an anguished cry, flung at Mir Jamal who had the misfortune of straggling back into the kitchen. "Yes, Allah be my witness, Mir Jamal, you would wear the noose of a traitor if you do not obey my orders before the dawn of another day? The guilty Bekawal over there, he must die, his body hewn to pieces. Ahmed too, must pay for his disloyalty, flayed alive and his limbs dismembered. And these harlots of treason, Yasmin and Rukhsana! You may butcher one with your dagger, and drag the other under the feet of the elephant. Would you execute my orders to the hilt, or should I summon the harem ladies? We have our own methods to cut down the sprigs of treason?"

"Your orders would be honored most obediently, my Lady." Mir Jamal bowed double, awed and flustered.

"When all are committed to the tortures of the damned, Mir Jamal, you are to dispatch soldiers to the palace of Buwa Begum." Mahim turned to her heels. "The chief plotter must be arrested. Her palace and all her possessions are to be confiscated." She murmured over her shoulders.

This must be done before the emperor wakes. Mahim was plodding out of the kitchen, her legs weak and trembling. All her strength was drained, her anger replaced by fear and disconsolation. *His kind and generous heart would find means to spare the lives of the traitors, forgiving, always forgiving?* Her heart was thundering again. She was feeling like a young girl, alone and frightened. Carrying the weight of fear and loneliness, she was drifting toward the staircase, groping for the sanctuary of her bedroom, seeking oblivion and darkness.

32

Palace of Sikri

Would I were heaven that I might look on thee with many eyes.
— Plato

The Monsoon breeze with a subtle scent of ranunculus from the garden was filling the chamber of rose and ivory with its freshness where Babur and Bibi Mubaraka sat talking and laughing. They were drinking tea and luxuriating in the bliss-comfort of their solitude—togetherness! This bedroom in the palace at Agra had been consecrated by their love during several weeks of Babur's convalescence, affording them the luxury of precious moments they had not ever dreamed possible amidst the burdens of royal duties and royal intrigues. Babur had almost recovered from the affects of poisoning with the exception of occasional assault of enteritis.

I am the happiest man alive on the face of this earth, not the emperor of Hind, but a lover blessed with the gift of a Beloved sweet and nonpareil.

Babur was thinking, tossing a ball of majun into his mouth while admiring his Beloved in layers of chiffon broidered with silvery stars, her periwinkle eyes radiant as she sipped her tea most delicately. He himself was donned in the morning robe of white silk, as silvery as his hair, beard and mustache. No jewels adorned his royal person as he sat there bareheaded, only the stars in his eyes bright and ardent, caressing his Beloved. A Birdi table with the inlay of ivory and brass was separating the lovers in their velvety seats, its centerpiece of purple lotuses in a gold bowl the cynosure of their love and admiration. Babur replaced his cup in the silver tray, his gaze resting on the coronet of pearls as Bibi Mubaraka lowered her head to pour herself another cup of tea, oblivious to the flash of tenderness in his eyes which were lit up further with the light of amusement.

"Had I known that such bliss of spending hours, days and nights with you without the burden of royal duties was possible, I would have contrived to ingest poison with my own free will, sparing for sure Buwa Begum the indignity of exile and imprisonment?" Babur teased.

"My emperor!" Bibi Mubaraka protested, her eyes shining with the mingling of rebuke and gentleness.

"Such joy and bliss, rare as it is one can never imagine it exists until one experiences the purity and silence of love all-encompassing." Babur began dreamily. "That's how I feel, my love, craving only the sweetness of your love and presence. I have lost interest in titles and conquests, and have become wearied of etiquettes, so very cumbersome and superfluous. How can I leave this haven now, and resume the duty of sitting at jharoka morning, noon and night, just for the satisfaction of my subjects that the emperor is well and alive?" He concluded, eliciting a mock sigh.

"Mahim Begum has numbered your hours in this haven, my Emperor. You have no choice but to concede!" Bibi Mubaraka teased. "Bright and early tomorrow, jharoka would be your throne of judgment, demanding all your attention to heed the petitions of your subjects who have been deprived of long for the privilege of private audience. In the afternoon, of course, you would be holding court in the Hall of Private Audience, communing with your courtiers, and keeping abreast of the affairs in all quarters of your empire. Mahim Begum's orders, you are probably acquainted with this schedule?" A tinkling of mirth escaped her lips, noticing his expression of forced martyrdom, as if he was resigned to his fate of burdens tedious and onerous.

"You love to gloat over the power of Mahim, which holds us all prisoners, my mountain beauty, don't you?" Babur sighed again, his eyes spilling the light of poetry and wonders.

"Broken and sick, again I live
By death's task, I know life's worth."

He recited this couplet he had written a few days ago under some spell of inspiration both sad and joyous. "Why do I indulge Mahim in her whims and vagaries, I don't know? Forgiving her always—almost everything? By her orders, the gentle sinner of man—Ahmed, flayed alive! The other unfortunate cooks trampled alive under the feet of the elephants. And yet, my Pummock, succumbing to the most horrible of deaths! Men against beasts, and beasts staying faithful to the very end. And yet again, Mahim should not have acted so cruelly, staining her hands with the blood of violence and vengeance?"

"Mahim Begum is not to be blamed, my Emperor. Watching you suffer, she had gone mad with grief, and frightened. We all were." Bibi Mubaraka murmured in defense of the Begum, her gaze tender and profound.

"Mahim grieves only for the living!" Babur exclaimed, his eyes gathering rills of laughter. "She loves no one, but prince Humayun. Your grief was greater than your love, my Afghan Lady, though you betrayed me most excruciatingly, clinging to the curtain of death while I kept calling you back to the stage of life. You can't even begin to imagine my agony when I thought you were lost to me, my very soul pounding the throne of Allah with supplications most terrible and heart-rending. And when I knew you would live, I was humbled, almost collapsing under the weight of bliss and gratitude." His look was dreamy, as if the poet-mystic within him was seeking the magic of serenity. "Though I love life with all its joys and sorrows, I am getting wearied of pomp and ceremony. I wish to retire to that palace at Dholpur—that marble haven with lotus gardens for your sole delight alone. If you would agree to live there, that would be our paradise."

"Any place is a paradise for me, my Emperor, wherever you take me." Bibi Mubaraka smiled, her voice small and tremulous. "But Allah has assigned you the task of building a great empire, and He would lend you strength to accomplish what you must."

"Allah would wrench out this little strength which is left in me, if he chanced to look into my soul?" Babur smiled back, his look profound and enigmatic. "Of all the deaths, losses and agonies, what haunts me the most is the death of Pummock. Mir Jamal's account how Pummock suffered before dying, I can't efface from my thoughts. Strange, passing strange that I can't stop thinking about it! It reminds me of a story Khwaja Kilan told me, though this story has nothing to do with what Pummock suffered." He tossed a pallet of majun into his mouth, and eased himself up thoughtfully. Holding the gold of memories in his eyes, he was drifting toward the latticework window overlooking his palace garden with terraces wide and gleaming. "I was young then, on a hunting expedition with Khwaja Kilan in the woods of Ferghana. Proud and thrilled I was when I shot one hare, gloating over my prize and triumph. Khwaja Kilan with his usual flare for humbling his students through the medium of story-telling made me sit beside him, knowing fully well my weakness for stories, and commencing as always with a look most tender and profound. It was not just a story but a lesson in love and compassion which I understood even at that tender age on the first rung of teens. I don't remember the exact words, but the origin of this story is ascribed to Prophet Muhammad, who made his disciples sit with him after he saw one of them kicking a dog with a stick. There was a merchant passing through the desert in quest of riches, but midway to his destination he became very thirsty, and was on the verge of dying while hoping for miracles. Fortunately, he found a well and quenched his thirst. Gratefully, he resumed his journey, but had not gone too far when he espied a dog, suffering the same pangs of thirst he had suffered a few moments ago. So, he retraced his steps, filled his shoe with water, going back and forth several times to quench the thirst of the dog till it was revived. This dog as his faithful companion followed him till he reached a town, bustling with markets to trade and barter. Soon, he was blessed with riches beyond imagination, as if the heavens itself had opened its coffers for him to gather and invest. But deep down, he knew that as long as he clung to the virtue of love and compassion, his business would thrive and prosper. Why do I have this feeling that I have repeated this story so often and to so many friends?" His gaze was arresting the marble pools with jets of blue fountains, but he turned abruptly, his eyes spilling the wine of love. "Since I am to be torn away from you early at dawn tomorrow, I suggest we spend this afternoon and evening together in our lovely garden of Baghi-Zar-Afshan. With you beside me, I would be able to write my treatise on poetry, snatching inspiration from your lovely eyes, or just reading couplets?" He drifted toward her as if drunk with the soma of adventure and anticipation.

"My Emperor!" A cry of incredulity escaped the lips of Bibi Mubaraka. "You surely have not forgotten? Your promise to princess Gulbadan to show her the garden of Baghi-Zar-Afshan! She has been looking forward to this excursion since days."

"Mahim must have instructed you to refresh the emperor's memory?" Babur quipped, his expression deflated. Recalling with clarity that the ladies of his harem were to go sightseeing in Agra this very afternoon! And that he was taking Gulbadan to Sikri with him—his pleasure retreat where he indulged in contemplating or writing his memoirs.

"Mahim Begum doesn't instruct me, my Emperor, but keeps me abreast of all affairs in this household!" Bibi Mubaraka declared, laughter trilling down her lips. "I also know that she has dispatched a team of workers to erect a marquee in the middle of Baghi-Zar-Afshan for the sole comfort of you and the princess. You would find it furnished like a kiosk, with rugs, chairs and cushions, the marquee itself a grand protection against sun and heat."

"Nothing can compare to the grandeur in that garden but its gold-scattering blooms, and yet there are none at this time of the year." Babur's eyes were lit up with the warmth of ardor and nostalgia. "Those blooms which welcomed you once are late in returning, and yet I have made that spot the altar of my devotion, where I feel most inspired to write my memoirs." The warmth of ardor in his eyes was replaced by sadness all of a sudden as he began almost prophetically. "Mahim would bury me in Agra, if I was to die tomorrow, I am certain. Promise me love, that you would take my body to Kabul. I wish to be buried in my favorite garden, Aram-bagh. No great tomb over my grave. I would like to feel the warmth and beauty of sunshine, and I know I would even in my—" He couldn't continue, noticing great, big tears in her eyes. "My love!" One agony of a prayer escaped his lips as he crushed her into his arms. Would you waste these pearls on this mad raving fool of an emperor?" He kissed her wet cheeks. "Your laughter is much more precious than these pearls which I better swallow lest you claim them back. My heart longs for love and laughter, yet my thoughts have been chasing bleak shadows lately. And yet, love dissolves all, the malady, the sickness, even the morbid thoughts." He carried her in his arms into the adjacent bath with tiles of blue and white marble.

"My Emperor, at this hour of the day!" Bibi Mubaraka protested, as he undressed her most gently in great contrast to the violence deep within his soul and psyche.

"Emperors have the privilege of choosing any hour of lovemaking when whipped by the hands of their wild desire." Babur's kisses were hot and scalding, even the scented waters of the bath cooling not the fire of his passion.

The afternoon had descended quickly for both Babur and Bibi Mubaraka, their passion still greedy for time before they parted. Bibi Mubaraka accompanying the ladies of the harem, and Babur heading for Sikri with princess Gulbadan! This was Gulbadan's first trip to Sikri, and she was awed by the silver-domed palace with its spandrels of gilded finial' spilling over and under a host of parapets and merlons. She was literally transfixed by the pavilion ceiling inlaid with the patterns of morning glory in lapis lazuli, further enhanced by clusters of carnelians over slim panels into bouquets of carnations. Cradled in the crook of Babur's arm, she was now stepping out of the palace, proud of her red velvet dress with billowing sleeves, her matching cap studded with pearls and rubies. Babur was donned in blue silk robe, his matching turban with a large sapphire in the middle lending him the aura of youth and vivacity.

The vast, gleaming garden with its terraces and fountains was welcoming Babur and Gulbadan. They were lost in the scent and color of exuberance, as if drunk by the perfume from jasmine, genitian and edelweiss. A bower of Damascus roses was luring them toward its scented glory, but Babur had snatched Gulbadan's hand into his own, almost dragging her toward the grove of poplars. Gulbadan was wide-eyed and breathless, her gaze following the flight of parakeets and kingfishers, while doves fluttered close to her, friendly and fearless. Babur's attention was arrested to one pomegranate tree, swooning against the spiral embrace of a cypress, as if both were eager to experience the bliss of union and rapture. Babur didn't know he had stopped abruptly, bringing Gulbadan to a stumbling halt before this marvel of nature's own handiwork.

"Look, my Rose, nature's own miracle most sublime and wondrous!" Babur smiled into the eyes of his daughter. "You are too young to understand this, but since you are my only audience, I might as well share this knowledge with you. Pomegranate trees represent life, many seers in Hindustan believe, and cypresses represent death. If we cut a branch from cypress, and keep it in water, hoping for fresh roots, nothing happens. That branch wilts and dies. But if we cut a branch from pomegranate, keeping it in water, fresh roots grow out of its stem, making it a sapling for another pomegranate tree. That's why each pomegranate is planted beside a cypress, as if to honor the cycle of birth and death in life as well as in nature. Birth, death, resurrection!" He claimed her hand, resuming his stroll. "By the light of wonder in your eyes, my Rose, I can tell you understand more than any adult with a bagful of curiosity! But I must work on my book. You are free to roam in the garden, or chase the butterflies?" He hastened toward the marquee Mahim had it installed so lovingly.

"I would sit with you, my Emperor!" Gulbadan chirped precociously. Her thoughts chasing the alien word, *resurrection*! "I would read, or dream, as Mahim Begum says when I just sit and watch?" She sang merrily

"And what would you dream about, my lovely Rose?" Babur indulged happily.

"Dream, I don't know? Dream this dream!" Gulbadan declared innocently.

"My little dream-poet!" Babur's thoughts were a mingling of delight and incredulity. "My little princess, a mystic and a scholar, and doesn't even know of her talents! You learn quickly, my Rose, and before you know you would be a great author?" His feet came to a slow halt by the bed of Damascus roses, his sight alone absorbing their scent and beauty.

"What is resurrection, my Emperor?" Gulbadan asked, glowing with joy at Babur's praise and endearments.

"It means to be born again, after death." Babur smiled, trying his best to explain simply, his senses catching the ripple of fountains, against which the roses blushed and swayed. "You see this dark soil, my Rose?" He bent down, scooping a handful, and then letting it slip through his fingers back to the ground. "These clods of earth were leaves and flowers once just like these roses, but they withered and died, giving life to fresh leaves and flowers. Death becoming the food for life, living again and again! A time would come when you would think about these words, but for right now enjoy the beauty of this garden. Do you know why it is called Baghi-Zar-Afshan?" He proceeded gaily toward the marquee, infused with the euphoria of imparting knowledge to his daughter. "Baghi-Zar-Afshan means the gold-scattering garden, and do you know why? You see those trees towering high over the marquee? Gul mohur trees, remember that, not in bloom right now, but in spring they are loaded with flowers the color of gold with a scarlet heart in the middle. Every little whiff of breeze makes these flowers swing and scatter, falling on the ground in a shower of gold! Enough of tutoring, my love, and now the emperor must labor for scraps of inspiration!" He approached the marquee, Gulbadan racing ahead to claim her seat against one crimson pillow.

An evening with pale tremor of a haze had descended quickly while Babur seated under the marquee at his teakwood desk was still absorbed in writing his memoirs. Small gusts of wind were picking speed, not noticed by Babur. Gulbadan too, immersed in her book, Bostan by Saadi, was utterly oblivious to the dusk or to the caprice of the wind. This book was her birthday gift from Babur, lacquered and illumined with jade gilding, and one of her favorites since she loved to read stories. Before commencing to read she had helped Babur sort his papers in neat piles under the headings of Turki Diwan, Turki prosody, and a large pile of his odes and poems written in Persian. All those heaps now lay neglected at his feet as he sat writing his memoirs. Gulbadan had almost finished reading her Bostan, her senses becoming opiate and languid. She had closed her eyes, but her thoughts were awakening to the turbulence of curiosity and restlessness.

Mahim Begum adopted me, why? Padishah came to Hindustan with only Bibi Mubaraka and all the other begums were jealous, not my Dear Lady? Dildar Begum doesn't love me, yet she always talks about prince Hindal? Mahim Begum, always talking about prince Humayun! Prince Askeri and prince Kamran, I don't like them! They are always teasing me, and Gulrukh Begum doesn't believe me—she was falling asleep.

Suddenly, the sky was overcast with grey potbellied clouds. Babur had barely time to look up against the drums of thunder and lightning. A solid sheet of rain came pelting down, followed by andhi—the great storm with winds as violent as a hurricane. Babur's manuscripts were blown away like chaff, Gulbadan clinging to him terrified. He himself stood there numb with grief, watching his precious works of love lost to the winds.

The evening had descended over the palace at Sikri drenched with rage and bitterness for Babur, and with fatigue and bewilderment for the machalchis driven mad by Babur to salvage each scrap of paper from all corners of the garden. Now a great fire roared under the marble hearth in the parlor of the Sikri palace as Babur bent double with fatigue kept drying page after page with utmost patience. It was almost midnight, though Babur had lost count of time, his dinner neglected over the table brought to him hours ago, yet he was not hungry. Gulbadan had done justice to her meal, though distracted and shivering, but now she lay comforted on her gilded davenport under warm blankets. She was wide awake, fascinated by her father's absorption as he pressed the papers in layers of blankets and under the woolen rugs before holding each page against the blaze for drying. Her thoughts were wandering after Maywa Jan who had helped her change into the night robe of creamy silks, almost vanishing like a fairy godmother after she had tucked her under blankets. Babur himself had donned the pale robe of Chinese silk, his sleeves rolled up while he worked trancelike. Gulbadan's eyes were stinging for lack of sleep, but she didn't want to sleep, her thoughts a whirlwind of curiosity.

"Are you going to write a big, holy book like the Quran, my Emperor?" Gulbadan ventured forth softly. Since Babur didn't respond, she added. "Mahim Begum makes me read that book, and I yawn and yawn."

"Ah, my sleeping beauty, I thought you were sleeping!" Babur was startled out of his sad plight, the mystic poet within him awakening to the sense of the sacred and the unfathomable. "I don't have the divine inspiration to write such a poetic wonder!" He drifted toward her, divining with clarity her thoughts unspoken. "So, Mahim Begum forces you to read the Quran?" He lowered himself over the edge of the davenport thoughtfully. "And the reading makes you sleepy, or afraid, perhaps? Wish you had a friend like my friend and teacher, Khwaja Kilan. He taught me the love for learning by telling stories, reading poetry to me, and teaching me to love all through anecdotes all witty and wonderful. I was eleven when he taught me to read Quran as well as understand it. By then, it was sheer poetry to me, and I wanted to read more and more. Young children should not be taught to read Quran until they have learned enough to admire its beauty. Well, you are too young. Mahim would not make you read it, I assure you. I would guide you toward its light by making it interesting. Now, my sweet rebel, you better sleep, or I would make you read the Quran contrary to what I just said?" He got to his feet laughing.

"I promise, my Emperor, I would sleep if you eat your dinner?" Gulbadan chanted with a sudden burst of animation.

"You would rule the world, if not men?" Babur tossed a grape into his mouth on his way to the hearth, commanding over his shoulders. "You better sleep, my Rose, or I would summon Maywa Jan to take you to the bedroom.

Babur had grown oblivious to time, working tenaciously to dry each salvaged page, even forgetting his adored princess who had finally fallen asleep, soundly and blissfully. Watching one brittle page with smudges instead of letters, Babur sighed to himself, becoming aware of the light of dawn filtering through the latticework window to his left. The morning sky slashed with flaming streaks much like the licking tongues of flames under his hearth, had sucked his breath, his heart smitten with awe and bewilderment. The sky was changing colors before his rapt gaze, as if brushstrokes of nature were splashing it with gold and vermilion.

So serene and beautiful, this painted sky, as if it has never tasted the fury of the winds and the storms, Babur swayed toward the cushions piled over the Persian rug as a makeshift bed. *The caprice of nature, both awful and awesome! Gentle and violent!* He collapsed over the pillows, his thoughts ripping apart the mantle of memories where tragedies of his youth lay sleeping. He was hurled straight into the mouth of his ruined altar where Sweet Absent stood holding out her arms, inviting him to the abode of peace and silence.

33

Humayun Exiled

Ah, Love! Could you and I with him conspire
To grasp this sorry scheme of things entire
Would not we shatter it to bits—and then
Remold it nearer to the heart's desire
    — Omar Khayyam

I am wearied! Wearied of wars, intrigues, rebellions! Babur was thinking while pacing the length of his library in Agra palace under some spell of fever and loneliness. *I should visit Kabul, just me and my Afghan Lady! The cargo of time is foundering down the waters of love and longings, deep and abysmal, as if another day would never knock at the door of tomorrow, hugging the mantle of yesterday and greeting no fresh dawns.* His feet were coming to a slow halt by his desk cluttered with papers which were salvaged from the dust-storm in Baghi-Zar-Afshan. Most of the manuscripts were partially restored, and the rest neglected for the lack of time and inspiration.

This library of rose and ivory was wafting the scent of roses arranged artistically in jade bowls. Babur turned abruptly, inhaling deeply, his gaze studying the intricate details of the bowls encrusted with rubies and lapis lazuli. He was trying his best to tear the tapestry of wars to rags, but his thoughts were bent on chasing the dust of defeats and conquests. Five seasons had flitted past since his grief over his manuscripts at Baghi-Zar-Afshan, and intrigues and rebellions had adopted the caprice of the seasons. Summer over the edge of Monsoon had fallen into the well of Fall and Winter and Spring had faded against the onslaught of summer once again. He was becoming aware of the oppressive heat, his feet commencing the ritual of pacing along with his thoughts.

The reports of unrest in Kabul were a distant murmur in Babur's head, but his thoughts were hovering over the bridge of Irej from where he had returned recently after a decisive battle with Rana Sanga. Rana Sanga had emerged once more as a formidable foe, gathering his forces in the city of Irej where Ganges surged and swelled as the fortress of defense. But no fortress could keep Babur away from the foe, who had plotted to attack the Moghuls with the intent of killing and plundering. Instead of remaining in defensive position, Babur had launched the offensive by mobilizing his forty galleons laden with armor and armaments. His large cannon—Dig Ghazi alone had secured the victory, it seemed, killing Rana Sanga amidst the pandemonium of his own troops, frightened and fleeing.

Another victory was coming to Babur's head, that of Etawa, its king surrendering, followed by a loss on the field of Laknau, resulting in loss of the kingdom of Bihar. That loss was compensated by the conquests of Banaras and Ghazipur , his two strongholds to rule over the entire state of Bengal. One more victory was entering Babur's thoughts, where prince Askeri had accompanied him to the battlefield at Haldi overlooking the right bank where waters of Gorgu meet the river Ganges. The Moghul troops in ranks of a solid V had attacked the enemy, who were quick to flee in their ill-equipped boats in hope of reaching the shore of safety.

Ah, the doomed rebels, and now prince Askeri rules the entire state of Bengal! Babur's thoughts were weaving their way back into the valleys of unrest in Kabul, his pace slackening in rapport with his thoughts. *Uzbeks against the Moghuls, and Moghuls against the Moghuls.* His thoughts were closing shut the gates of wars, and entering the sanctuary of his royal household. *I must announce the betrothal of princess Gulrang with Aisan Timur, and princess Gulchihra's with Tukhta Bega, this very day? Khwaja Khizr gazing at princess Gulbadan adoringly? Oh, no, my Rose princess, she is still a child, my precious and adored!* His thoughts now were gathering his sons in one aching embrace. *Kamran, Askeri, Hindal, Humayun, all loved, yet I am harsh with Humayun, why? Dearer than my own life he is to me, is that why? Mahim thinks I favor Mehdi Khwaja over Humayun? How can such a thought enter her head, and why would I deprive my legal heir of his rightful legacy in favor of my sister's husband?* He didn't even know his feet as well his thoughts had come to a subtle halt, while he stood by the latticework window, contemplating his garden. The garden below with its wealth of topiaries and gurgling fountains was pouring sadness into his heart, aching suddenly for the nearness of his Afghan Lady. He turned abruptly, thinking of Bibi Mubaraka, but his feet were carrying him toward the chamber of Rose princess. Gulbadan had sprained here ankle the night before last, and he had sat with her half the night, consoling and comforting.

The rose chamber where Gulbadan lay resting was invalid's paradise with all its trappings of silks and damasks. Babur drifted toward the bed dreamlike, not even noticing the swift curtsy of Maywa Jan. Maywa Jan made a hasty retreat toward the door, while Gulbadan sprang to a couchant position, her face transfigured with joy.

"You are not to leap like a gazelle every time you see the emperor, my sweet Rose!" Babur bent down to hug her, and then stood laughing. "Though gazelles don't leap, maybe the wild ones? You are the wild one, jumping from terrace to terrace, and one little jump has cost you a month's confinement. And you would remain confined if you didn't learn the graceful manners of a Moghul princess."

"I had the grace not to cry, my Emperor, not even when Dildar Begum pulled me by the arm, and I had to wear a sling for one month!" Gulbadan chirped happily.

"I regret now that Dildar Begum was confined inside the harem for a month for pulling your arm so roughly, by my orders, and without your company!" Babur laughed without regret, his look tender and contemplative. "She didn't complain? And now you better rest and get well if you want to have a picnic on one of my grand safinas?"

"May I ride a pony, my Emperor, when I get well?" Was Gulbadan's abrupt request, her eyes shining.

"A great scandal it would be if a royal princess went riding in public here in Hind, or any female, for that matter?" Babur declared with a touch of nostalgia. "I would take you to Kabul, and there you could ride to your heart's content. Your aunt whom you call Dear Lady used to race with me on her pony! We grew up in Ferghana, riding our lives away, it seemed, form ponies to horses, and she can still ride with ease and grace, I am sure."

"My Dear Lady says I am not to wear saris?" Gulbadan's mind was bent on getting something, though she didn't know what she wanted the most. "May I have one sari, my Emperor, even if I can't wear it?"

"You would have a whole bazaar of saris in your very room, my sweet Rose!" Babur promised generously. "Saris of silk and gold all the way from Benares, and you would wear them too! I am afraid though you would twist your precious ankles quite often if you wore saris?"

"I won't, my Emperor!" Gulbadan protested, her eyes lighting up with anticipation. "When I wear saris I would be carried in a palanquin, and picnic in your safinas!" Her eyes were gathering dreamy stars, soft and twinkling. "I don't like going on Brave, it's noisy. Useful is very big, but my favorite is Baburi. That must be your favorite too, my Emperor, sounds like your name? May I go on Baburi?"

"Baburi, sure, is named after me, my elf, but it would refuse to stir if you don't invite the emperor as your royal guide?" Babur laughed, noticing Tahir curtsying his way toward him.

"My Emperor, Begums request your presence at dinner!" Tahir extended his curtsy into a somersault to please princess Gulbadan, knowing too-well that the emperor would be pleased in return.

"For you, my Rose, the emperor lets Tahir play the fool!" Babur turned laughingly. "Rest and dream about saris." He sprinted toward the door. "When you are well, we would dine on Baburi."

Babur had dined in the House of Pleasure with his mountain-brides in great splendor. Even now as he sat with his wives amidst the flickering of candles from gold and silver candelabras, he could see the trays of sweetmeats and fruit arrangements piled high on the tables, replacing the dishes of sumptuous viands enjoyed by his royal household. Bibi Mubaraka was seated to his left, gulfs apart, separated by an ocean of princes and princesses, it seemed. But he was content, arresting his beloved in his gaze when not talking with Mahim to his right, or heeding the comments of his other wives seated across the table, mostly entertained by Mir Jamal and Mehdi Khwaja. Actually, all were being entertained by the musicians and the dancers with studs in their noses and bright tilaks on their foreheads.

"My Emperor, do you know why Rana Sanga died while fleeing the Moghuls?" Mehdi Khwaja's abrupt inquiry and enigmatic smile was gaining Babur's attention, so he continued mysteriously. "The night before his defeat he was visited by a sage in his dream. This sage was no ordinary man but a giant with a terrific form, his expression at once menacing and encompassing. When in full retreat, that same dream-sage stalled him, frightening him out of his wits, and he breathed his last amidst spasms of convulsions."

"Not even a demon could pour fear into the heart of that man!" Babur laughed, tossing a pallet of majun into his mouth. "Battle of Jam could have cured Rana Sanga of shock from any nightmare, and he might have lived. The Uzbeks are a mighty foe, and they are not superstitious. I believe they have mastered the art of killing superstition. I should send you to Jam to fight the Uzbeks, Mehdi Khwaja, your valor are getting rusted."

"Even my rusted valor would dishearten the Uzbeks, my Emperor." Mehdi Khwaja smiled. "Uzbeks are doomed, rather defeated by Kyzylbashes, their leader Ubaid Khan dead, and their other leader Abusaid Sultan captured alive."

"Bain Shaikh brings encouraging news, my Emperor!" Mir Jamal seemed anxious to drain his cup of news. "Shahzada Tahmasp who besieged Iraq last week has subjugated the Uzbeks entirely, and they have offered their total submission."

"Submissions carry within them the seeds of anger and vengeance, which sprout forth sooner or later." Babur demurred aloud, his eyes gathering rills of sadness. "Afghans are a querulous lot. We have won Fatehpur, no doubt. Biban and Bayazid have fled. But Lahore is rigged with insurrections. I wish to retire—entrust all these warring kingdoms into the hands of my sons to rule and subjugate?" His gaze was profound and restless as he continued. "I have grown old. The burdens of these kingdoms are too heavy for my shoulders anymore. My sons are young and healthy. They are capable of dividing and sharing such burdens. I long for rest and quiet before I die, retire to Sikri, perhaps? Write couplets and serenade the beauty in nature." He was oblivious to the quick surge of tears in the eyes of his wives.

"My Emperor!" Mahim sobbed aloud, her voice choked against the deluge of tears.

"My beauty!" Babur was startled out of his reveries, his gaze embracing the tear-streaked eyes of his wives with a sense of awe and incredulity. "The emperor is not dead yet! He is going to live and rule, and be ruled by you, my precious loves!" His eyes were spilling joy and sunshine. "Wipe your lovely eyes, my beauties!" He gasped for breath, catching the star-dance of mischief in the eyes of his brother-in-law. "Tell those Uzbeks beyond the steppes of Kabul, Mir Jamal, that the emperor's rule extends from the highlands of Badakhshan to the junction of Gorga River with Ganges. And that his empire stretches from the Himalayas to Gwalior and Chanderi, and from the Oxus to Bengal!"

"I would tell the whole world, my Emperor!" Mir Jamal sprang to his feet, more so by the impact of the gilded portals thrown open than by the outburst of his passion.

One young messenger in liveries of pale silks bounced right through the open doors, curtsying and announcing the arrival of prince Humayun. He was quick to retrace his steps as the Prince himself emerged forth, royal and graceful.

"My Emperor." Humayun offered a gallant curtsy, accepting Babur's smile as a mark of favor.

Humayun was claimed by Mahim Begum, her eyes shining with tears of joy and welcome. Soon, he was swept into the arms of other begums, thrilled by the shower of hugs and kisses. Watching this handsome prince, the dancing girls were caught in abeyance, rapt and dazzled. Even the melodious tunes from the flute of Shaikhi were attaining the quality of flight and surrender. Babur was not even smiling anymore, his gaze reaching beyond the cameo in his son's gold turban and searching the kingdoms exposed to assault and annihilation.

Kabul exposed to the danger of riot and plunder! My own son, unwise and heedless, flying to Agra and exposing Badakhshan to the war-mongering lusts of the Afghans! Babur's thoughts were a whirlwind of pain, chaos, longing. He was becoming aware of Mushin pouring wine into the jeweled cup of Humayun, while Mahim Begum stood there rapt and fawning.

"Come here, my charming prince, sit by the emperor!" Babur commanded, his voice sending chills and fears into the hearts of all present.

"Yes, my Emperor." Humayun took a quick gulp of his wine before gliding toward his father with the ease of a gymnast.

"Could you satisfy my curiosity, my young Prince! What made you grace Agra with your royal presence, when raids and insurrections are rampant in Hind and abroad?" Babur's look was profound and compelling.

"Why did I expect a much different welcome than this, my Emperor!" Humayun murmured to himself. He lowered his gaze, his lips sealed after he took another swig of his wine.

"How presumptuous of me that I expected the virtues of loyalty and integrity from the heir-apparent to my throne!" Babur was trying his best to control his anger. He claimed the jeweled cup from his son, his very eyes commanding. "You have not answered me, my prince, what made you come to Agra?"

"My love for you, my Emperor!" Humayun murmured. "I heard, you were ill, and I—" He was discomfited by sudden blaze of anger in the eyes of the emperor.

"Ah, my foolish Prince!" Babur's voice had the rumble of a distant thunder as he began to pace. "Your indolence and insufferable neglect in writing to me is the cause of all this misunderstanding. I was ill, yes, but that was a year ago! All those post-houses built by my command every eighteen mile from Kabul to Agra, and furnished with relays of six horses each post-house, why? Why, I tell you, so that we could communicate. A jungle of raid and rebellion all around, and the clouds of intrigue and stupidity, and you decide to leave Badakhshan exposed to the raids of the rebels and plunderers? Why, my heedless Prince, why?"

"My Emperor! I sent prince Hindal, he is to—" Humayun's thoughts were silenced by another thundering exclamation from Babur.

"Hindal, my besotted Prince!" Babur seemed not aware of his raging expression, or of the stunned silence of the all present. "He is not schooled yet in the art of warring intrigues. Hindal is barely eleven! You have left your child-brother at the mercy of the foes—vile rebels and cutthroats. For this blunder alone, you are exiled to Sambal beyond the Ganges for six months. This is not your punishment, but a discipline, if you are to inherit this kingdom after me? And dare not set foot in Agra, until I summon you." He drifted toward Bibi Mubaraka, his gaze wild and unseeing. "Come, my Afghan Lady, I need to cool the fire of my anguish with the scent of roses in our garden." He assisted her to her feet, almost dragging her along outside the House of Pleasure.

The garden with its marble terraces, flanked by fountains had claimed Babur and Bibi Mubaraka as its honored guests, and yet both were silent and contemplative. They were strolling side-by-side, inhaling most blissfully the scent of roses and oleanders. An evening hush had fallen over the garden, though yellow finches and kingfishers could be heard chirping. Suddenly, the perfume from Rat-ki-Rani was pervading Babur's senses, and he was awakening to the poetry of his lone contemplations.

The irony of love—this paradox! Love's mockery, rather its silence! What does love mean? Can one truly love? Can one die for love? Is love nourished by self-denial and suffering? Do I not love Humayun with all my heart and soul? Would I not suffer when he is in exile, and my heart longing for his presence? Are kingdoms greater than life, greater than love, greater than Humayun? More powerful than death! Babur was thinking, watching the shadow of poet-mystic within him shudder and disappear.

Inside my grave when I finally die
One heartrending cry would fill my soul
Telling the whole world I have lived a lie
Polishing emptiness from the soot of hot coal

This quatrain in Babur's head was carving rills of memories, stark and distant. Sweet Absent was with him, yet he was comforted by the presence of his Beloved alive and beautiful.

Was it a lie that I loved? Is it a lie that I love? Do I love? Is love many in one? Love for life! For wealth! For joy and beauty! For family and friends! For wisdom and learning! Who do I love the best? Humayun, Afghan Lady, Gulbadan? Am I not accursed in love, courting—

"My Emperor, you were harsh with prince Humayun." Bibi Mubaraka's sweet voice had claimed Babur's attention.

"Harsh, my love, yes! Cruel, even to my own self!" Babur flashed her dreamy smile. "Just because I love him! Love is a revelation, my love. A revelation which comes and goes like the changing of the seasons! Each revelation dear, sweet and more tender, more profound! More painful than the ones lost in timelessness! Strange that my love for Humayun manifests itself in harsh rebukes! I was longing to hold him into my arms and I couldn't, and yet again I can count the ones I love on my little finger, you, Humayun and Gulbadan. And yet again, I love all my wives and children."

"Why were you unkind to Humayun this evening, my Emperor?" Bibi Mubaraka opined aloud as if searching her thoughts.

"Another revelation, my mountain beauty!" Babur laughed. "Or is it? Love feeds on perfection in the one whom we love. Your beauty is perfection, the highest of all perfections. Gulbadan's innocence is her perfection, the purest of all perfections. Yet, Humayun is fair and handsome, valorous and intelligent, and yet I demand more than that in him, some sort of wisdom and discipline beyond praise or reprimand?"

"You would forgive, prince Humayun, my Emperor?" Bibi Mubaraka sang this plea.

"If I have a thousand lives with thousand souls, I would cut them all to pieces till they were three thousand! Dividing them between you, Gulbadan and Humayun, and praying to all the deities in Hind to keep alive the breath of life in the souls of all my beloveds! That is how precious—dearer than life, is the life of Humayun to me. Forgive him, no, not as yet. Forgiveness breeds sloth, pride, vanity, stupidity."

"You would embrace him, my Emperor, before he leaves, won't you? Otherwise, you would grieve his absence more than ever before!" Bibi Mubaraka murmured, knowing the well of pain inside the emperor's heart.

"Not too ardently, I hope, lest I keep him at Agra!" Babur murmured back.

He caught her into his arms, kissing and murmuring endearments. The scent of the night and the glittering stars were serenading the lovers. Bibi Mubaraka was swooning with joy, and Babur's heart was humming the song of longing and surrender.

Inside my grave when I finally die
One heartrending cry would fill my soul
Telling the whole world, I have lived a lie
Polishing emptiness from the soot of hot coal

34

Great Sacrifice

All human bodies yield to death's decree
The soul survives to all eternity
— Pindar

Babur pacing in his bedroom of rose and ivory inside his Agra palace seemed oblivious of his Afghan Lady seated in his own gilded chair, bemused and motionless. She was watching him under some spell of hopeless, helpless pain, her pallor accentuated by the sparkle of sapphires in her hair and around her throat. In contrast to the stillness of his beloved, Babur was whipped by the madness of his grief and despair. Six grueling months had slithered past since Humayun was exiled to Sambal. And now when the Prince was about to return to Agra, the news had reached Babur that his son was afflicted with some serious illness. He was brought to Delhi, ministered by skillful physicians. Mahim, afflicted with her grief had hastened to Delhi to bring her son back to Agra where he could be treated under her strict vigilance.

I have killed my son! My beloved prince is dying! Babur's very soul was kindling a blaze of agony.

Babur was becoming aware of the ritual of his pacing, his senses inhaling the reek of death. Death was pacing along with him, chasing his very shadow. It was seething inside his very soul and psyche. A death which had nothing to do with Humayun, but with the pulse of grief within him, above and beyond! Surcease was hovering above, grinning at the mockery of life, and holding out some sort of spurious challenge! His thoughts were defying death, kneading the dust of the world into a ball of clay and feeding it to Humayun, bestowing upon him the gift of life eternal and life blessed. His thoughts were entering the conduit of hysteria, knowing the unknowable, forgetting the unforgettable, seeking some essence supreme and inconceivable—

"My Emperor, you are suffering more than prince Humayun under the assault of fever!" Bibi Mubaraka ventured again as she had done several times before to appease the suffering of the emperor. "Everyone gets a fever at one time or the other. I had it many times, and you did too, but we prevailed. The Prince would be here any moment now, and you would watch him getting well and gaining strength."

"My son is dying, and I am his murderer!" Babur groaned, mired deep in his sorrow.

"How could you say that, my Emperor?" One incredulous protest escaped the lips of Bibi Mubaraka. "Sambal has not been his exile, but a retreat. He didn't live like some prisoner inside a tower of gloom, but like a prince in a palace. He stayed healthy and cheerful, visiting the shrines and studying astronomy. His letters to Mahim Begum are full of wit and gaiety, she showed them to me. Would you like to read?" Her thoughts were disrupted by the fire of anguish in Babur's eyes and upon his lips.

"If Kamran, Askeri, Hindal had come to Agra after deserting their posts, would I have punished them, sending them to exile?" Babur's feet were coming to a slow halt, but he was turning abruptly toward the marble latticework window. "No, I wouldn't have, and yet the most beloved of my—" He ceased to speak, his hands knotted behind his back.

Only the abysmal, profound sadness was Babur's companion as he stood watching out of the latticework window at the caparisoned elephant. Mahim Begum was alighting form the gilded howdah, cradling the Prince most possessively. The gold turbaned mahout was neglected behind, as Mir Jamal and Mehdi Khwaja materialized in the garden. More princes and servants in liveries of gold were appearing, eager to assist, but Mahim Begum was holding on to Humayun, while keeping everyone else at bay with her eyes alone.

Just like Virgin Mary and Jesus! One cold thought in Babur's head was crackling and splintering. He was not even aware that Bibi Mubaraka had crept behind him, following his gaze where Humayun was lumbering along under the protective support of his mother and uncles. Something inside him was snapping loose, ripping open the veil of his psyche with the knife of fear and presage. White peace in death was rising like the mists silvery and blessed. The bud of life just a fleeting promise! The flower of life inside the kernel of death swirling against the cosmic dance of dewdrop dreams!

Yes, Mary and Jesus! But Jesus died, and then lived, still living! My son is dying— no resurrection for us unholy mortals! Babur swung around, almost knocking Bibi Mubaraka down, but catching her into his arms before she could lose her balance.

"Humayun has come home." Babur murmured, releasing her quickly and dashing out of the room as if fleeing his own shadow.

The scene upon which Babur landed in the parlor was one of doom and gloom, and he stood there in a daze, unable to move or speak. Sayyid Tabib was offering his services, but Mahim Begum was ignoring him, commanding others all around her to prepare a bed for the royal Prince. Babur's senses were getting numb, his gaze alone caressing the dear face he could not recognize. Humayun's gaunt features were almost cadaverous. His lips livid, and dark circles under his eyes digging deep trenches, much like his sunken cheeks all sallow and transparent. Mahim Begum, noticing the presence of her husband cried all of a sudden.

"You didn't think of bringing your ailing son to Agra, my Emperor, because you have other sons!" Mahim's eyes were flashing accusations.

"Yes, my dear Lady, I have other sons, but they are not Humayun!" Babur was jolted out of his daze, leaping to his feet suddenly.

In a flash, Babur had scooped Humayun into his arms, carrying him like a babe down the hall toward a room he admired for its aura of peace and serenity. This room with its carved panels of vines and flowers was welcoming the emperor and his son, as Babur lowered Humayun over the gilded bed, propping satiny pillows under his head most gently. Haze and bewilderment were visiting Babur, his hands fumbling for the sheets over the legs of his son, his gaze fixed and unseeing. Mahim Begum, followed by other members of the royal household had drifted into this chamber under some spell of silence and dream-haze.

Humayun lay listless while attended by the royal physicians, swallowing concoctions of sweet herbs obediently. A few servants stood fanning the invalid prince most fervently and diligently. Mir Jamal, assisted by Gulnar Aghacha was pressing cold compresses over the feverish forehead of Humayun. Mehdi Khwaja had brought his concoction of rose and borage tea, and stood feeding the Prince most patiently. Sayyid Tabib was intent on feeling the pulse of the Prince, his expression one of woe and misery.

"Sayyid Tabib, you are to answer to Allah for the life of my Prince!" Babur exclaimed suddenly, his voice carrying the whip of threat and challenge.

A gong of death was swinging in Babur's head as he sought the sanctuary of his marble terrace. He was almost blinded by the coppery haze of dusk, but his sight and senses were getting accustomed to the hush and beauty of his gardens. The gardeners bare to the waists were pruning the bushes while joking and laughing, some planting the new saplings. The marble terraces were left behind, and he didn't even know that he had straggled far into the groves of pear and apricot. His senses were awakening to the assault of pain, his gaze reaching out to the orchards of loquat and pomegranate. But his feet were carrying him toward the fountains flanked by clusters of roses and daisies. The slates of fretted stone displaying a network of zinnia and dianthus were luring his attention, but he was seeking the solitary trail of his garden where pipals and poplars could stand guard over his solitude, witnessing not the measure of his pain splintering into the fireworks of agony.

Something larger than pain and greater than agony was entering Babur's soul and psyche. It was the blight of hope, cowering against the glacier of despair. The doom of death was hovering over his shoulders, not around or beyond him, but within him. This feeling had nothing to do with Humayun! He was not even thinking about him, rather his thoughts willing themselves not to think about his beloved prince. The razor-sharp pain within him was the death of hope, hemmed in by thistles of doubts, his heart holding on to the link of life which was Humayun. The knife of pain poised over his heart was telling him some secrets, commanding his attention. It was demanding a great sacrifice from him, holding him in pincers of fear and apprehension, yet unveiling the sacred altar within him where his Sweet Absent slept under the shroud of white peace in death.

I must pray! I haven't prayed since sweet Zainab died. And yet I know at times when I prayed in utter hopelessness, my prayers were answered. When I was in exile, grieving and mourning the loss of my father and his kingdom, I had prayed without hope, without words, and I was consoled. I had become the king of Kabul.

Babur's very thoughts arrayed in rags of misery were succumbing to fatigue and hopelessness. He was seeking the comfort-support of the mighty poplar. Leaning against its trunk, his eyes were closing. Behind the closed shutters of his eyes, his spirit was coming alive, emerging fresh from the baptismal waters of darkness, and darting aloft toward the rainbows. The gates of his psyche were thrown open, revealing doors and corridors within the gulfs vast and boundless. Surcease was only a whisper away, whispering *life for life*! Bright, emerald eyes from the ether of his thoughts were comforting him, pouring the light of wisdom in his psyche. Yet the conduit of knowledge was slipping and sliding, it was fragmented—his whole being was effaced.

"My Emperor, my Emperor!" Abal Baka was repeating this mantra in an effort to awaken the emperor from his deep repose against the tree-trunk. "Bibi Mubaraka Begum is requesting your presence at dinner."

"When life becomes a glutton to pain, it ceases to hunger for food." Babur murmured, his eyes shot open! "Feed me with your wisdom, my sage, if you must! The only remedy to the violence of my anguish! Lend me hope. How is prince Humayun?" He stirred, retracing his steps toward the palace.

"My Emperor, I wish I could—" Abal Baka's voice was choked in his feeble attempt to console the emperor. "When all human assistance fails, my Emperor, the sages recommend that an offering made to Allah of the most valuable thing belonging to a person who labors under the affliction is most graciously accepted by Allah. I have seen miraculous recoveries after such offerings are made. The most valuable thing in the possession of prince Humayun is Koh-i-Noor. It would fetch a great price if you sell it, and feed the hungry. I have heard that this diamond is of great worth, and its price could feed the entire world at least for one whole week! Prince Humayun would be on his feet in no time after this offering his made."

"The brightest of diamonds in the heavens!" A volley of strident mirth escaped Babur's lips. "The suns, the stars, the moons and the galaxies! Does Allah lack wealth from the coffers of his bounteous treasures? Does he covet vain offerings? Does he crave to possess this pebble on earth—Koh-i-Noor?" He sprinted onward, his thoughts whipping up a storm.

Has any man ever earned anything precious in his life which he could claim as his own? Absolutely his own! Something invaluable and priceless! Some sort of treasure worthy of an offering to God! What is the most precious thing on earth? Nothing but love! My love for my Afghan Lady! Does she belong to me, do I possess her? What right do I have to lead her toward the altar of death in exchange for the life of my son? Gulbadan, isn't she the most precious of my loves? Could a father offer the life of his beloved daughter to Allah to save the life of his son? Love for love? Beloved for beloved! Death for death! Life for life! What is the most precious to me? My life, my life! A jubilee of joy and agony was in Babur's head, dancing and swirling. His heart was beating like a drum as he sought the red sandstone steps.

"My life! I am going to offer my life in exchange for the health of my son!" Babur floated right into the House of Pleasure where the members of the royal household sat numb and chilled. "Your wisdom, Abal Baka, has opened a window of perception, to greet death—for the sake of life."

"My Emperor!" Was Abal Baka's stunned response, only his gaze roving over the bowls and platters laden with a variety of viands and vegetables!

"At least suffer not the pangs of hunger, my beloveds!" Babur coaxed, forcing a smile, his gaze lingering over Bibi Mubaraka. "The emperor would dine late." He plodded away toward the room where his son lay dying.

Sayyid Tabib greeted Babur most solemnly as soon as he entered the chamber where his son had fallen into a coma. Humayun's eyes were closed, his breathing even, his expression peaceful. To Babur, Humayun looked like a child, cradled into the comfort of sleep. But carved vines and flowers on wood paneling had lost its serenity to Babur's anguished awareness as he began pacing. Princes, Begums and princesses were entering this chamber, mute and crestfallen. But Babur seemed oblivious to all, pacing, rather circling the bed. Mir Jamal and Mehdi Khwaja stood whispering with the physicians. Babur seemed to be hugging the grey mists of mournful silence in this room, his gaze alone pleading with his son to open his eyes and respond to his love.

Mahim Begum and Bibi Mubaraka Begum were standing side by side, though gulfs apart from each other, praying silently. Gulrukh Begum and Dildar Begum had abandoned themselves upon the rugs by the window, joining Gulnar Aghacha and Nurgul Aghacha. Princess Gulrang and Gulchihra had effaced themselves in one corner, frightened and grief-Stricken. Suddenly, Babur was on his knees, snatching Humayun's listless hands into his own, and closing his eyes.

Allah, I offer my life to Thee. Grant me this last wish, let my son live! Thou hast been gracious to Thy servant in all his life, hold not Thy mercy from him in his last extremity. This soundless prayer was Babur's only link to his son, as he stayed on his knees, relinquishing not the hand of his beloved son. He himself felt like a child unloved and child abandoned, seeking some divine intercession for the boon of life and love. A cry of agony was ripped through his heart, though no sound had escaped his lips. His soul had heard the voice of its own shattering, overwhelmed by the agonized cries of the mind gone insane.

"My— Emperor—" Humayun murmured feebly. The eyes of the son and the father were fluttered open, gazing, gazing.

Babur sat there smiling, awed and entranced. He could feel the strength draining from his hands, and flowing into the bloodstream of Humayun. His soul itself had broken loose the fetters of time, and was sailing aloft. Seeking another abode, another life! Fire was coursing in Humayun's veins, and ice was chilling

Babur's heart, yet his whole body was racked by pain so excruciating that he bit his lips. Against the assault of nausea, he could hear the edict of his thoughts: *your son is greeting light, but you would be courting darkness.* Babur was collapsing on the same spot where he sat kneeling.

The emperor is ill! Some muffled, formless sounds were reaching Babur's darkness, yet his body and soul was ravished by pain savage and intolerable.

35

Life for Life

Gone from each flame, each sacred shrine
Are those who made this realm divine
— Aneid, Virgil

The imperial throne embellished with silks and damasks was converted into a bedstead for Babur. He was ailing—perceptive of his brief sojourn in this world, and had chosen Mystic House as his luxuriant abode to spend his last days. This particular evening, he had decided to name Humayun his successor since most of his family had come to Agra with the exception of Hindal.

Prince Hindal was in Kabul, expected to arrive in Agra. Babur was losing patience, fearing that he would die before he could name Humayun his successor. He was rather longing to see the sweet face of his youngest son, his heart tender and aching. His eyes were closed, yet he was aware of the sweet presence of Bibi Mubaraka in this room. Grateful that the members of his royal household had fulfilled his wish for privacy, granting him the privilege to spend some time with his beloved! Hugging this knowledge with aching tenderness within him, his thoughts were commencing the journey of farewell by lending substance to the memories before they could be engulfed into silence.

Babur's sacrifice of his life to God in exchange for the life of Humayun that fateful evening had become a reality for him. His ailing self welcoming the beauty of one last summer and embracing the purity of short-lived winter, surrendering his body and soul to the dictates of death and dying! Paradoxically, the miracle of his prayer had blossomed into an astonishing recovery for Humayun, while his illness had no hope for healing. He could endure his physical pains as long as his mind validated the fact that by relinquishing his life to death, he was nourishing the life of his son so that Humayun could live and prosper.

Humayun, though completely restored to health had grown reclusive and more than ever superstitious. He was bewildered by the presence of duality in man and nature, yet trying his best to understand the paradox of oneness on the metaphorical level of mystery and mysticism. And yet again, duality was hemmed solid inside the globe of non-duality where joy and pain, much like love and hatred were one entity, one essence. Revealing light only when darkness was present. The Prince had grown vain, believing himself to be the center of the universe where the world kept spinning and laughing. But there was no laughter in his heart, suffering still the pain of life, with his father, oblivious to the pangs of fear and exaltation within the abysmal deeps in his soul and psyche.

Babur, with the crystal-clear prescience of his lone contemplations, somehow could peer into the soul of his son much more easily than the Prince stumbling down the road to self-discovery and self-adulation. But he dared not indulge in such luxury lest he be disappointed. Besides, the physical afflictions, such as fever, dyspepsia and dysentery had become the unwelcome guests, invading his body quite frequently after his initial illness at the bedside of prince Humayun. A succession of pain-filled days merging into weeks and months had drained Babur's store of strength and vitality. At times, under the assault of fever, boils would sprout on his arms and legs, and his eardrums bursting with pressure from viscous discharge he dreaded the most. And yet sciatica was much more savage, and spitting of blood intolerable.

Bibi Mubaraka, watching her husband under the satiny sheets was trying to imagine how he looked like when invested with the title, Tiger of Ferghana, or the Lion of Kabul! She couldn't even recognize him as the emperor of Hindustan, looking more like a King-Kalendar, his lips still the color of poppies under the bushel of his white mustache. No jewels adorned his royal person with the exception of jewels in his sherry-brown eyes, if he deigned to reveal them, Bibi Mubaraka was thinking. Her thoughts were edifying further that his eyes had retained the sparkle of youth, and they could still flare into flames of love, anger or laughter in conformity with his mood or temperament. Noticing a subtle tremor under the satiny sheets, Bibi Mubaraka's heart was reaching out to Babur, her eyes gathering tears. And yet her thoughts were murmuring consolations that he was not suffering, looking so peaceful, as if dreaming pleasant dreams.

For sure, Babur was accosting pleasant dreams, greeting his sons, prince Askeri who had arrived from Bengal, and prince Kamran from Kandahar. Hoping beyond hopes that prince Hindal would arrive soon. His thoughts were comparing his love for Hindal with Jacob's love for his son, Joseph. Another sprig of a thought was awakening to self-inquisition— was Ibrahim not ready to sacrifice his son Issac at the altar of faith by God's explicit command? Do my subjects think that I am offering my life as a sacrifice to save Humayun's? Allah didn't command me, and yet didn't I offer this wordless sacrifice? Suddenly, his thoughts were gathering his daughters into their arms, sealing their fates with bridegrooms he himself had chosen before his breath could expire into the ether of nothingness. He was opening his eyes, gazing into the tear-streaked eyes of his beloved and murmuring.

"No use grieving, my love." Babur's voice was barely a low moan, warm and tender. "I love you more than Humayun. Yet, if he was lost to me, I would have been inconsolable, making you wretched. Forgetting my true love—even my duty to my own soul!" His eyelids were getting heavy, yet he was willing them open. "I will love you always, be with you forever. Never be parted from you, you know that? Allah never abandoned me, he sent me a houri straight from the heavens. And you are that houri. You would take me to Kabul, to peace. We would be together." His eyes were closed, his lips silent.

Bibi Mubaraka stirred, feeling his pulse, sucking her tears back and crashing into her former seat under some burden of grief she could neither carry, not discard.

"Must name Humayun my successor this very evening!" Babur's eyes were shot open, this time sparkling with the fire of commands. "Gulrang, Gulchihra—must be married!" His gaze was flying over his beloved toward the royal procession.

Begums, princes and princesses were sailing in as was their wont to cheer the emperor. This evening all seemed to be cheerful, consoled by a false belief that the emperor was recovering from his bouts of prolonged illness. Foremost amongst the princes were Humayun, Kamran and Askeri, followed by princesses old and young.

"Mahim." Babur's voice was choked by an abrupt fit of coughing, his eyes stinging. "Mahim." He managed another murmur, wiping his eyes with a gold-broidered handkerchief.

"Yes, my Emperor." Mahim floated closer to the bed, her rather chunky figure impeding her progress.

"Make room for Gulrang and Gulchihra here close to me." Babur intoned feverishly, summoning Karman to his side by a swift wave of his arm. "Go, find both Aisan Timur and Tukhta Buga, and bring them to my presence in all haste."

"They are gracing the Mystic House with their presence this evening, my Emperor." Kamran bowed ceremoniously. "I would pull them away from the latticework window where they are standing right now, enjoying the beauty of the garden."

"Askeri, fetch Maulana Kazi as quickly as his feet would carry!" Babur commanded, easing himself up, while Mahim propped a pillow behind his back. "Our daughters are to be wedded tonight, my beauty, songs and feasting could wait." His eyes were seeking the approval of the Afghan Lady.

Maulana Kazi, hugging a copy of Quran to his breast was performing the nikkah ceremony for the couples with two witnesses each for each married couple. Gulrang was married to Aisan Timur, and Gulchihra to Tukhta Buga, both couples signing their names on gold-sprinkled papers as nikkah contracts.

Dildar Begum was hugging and kissing both her daughters and sons-in-law. Momentarily, forgetting about Babur's illness and about the paucity of this festive occasion. *This festive event which demands songs and feasting, not tears and sadness!* Dildar Begum was thinking, while watching Gulrukh Begum whose tears were flooding down her cheeks as she bestowed one silk robe on Maulana Kazi, just a small reward for his services of nikkah ceremony.

Babur's thoughts were lulled to peace and serenity, his gaze imprinting each beloved face on the canvas of his soul to take it with him on his journey to death. His tinsel-peace was short-lived though, splintering into raging flames as soon as his gaze espied Mir Birdi. Mir Birdi was commanded to fetch prince

Hindal from Kabul, and now as he approached closer to the bed, Babur's rage was on the verge of exploding.

"My Emperor." Mir Birdi smiled, bowing profusely.

"Where is prince Hindal?" Babur's eyes were flashing accusations.

"Prince Hindal is in Lahore, my Emperor." Was Mir Birdi's flustered response! "At Kila-zafer. He would be here before the night is over." He couldn't continue against the flood of rage in the emperor's eyes, forgetting even to impart the news he was supposed to deliver.

"You ingrate wretch!" Babur exclaimed, overwhelmed by one spasm of coughing he was trying to control. "The steel of deceit is your armor, and the weight of indolence your dowry." He was holding his coughing at bay, and in haste to drain his bucket of rage. "Prince Hindal would have been here days earlier if you were not such an imbecile and a glutton. Are you not the author of this shameless delay? Were you not sent to Kabul by my express command to bring prince Hindal here? But I have heard you were extending your visit at Kabul even after the wedding of your sister, and then indulging in days of feasting at the wedding of your other sister in Lahore? You didn't have time to arrange for fresh horses for prince Hindal's journey, is that it? What do you have to say in your defense?"

"My Emperor." Mir Birdi murmured wretchedly. He was shocked by Babur's shell of a body, not ever imagining before leaving Agra that the emperor would age so quickly. By the sheer weight of his love for the emperor, he could neither move, nor speak.

"How tall is prince Hindal?" Babur asked, noticing an ocean of love in the eyes of his governor.

"As tall as me, my Emperor!" Was Mir Birdi's tremulous response. Encouraged by the emperor's kind and wistful gaze, he added. "I am wearing his jacket. He made me wear it, saying he chose the material himself— white satin embroidered with gold thread."

"Come close, you maudlin lout! Let me feel the jacket my son had worn." Babur commanded. He caressed the sleeve of the jacket lovingly as Mir Birdi came close. "Now begone and don't dare come into this room until you bring prince Hindal with you!" He espied Gulbadan standing to his right, sad and forlorn. "Come, sweet Rose, sit with the emperor on his bed." A tender, whimsical smile was lingering upon his lips.

Gulbadan drifted toward her father as if sleep-walking, easing herself into the crook of his arm, and smiling most blissfully! Babur had kissed her on the brow before letting his gaze wander and sweep over his sons, wives and princesses into the haze-warmth of his love and sadness. His gaze seemed to be fluttering from one face to the other, as if arresting the very essence of life into his eyes, but it was lingering over Bibi Mubaraka before returning to Humayun.

"Come, my beloved prince, take your seat on this makeshift throne which has become a part of my bed." Babur commanded, his gaze tender and smoldering.

The Mystic House itself was plunged in utter silence as Humayun drifted toward the bed, mounting one little step, and settling himself on the throne facing his father. All eyes were turning to Humayun against the curtain of awe and silence, and yet they were shifting toward the emperor with princess Gulbadan cradled into his arms—his white Rose, dreamy and fragrant. Babur's eyes were caressing the features of his son, as if painting each nuance and moment over the canvas of his soul. The sharp nose and the full lips, made more prominent by the high cheekbones. Amber eyes shining much like the sparkle of jewels on his cummerbund. His purple robe and ropes of pearls around his neck down to his waist were lending him the aura of a dream-prince, waiting patiently for the arrival of his dream-princess.

"My son. My Beloved prince! You would be the next emperor of Hindustan, and I would lend you advice as along as even one spark of life in me stays kindled." Babur could barely keep his eyes open, his voice the ebb and flow of his pain and sadness. "Vainglory is the vilest of vices, shun it. Compassion is the noblest of virtues, embrace it. Be affectionate toward your kin, deal kindly with your brothers. Whatever their offences might be, never let your resentment lead you to the last extremity against any of them." His voice was sounding hollow and distant. "Do naught against your brothers, even though they may deserve it—" One soundless tremor upon his lips and his lips were silent, his head lolling toward the shoulders of Gulbadan.

The breath of life was no more, peace and pallor was Babur's death shroud, his body limp and lifeless. A wall of laments came crashing over the head of Babur in an effort to snatch him from the doors of death, but he was beyond earthly grief and sorrow. The forty-eight year old emperor, who had ruled for thirty-six turbulent years, now lay embalmed in bliss everlasting.

Bibliography

Amini, Iradj. *The Koh-i-noor Diamond*. Roli books, 1994.

Augustus, Frederick. *The Emperor Akbar*. Vol. 1. Atlantic Publishers, 1983.

Beveridge, Annette, trans. *Humayun-Nama*. Sang-E-Meel Publications, 1987.

Berinstain, Valerie. *India and the Mughal Dynasty*. Discoveries Series. Harry N. Abrams Inc., 1976.

Burke, S. M. *Akbar: The Greatest Moghul*. Munshiram Manoharlal Publishers, 1989.

Early, Abraham. *The Lives and Times of the Great Moghals*. Viking, 1997.

Jarrett, Colonel H. S., trans. *The Ain-i-Akbari*. Vols. 1 & 2. Atlantic Publishers, 1989.

Majumdar, R. C. *The History and Culture of Indian People*. Bhaharatiya Vidya Bhavan, 1994.

Index

About the Author

Farzana Moon is a teacher and a bibliophile, a poet, historian, and playwright with a Masters in Education. She writes Sufi poetry, historical, biographical accounts of Moghul emperors, and plays based on stories from religion and folklore. She has written several books, including *Sufis and Mystics of the World* based on her lectures at Clark State Community College. Most of her Moghul sequels are published with the intent of exploring markets for documentaries. She is the author of *Holocaust of the East* published by Cambridge Scholars Publishing. *Answers from Mount Hira* is a biography of Prophet Muhammad, the first volume in a trilogy published by Dreamcatcher Books. She participated in author/panel discussions at Columbia University. A collection of her plays are archived at Ohio State University. Her most recently published book is *Irem of the Crimson Desert*. She is currently researching for a book about Bahadur Shah Zafar—the last of the Moghuls, adding another century and a half after the sixth Moghul emperor of India. Born and educated in Pakistan, Farzana is a US citizen. She is being considered for a Fulbright Scholarship to continue her research about Bahadur Shah Zafar in India.